Lucy Lord is a journalist and columnist who has written for *The Times*, *Guardian*, *Independent*, *Evening Standard*, *Time Out* and *Arena*. Her favourite pastimes are reading, writing, lying in hammocks, lunching on beaches and throwing parties. She lives in London with her musician husband. *Revelry*, her first novel, isn't autobiographical in the slightest.

LUCY LORD

Revelry

HARPER

Harper
An imprint of HarperCollins*Publishers*
77–85 Fulham Palace Road,
Hammersmith, London W6 8JB

www.harpercollins.co.uk

A Paperback Original 2012
2

A catalogue record for this book
is available from the British Library

ISBN: 978-0-00-744172-3

Set in Meridien by Palimpsest Book Production Limited,
Falkirk, Stirlingshire

Printed and bound in Great Britain by
Clays Ltd, St Ives plc

MIX
Paper from
responsible sources
FSC™ **FSC™ C007454**
www.fsc.org

To my husband, with love.

Last summer was meant to be perfect. Unbridled sunny hedonism with all my favourite people in Ibiza, Glastonbury and the rest of the latter-day Sodom and Gomorrah hotspots we creative, *civilized* people have colonized over the last few decades. How we were looking forward to indulging in excesses that Nero's subjects might have considered over-the-top, smug in the knowledge that tiresome, bourgeois rules didn't apply to professional free spirits like us. As I say, it was going to be perfect. But somehow, somewhere, something went wrong.

Chapter 1

Let's start in Ibiza. It's the beginning of June and we've hired a villa for a week to coincide with the Space and Pacha opening parties. A fairly loathsome thing to do, I'm sure you'll agree, but some of my friends have started to think they're so cool it hurts. The renovated *finca* is a typically Ibicenco whitewashed cuboid affair, with roof terrace, tropical gardens kept verdant with horribly eco-unfriendly sprinklers and a big floodlit pool. Divided by ten, it wouldn't have been too pricey were it not for the dreaded strong euro. But hey – that's what credit cards are for.

In varying states of undress, sobriety and attractiveness, my fellow revellers lounge around the pool. To my right, talking nineteen to the dozen, feet dangling in the water, is my oldest and dearest friend Poppy. We were new girls at school together and bonded at the age of ten over a shared love of Frazzles and Enid Blyton. The rest of the class thought we were weird.

Tiny, with long, straight, honey-blonde hair (dyed, but not obviously) and smooth golden skin, Poppy's the sort of girl you could easily hate if you didn't already know and love her. After getting a first in History from Oxford, she travelled round the world on her own, bribing bent Colombian border guards, replanting rainforests in Borneo and volunteering in a Zimbabwean lion sanctuary. She's now doing very nicely thank you in TV production. Her apparent fragility belies enormous resources of stamina. How she manages to combine outrageous partying with her high-flying job is anybody's guess.

I suspect she's still pissed from last night. It's just gone 2.30, we haven't been up for long, and she should, by all rights, be feeling like death. Instead, she's babbling away like nobody's business, and – sure enough – finishes her sentence with '. . . I think the sun is well and truly over the yardarm by now, don't you?' She jumps to her dainty little feet, making for the bar the other side of the pool. I hear a heavy sigh and look up to see Alison rolling her eyes at Alison.

Alison and Alison are a pair of killjoys if ever there was one. Not people I'd ever have chosen to come on holiday with, they are the girlfriend and fiancée of Charlie and Andy, who have been my brother's best mates since their Cambridge days. Max and I unwisely decided to hire the villa together, to share with our respective friends – then the bugger bowed out at the last minute over a bust-up with his latest boyfriend.

Skinny Alison is in full-on Bridezilla wedding planning mode. If I hear another word about bridesmaids, flowers or seat placements, I won't be responsible for my actions. And somebody really ought to tell her that the strings on string bikinis are adjustable for a reason. I'm itching to give her boobs a good hoick.

I'm not normally such a bitch, honestly, but the Alisons have been determined to ruin everyone's holiday from the moment we arrived. Moan, moan, moan – and another bloody moan for good measure. It's too hot, they don't want to stay out too late, the food's not up to scratch, they *don't like beaches*. I mean, how can you not like beaches? They didn't like it at all when Poppy and I brought a Croatian couple back to drink absinthe by the pool at dawn, I think, giggling to myself at the memory. But really – if neither beaches nor a laissez-faire attitude to partying is your bag, the question remains: why come to Ibiza in the first place?

'The problem is that Andy wants to invite some old school friend who I haven't even met, and who'll probably turn up drunk anyway. It's not meant to be a hooley, it's *my day* . . .' Skinny is telling Plump Alison, who is hanging on her words, seemingly enraptured. I shut my eyes and turn my face up to the afternoon sun, allowing myself to drift off for a second.

'So I've told him, *we just don't have the numbers.*' It's no use: sleep is not an option within earshot. Andy and Charlie have driven into the village to buy provisions. I'd bet my life's earnings (not a lot, I grant you) that they've stopped for a couple of sharpeners, if only to escape Alison's inane witterings for half an hour.

'Drinks, anyone?' asks Poppy, and two prone male bodies show faint signs of stirring.

'A beer might just save my life,' croaks the lithe, brown one with messy black hair. Damian is Poppy's long-term boyfriend, and they couldn't be more compatible. As a journalist on a men's magazine he is the epitome of the work-hard, play-hard lifestyle that suits my friend so well. And if ever the reams of misogynistic drivel he is required to churn out for work start creeping into his extracurricular chat, Poppy pulls him up short pretty sharpish.

They make a fine-looking couple, I reflect, not for the first time, as Poppy opens a bottle of San Miguel and takes it over to him, crouching down to ruffle his hair and give him a kiss. Damian has his half-Indian heritage to thank for his permanent stubble and soulful dark eyes, hidden, at the moment, by a pair of classic Ray-Bans. The other half is Welsh, and the unlikely sounding genetic combination has proved a winner. Poppy has chosen her Missoni string bikini with typical nous. Its zigzag stripes of emerald, lime, khaki and aqua add curves to her slender frame and enhance her green eyes. Despite the heavy night, she is the picture of health and vitality. 'Beer, Ben?' she asks. 'Or does the Pope shit in the woods?'

'Cheers babe.' Ben drags himself into a sitting position. I try not to gawp.

Ben Jones is probably the most gorgeous specimen of manhood I have ever laid eyes on. A classically trained actor, he supplements his fluctuating income with the odd modelling stint (as you do), his full pouty lips, high cheekbones and long-lashed blue eyes lending themselves perfectly to preppy Gap-style advertising campaigns. He and Damian were at school together, so I've known him for as long as Poppy's been with Damian, which must be getting on for . . . Jesus, nearly five years now. And even after nearly five years, it's sometimes hard to believe that I count this Adonis amongst my closest friends; in fact it's sometimes hard to believe that I count any of these people amongst my closest friends. But I'll come back to that later.

'So what happened after I left last night?' he asks us all. Unusually for him, Ben left early last night as his nightmare current squeeze, an Australian model called Kimberly, wanted to get her beauty sleep (and presumably her fill of Ben, lucky bitch).

Both Alisons sit up straighter, I notice. Fuck it, who am I trying to kid? *I* sit up straighter, and pull my tummy in too.

Poppy starts to laugh. 'Good question. Who do you want to hear about first, Mark or Bella?'

'Start with Mark please,' I say, getting to my feet. Joining Poppy at the bar, I pour myself a large gin and tonic and light the first fag of the day.

'Christ, Mark's a dick,' says Poppy, and we all laugh.

Mark is the art director on Damian's magazine, all shaved head, biceps bulging out of racer-back vests and crotch attempting to thrust through the flies of his Diesel jeans. On anybody less pulsating with testosterone, this would look gayer than Elton and 'my partner David Furnish' on a campsite in Mykonos. Mark presides over shoots of naked women and says things like, 'Man, Kelly's minge is sweet' without shame. It pains me to admit that I find him extremely sexy.

'Yes, he really excelled himself last night, didn't he?' I say. 'What would be your reaction, Ben, to eighteen-year-old Brazilian twins?'

'Fuck me!' Ben chokes on his beer. 'Lucky bastard. Where did he find them?'

'Pacha, of course. The last we saw of him, the three of them were heading off, arm-in-arm, to the marina, making for the girls' parents' yacht.'

'They were bloody fit,' says Damian. Poppy sighs patiently.

'They were eighteen, darling. And Mark is thirty-two. Don't you think it's a tad pathetic?' Poppy is lucky enough never to have suffered from jealousy. I suppose she's so secure in her own achievements and beauty that it's never been an issue. Which is more than you can say for me.

'I really hope their father – who I am assuming, with my penchant for racial stereotyping, has a macho and fiery Latin temperament – catches Mark in the act with his darling daughters,' she muses.

'You messa with my bambinas, I cut offa your cojones,' I add, and everybody laughs, even the Alisons. I glance over at Ben. Christ, he's gorgeous.

'So what did you get up to then, Bella?' he asks. I sigh theatrically, trying to mask the shyness that used to be so incapacitating and which still occasionally rears its ugly head at entirely inopportune moments. Like at job interviews, or when talking to handsome men. I deal with it by drinking more than is seemly (not at job interviews), hanging out with people way cooler than me and hoping some of their attitude will rub off. But, deep down, I've a strong suspicion I'll always be a bit of a loser.

'It was my favourite dress.'

'That short white lacy number you had on last night? Yes, it looked great on you. Really showed off your tan.' He noticed what I was wearing? Result! 'So what happened to it?'

'Well . . .' I'm starting to feel a bit sheepish now, as I don't want Ben to think I'm a complete slag, even though he is by no means Mr Whiter-Than-White himself.

'It's classic,' says Damian, grinning. His teeth are dazzlingly white against his brown skin. 'Come on Belles, spill.'

'OK then. I met this American guy – can't even remember his name now . . .'

'It was Randy,' says Poppy. 'Can't believe you've forgotten that bit.'

'Oh God, yes, of course! I can't believe I've forgotten that bit either. Anyway, *Randy* and I decided to go to the loo for a line, and while we were in there we had a quick snog. In the course of the snogging, my dress came off – *I did not shag him*, by the way . . .'

'Of course not,' mutters Skinny Alison and Poppy glares at her.

'I didn't. Anyway, by the time we were ready to go back and have another drink, I looked on the floor and my dress was gone. Someone must have put their hand under the partition from the next cubicle and pinched it. I mean, really – what on earth would possess you?'

'Was it the Ladies or Gents?' asks Ben. Such a pertinent question makes me go all gooey.

'The Gents. Not sure if that makes it better or worse. It must have been some sort of prank, rather than a random opportunistic cheapskate stalking me and thinking *I really really must have that dress* – fab though it was. Ha-ha very fucking funny.'

'Actually it is,' says Damian. 'And you never know, transvestism isn't unknown in Ibiza.'

I ignore him.

'Anyway, I was stranded in my bra and knickers, so had to get Randy to go and alert the bar staff to my plight. They all thought it was bloody hilarious, but the barmaid did lend me a towel, which I fashioned into a mini toga and wore for the rest of the night. No one batted an eyelid, of course.'

'Excellent stuff,' says Ben. 'What happened to Randy?'

'Dunno – I lost him in the crowds.'

'Poor bloke, he's probably brokenhearted.' I glance up suspiciously. Is he taking the piss? Ben simply doesn't do gratuitous compliments. Not towards me, at any rate.

'Hi guys,' coos a breathy voice from the direction of the French windows. 'How's it going?'

Nearly six feet tall, with curly, almost ringleted auburn hair and even whiter teeth than Damian, Kimberly likes to make an entrance. Now she poses languidly for a second, allowing us to take in the length of her legs, before slinking across the terrace towards Ben. He leaps to his feet.

'Drink, darling?'

'Ew, no!' She wrinkles her retroussé nose in disgust. 'I can't believe you're all drinking in the sun? Don't you know how dehydrating it is? Your skin's not going to thank you, babe.' She gives a little tinkly laugh and I want to punch her. Her skin is an unlikely bronze spattered with tiny freckles. Surely redheads don't tan? 'Organic OJ will do me just fine?'

I haven't seen Kimbo swim the entire time we've been here, despite her vast collection of tiny bikinis, and suddenly realize why. If her hair went anywhere near water without the aid of a hell of a lot of Frizz-Ease and an hour's attention it would surely be a ginger afro. I'm tempted to chuck my drink over her just to check, but reconsider. It would be a waste of perfectly good gin.

'I just had a call from my agent?' she says. 'And US *Playboy* is interested in me doing a centrefold? And although I'm perfectly happy with the human body as a sexual and sensual instrument –' Excuse me while I puke. '– I'm more in touch with my inner spirituality? Y'know?'

The Aussie upward inflection is doing my head in. We may be hungover, and she may be talking utter crap, but it's not as if we don't understand the English language. Y'know?

'Babe, that's amazing,' says Ben. 'I can't believe I'm knobbing a potential *Playboy* centrefold. You've got to accept.'

'Oh, I don't know,' says Poppy. 'As you're such a spiritual person, maybe you should concentrate on less *obvious* things.'

'Oh you naughty boy,' says Kim simultaneously, tapping Ben's nose playfully, as I suppose a *Playboy* centrefold might. 'But the shoot clashes with my yoga retreat in Kerala next month – Goa's just *sooooooooo* touristy these days – and I need to, like, reconnect with my soul?' She starts doing some ostentatiously arse-revealing yoga moves and Poppy catches my eye.

'Anyone up for Sa Trinxa?'

I was hoping someone would moot this. The gin has already topped up the toxic fluid that is my blood and I want to party on. Sa Trinxa is the coolest bar on the coolest beach in Ibiza and I defy anyone not to have a good time there. Apart from the Alisons, of course, who'd rather talk weddings around the pool.

'I'm game,' says Damian.

'Me too,' says Ben.

'I think I'll take a rain check? I need to, like, catch up with my meditation? You guys have fun, OK? But not too much fun without me, gorgeous? Remember the Tantra?' Kim licks Ben's face in a frankly horrible display of intimacy and slinks off.

Sa Trinxa it is then.

I'm basking in the clear water off Las Salinas, favoured beach of Ibiza's beautiful people. It's a fifteen-minute walk from the car park to Sa Trinxa, at the far end of the beach, but boy is it worth it. Looking back at the beach from my watery vantage point, I'm faced with a scene right out of a soft-focus Seventies fashion shoot. Nestled into the rocks at the back of the sandy white beach, the bar is built up on a wooden platform, with bamboo and banana leaves providing shelter from the fierce Balearic sun. Exquisite semi-naked bodies of every nationality laze on the shore, tattoos and anklets much in evidence. Impossibly slender and tanned girls in tiny bikini bottoms are starting to dance on the water's edge, swaying in time to the ambient music the bar's sound system is pumping out. They know that everybody in the bar is looking at them; that's the point.

I do a somersault underwater. I could swim before I

could walk, as my parents had a pool when I was a baby (when they were still together), and I'm still better at swimming than walking. The former has fewer falling-over opportunities. I come back up for breath and let my mind drift back to last night. I was a little economical with the truth when I said I hadn't shagged Randy. It seems a tad sordid to admit you've done it in a nightclub loo, after all. Even if the club in question is Pacha. But hey, he was fit as fuck, and seemed to think that I was too, which is always a turn-on. He was from California, and looked like a surfer, with a broad jaw, shoulder-length, sun-streaked hair, darker eyes, lashes and stubble, perfect American teeth and mid-calf, Hawaiian-printed board shorts. One of the best things about Ibiza is that you can meet so many globally gorgeous men here.

He approached me on Pacha's absurdly jet-set terrace, complimenting me on my eyes, dress and legs. I lapped it up, then told him I had some coke if he fancied a line. I'm always so euphoric on Charlie (not least for its confidence-boosting properties) that I want to share it, for whomever I'm with to be on the same wavelength, to *share the joy man*. I'm a bloody idiotic hippy at times. Anyway, we made our way to the Gents, waiting until nobody was having a piss in the urinals, before sneaking into one of the two whitewashed stone cubicles, laughing as we locked the door behind us.

I felt another rush of euphoria after we'd done the lines and Randy seemed to too, as he grasped my shoulders and started kissing me, tracing the inside of my mouth with his tongue. It felt great and I responded in kind, offering little resistance when he slid my dress off my shoulders and onto the floor, leaving me standing there in my bra and knickers. He undid his board shorts, which also fell to the floor. He wasn't wearing anything underneath and his cock was impressive. He pushed me against the wall, and tried to get my knickers down, but we were both hampered by the garments around our feet. We laughed, and kicked them aside.

Realizing that in such a confined space there was no other option, Randy sat down on the loo seat and pulled me down on top of him. He'd already managed to get a condom on (something told me he'd done this before). I felt his great American cock going deeper inside me, as I manoeuvred myself up and down on him, turned on as much by the naughtiness of it all as by his calloused thumb rubbing my clitoris. God, it was good.

But when I told Ben that I'd lost Randy in the crowds, I was lying about that too. When we eventually emerged from the loo, with me in the towel the barmaid had lent me, he kissed me, apologized and said he couldn't be seen with me in case his friends told his girlfriend back in Santa Barbara. Bastard. It was the first time he'd mentioned a girlfriend.

You know what though? I've been treated worse. God, the hours I've spent agonizing over why some chap or other hasn't called, what I might have done to put him off me. What it is that other women have that I don't; something that keeps the opposite sex interested in them for more than just a few cheap shags. Endless, painful self-analysis. At least Randy had the decency to tell me to my face immediately after the event. OK, so decency is probably not quite the right word, but you know what I mean. It's that being kept hanging on for weeks, sometimes months on end – because they don't have the bloody courage to tell you to your face – that really hurts.

Here, in the beautiful sea that surrounds this beautiful island, Randy's nothing more than a delicious (if somewhat seedy) memory. Ships that pass, and all that. I do a backward somersault, then swim out towards the horizon for a bit, going deep underwater like a fish before heading back to the shore. It's time for another drink.

The jetty that sticks out into the sea in front of the bar acts as a kind of catwalk. The rocks that account for the very clean water make it difficult to get in and out of the sea without using the jetty, so every time you have a swim you know that at least someone will be observing, and quite possibly commenting on you. In the old days I'd have been horribly self-conscious hauling myself out of the water in front of such a pulchritudinous crowd. Today, emboldened by the five bottles of wine we seem to have got through with our lunch, I am the picture of insouciance. I may be nowhere near Poppy's league of beauty, but I scrub up OK and am feeling happily confident in my fuchsia and orange halterneck bikini, my long dark hair dripping down my back. It's great how sexy sunshine and booze can make you feel when there are no mirrors around.

Lunch was to die for. Griddle-blackened tiger prawns pulsating with garlic and parsley, fantastically crunchy chips to soak up the juices and a lovely fresh salad to make us feel virtuous. The food, wine and swim (not necessarily in that order) have certainly sorted out my hangover, I think, as I weave my way through the bodies on the sand back to our table.

'How was the water?' asks Poppy.

'Absolutely gorgeous! So refreshing, I feel like a new man. What's the wine situation?' I pick up my empty glass.

'Don't panic, we've ordered a couple more bottles,' says Ben, laughing.

Looking around the table I feel a moment of pure joy. I'm with three of my favourite people in probably my favourite place on earth, mellowed with sun and wine, with nothing but more pleasure to look forward to until we leave this magical island. It's so hot I'm drying off already, salt crystals forming on my sunbaked shoulders, my wet hair keeping me cool. Whichever direction I look, I am confronted by sunshine, beauty and laughing faces. It seems as if nothing can pierce my bubble of happiness.

And then I see him. Walking up the beach towards us, skinny brown legs in way-too-short denim cut-offs, barrel brown chest revealed by a batik silk shirt left open to the waist. His shoulder-length hair is thick and grey, his chest hair white and wispy. A shark's tooth dangles from a leather string around his neck, above which his strong mahogany face is etched with deep vertical grooves. He is carrying – oh God – a guitar in one hand and what looks like a spliff in the other.

'Bella,' says Damian, following my gaze. 'Isn't that . . .?'

Yes, the ageing hippy openly checking out all the topless babes on the beach is my much-loved but thoroughly disreputable father.

Chapter 2

'Wow Bella, that smells fantastic. What's cooking?' asks Charlie, dipping a slightly podgy finger into the *rouille* I've just prepared. I slap his hand away and smile at him. Thick, sandy blond hair frames his good-natured, ruddy-cheeked face. He'll have a double chin in ten years' time, you mark my words.

'Bouillabaisse.'

After boozing all day yesterday, an early(ish) night was in order, so I got up at the supremely civilized hour of 10.30 to go to the market. There I had a lovely time trading banter with the stallholders and getting their recommendations on what was freshest in. I spent most of my childhood holidays in Mallorca (where Dad still lives in a thirteenth-century hermitage) so my Spanish is passable. I stocked my pretty wicker basket high with prawns, mussels, clams, scallops, red mullet and the scraps of small fish that are so essential for depth of flavour in a good fishy broth. I'm not actually making bouillabaisse, which is of course indigenous to the south of France, but a kind of generic Mediterranean fish stew.

I love cooking. I've chopped onions, garlic and fennel,

skinned and seeded some overblown, sun-infused old tarts of the tomato world, and glugged in some Pernod, saffron and thyme. Now the fish is simmering away and I stop for a fag break.

The insistent chirruping of crickets vies for attention with my friends' laughing voices wafting through the balmy air from the terrace outside. The old stone floor is cool against my bare feet as I pad about the enormous room, wishing my tiny kitchen in London could compare. There is a huge scrubbed oak table in the middle, piled high with the usual holiday detritus of suntan lotion, shades, hats, wet towels, cameras and unwritten post-cards. All the cupboards are finished in the same oak, the walls are whitewashed and the white enamel double sink has elegantly curved stainless steel tap fittings. A fireplace vast enough to roast several ten-year-olds is stacked with currently redundant logs, giving the room an almost cosy feel, despite its size.

I'm feeling wonderfully wafty in my new multicoloured maxidress, fondly imagining I'm channelling a Seventies socialite, Talitha Getty/Bianca Jagger vibe as I float through the French windows – only to trip over the hem and fall flat on my face at Ben's feet. Everyone creases up laughing.

'Ow, that bloody hurt. Shut up, you buggers, it's not funny.' I sit up and rub my knee, where the skin has split and a purply bruise is starting to form. I pretend to laugh but am actually feeling a bit stupid and in genuine pain.

'Shit, that looks nasty,' says Ben, crouching down beside me. 'You need to clean it up. Does anyone have any antiseptic?'

'There's some Savlon in my sponge bag. Poor love.' Poppy bends over to kiss the top of my head as she makes her way inside the villa.

Ben helps me to my feet and I go hot all over. I can't

help it: his proximity is overwhelming, even after all these years.

'Have a drink, darling,' says my father, pouring me a glass of wine as I sit down at the table. 'Best anaesthetic there is.'

It turns out that Dad heard from my mother that we were on the island, so he thought he'd pop over to surprise us. It's only a short ferry ride from Palma, after all. Feeling mean not to have mentioned it to him, I immediately asked the others if they'd mind if he stayed on the sofa for a couple of nights. Everyone seemed to be cool with it, though I thought I detected some sniffiness in the Alisons' corner. No surprise there then. As it happened, Dad didn't need the sofa as he was travelling, as he often does, with his trusty hammock and sleeping bag – 'I much prefer to sleep under the stars, angel face.'

'Here you go,' says Poppy, handing me the tube of Savlon, a roll of lint and a packet of plasters. Trust her to come prepared. It just wouldn't occur to me to bring first aid stuff on holiday.

'Let me do that,' says Ben, crouching down again, gently pulling my skirt up over my knees. I can barely breathe as I glance over at Kim, but she seems entirely unperturbed, twinkling and laughing at something my father's just said. She and Dad have been all over each other all day, and while it's pretty obvious what he sees in her, it's also, sadly, all too obvious what she sees in him. My father's a photographer, you see, and a pretty influential one at that. In the Seventies he ran amok with Bailey, Donovan et al., and was never without several pretty girls on either arm. It's amazing his marriage to my mother lasted as long as it did.

He's shot everyone from the Stones to Iggy Pop, Gwyneth Paltrow to George Clooney – and got pissed with them all afterwards too (except for Gwynnie, whom he called 'lovely to look at, but probably the most boring woman in the world'). He's stayed for nothing in the best hotels in the best locations, and is endearingly blasé about high-end glamour, preferring to rhapsodize over waterfalls or deserts. When he occasionally emerges from semi-retirement in Mallorca, the glossies fall over themselves trying to persuade him to shoot for them. Kimberly's in the process of proving herself to be nothing more than a nasty little opportunist, and while part of me is delighted she's showing her true colours, I'm mortified that my father should be the cause of it.

I'm also pretty sure this is why Ben is being so unusually solicitous, but am not about to look a gift horse in the mouth. Now he tenderly cleans my wound, looking up at me with those delicious blue eyes, and it's all I can do not to grab him right here and shove my tongue down his throat.

I am distracted from my lascivious reverie by the sound of Kim squawking, 'Oh my God, Justin, you crack me up. You're just sooooo witty,' and laughing as if my dad were Peter Cook and Dorothy Parker reincarnated and rolled into one. When she smiles, her pink pointy tongue peeps through her teeth, in a cutesy manner she clearly imagines is both endearing and provocative. It might just provoke me into a spot of GBH. Dad smiles smugly and relights his spliff.

Dad and Kim are both sitting with their legs propped up on the table we've laid this side of the luminously turquoise pool, just to the left of the French windows. This is Dad's default position so it doesn't bug me too much. For Kimbo it is another excuse to show off the length of her horrible legs. She is wearing a cream backless jersey minidress, cut away at the sides and held together with a large gold ring that showcases her pierced belly button and matches her gladiator sandals. She's piled her copper curls up in a faintly Grecian style that emphasizes both her height and the swanlike quality of her neck. Her skirt is so short that the legs-on-table pose is a blatant invitation to look at her knickers. Oh well – at least she's not going commando. One must be thankful for small mercies.

Poppy's perched on one of the sun loungers, a very contented-looking Damian sitting on a fat cushion on the ground between her legs. He occasionally turns his head to kiss her slender fingers, which are massaging his shoulders. In denim hot pants and a little white broderie-anglaise camisole, her surfer girl hair streaked white by the sun, Poppy is the picture of butter-wouldn't-melt gorgeousness (if you discount the fag in her hand and enormous margarita at her feet). Damian is his usual understated cool in long shorts and a close-fitting Superdry T-shirt.

To the other side of my father leers Neanderthal Mark, resplendent in crotch-hugging Daniel Craig-as-Bond shorts and a grey marl racer-back vest with 'sit on my face' emblazoned in neon pink lettering across his enormously worked-out chest. He and Dad have worked together on several shoots and were having a lovely time reminiscing about various tits, arses and pudenda they've come across (if you'll pardon the expression) until Kim appeared, fresh from her ablutions.

Alison and Alison are in their usual sun loungers, engaged in a crisis meeting as the woman making Skinny Alison's wedding dress has had the temerity not to be available at the end of a phone twenty-four/seven, even though Skinny is on holiday herself.

'I mean, I'm paying her enough,' she's fuming. 'I just want to know that everything's going according to plan. That's not really too much to ask, is it? It's absolutely vital

20

that we get the second fitting done the minute we get back. Oh God, I shouldn't have come to this bloody island. There's just too much to do. And I do want everything to be perfect on *my big day*.'

'Of course you do, sweetie,' says Plump Alison, who is awfully wet but the only one showing the self-obsessed hag any kindness, I suppose.

Indeed Andy seems blissfully unaware of his fiancée's latest gripe as he sits playing chess with Charlie at the circular stone table in the bar. Andy is quite a good-looking man, in a saturnine sort of way. Tall and rangy, with short dark brown hair and rectangular, dark-framed specs, he looks exactly like the hard-hitting investigative reporter (or 'proper journalist', as Poppy puts it when she wants to wind Damian up) that he is.

Though you wouldn't guess it given her asinine wedding obsession, Skinny Alison is a high-flying lawyer. She too is tall and dark, with a severe black bob and droopily melancholy features set in a long face. She looks surprisingly elegant with her clothes on, I have to admit, clad tonight in white linen palazzo pants and navy and white striped boat-necked T-shirt, her lips defined with a slash of scarlet that matches the silk scarf wrapped around her narrow waist. The fact that she isn't pouring with sweat in such a get-up is testament to her reptilian cold-bloodedness. She and Andy must have awfully grown-up, intellectually superior dinner parties, I reflect, as I eye them over my drink and wonder what on earth they have in common with my darling, laid-back brother. I've met Andy on and off over the years and he's always struck me as nice enough. But still.

'How's that?' asks Ben as he gives my knee one final wipe and sticks a plaster on it.

'Much better – thanks so much.' I will him never to stop

21

manhandling my legs. 'I'll just have a fag out here, then go back and finish the food.'

'Great, I'm starving,' says Charlie from the bar. 'What's the ETA?' So they *can* hear what's going on from there, then. Interesting.

'God, Charlie, do you ever think of anything but your stomach?' says Skinny Alison. 'You really should start looking after yourself. You're not getting any younger, you know.'

'Well, I love him just the way he is,' says Plump Alison in a rare moment of defiance. She walks over and gives him a cuddle from behind.

'Thanks babe,' says Charlie, kissing her forearm. 'Does that mean I can have seconds?' He roars with laughter. He's a pretty good sort, as Sloaney accountants go.

'I've never had to worry about my weight,' says Kim smugly. 'I guess I'm just lucky – good genes? My mom and grandma both had great skin too? And they both look soooo young for their age? My guru says you get the face you deserve, and I've been so lucky I always try to give something back.' She beams around complacently.

'So, what's the score tonight then?' interjects Poppy – who's never had to worry about her weight either – into the flabbergasted silence. 'Dinner in – what? – twenty minutes or so, Belles?' I nod. 'Cool, then we'll just chill for a bit, then hit Ibiza Town, then . . . does anyone have any particular debauchery in mind?'

We ascertain that Mark wants to hit the Rock Bar, as the Brazilian twins said they might be there, Damian needs to score from some bar in the gay quarter and the rest of us are keen to go to Amnesia as it's Manumission night. I finish my fag and go inside to put the finishing touches to dinner, Poppy hot on my tail.

'Christ, have you ever met such a self-satisfied, *vacuous*

22

little tart,' she rants, opening the fridge in search of another bottle of tequila. 'OK, tall tart.'

'Hmmm . . . let's think.' I put my head on one side and pretend to consider it. 'Nope, can't say I have. Surely even Ben must be starting to realize that by now?'

'Well, I don't think he was ever after her mind.'

'My dad and Mark slavering over her like a couple of randy old dogs isn't helping much either,' I ponder gloomily. 'God, I'd like to wipe that smug smile off her face.'

'Oh well, let's not let the bitch ruin our holiday.' Poppy brandishes the tequila bottle. 'How about a couple of mind-sharpening shots?'

'The shot glasses are in the bar. Can you really be arsed to go through and pour shots for everyone?'

'Nope. But I've found the perfect substitute!' cries Poppy triumphantly, producing a couple of egg cups from one of the cupboards. Giggling, we find the salt and lemon (right next to the stove as I was about to use them to season the stew) and embark on the ridiculous ritual beloved of party animals the world over.

'Eurgh,' I wince, screwing up my eyes and shoving the lemon wedge in my mouth as quickly as I can to get rid of the taste. Once the gagging reflex has stopped, I'm suffused with a warm glow and set about completing the fish stew with renewed vigour.

'I'll set the table, shall I?' offers Poppy, heading back outside.

'You're an angel.' I really mean it. The first stirrings of pissed sentimentality are creeping up on me, and Poppy certainly looks angelic tonight, with her lovely smile, big almond-shaped green eyes and perfect, straight nose, all framed by that silky, golden mane.

When Pops and I were at school, we were inseparable

and a trifle eccentric, not part of any of the cool bitchy girl gangs. It was just us against the world – and the world of an all girls' school can be horribly unkind if you don't conform. Poppy and I existed in our own little world of make-believe. After our Enid Blyton stage, we became obsessed with the 1920s and 1930s and devoured books by Evelyn Waugh and Nancy Mitford, Agatha Christie and P. G. Wodehouse, dressing in homemade flapper dresses, cloche hats and character shoes. My fourteenth birthday present from my mum was an old gramophone player with a horn and a pile of dusty 78s that we played over and over, dancing the Charleston and giggling till we were breathless. We even spoke like characters from the books. Things were either 'beastly' or 'vile', 'divine' or 'too, too happy-making'. Our catty, boyband-obsessed classmates had no idea what to make of us, but we were absolutely content in our anachronistic, self-contained bubble. We never felt the need to befriend anybody else in that stuck-up girls' school.

By the time we'd hit the sixth form and discovered booze and boys, our shared obsession had died down a bit, but we were still both terribly excited at the idea of Poppy going to Oxford, and all the Brideshead-style punting shenanigans that this would entail. But the first time I went to visit her, towards the end of the Michaelmas term, I was in for a shock. Poppy had always had a pretty face, but the mouse-fair shoulder-length bob and old-fashioned clothes that swamped her tiny body meant that up until now her prettiness was very much of the girl-next-door, unthreatening variety.

The stunning undergraduate holding court in the Christ Church bar, surrounded by sycophants seemingly hanging on her every word, was a different proposition altogether. Her recently highlighted hair had grown, and now flowed – silky, blonde and streaky – down her back and over her shoulders. In keeping with the Britpop look of the time, khaki hipster cargo pants and a black crop top showed off her pert tits, flat brown tummy, narrow hips, and . . . Good God, she'd had her belly button pierced! And she was smoking! I was in such a state of shock at Poppy's transformation that I just stood there gawping for a bit, until she noticed me and squealed, running over with her arms outstretched for a hug.

Pops did her best to make me feel welcome that weekend, but there was a definite change in her. The way she spoke, the way she lit her fags and tossed her hair – it was as if that first term at Oxford had bestowed on her an unshakeable sense of self, a glamorous patina that has not left her to this day. Her fellow students, still high on the glory of having been chosen as the crème de la crème of the country's intelligentsia, were clearly not impressed by me, a shy, somewhat dumbstruck, London art student. We never did get to go punting.

Back at Goldsmiths, things were hardly better. I'd been so excited about the prospect of art college, imagining I'd meet all sorts of interesting, like-minded people, my head full of romantic notions of Art, and Beauty, and Love. But once I was there, I couldn't believe how full of themselves everybody was, how obsessed with being trendy. If I'd thought my all girls' school was cliquey, this was ten times worse, in its shallow, sniggering, look-at-me arrogance. I was horribly conscious that I'd never be skinny enough to be properly fashionable. Not that I'm fat (a perfectly reasonable size 10–12 for my five foot seven height), but you had to be pretty bloody emaciated to make the outlandish garments favoured by my peers look anything other than downright hideous.

No doubt, if they'd realized who my father was, things

would have been different. But Brown's a pretty common surname, and I was buggered if I was going to ride on Dad's coat-tails. Actually, I lie. I'd gladly have ridden on his coat-tails, but couldn't exactly start saying to all and sundry, 'Don't you know who my dad is?' without looking and sounding like a total dickhead.

Part of me hated the lot of them; another part, the insecure eighteen-year-old girl part, longed to be accepted. Sometimes I'd drink too much to kill my insecurity and make a complete arse of myself in the college bar. Sniffing out vulnerability the way a shark sniffs blood, my male contemporaries soon realized that I could easily be sweet-talked into bed; pathetically naive, and longing to be loved, I fell for it every time. Disappointment inevitably followed crushing disappointment.

By the time Poppy returned from her round-the-world travels and came to live in London, I had a pretty low opinion of both myself and the entire opposite sex. I was temping at a post-production house in Soho; the married boss, a loathsome piece of work with a shaved head, goatee and penchant for black polo-neck jumpers, had already tried to shag me. Pops took one look and kindly swept me up in her groovy new life, introducing me to her terrifyingly successful new friends as 'Bella, my best mate ever'. Slowly I began to be assimilated, to develop my own style and something approaching confidence. I've never shaken off the feeling that if it wasn't for her, I'd still be that twat embarrassing myself in the Goldsmiths bar, desperate to be loved and accepted.

I owe Poppy a lot, I think now with a huge rush of affection, as I taste the fish stew. It's sublime. The basic Mediterranean triumvirate of tomatoes, onion and garlic underpins the delicate sweetness of the fish, whose variety yields a beautifully complex balance of textures and flavours.

I have elevated my ambrosial mire to heady aromatic heights with saffron, thyme and the aniseedy kick of fennel and Pernod.

I go out of the door at the back of the kitchen to get some flat-leaf parsley from the herb garden. Away from the floodlights of the pool, the stars are stupidly bright, twinkling their little hearts out against the velvety purple sky. Pulling up great leafy handfuls (I'm a strong believer that more is more when it comes to herbs), I notice a shadowy figure making its way in the direction of the outdoor loo. Having known that figure all my life, I recognize my father instantly. I'm about to say something when I hear a ghastly giggle. Stepping back into the shadows, I watch as Kimberly grabs him from behind, running her long fingers over his crotch and biting the side of his neck.

'Kimberly?' asks Dad, his voice hoarse with lust. She continues her lewd manoeuvres for what seems like minutes but is probably only thirty seconds or so, until Dad says, 'You shouldn't have followed me. It'll be too obvious what we're up to.'

'This is just for starters, big boy,' breathes Kim. 'We're going to have a ball later.'

And she turns on her elegant heel and saunters back to the party.

I wait until Dad has continued towards the loo before bolting back into the kitchen, feeling deeply queasy. You'd think I'd have become inured to my father's various peccadilloes over the years, but actually witnessing the full sub-porno horror, and with somebody I hold in such low regard, is unpalatable on every level. And then there's the little matter of darling, gorgeous, soon-to-be-cuck-olded-by-a-much-older-man Ben.

I chuck the parsley down onto the worktop and start chopping furiously.

'Jesus, what has that poor parsley ever done to you?' says Poppy, then stops when she sees the look on my face. 'Christ Bella, what's up?'

I tell her and she starts to laugh. 'Oh, I'm sorry, but you must admit it's quite funny. I mean, look at Ben. I can tell you with my hand on my heart that this is going to be an entirely new experience for him.'

'I know, that's what makes it so awful. Poor Ben . . .'

'Oh I don't know, it'll probably do him good, vain bugger. Come on, Belles, you know what he's like! Mr Irresistible . . .' She starts laughing again. 'It's really quite priceless.'

'But it makes Dad look like such a silly old fool. It's not as if she can actually fancy him more than Ben, and for him to think she can is *so* deluded. Aaaaargh, cringe!' I light myself a fag and puff away like something demented.

'I'm not sure your father's that stupid,' muses Poppy. 'He's been in the game for years, and he's just taking advantage of the situation. Most men would probably do the same – silly fuckers, the lot of 'em. No, let's be realistic, babe. The only person who comes out of this badly is Kim . . . Big Boy, indeed!' And she starts spluttering again. This time I join in, feeling an awful lot better. Thank God for Pops, I think, giving her a grateful hug. She hugs me back, then says, all brisk and businesslike, 'Right, let's get this food sorted. And don't worry your pretty little head about things. It'll just add to the evening's entertainment.'

I take another couple of drags on my fag before stubbing it out and picking up the chopped parsley. I watch the emerald confetti cover the surface of the pan in a grassy blanket, then give the whole lot a good stir. A hefty grinding of black pepper, a final squeeze of lemon and it's ready.

I carry the vast pot out to the table that Poppy has laid

beautifully, with candles, proper napkins and jugs of flowers nicked from the garden. A couple of crusty white loaves, fresh that morning from the *panadería*, share table space with a happy clink of bottles, red, white and rosé. Managing not to trip over my hem this time, I put the stew in the middle. It does look and smell sensational, if I do say so myself.

'Who's my clever, beautiful, darling girl?' says Dad, reaching up to give me a hug. I hug him back, seething with mixed emotions.

Chapter 3

It's ten to midnight and Ibiza Town is heaving. We amble slowly through the harbour, taking in the bustling bars and restaurants to our right, the Old Town climbing up the hill behind them, crowned by its ancient stone fortress. To our left, yachts sit imperiously on the inky calm sea, their polished wood and gleaming white bodywork a constant taunt to those yet to make a billion dollars. Palm trees line the water's edge, and everywhere you look is a seething mass of humanity, determined to get its money's worth of fun. Immaculate, gesticulating Italians in faded jeans and shades; evidently Scandinavian blondes with deep golden tans and suspect neon fashion sense; less attractive but edgier Brits. Every European cliché is covered here.

We are overtaken by a procession on stilts – models in bikinis and fabulously bewigged transvestites in full evening dress; it's hard to say which are the most gorgeous. They are promoting Manumission at Amnesia, which won't really get going for at least a couple more hours. We pass stalls selling silver and turquoise jewellery, batik sarongs and limited edition CDs. Finally we reach the

Rock Bar, with its too-cool-for-school clientele and water-front tables and chairs. As luck would have it, a large group of Americans is leaving as we arrive, so we quickly nab their table, to the evident disgruntlement of some unfeasibly attractive French girls just behind us. Ben flashes them his most gorgeous smile, and their disdainful Gallic shrugs melt into coy giggles.

As there aren't enough chairs to go around, Mark, Ben and Andy make a big show of looking for empty ones. Poppy nudges Damian.

'Go on, you lazy bugger. Make yourself useful.'

'Why bother?' asks Damian idly. 'Mark and Ben just want to flirt with some randoms and Andy loves to do a good turn.' There is a slight edge to his voice when he gets to the last bit. Perhaps Poppy's comments about Andy being a 'proper journalist' have been a little too close for comfort. He plonks himself down onto one of the free chairs and pulls Poppy onto his lap. 'Just sit down and shut up, beautiful.'

'Good idea, that man,' says Charlie in his public school way, pulling up a chair and beckoning Plump Alison to sit on top of him. Skinny Alison helps herself to a chair, leaving two left, between my father, Kim and me.

'Ladies,' he starts, but Kim is having none of it, insisting that he take the chair, while she perches on his lap like a great ginger giraffe. I sink into the final chair gratefully, my decision to wear my Terry de Havilland platform wedges not having been the best of the holiday so far.

The three men return from their search empty-handed, which is not surprising at this time of night. At the sight of us all, with the exception of yours truly, sitting on one another's laps, Andy approaches Alison with a rueful grin, saying, 'Go on darling, indulge me.'

'If I must,' she huffs. 'But we all look bloody silly.'

Ben takes one look at Kimberly sitting on Dad's lap and slopes off to flirt some more with the French girls, which leaves – oh shit – Man-Mountain Mark.

'Babe?' he asks me, arms stretched out, pleading. He looks so silly in his little shorts and offensive T-shirt that it's hard not to laugh out loud, but he's also extremely fit and muscly and I reckon if anyone can withstand me using them as a chair it's him. I stand up to let him sit down, then settle down comfortably on his enormous lap. He casually puts his arms around me and I get a pleasing tingle, despite myself. There is something about Mark's overt maleness that is both reassuring and arousing at such close quarters.

'I'm not squashing you, am I?' I ask stupidly, and he laughs.

'Light as a feather, babe.'

Perhaps it's the hefty post-prandial line we all found so essential, perhaps it's the booze, perhaps it's the balmy evening, but his response turns me on way more than it should. I hope I don't slide off his lap. Remembering my similar reaction to Ben earlier in the evening (and to Randy last night, for that matter), there is a brief moment during which I wonder at my fickleness before thinking, fuck it. I snuggle closer back into his chest.

The highly camp waiter comes to take our order and we plump for vodka *limóns* all round. It's not something any of us would order at home – in fact it's not something any of us *could* order at home as the *limón* in question is a lemon Fanta, neither as sweet nor bitter, respectively, as lemonade or bitter lemon, but wonderfully tangy and refreshing in the heat. The generous Spanish spirit measures help too, of course.

'Well, this is all very cosy, isn't it?' says Charlie, who's sweating slightly in his chinos and polo shirt. Plump Alison, who has caught too much sun and looks pink and sore, shifts uncomfortably on his lap and he tightens his arms around her. Those shorts really weren't a wise choice, I find myself thinking meanly, then pull myself up. *Stop being such a bitch, Bella.*

As if she'd read my mind, Skinny Alison suddenly says, 'I hope you're planning to lose some weight before the wedding, Alison. I don't want you bursting the seams of your dress.' Alison, it transpires, is to be Alison's bridesmaid, which seems odd as they only know each other through their respective other halves. Clearly Skinny Alison is not one for extensive female bonding.

'I've got a great detox programme I can recommend?' says Kimberly, leaning forward with deep faux-sincerity. 'I always follow it for a week before the Victoria's Secret show and it really makes a difference.'

As everybody now has a clear mental image of lean, lithe Kim in her exotic underwear, compared to poor Alison in her ill-fitting shorts, I suddenly snap, 'Oh for Christ's sake, leave the girl alone. We're meant to be on holiday.'

'Well,' huffs Kim, all affronted. 'I was only trying to help.' Alison, who was looking on the verge of tears, smiles over at me gratefully and I instantly feel guilty.

'Still,' says Skinny Alison, 'you will think about it, won't you? I don't want to have to worry about getting your dress altered, when there's so much more to think about for *my big day.*'

'Jesus, Al, give it a rest, won't you?' says Andy sharply. 'Get off me, please. I'm going for a walk.'

'Wha . . .?'

I catch Poppy's eye and try not to snigger at the look on Alison's face.

'I'll be back in ten minutes, just need to clear my head,' he says, lighting a fag and striding off towards the harbour, his long legs in their old Levis covering ground quickly. He looks rather dashing, and he's certainly gone up in my estimation for standing up to his witch of a fiancée.

Ben comes over with one of the French girls. 'Hey guys, this is Veronique. She's never been to Manumission before so I suggested she comes with us. Her mates want to go to El Divino.'

'Hi Veronique,' we chorus, as I consider how much less attractive Veronica sounds in English.

If you didn't know Veronique's nationality, French would be your first guess. Her long dark brown hair is dead straight, with a choppy eyelash-skimming fringe. Though her dark almond eyes are thick with kohl and mascara, she doesn't appear to be wearing any other make-up, her clear olive skin and pillowy lips needing little enhancement. Stick thin in skinny black jeans and braless in a black vest with a couple of studded belts encircling her narrow hips, she is the picture of rock-chick insouciance.

Ben has certainly upped his game here, I think dispassionately, wondering how Kim will react now and rather hoping for Dad that she doesn't immediately switch allegiance back. Then my father, as tends to be his wont, surprises me. Gently pushing Kimbo off his lap, he rises gallantly to his feet and kisses Veronique's hand, murmuring, '*Enchanté*, mademoiselle,' before launching into fluent French. Within seconds the sulky pout has been replaced by a delighted, slightly gappy smile. To give him his due, Ben laughs good-naturedly and tries to join in the conversation in schoolboy French.

'What are they saying, what are they saying?' asks Kim, as Ben looks over in her direction and says something, laughing. Dad puts his arm around her waist and says, 'Veronique was saying you look like a model. We were just telling her how right she is.'

34

By the look on Veronique's face, it wasn't a compliment, but it is so beyond Kim's intellectual capabilities to consider that some people might not be impressed by her profession that she is temporarily mollified and preens herself unnecessarily.

'And what do you do, babe?' she asks Veronique, launching back into faux-sincere mode.

'I sing. I write. I paint,' breathes the Frog in a seriously sexy accent. 'I was – 'ow you say? – discoverrrred by a model agency – during my Baccalaureate. But I told zem no – I am an artiste.'

Mark gives me a squeeze and whispers gleefully in my ear, 'This is awesome. I fucking hope it turns into a bitch fight. Couple of hot babes too.'

I laugh and whisper back, 'Who do you think would win? The Frog looks pretty scary, but I reckon Kim's as tough as old boots.'

'Difficult call.'

'Yeah, well . . .' says Kim. 'You probably did the right thing, babe. It's only a few *short* girls who ever really make it. In fact, I can only think of Kate Moss. And I'm sure you'd agree you're hardly in her league.' She looks around at us all and laughs gaily.

'Pouf, whatever . . .' shrugs Veronique, lighting a fag and turning her back on Kim. 'Ben, *chéri*, you said somezing about a drink? *Vin rouge, s'il te plaît.*'

'I'll get it,' says my father, taking Kim by the hand. 'Why don't you come with me, Kimberly?' And he leads her through the heaving crowds towards the bar.

With Kimbo out of the picture, we all relax for a bit.

'No disrespect, mate,' says Damian to Ben. 'But where the fuck did you find her?' Then, as Veronique raises her eyebrows, 'Not you, darling – the other one.' Poppy rolls her eyes and stage-whispers to me: 'Lord Tact of

35

Tactville strikes again.' I giggle and whisper back, 'This is hilarious.'

Poppy looks at me curiously. 'So you're feeling better about everything now?'

'Oh yes, water off a duck's back.' I wave my hand about airily.

'Ow,' complains Mark as I bash him in the nose, at which Poppy and I laugh so much that I nearly fall off his lap. The various intoxicants have made us awfully silly, I am nearly coherent enough to reflect.

Andy returns from his strop.

'Right, when are we off to Manumission?' he asks, looking at me and Poppy.

'Oh God, not for another hour or so at least,' says Poppy. 'Anyway, Damian needs to go and score first, don't you sweetheart?'

'Too right I do,' says Damian, getting to his feet. 'In fact, no time like the present. Anyone else fancy a walk?'

'I'll come,' says Andy, surprising us all.

'Actually, darling,' says Skinny Alison, 'I think I'd rather have an early night. I need to get up early to try and get hold of that incompetent bloody seamstress in the morning.'

'OK darling, go ahead. I fancy a night out.' Skinny Alison's features droop, and I almost feel sorry for her, but it soon passes as she bullies Plump Alison and Charlie, who were clearly also looking forward to a night out, into escorting her back to the villa.

Multicoloured lights flash through the darkness, the sweat of 20,000 revellers fills the air and the insistent beat of electro house pumps through our veins. Nazi officers, sexy nurses and PVC-clad beauties mingle with only slightly less exotically dressed clubbers. A naked couple is almost shagging on stage – they put a stop to the live sex shows a few years ago, but the simulation is pretty realistic. Dwarfs fondle girls in stockings and suspenders carrying whips. Nice work if you can get it, I suppose, if you're a dwarf.

The popularity of Manumission is staggering. Queuing time for your average Joe is generally a couple of hours, but we managed to blag our way to the front of the guest list queue in ten minutes. This was not, as you might expect, due to the extreme beauty of Kim, or Ben, or even Poppy; people are used to extreme beauty here. No, we managed to swan past a whole load of satisfactorily put-out models entirely thanks to my father's longstanding notoriety in the Balearics.

'You've got to hand it to him, Bella, he's a groovy old bugger,' were Poppy's words, as my heart swelled with a weird kind of pride.

Now we're all on the dance floor, vaguely paired up – me with Mark, Damian with Poppy, Dad with Kim, Ben with Veronique and Andy kind of hovering on the sidelines. He's a good dancer, I notice.

Mark puts his arms around me and starts gyrating unnecessarily, grinding his pelvis into mine. As any inhibitions I might once have had disappeared hours ago, I'm finding this mightily enjoyable and looking forward to what I'm assuming will be the logical conclusion to tonight. I close my eyes and let the sensations wash over me. Suddenly they stop and I open my eyes. Mark is looking over my shoulder. I turn round and follow his gaze. Two little brunettes in short dresses, one hot pink, the other orange, are attracting quite a bit of attention with some clearly South American hip undulations. Fuck. The Brazilian twins. Just my bloody luck, I think, any idea of my night culminating in some hot shagging disappearing in a puff of smoke.

'I'll be back in a minute, babe.' Mark can't get away fast enough. He practically runs over to them and they both squeal enthusiastically and throw their arms around him.

And in a flash the scene changes from divinely decadent to disgustingly decadent. Dwarfs leer repellently. The lingerie-clad babes seem to mock me, cackling as they crack their whips. The Nazis assume a terrifyingly sinister mantle. *Of course they do, they're fucking Nazis, for Christ's sake. Whoever thought that was cool?* I want to scream. My father has his hand right up Kimbo's skirt. It's the last straw. I mumble hasty goodbyes to a surprised Poppy and Damian and push my way past the crowds out of the club.

Outside I catch my breath and light a cigarette.

'Are you all right?' I look up to see Andy standing behind me, his intelligent eyes concerned behind the specs. He must have followed me out.

'Yes, I'm fine, thanks. It just all got a bit much, that's all,' I say, trying to disguise my humiliation. I'm feeling horribly frumpy in my maxidress now.

'Listen,' says Andy awkwardly. 'I saw what happened in there, and for what it's worth, I think Mark's a fool. Those two girls are . . . well, they're nothing special really.'

'Thanks,' I laugh, a trifle tearfully. 'However, they're practically half my age and there are two of them. You do the math, as our American cousins are wont to say.'

Andy laughs too, looking relieved. 'Do you want to go back inside?' he asks. I shake my head.

'No, I've had enough. I'll get a cab back to the villa.'

'OK, I'll see you back.'

'Don't be silly; you've got a pink ticket. You go back inside and enjoy yourself. I'll be fine.'

'Well, if you're sure. Let me see you into a cab at any rate.'

He is as good as his word and five minutes later I am sitting in a taxi, speeding along the motorway back in the direction of Ibiza Town. Now I'm away from the seediness of Manumission I decide I fancy another drink. I'm still buzzing from the various substances I've ingested and am certainly not ready for bed yet. The idea of chilling with the Alisons and Charlie just doesn't do it for me, so I ask the driver to take me back to the harbour, instead of taking the turn that would take us back to the villa.

He shrugs. '*Sí sí, claro.*' He's seen it all before.

Five in the morning is probably the quietest you'll ever see Ibiza Town. Most of the bars pack up around three, as everyone decamps to the clubs, and there's respite for a few hours before the bars and cafés start opening up for breakfast. I am starting to regret my decision not to go home, when I see a light glimmering in the distance. I walk towards it and discover a little bar, just behind the waterfront. It's distinctly unglamorous, with unflattering strip lighting and about ten customers, but it's a bar and it will serve me a drink. I go in.

'*Un vodka limón, por favor,*' I say to the barman, plonking myself onto one of the high bar stools.

'*Cinco euros,*' says the barman, handing me the drink. I look up in surprise. Very cheap, by Ibiza standards.

'Here, let me get that,' says an unmistakeably cheeky chappie cockney voice in my ear. I look over into a pair of very sparkly blue eyes set in a ruggedly handsome face.

'Well, if you're sure . . .'

'Yeah, no problem. So what's a lovely lady like you doing all alone on a night like this? Where are your mates?'

As I start to tell him, it dawns on me that there is something out of the ordinary about this particular fellow. The short arms, the large head, the . . . the . . . little dangly legs, swinging from the bar stool. Yes, I'm being chatted up by a dwarf.

He notices me noticing and says matter-of-factly, 'Yeah babe, I'm a dwarf. Just finished my shift at Manumission. All the industry workers come here after their shifts – it's the only bar left open in town. You were lucky to find it.'

'I just kind of stumbled on it,' I say, and we start chatting. He's a bright chap, it turns out, and I surprise myself by enjoying the conversation as much as any I've had in the last few days. He seems to think so too, as he says:

'I can't tell you how good it is to talk to an intelligent English girl. I meet so many gorgeous babes in my line of business, but they're Spanish, or Dutch, or Swedish, and I haven't had a good chat for months.' Just as I am wondering whether this is a compliment or not – nothing about *me* being a gorgeous babe, I notice – he pipes up, 'Hey, I've got some Charlie back in my apartment – just along the front here. Do you fancy coming back for a line?'

Without missing a beat, I say, 'Sure,' wondering how much weirder the night can get. I get off the bar stool and watch as he swings his little legs round and leaps down to the floor. Quite a lot weirder, it transpires, as I take his hand. It's like walking along with a toddler.

'Bye Joe!' 'Adios José!' 'Ciao Giacomo!' Everyone calls out their goodbyes. My diminutive friend is popular in these parts, it seems.

It's totally light now and the cafés are setting their tables with gingham cloths and laminated menus, in time for the breakfast rush. Surprised, I ask Joe the time.

'Blimey, it's eight thirty,' he says, looking at his watch. 'Time does fly when you're having fun.' He winks. *We've been talking for three and a half hours? Bloody hell*, I think, as I follow him up the narrow staircase to his flat.

On the first floor of a slightly dilapidated nineteenth-century building, right on the seafront, it is in a fab location. I tell him as much, as I look out to sea over his wrought-iron balcony.

'Being a Manumission dwarf must pay well,' I joke, and he nods seriously.

'It's the best job in the world. I mean, let's face it, being born a dwarf could be a serious bummer, but in my line of work I meet all these gorgeous babes . . .' He's off again, I think. '. . . I mean, I should spread the word to all dwarfs – move to Ibiza – but then I might be doing myself out of a job.'

As he can't reach the table, he racks a couple of lines out on the wooden floorboards and we both sniff greedily. Then he gets out a photo album and starts showing me pictures of all the 'babes' he's had over the years. 'She was my girlfriend,' he says, pointing out an improbably pneumatic blonde. 'And her,' gesturing towards a leggy brunette. And on and on and on.

By now I am wondering what to make of it all. He is clearly trying to pull me, I think. Could I go through with it? On the one hand, it would be a great story to tell the grandchildren. On the other . . . hmmm. In my defence, it's been a very long night.

I'm still trying to make up my mind when he excuses himself to go to the loo. I'm idly wondering if he has a special WC, half a foot off the ground, so he can reach it (or is his cock ENORMOUS? – surely nature compensates in some way?), when something catches my eye. Hanging over a chair that until now was partially obscured from my vision is a very familiar-looking dress. *My white dress*.

I pick it up and scrutinize it just to be sure. Yes, it's

definitely mine. Same neckline, same crochet, same red wine stain on the hem. Little bugger. It must have been him filching it from the next-door cubicle. More in his eye line, I suppose. He comes back from the loo.

Slightly disappointed I'll never find out about his cock, I hold up the dress and ask, 'What's this?'

'Oh some tart left it on the toilet floor, so I grabbed it,' he chortles. 'Sometimes we do cross-dressing dwarf weddings and I thought it would make me a beautiful bride.'

I start to laugh immoderately. The idea that my minidress could be floor-length on him is enough of a turn-off to bring me to my senses.

'Tee hee hee . . . hee hee . . . heee hee hee hee heeeee . . . sorry Joe, but I've got to go. See ya!'

Seeing the disappointment on his weirdly handsome face, I relent.

'I'm the silly tart whose dress it was, you see.'

He laughs too, then asks, a tad desperately, 'Go on gorgeous, what d'ya say – a quick shag, just for a laugh?'

'I can't,' I say, 'but thanks for the offer.'

'No hard feelings?'

'No hard feelings,' I say, as I bend down to take his hand.

I am still giggling as I walk down the harbour, clutching my crochet dress to my breast like the blue blanket Max used as a comforter when he was a toddler. And then something makes me laugh even more.

Mark, still in his horrible 'sit on my face' T-shirt, his lower flanks only in very tight briefs, is running down the seafront, a look of abject panic on his face.

We stare at each other.

'Well?' I ask.

'Their bloody father came back,' he pants, and I laugh some more.

'What happened to you?' he asks eventually. I tell him and soon we are both laughing so much that it feels as if we'll be mates forever.

'Let's go back to the villa,' says Mark. 'I've got a bottle of Scotch.'

'OK,' I say. 'But no shagging. You're a fucking slag.'

'Takes one to know one,' he says companionably, and we walk back, arm-in-arm, in search of a cab.

Chapter 4

I'm standing in the printing room, binding twenty long and extremely tedious presentations. This is the downside of being me. I've wanted to be an artist ever since I was tiny, and have sold a fair amount of my work over the years, but not nearly enough to keep me in the manner to which I'd like to become accustomed. My miserable time at art college coincided with the new-found notoriety of Tracey Emin and Damien Hirst, and a whole host of my contemporaries attempted to emulate their success with substandard parodies, sold to a gullible public as avant-garde brilliance. My less zeitgeisty approach to art (drawing and painting things I find visually appealing) sadly failed to grab the same media attention, as a result of which I am still that oh-so-romantic figure, the struggling artist. That is, skint.

In order to buy myself time to paint, have fun and pay the mortgage, I take on temping contracts – anything from a few days to a few weeks, depending how desperate I am. I started off temping in media companies, which I thought would be fun. And in the beginning they were: post-production houses in Soho, advertising agencies and

PR firms around Charlotte Street, breathtakingly pretentious record labels in Clerkenwell where all the fonts
were lower case. I liked going to work in jeans and
trainers and hanging out with wisecracking movers and
shakers who thought they were cool. Occasionally even
the temps were treated to very long lunches that turned
into druggy nights. But after a while I noticed everyone
was getting younger than me, and there's something desperately sad about making coffee for twenty-something record
execs when you're pushing thirty.

So fortuitously I discovered I could do a new type of
temping: desk-top publishing. DTP, as it's known in the
trade, involves making presentations look pretty, using
computer graphics packages like Photoshop and Quark.
It appeals to the artist in me. It certainly beats filing or
co-ordinating people's diaries (one of my pet hates – I
mean, how much more servile can you get? Besides, I'm
crap at efficiency). And it pays substantially more than
bog-standard secretarial temping. But – and it's a big BUT
– most companies that use DTP operators, as we are
glamorously called, are financial ones. Yes, even now, as
the reviled institutions desperately try to claw back business with hideously written dossiers, brimming with
management speak and graphs.

And, as far as atmosphere goes, financial companies
suck. They've always been life-sappingly corporate.
That's a given. From the horrible suits everyone wears,
to the icy air conditioning that makes you wish you
were wearing one, to the macho trading-floor filth that
masquerades as witty banter, everything about them has
always conspired to destroy the soul. Now, the added
frisson of grim fear and shoulder-sagging desolation
really make them the last place on earth any sane person
would choose to hang out.

And binding is about as dismal as it gets. At least if you're hiding behind your computer you can waste half the day pissing about on the internet. As it happens, the binding really ought to have been done by Sebastian, the dim, blond, posh gap-year intern. But he doesn't get asked when there's a perfectly good female around to patronize. It's on days like today that I feel a total loser compared to my friends in their high-flying careers, however tenuous such careers may now seem. The idea of Poppy binding is frankly laughable. But I just cannot contemplate what kind of 'real' office-bound career I might have chosen. Or what I could do instead. Become a tree surgeon? No, I decide grimly, if this is the price I must pay for my art, so be it. One day I'll be able to support myself without stooping to this.

So I punch another set of holes into another sheaf of paper.

'Bella,' calls Gina, PA to one of the directors, 'your phone's ringing.'

I make my way back to my hot desk and pick it up.

'Hello, darling. Can you think of anything that rhymes with erection?'

'Hi, Mum. How are you?' My mother writes erotic poetry and I love her to bits.

'Rough as a badger's arse, I'm afraid.'

I laugh. 'Lovely expression, Mummy.'

'I think it's rather good – I only learnt it recently. Anyway, it sums up how I feel perfectly, but it's entirely self-inflicted so I'm trying not to feel too sorry for myself.'

'What have you been up to?'

'Well, Tabitha and Valentine came to stay for a few days, which you know is always lethal. She's done something quite groovy to her hair. Then yesterday that ghastly little man with the squint – I think he's the new

46

postmaster or something – wanted me to sign some horrid petition so I fobbed him off with a couple of large whiskies. And then Auntie Charlotte rocked up on her motorbike – and, well, as you can probably imagine, it all went downhill from there. Anyway, what was I ringing for? Yes . . . erection . . .'

'Erm . . . deflection? Reflection? Rejection?' I proffer.

'Not really the mood I was after . . .'

'Perfection?'

'That's it!' she cries triumphantly. 'Thanks, darling. Love you! Speak later.'

I hang up and laugh. Mum can't really concentrate on anything else mid-poetry and I know she'll call back later. We speak at least once a day.

They were fabulous tabloid fodder in the early Seventies, my parents. Dad, the boy from the wrong side of the tracks, shagging his way round London on the strength of his winning way with a camera; Mum, the outrageously beautiful but seriously impoverished posh bird dabbling in modelling to try and boost the family fortunes. There are some wonderful photos of her in my old home near Oxford, all sepia-tinted, doe-eyed, floppy-hatted early Biba and Ossie Clark stuff. I think they really did love each other, but no one in their right mind could put up with my father's womanizing for long. Still, my childhood was happy enough. They divorced before I was old enough to realize what was going on, and Max and I had the fun of a dual existence, spending term time and Christmas with Mum in the English countryside and Easter and summer holidays with Dad in lovely, warm, beautiful Mallorca.

Forgetting all about the binding for a few blissful minutes, I decide to have a quick look at my emails. Ooh – a Facebook notification.

Ben Jones has tagged a photo of you on Facebook.

I click on the link with the usual just-been-tagged trepidation. Unlike my luminously photogenic mother, I either look absolutely horrific or surprisingly pretty in photos – nothing in between. People, even Ben, whom I'd forgive most things, shouldn't be allowed to tag one without one's consent, really they shouldn't. Facebook opens and I see that he's posted an entire album of holiday snaps. Christ Almighty. I click on the first one, which features Damian, Poppy and me sitting around our lunch table that day at Sa Trinxa, several empty bottles and ashtrays between us. Poppy and Damian are smiling into the camera, their usual shiny, gorgeous selves. I appear to be eating, drinking, smoking and cackling with laughter, *all at the same time*. My wet hair is plastered to my scalp and my halterneck bikini top has rucked up on one side, making my boobs go all wonky. It is quite hideous, something akin to a Hogarthian gin hag.

Frantically I detag myself, trying not to feel too depressed as I remember how attractive and confident I was feeling that afternoon. That'll teach me. Aware of the possible damage limitation now necessary, I start to click through the rest of the photos, most of which, I can't help but notice, are of Ben himself, unfailingly gorgeous in every one. Surely he didn't keep asking us all to take photos of him with his own camera or phone?

An adenoidal whine punctures my musings.

'Bella? Have you finished binding those presentations yet? You do know we need them for a meeting in ten minutes? Surely whatever you're doing can wait till afterwards?'

It's Stella, the other director's PA. Thank fuck she can't see my monitor from where she's sitting. She's right, of course, but I don't enjoy being spoken to like that by someone five years my junior who is content to

48

organize someone else's diary for the rest of her life. Nor one who thinks, 'Oooh I'm such a cheap date – a glass of wine goes straight to my head' is an acceptable conversational gambit.

Gina gives me a sympathetic glance as I hurry back to the printing room.

Roll on 5.30.

I heave an enormous sigh as I walk out. Being stuck in that place on such a beautiful day really pisses me off. There aren't even windows in my corner of the office. Last week Stella told me off for dressing 'like you're going to the beach. We wear smart business attire in this office.' 'Smart business attire' – now there's a phrase to strike ice into your heart in the depths of summer. I've compromised with my old black interview jacket over a pale pink shift dress with platform court shoes. God I'm a rebel. The black kills the baby pink stone dead but I'm buggered if I'm going to waste money on another suit jacket. Now I take it off and replace the uncomfortable platforms with a pair of flat leather sandals. It's not exactly cutting edge but at least I feel as if I'm in the land of the living. The land of the *summer* living. I shove the despised items into my handbag, which now bulges so alarmingly I have to carry it in my hand rather than over my shoulder.

If my current place of work has one saving grace, it's its Mayfair location, the majority of financial institutions being stuck in the City, or, worse, stranded in the vampirically bloodless no-man's-land that is Canary Wharf. East London may be hip but the Square Mile depresses the hell out of me – except at weekends, when you can appreciate the buildings without the suits.

Not wanting to waste a moment of sunshine, I decide to walk home. It'll only take an hour or so and I'm not meeting Poppy till 7.30. People are beginning to throng the pavements, spilling out of pubs and bars. I amble through the grand streets of Mayfair to Hyde Park and the rose gardens, whose overblown beauty at this time of year transports me to some far-off fairyland. Then the long walk past the Serpentine, teeming with ducks, geese, swans, gulls, runners, Rollerbladers and tourists. By the time I hit Portobello Road I'm thoroughly invigorated by the sheer buzz of London in the summertime, Stella and binding far from my thoughts.

When I first started coming to London with Poppy, in our teens, we'd always hang out on Portobello Road – initially to browse the market for 1920s and 30s memorabilia, then to gaze at cool boys in pubs and bars. Neither of us had the confidence to chat to them in those days. Anyway, I always loved the area, and was determined that it would be my home one day.

It wasn't as simple as that, but a couple of years out of Goldsmiths, living in a grimy flat-share in Balham, I saw an ad in the 'For Sale' section of the *Standard* for a 'tiny, run-down one-bedroom flat with balcony in the heart of Notting Hill'. Balcony? This was beyond my wildest dreams. So I hopped on the Central Line on a lovely summer evening and went, heart in mouth, to the address I'd scribbled down on a Post-it note. The location was perfect – a winding side street off the dodgy end of Portobello Road, with a row of pastel-painted terraced early Victorian houses. 'Run-down' was accurate enough, though. The pink stucco was peeling badly and it smelt as if the rubbish hadn't been taken away for weeks.

Yet up four flights of rickety stairs lay the flat of my dreams. Yes, it was tiny, and yes the swirly carpet was hideous and the kitchen units painted the most revolting orangey salmon pink, but there was a little stone balcony leading out from the kitchen with views over the rooftops of West London and I just knew I'd be happy there.

My darling nan (my mother's mother is still 'Granny') had left me a small nest-egg which just covered the deposit. When she died, she was still living in the terraced house on the Hoxton/Dalston borders where my dad was brought up, one of the few slums to have survived Hitler's bombs. Dad offered to buy her a nice place in the country but she always stubbornly refused. The East End was what she knew and loved. It came as an enormous shock to discover she'd squirrelled away fifty grand to be divided equally between me and Max, her beloved grandchildren. Dad inherited the house, which he rents to Max as premises for his hugely successful bar/restaurant business. Funny how Nan was sitting on a goldmine for all those years. I still miss her.

Now I let myself in and look around contentedly. One of the first things I did when I moved in was to rip out that horrible carpet and paint the floorboards white and, though I say so myself, the effect is pretty damn cool. There wasn't much cash left for decorating, but I replaced the salmon-coloured kitchen units with some inoffensive ones from Ikea, laid blue and white mosaic tiles over the splash-back and put up some French art nouveau posters in second-hand frames. With my little herb garden on the window ledge and balcony door open so you can see all my flower boxes, I like to think the effect is artfully bohemian.

My living room is a mishmash of old and new, but that's the way I like it. There are books everywhere. One wall is completely lined with bookshelves but that's not nearly enough, so they tend to pile up on the floor. A zebra-print Sixties beanbag and sheepskin rug look incongruously Austin Powers against the antique chandelier, huge fake

Venetian mirror and chaise longue I've picked up in the market over the years. I found my most recent acquisition, a fairly nasty repro Forties chest of drawers, in a skip. Now that I've painted it bright lacquer red, changed the handles and put some gorgeous chinoiserie silk under a sheet of glass on its surface, I adore it. I'm considering upholstering the chaise longue similarly, but that might drain my beer resources.

White muslin curtains flutter around the sash window, which looks out onto a window box crammed with colourful geraniums. My beloved oils hang from the walls that are not lined with books, and overgrown houseplants take up probably more floor space than they should.

I go into my bedroom to get changed and my smugness evaporates. Christ, the mess. When my flat is tidy it can look very pretty indeed. I tidied up the living room yesterday. But it's so small, and OK, I'm such a slut, that mess does accumulate extraordinarily quickly. I start rummaging through the clothes on the floor in search of something to wear. Poppy said that Damian and Ben might be joining us later, so I need to look good. Or, at least, not like a Hogarthian gin hag. After trying on and discarding several options, I settle on a short halterneck floral tea dress in shades of mauve, navy and white that shows off the remnants of my Ibiza tan. I'll pair it with my old navy Converse to stop it looking too girly, but in the meantime I wander barefoot to the fridge and pour myself a glass of wine.

I pick up my phone to look at the time. It's only 6.45; still plenty of time before I meet Poppy at The Westbourne, so I go out onto my balcony and gaze over the treetops. It really is a gorgeous evening. I do a lot of my painting out here – so much so, in fact, that I've probably exhausted this particular view. I really must get a studio sorted, but

I'm absolutely broke, especially after the Ibiza shenanigans. And there's Glastonbury, Bestival and all sorts coming up. *Priorities, Bella.* Sometimes I wonder how much I really love my painting if I'm happy to spend so much time and money partying. If I could dedicate my life to lotus-eating, would I? I probably need to be way more dedicated to ever really succeed, especially in the current dreary climate. On the other hand, artists are meant to be hedonistic, aren't they?

Suddenly I laugh. Come on, Bella, snap out of it. *Artists are meant to be hedonistic* indeed! A pretentious excuse for getting off your tits if ever there was one.

I go inside to redo my make-up, brush my hair, drain my glass, shove my feet into my battered Converse and pick up a denim jacket in case it gets chilly later. Money, keys, fags in pocket. No need for a handbag as I'm not going far.

As I head towards The Westbourne, it strikes me how much the area has changed since I moved here. I still love it. The architecture is fab and nothing beats getting one's vegetables from the market on a Saturday morning (if one is up, that is), but the fabled 'cultural diversity' has become a bit of a joke. Whatever you may feel about American bankers, culturally diverse they are not. And now half of them are out of work, the streets are crawling with them, like expensively shod vermin. (Actually, running with them, as they can no longer afford their gyms. The heart bleeds.) Still, while Notting Hill's no longer the in place to live, for me it still has that slightly arty loucheness that an entire plague of penny-loafer-wearing Chad Jnr IIs would be hard pushed to destroy.

The USP of The Westbourne is its relatively sizeable beer garden, all too rare a commodity in central London, which opens directly onto the street for maximum posing potential. It's predictably heaving, but Poppy has managed to secure a table outside. The cream of London's beautiful people jostles for standing room on the pavement, spilling pints of expensive lager on Sass & Bide jeans. A white E-type Jag, circa 1972, provides some much-needed extra seating. Three skinny girls perch on its bonnet and a ridiculously handsome black guy grins from the driving seat. This summer a disproportionate number of people are wearing Stetsons. Wild West London indeed.

Poppy stands up and waves enthusiastically. She's wearing a very short navy and white striped Christopher Kane bodycon dress with outrageous vintage Vivienne Westwood silver platforms. And a trilby. No cloned headwear for my best mate.

'Hello lovely, how are you?' She envelops me in a bear hug with a strength that belies her tiny frame, a result of the boxing lessons she's been taking for the last couple of years.

'All the better for seeing you. Horrendous day in the office, as usual. *Save me from those people!*'

Poppy laughs. 'Awww, try and rise above it, sweetheart. It's only a couple more weeks now, isn't it, till you're free again? Just think of all that lovely money.'

I smile. She knows me so well. There are two large bottles of Magners on the table, with their accompanying ice-filled pint glasses. 'Is this for me?' I ask, and she nods, so I sit down.

'How are you anyway? Looking gorgeous as ever. I love the hat.'

'Hides a multitude of sins. Heeeeavy night last night.' Poppy grimaces, miming shooting herself in the head, and I laugh sympathetically. Within seconds the grimace is replaced with a radiant smile. 'But I've got some good news – I've just been promoted!'

'Oh yay, well done Pops. Congratulations!' I lean over to give her a hug. 'But I thought you were promoted only a couple of months ago?'

'I was,' she grins. 'And they've decided to promote me again! You're looking at the new Deputy Head of Production for Europe.'

'Fucking hell, Popsicle. That's brilliant! I'm so pleased for you. This calls for champagne. Don't go anywhere.' And I elbow my way through the packed pub to the bar. I certainly can't afford to be buying champagne in pubs, but if ever an occasion called for it, this does. I am hugely impressed by Poppy's achievements and not jealous in the slightest. OK, there may be a teensy bit of salary envy, but overall I'm delighted.

After waiting for about fifteen minutes, I am finally served by the way-too-attitudey staff. I lug the champagne bucket back outside and plonk it on the table. 'Sorry to take so long. It's mad in there.'

'Don't be silly. And you shouldn't be buying me champagne either – I'm the one with the obscene salary.' She tries to give me a couple of twenties, but I wave them away. 'No no, this is on me.'

'OK, but drinks on me for the rest of the night.'

'It's a deal.' Big relief.

I pour the champagne and we clink glasses.

'Cheers!'

'To Poppy's staggering success,' I intone solemnly.

'To my staggering success,' she concurs, knocking back the glass in one. 'God, I needed that. I only had three hours' sleep last night.'

'Anything exciting?' I top her up again.

'Oh, just some naff awards do. Angelina Jolie was there, minus Brad and weird rainbow tribe. She's a bit gaunt in the flesh. Very pretty, though. I got through a lot of caipirinhas. Funnily enough, Damian was also invited, in misogynist hack capacity, but obviously we were put on different tables. He kept pulling faces at me, trying to make me giggle while I was schmoozing the big cheeses at Channel 4. Prick,' she finishes fondly.

'You know you love him really.'

'Yeah I do. Great big kid.' Poppy laughs.

'So what does the new job involve? What was the title again? Deputy Head of Production for Europe? Isn't that a new area for you?'

'Well, yeah, as far as Europe's concerned.' She shrugs. 'I'll need to brush up on my French, Italian and German, of course . . .' All three, you notice. 'But in principle it's the same thing I've been doing over here – I just have to research the markets thoroughly. The main thing is, it's going to involve a *lot* of travelling – yippee! Via Condotti, here I come.'

'You lucky bugger.'

'Actually, there was one thing I wanted to suggest.' She sounds serious for a moment. 'As I'll be away quite a lot during the week, how would you like to take over my spare room as a studio? It's a bit of a hike, I know, but the light is great and you'd have loads more space than on your balcony. I'll give you a spare set of keys and you can always kip over if it gets late and you can't be arsed with the journey back.'

'Bloody hell, that is so weird! I was just thinking earlier how bored I'm getting with the view from my balcony and how I should get a studio sorted. Oh Pops, I'd love it! Thanks so much. Psychic, or what?'

'Or perhaps I'm just getting as bored with the view from your balcony as you are,' Poppy laughs, winking from under her hat.

'Ow, bitch!'

'Not really, silly. But it is about time you had a studio, don't you think?'

'Didn't I just say so? Thanks again, from the bottom of my heart.' And I stand up to give her the third hug of the evening so far. Then something occurs to me:

'Are you sure Damian's cool with it? I would hate to be an imposition . . .'

'Oh, he's fine about it. He's always flying off to do his dreadful "interviews" with Z-list slappers, anyway.' Poppy does the inverted commas fingers gesture. 'And, as I pay most of the rent, he wouldn't have much say in the matter . . . even if he *did* object, which he doesn't,' she adds hurriedly.

Poppy and Damian, being a million times cooler than I am, live in a huge warehouse conversion overlooking Hoxton Square. It *is* a bit of a trek from here, but she's right about the light in the spare room. The windows are enormous and, joy of joys, it has a skylight.

We discuss the practicalities of the studio for a bit, until I remember something.

'Oh Pops, I'm sorry. I should have asked as soon as I saw you. How's your dad? Didn't you go to see them last weekend?'

Poppy's father has Alzheimer's, and in the last year or so his decline has become much more apparent. It was a particularly cruel twist of fate a few years ago that led him, a doctor, to diagnose himself with early symptoms of the disease, acutely aware of the long-term implications. For Poppy, always a daddy's girl and an only child to boot, it was devastating. They shared the same keen intelligence and Dr Kenneth Wallace was always so proud of his clever little girl, encouraging her to apply for Oxford, planting the seeds of the self-belief that has served her so well as an adult. Despite her devastation, Pops has until recently remained staunchly upbeat about it, researching new break-throughs in treatment and medication, and supporting her mother Diana with as much of a positive outlook as she can muster. Ken still lives in the family home, looked after by Diana (with the help of carers), but it's becoming increasingly apparent that this won't be possible for much longer.

'Not great, to be honest. Oh Belles, sometimes I can hardly bear it when I remember how he used to be.' Poppy's large, almond-shaped green eyes fill with tears, which she angrily wipes away. 'It's such a bloody horrible disease.'

'I know, lovey, I know.' I reach over and squeeze her hand, thinking of the tall, bespectacled gent with his wonderfully dry wit and endless thirst for knowledge. It was always hugely entertaining around the Wallace dinner table, even when we were kids. 'He did . . . recognize you, didn't he?' I falter, as it's the big one; the big, big horror that one day her own father won't know who she is.

'Oh yes, he still recognizes me, bless his dear old heart.' Poppy smiles sadly. 'It's just the other things he doesn't recognize that are so scary.'

'Like what?'

'Like last weekend we were watching telly – that's all you can do with him any more, really, as conversation is so bloody impossible – and he thought the people on the box were outside the window, trying to break in. He got quite agitated about it and I just had to keep saying, "Dad, it's the TV, we're watching telly, remember?"'

'Oh Pops.' I squeeze her hand again, not knowing how else to proffer comfort.

'I honestly don't know how Mum copes. Remember I told you she was feeling guilty for getting irritated because he kept repeating himself?'

I nod.

'Well, it's way beyond that stage now. He isn't really a properly functioning human being at all any more. Jesus, Belles, if I ever get like that, please just give me a lethal injection.'

'You're on. And vice versa?'

We shake on it and Poppy continues.

'Dad hates the carers – keeps going on about what are all these strangers doing in my house, which you can't blame him for really. But he's very fond of the chap in the mirror. Keeps introducing his "new friend" to Mum. When he waves and smiles, the chap in the mirror waves and smiles back, you see.'

'Oh Pops, your poor mother. Surely it must nearly be time for him to go into residential care?'

'From a purely selfish point of view I'd like him to stay at home until he dies.'

'Why?'

'Because sometimes we can pretend things are like they used to be – say if Mum and I are cooking Sunday lunch and we've put Dad in front of some documentary on the telly. But it's simply not fair on Mum the rest of the time. She's being a complete bloody martyr though – reckons it would be a betrayal to put him in a home.'

I think of blonde, soignée Diana, an ex-Radio 4 presenter, still glamorous at sixty-two. Jesus. What a life sentence. For both of them.

'Damian's been looking into residential homes that specialize in dementia,' Poppy continues. 'Even though they are, by their very nature, fucking grim hellholes, some are so much better than others – actually the discrepancies are astounding. There's one he's found near enough home for Mum to visit daily that looks quite promising. We're going to go and have a look the weekend after Glastonbury.'

'He's a good chap, your man.'

'My rock.' Poppy faux-swoons, then visibly cheers up. 'Ooh look, talk of the devil. There he is with Mark! What does the sexist cunt think he's wearing?'

I follow her gaze and laugh. Mark's huge chest is clad in a T-shirt announcing *10 reasons why beer is better than women*. The last time I saw something similar was about twelve years ago, on an ill-advised student trip to the Greek island Ios. It involved an awful lot of booze and shagging randoms, and my (only) Goldsmiths friend Emma and I ended up running out of money and sleeping on a roof for a week with an entire rugby team from Halifax. Happy days.

'Is it meant to be ironic?' Poppy asks as she stands up to greet Mark.

'I've been telling him it's crap,' says Damian. 'But he insists it will get him birds. How are you anyway, my lovely?' As ever, he looks effortlessly cool in dark jeans and a close-fitting scarlet T-shirt by some obscure Japanese label, his eyes hidden by yet another pair of expensive shades. They get the pick of the latest designer kit at *Stadium*, the magazine they work on, which makes Mark's choice of garb even more baffling.

'Well, apart from this Neanderthal seriously comprom-ising my street cred, I'm fine,' says Poppy equably as she gives her boyfriend a hug.

'Just you wait,' says Mark.

'Actually, I think it's hilarious,' says a voice, and my heart jumps into my throat. It's Ben, looking like a film star. 'I especially like number six – a beer still looks as good in the morning as it did when the bar closed.'

'All right, mate,' says Damian, as they high-five each other.

'What's this in aid of?' Ben picks up the nearly empty champagne bottle.

60

'Poppy's been promoted,' I say, as she doffs her trilby and says 'Deputy Head of Production for Europe to you, sir.'

Ben breaks out in a big grin and lifts her off the ground in a great bear hug. 'Oi, put my missus down,' says Damian, as I try to ignore the brief stab of jealousy in my heart. I'd die for Poppy's casual flirtiness with Ben. It's easier when you're already taken, I suppose.

'Aren't you going to congratulate her?' he asks Damian, who laughs.

'She actually found out a couple of days ago. We celebrated then, didn't we, sweet thing?'

'Oh, we most certainly did.' Poppy smiles and puts a finger to her lips. Even after five years, the chemistry between them is obvious.

'Enough, enough – I *so* don't want the sordid details,' says Ben camply. 'Who's up for beers?'

He goes to the bar and returns minutes later with three pints of Stella.

'That was quick. It took me bloody ages to get served,' I say.

'I think the barman took a shine to me,' Ben smiles, and he's probably right. He's looking absurdly handsome in a slim-fitting navy blue suit with an open-collared white shirt that shows off his tan and incredible blue eyes. The narrow lapels and old-skool Adidas trainers neatly sidestep any suggestion of banker wanker.

'What's with the whistle, mate?' asks Damian.

Poppy groans, 'Get him with the Mockney.' Damian's Welsh lilt has just about had all its curves sanded down to standard men's magazine estuary, which is a shame. Occasionally it resurfaces when he's tired or upset. I imagine Ben's accent disappeared the moment he walked through RADA's doors (though he can apply it on demand, just as he can Scouse, or Geordie, or Glaswegian).

'Audition. A new BBC sitcom – it's being touted in the biz as the *This Life* of the new decade, and I haven't a hope in hell of landing a part. But it would be churlish not to try.' His boyish modesty is so endearing it makes me want to race right over to White City and shake the execs by the scruffs of their stupid necks. How can they be so blind not to realize what delicious gold dust they're in danger of letting slip through their fingers? But he's probably got it down to a fine art.

'Don't be a cunt,' says Mark. 'You know you're in with a chance with your *big blue eyes*.' He tries to widen his little brown ones to illustrate. 'Talking of big blue eyes, I shagged the work experience girl last night.'

'Poor little thing,' is my immediate response, and he grins. 'Yeah, I gave her a fucking nosebag full, put on some porn and soon she was letting me piss on her.'

'*What?*' Even Damian looks shocked. 'Sweet little Amy?'

'Not so sweet, mate.'

'But why did you want to piss on her?' I ask.

'Never heard of golden showers, darlin'?'

'Good God almighty, you really are a wanker, aren't you?' says Poppy.

'Not really. I made her laugh.'

'Yeah right.'

'No really, I did. I couldn't piss because of the coke, so she had to put the bath taps on full flow to encourage *my* full flow. She was giggling all over the place, little minx.'

'I hope you were nice to her in the office today,' I say sternly.

'She called in sick.' Then, seeing our combined horror and amusement, he adds, 'C'mon, it's not like she's a kid or anything. She knew what she was letting herself in for. She probably just had a hangover.'

'I'm just wondering how much lower you can sink,' says

Poppy. 'Never mind, let's at least give the poor girl the dignity of not being discussed like this any more.'

'But tell us what her tits were like first?' says Damian, leaning back nonchalantly in his chair, one foot crossed in his lap. Poppy slaps his leg, laughing.

'Fucking gorgeous.' Mark makes melon-squeezing gestures with both hands. 'Pierced nipple too. See, I rest my case for the defence – not so sweet.' Everyone laughs and I have a hideous moment of clarity.

Is this what we have come to?

I am actually quite shocked by Mark's revelation, and feel hugely sympathetic towards the work experience girl. I remember myself at that age, vulnerable and desperate to please, and can only imagine how ghastly she must be feeling today, to the extent that she couldn't face going into the office at all. Being *peed on*, for God's sake?

'Oooh Ben, loved the Ibiza Facebook pics,' says Poppy, snapping me back into reality.

'Except I had to detag myself in that one of us at Sa Trinxa,' I say grumpily. 'That was possibly the worst photo I've ever seen of myself.'

'Oh, it wasn't that bad,' says Ben, laughing.

'You know which one I mean, then?'

'Well, I know which one you detagged . . .'

'Ben, it was an awful photo,' says Poppy. 'Don't worry, Belles, you look nothing like that in real life.'

'Thank you.' I smile at her. '*That's* what I wanted to hear.'

'Talking of Ibiza, mate, did you ever hear from Kimberly again?' Damian asks Ben.

The day after my encounter with the dwarf, Kimbo and my dad said their goodbyes and left the island, leaving me hot with vicarious shame.

'Nope,' says Ben, grinning.

'Oh God, I'm so sorry,' I say, ad nauseam. 'I can't believe Dad did that. No, scrub that. I can perfectly believe Dad did that, but I really can't believe that Kim did.'

'Listen Bella.' Ben looks into my eyes with such sincerity I could melt. I wish I'd bothered to pluck my eyebrows before I came out. 'It's not your fault your father's a randy old goat. And it's certainly not your fault the bird I was shagging turned out to be such a gold-digging slag. So, for the last time, stop apologizing.'

'OK,' I smile.

'In fact he did me a favour. Veronique was hot as fuck,' he goes on, and my heart sinks again.

'Have you kept in touch with *her*?' asks Damian, taking a swig of his pint.

'Well, let's just say she has an interesting interpretation of the text medium.'

'Meaning?' asks Mark. 'Photos? Videos?'

'Both,' says Ben smugly.

'Go on, show us,' pants Mark.

'Shall we just leave them to it?' Poppy says to me, but Ben surprises us, saying, 'No, it wouldn't be right. She sent them for my eyes only.' Drop-dead gorgeous and an old-fashioned gentleman to boot. Could this man *be* any more perfect?

'Spoilsport,' sulks Mark, and Ben laughs.

'Surely you get to see enough of that sort of thing at work anyway?'

'No such thing as enough, mate.' Not for the first time, I thank the Brazilian twins for my lucky escape.

'Yeah yeah, you boys and your ludicrous conquests,' says Poppy. 'Can we talk about something a tad more interesting for all of us? Like a certain festival that's happening next week, perhaps?'

'Yay, Glastonbury!' I shout happily, more than a little pissed by now.

The Daddy of all festivals is next weekend and I'm looking forward to it enormously, despite vowing 'never again' after last year's washout. It really was repulsive, with constant, relentless rain, and mud so deep it came over the top of your wellies, which made every step a Herculean effort. Some people had their tents washed away, and were left standing in their knickers: no possessions, no money, no nothing. None of us fared that badly, but my tent was not waterproof in the slightest (not least because I kept getting too wasted to remember to zip it up properly), and I had to sleep inside a bin liner inside my sleeping bag. The irony of a bunch of middle-class twits with lovely warm homes paying through the nose to endure such miserable, Somme-like conditions was lost on none of us. Still, with that uniquely British triumph of hope over experience, we duly paid through the nose again this year. And at the beginning of April it's a gamble, as you have no idea how the summer's going to pan out. So far it's been an absolute scorcher, so fingers crossed.

'Remember Mark's trench foot last year,' laughs Damian. Mark had refused to buy wellies, claiming they were for poofs.

'Fuck me, that was painful. It took about a week to unmesh my trainers from the flesh of my feet. And another week to dry off.'

'Oh, it wasn't all bad,' says Ben. 'That first night, before the rain had really set in, was a hoot. Remember we found that random field with the tiny sound system playing some banging house? And Bella said something funny about sinking literally and metaphorically into the quagmire.'

I look up, shocked that he remembers something I said in a drug-fuelled moment nearly a year ago. I have a distinct recollection of him looking like a rock star in a fake fur coat, cowboy hat and shades, his long legs in mud-spattered jeans tucked into long black wellies. Film star, rock star, whatever . . .

'We had a laugh all right,' says Poppy. 'It just wasn't terribly comfortable. But this year is going to be beautiful, *isn't it*? Come on, let's all just will this gorgeous sunshine to continue.'

'What day are you all going down?' I ask.

'I'm shooting next Friday so can't get there till Friday night, which is a pain in the arse,' says Ben. 'I don't suppose any of you could reserve a place and set up my tent for me? All the spaces will be gone otherwise . . .'

'You lazy cunt,' says Damian. 'Course we will, mate. Mark and I have Press passes anyway, so I'll see what privileges we're entitled to this year.'

'We'll probably drive down on Thursday if you need a lift, Belles,' says Poppy.

'Thanks, Pops. Where would I be without you?'

Chapter 5

'Bella Bella, *che bella*,' says the head waiter as, an hour or so later, we walk into Osteria Basilico, the much-loved Italian on Kensington Park Road. It's a longstanding joke he's kept up ever since I first moved to the area. 'And the beautiful Poppy. Why should we be so honoured tonight?'

Poppy and I grin at each other, aware that it's pathetic to be flattered by the blandishments of Italian waiting staff, yet enjoying the compliments nonetheless.

'Hi Giovanni,' I say. 'Any tables downstairs?' Of course, all the tables outside are already taken.

'For you, anything!' He kisses his fingers. We follow him down the stairs.

Osteria Basilico is a proper old-fashioned phallic pepper mill Italian eaterie, serving classic stalwarts in lively, cavernous surroundings. The free-flowing wine and candlelit gloom encourage you to let your hair down. Not that we are in need of much encouragement.

It's pretty full but, true to his word, Giovanni finds us a table for five in the furthest corner from the bottom of the stairs.

'Shall we order some wine before we start?' asks Damian,

and as we all nod our assent, 'A white and a red to kick off with?'

He selects a Chianti and an Orvieto without bothering to look at the list. We've been here enough times by now to know it pretty comprehensively. I pay lip service to the menu, despite knowing I'll be going for the melt-in-the-mouth carpaccio and sublimely garlicky spaghetti vongole.

'Don't you understand, Max, that money is no object when it comes to making my day absolutely perfect?' comes a strident voice from the next table.

'OK OK, I was only offering you a couple of options,' retorts a laid-back and wonderfully familiar voice. 'Jesus, woman, take a chill pill.'

'Max!' I cry, jumping out of my chair. I hadn't noticed in the gloom, but sitting right next to us in this subterranean corner of West London is my resolutely East London brother, dining with Andy and Skinny Alison.

'Bella!' He rises languidly to his feet and gives me a hug. 'What a coincidence.'

'Why didn't you let me know you were in my neck of the woods? We could have hooked up for a drink.'

'You must know I never mix business with pleasure, sis.' Then, seeing the look on Alison's face, he adds, 'Just kidding. Did you know I'm sorting out the catering for Andy and Alison's wedding? As I'm Andy's best man? We thought we'd discuss it over a nice, relaxed dinner.' He rolls his eyes at me and I try not to laugh.

I know I'm biased, but Max is gorgeous. His curly blond hair used to be the bane of his life. He looked like a cherub when we were kids and spent years trying to tame it – tying it back, slicking it down, shearing it into brutal military-style No. 1s – but always the curls sprang back, a life unto themselves. Now he's come to accept them and wears them in a kind of honky afro/golden halo. He's very tall (six feet four), broad shouldered, and keeps himself in shape, but without Mark's ridiculously pumped-up look. His big long-lashed brown eyes, so similar to mine, give his face a sweetness that reflects his personality probably a lot more accurately than he would like.

'No, I didn't know, although I probably should.' I smile at Andy and Alison, willing them not to realize how comprehensively I switched off whenever Alison started boring on in Ibiza. 'Why don't you join us once you've finished eating? There's plenty of room at our table.'

'Thanks, but we haven't finalized the catering arrange-ments,' begins Alison, when Andy cuts her off. 'We'd love to,' he says firmly, smiling at me. 'I'm sure we can wind this up in the next five minutes or so while we finish our food.'

'Great,' says Max. 'We'll be over soon.' He rolls his eyes at me again. 'Right, back to business . . .'

We order our food and settle down convivially with the wine and breadbasket.

'Why the fuck did you ask them to join us, Bella?' says Mark, as everyone shushes him.

'Max is her brother, Mark,' says Poppy quietly. 'Why the fuck do you think?'

'I don't care about the shirt-lifter,' says Mark. 'But that bird. Jeeezus, she could wipe the hard-on off Hugh Heffner in a Jacuzzi full of Playmates. Does she ever smile?'

'Sssh, sssh, sssh,' we say, trying not to giggle.

'Andy's the one I object to,' says Damian, dropping his guard momentarily. 'Fucking do-gooder with his "insightful and intelligent" pieces.' His voice is sounding more Welsh by the second.

'You sound like you're quoting,' says Poppy.

'I am,' says Damian morosely. 'The National Press Awards.'

Poppy laughs. 'C'mon, sweetheart, you could have gone down that route if you wanted. You chose the sex, drugs and rock-'n'-roll path of no-resistance journalism instead, and you love it.'

'Yeah, I suppose. He doesn't have to be such a fucking smug prick about it, though . . .'

At this inauspicious juncture, the three of them join us, and we all shift around to make space.

'So did you finalize the catering arrangements?' I ask Alison, as Poppy kicks me under the table. Alison is looking quite the elegant solicitor tonight, in a beautifully tailored white cotton shirt with three-quarter-length sleeves and oversized, pushed-back cuffs. Narrow black 7/8 trousers show off her slim thighs and bony ankles. Her shoes and Mulberry handbag have been expertly and expensively crafted from the same soft tan leather, while a touch of turquoise jewellery lifts the outfit from classic boredom. Yup, the bitch looks good.

'No, not really,' she sighs. 'Nobody seems to understand how stressful it is, planning a wedding. There are so many things to consider.'

'Erm, maybe I'm being stupid, babe, but why don't you just choose some grub you like and lay on plenty of booze?' asks Mark, shoving half a bread roll into his mouth.

'People have different dietary requirements,' explains Alison patiently, as if to a five-year-old. 'Half of my friends are gluten-free, about a third don't eat dairy, loads are vegetarian and most won't countenance intensive farming, so knowing the food's provenance is vital.'

'Fucking Stoke Newington lesbians,' grunts Mark, and I try not to laugh again as I recall that Andy and Alison live in Crouch End, North London's liberal enclave, barely a stone's throw from Stoke Newington.

'Then there are the favours,' she continues earnestly. 'We

can't decide whether edible favours are the way to go – and, if so, should they come out of the catering budget?'

'I'm sorry,' says Poppy. 'But I think favours are utterly preposterous for adults.'

'What are favours?' asks Damian, speaking for the rest of us.

'Oh, ridiculous twee little gifts – sugared almonds, or packets of seeds, or horrid little gift soaps that most people will only throw away anyway and end up costing you a fortune. Honestly, Alison, save yourself the bother and expense.'

'I have to say I'm inclined to agree,' says Andy. 'If we're averaging three quid each and two hundred people, that's six hundred pounds on stuff that's only going to get chucked.' He takes a swig of his red wine.

'He can do mental arithmetic too,' says Damian, just a tad too loudly.

'I told you, money is no object,' says Alison. 'All the weddings I've been to over the last five years have had favours, and I will NOT have a second-rate, *budget* version.'

'Suit yourself,' says Poppy equably.

'I'm sure whatever Alison chooses will be perfectly delightful,' says Ben, smiling at her. 'And I for one won't be throwing mine away.' As far as I'm aware, he hasn't been invited, but nobody points this out.

For the first time since we arrived (I suspect the first time all evening), Alison smiles. It sits uneasily on her long face, the scarlet lips parting to show both top and bottom teeth. In fact, it doesn't suit her at all, and I wonder if this is partly why, like Posh Spice, she has perfected the art of looking miserable.

'Well, the jury's still out on whether we're getting them or not,' says Andy, and Alison's features revert to their habitual scowl. Thank Christ for that. Andy turns to Poppy. 'How's your father getting on?'

I had no idea Andy knew about Ken. Poppy must have confided in him in Ibiza. I can understand why – with his height, specs and obvious intelligence, Andy must remind her to an extent of her beloved daddy, the daddy she used to know.

'Bloody awfully, but thanks for asking. Last weekend was the worst so far.'

'You poor thing,' says Andy seriously. 'I don't have any personal experience of it, but I wrote a piece about dementia a few months ago and it does seem to hit the family very hard, from what all the people I interviewed told me.'

Alison is looking daggers at Pops.

'And so does cancer, and heart disease, and diabetes, all of which can be prevented with a little more self-restraint in one's life,' she says, taking a tiny sip of her red wine. I can hardly believe my ears at her insensitivity.

'Oh for Christ's sake, Al . . .' starts Andy, and Poppy smiles at him.

'Thanks, you nice man, but I can fend for myself.' She turns to Alison, and hisses, 'I suppose you also think that if he'd done the fucking crossword or Sudoku or something more often, he'd still be right as rain. My dad is a doctor, who knows all about prevention and cure, thank you very much. Can you imagine what it felt like for him to diagnose himself? He has more intelligence in his little toe, even with his illness, than you'll ever have in your whole body, you cow.'

Alison puts up her hands in mock surrender.

'No need to get personal. I didn't realize he was a doctor. I apologize. It's just that people who don't look after themselves cost the state so much money, don't you think?'

'The tax on smoking practically pays for the NHS,' says

Mark, who's enjoying this exchange thoroughly. 'More wine, anyone?' With a flourish of his huge arm, he summons the waiter and asks for four more bottles.

'Four? Are you insane?' asks Alison, askance.

'You don't have to drink them babe, do ya?' Mark turns his back on her and starts chatting to me again.

'What the fuck is her problem?' I whisper.

'She doesn't like Andy talking to Pops, is all. Stupid bitch.'

'But that's absurd. He was only being nice about her father. And anyway, even though Pops is more gorgeous than that bitch could hope to be in a million years, she's not exactly what you'd call a threat. She and Damian are devoted to each other.'

'*We* know that, gorgeous, but she doesn't.' Mark and I clink glasses and down them in one in a moment of complete solidarity. I think I might love him, despite the Brazilian twins and the intern with the pierced nipple.

After a bit, Alison turns to me.

'Remind me what is it that you do again, Bella? Isn't it something *secretarial*?' Her pale blue eyes bore into me. Her colouring is really quite striking, I find myself thinking irrelevantly, the black hair and precisely plucked brows a vivid contrast to her pale skin and eyes.

'Erm no . . . I'm an artist, but sometimes I have to do a bit of temping to help pay the bills.'

'And you really think that's any way for an adult to earn a living? Don't you think it's time you got a proper job and left the painting as a hobby? I mean, frankly, if you haven't made any money out of it now, I can't imagine you ever will. You're what? Thirty-two?'

I am stunned into silence. Not only because Alison thinks she has the right to speak to me with such vitriol, but also because she has pinpointed my Achilles heel with painful accuracy. She is beyond poisonous.

'I don't know how you can say that when you haven't seen Bella's work,' says Damian loyally. The others are all laughing loudly at something Ben's just said, so only he and Mark have heard this delightful exchange. 'She's extremely talented and I know her big break is just around the corner.'

I flash him a grateful smile. Luckily our food chooses this moment to arrive and I am spared having to defend myself further to the witch. We eat our food, and drink all the wine that Mark ordered. Then we order brandies.

'Andy,' says Alison. 'We really should be getting home. I've an early start tomorrow and I'm working on a very important case.'

'Oh yes, your job's so grown-up and important, isn't it?' I slur, completely pissed by now. 'It must be a total nightmare for you having to hang out with plebs like us.'

'Oh, I think most people around this table have pretty important jobs, Bella,' says Alison nastily. 'Don't kid yourself.'

'For God's sake, Al.' Andy looks and sounds deeply pissed off, even more than when she was going on about Poppy's dad. 'I'm sorry, Bella. Sorry Poppy, too, for earlier.'

He pulls an apologetic face at us both, but I take no notice. It's too much. After my shitty day in the office and gallons of booze, this sniping at both Poppy's deepest sadness and my deepest insecurities makes my reaction just a smidgeon over the top.

'You fucking bitch.' I chuck the remains of Alison's drink at her. 'At least I'm not a dried-up old hag who can't speak without hurting people or even smile without looking like a fucking gargoyle.' I am mesmerized by the red wine dripping down her pristine white shirt. Then I come to my senses and burst into tears.

Getting up with as much dignity as I can muster, I say,

'Max, could you cover my share of the bill, please? I'll sort it out with you tomorrow.'

And I stagger upstairs, sobbing. I am halfway down Kensington Park Road when I hear footsteps behind me.

'You left your jacket behind,' says Ben, holding it out to me with a smile.

'Oh, thanks so much, I'm such a twat. My keys and wallet are in the pocket.' And I cry some more, as Ben strokes my hair, standing there in the street, going, 'Sssh, sssh, it's going to be OK, everything's OK.'

After a bit he laughs. 'You certainly told Alison where to go.'

'I'm already regretting it.' I look up at him through teary eyes. 'I seem to have sobered up in the last couple of minutes.'

'Silly bitch deserved it, going on at you and Pops like that. Oh, I know I was nice about her stupid favours, but I was bored shitless by the conversation and it seemed the only way to bring it to a close.' We both laugh.

'Well, goodnight then,' I say reluctantly.

'Don't be silly, I'm walking you home,' says Ben, and my heart starts to beat alarmingly fast. *Don't be silly, Bella, he's just being nice. Remember what a gentleman he is.*

He lights us each a fag. We turn right into Portobello Road and continue down through the market-stall debris, under the Westway and finally into my street. Ben is talking easily about Poppy's promotion, laughing about Mark's appalling behaviour, bitching about Alison. I am tongue-tied, but happy to listen, nod and laugh when required.

'Well, here I am then,' I say stupidly. 'Thanks for looking after me.'

'It was my pleasure, darling.' Ben smiles that knee-trembling smile again. And very slowly, bends his head to kiss me. His lips are soft yet insistent. Involuntarily my own mouth opens just a fraction and he lingers a moment longer, running his tongue ever so lightly against my trembling bottom lip. Reluctantly, it seems, he pulls away, holding me in his electric blue gaze.

'You looked very pretty tonight, you know.' Then he turns on his heel and walks back down the street, turning once to blow me another kiss.

Bugger me.

Chapter 6

Remember waking up on Christmas morning when you were a kid? That manic overexcitement that got you out of your own bed and into your parents' at 5 a.m., only to be told to go back to sleep for a couple of hours? Well, that had nothing on the hyperactive frenzy I seem to have worked myself up into this morning. I am a Ritalin-dependent attention-seeking seven-year-old, without the compensating cuteness.

For today we are going to Glastonbury. It is a glorious, glorious sunshiny day, I've been packed since 8 a.m. and Poppy and Damian are picking me up in half an hour. I always get excited about Glastonbury, even when it's raining, but this year is different. This year I have been kissed by Ben, and the next four days stretch out in front of me, reverberating with romantic opportunity.

I haven't seen or spoken to Ben since he walked me home the other night, and neither have I told anyone about *the kiss*. I don't know why. Normally I'd be straight on the phone to Poppy, but she is so much closer to Ben than I am because of Damian that I've never really confided in her about my feelings for him, though I imagine she has a pretty shrewd inkling. No fool, our Pops.

It's my wonderful little secret. Again and again I play over those few seconds. 'It was my pleasure, darling.' . . . Smile. Kiss. 'You looked very pretty tonight, you know.' He called me pretty! He kissed me! I realize I'm possibly reading too much into what was most likely just a drunken flirty moment, but I don't care. I've been on Cloud Nine for the past week and am full of joyous optimism for what the next few days may bring.

Unable to sit still for a second, I go over my packing for the twentieth time to see what I've forgotten. Three bikinis (did I mention the joyous optimism?), four pairs of knickers, three vest tops, two miniskirts, black leggings in case it gets cold, black polo-neck jumper ditto, yoga pants, T-shirt and hoodie for sleeping in if I get the chance, waterproof jacket and trousers, wellies, which take up far too much room in the rucksack but I'm not taking any chances after last year, flip-flops. I am wearing ancient cowboy boots and a white sundress printed with red cherries.

Satisfied that my clothing covers every eventuality, I turn my attention to sundries. Wipes, wipes and more wipes; toothbrush and toothpaste; moisturizer; sun block that I'll forget to use; dry shampoo that after a couple of days my greasy barnet won't allow me to forget to use; deodorant; make-up. Come on, I'm hardly going to be slumming it to that extent, especially with Ben around. Strapped to the outside of my rucksack are my sleeping bag and pillow. Yes, a real one. I don't care if I look a pillock, it makes the biggest difference in the world to comfort. Oooh, bin bags and loo paper! I suddenly remember and dash to the kitchen and bathroom. I'm out of both. I'll have to remember to get some from the Tesco megastore we always stop at on the final leg of the journey. A 1.5-litre bottle of Evian and 1.5-litre Evian bottle filled with vodka as glass isn't allowed on site; 3 grams of coke and 12 pills secured inside my bra, the only place security won't look if I'm unlucky enough to be stopped; 60 Marlboro Lights.

I look at the time on my phone. Still twenty minutes until they're due, and Poppy and Damian aren't the most punctual of couples at the best of times. I pick up an old copy of *Stadium*, Damian's magazine, and go out onto the balcony to kill some time. The cloudless sky is already a medium denim hue and it's only ten past ten. Feeling the sun warm on my shoulders, I heave a deep sigh of satisfaction. The next few days are going to be fabulous. Trying to quell my impatience, I flip through *Stadium*. It falls open randomly at *17 things you should have grown out of by now.* Hmmm, let's see. *No. 3. Pretending to find older women attractive. Let's face it, nineteen is their optimum age. Saggy tits and wrinkles are never a good look.* Oh charming. No wonder Mark's like he is. I have a look at the tiny by-line to see if Damian's responsible. No, not this time. I'm sure Poppy would have something to say if he were.

Slightly depressed now, I shut *Stadium* and gaze out over the leafy view for a bit, before going back inside to pick up the card I've made to thank Poppy for offering me her spare room as a studio. On the front is a highly stylized pen and ink illustration of Pops herself, hair in a ponytail, jaunty scarf around her neck in the manner of a 1950s fashion drawing, heading towards an old-fashioned aeroplane, an old-fashioned suitcase with labels spelling out *Paris, Barcelona, Milan* and *Capri* swinging from her hand. On the back, in the same style, is a drawing of me standing at my easel, wearing a checked artist's smock and a headscarf around my head like a turban. Inside, in large, glittery writing, I simply wrote, *Thanks, dear friend xxx.*

I love making cards for people. I like making presents too. Last Christmas I found an old dolls' house in a junk shop, which, I decided, with a bit of TLC, would make a perfect present for Milly, my Goldsmiths chum Emma's five-year-old daughter. I painted it white, with a pink roof, and big, blousy cabbage roses around the door, getting carried away with a riot of hearts and flowers on the shutters and climbing up the side of the house. After spending a happy afternoon seeking out remnants in the fabrics and wallpaper departments of Peter Jones, I hung pretty pink and white gingham curtains at the windows, and had a real blast with the interior, wallpapering each room in different shades and patterns of pink and even laying tiny bits of cream carpet. The *pièce de résistance* was the installation of battery-operated fairy lights throughout, so that the house lit up when you pressed the switch on the back. Of course it was beyond kitsch, but Milly absolutely adored it, and the delight on her face when she opened it was worth every penny I'd spent on it (in the end, it worked out significantly more expensive than it would have done just to have bought her a new dolls' house).

I felt slightly sheepish about the hours I'd put into my labour of love – let's face it, it was a pretty bloody twee thing to do – and was reluctant to tell Poppy and the others. As it happened, I needn't have worried. They all thought it was brilliant, and Pops even insisted Damian drive me all the way over the river to Emma's terraced house in Stockwell to deliver it, all wrapped up with a pink bow on top, one cold December evening. Mark did take to calling me Polly-Bella-Anna for a few weeks afterwards, and often asked if I'd done my good deed for the day, but all the piss-taking was affectionate.

My phone rings. I look at the display. It's Poppy.

'Hi babe, we're downstairs.'

'Yay! You're early! I'll be down in a sec.' I lock the balcony door, plonk a pair of oversized shades on my nose, heave my rucksack over my back – fuck me, it's heavy – pick up my tent and card and stagger down four flights of rickety stairs.

I love Damian's car. He bought it last year when he was upgraded from staff writer to features editor and columnist on *Stadium* (Poppy refers to the promotion as 'the Faustian pact'). It's a navy blue convertible late Sixties Merc and today will be the first time I've been in it with the top down. Hendrix is blaring from the stereo. We are going to look like such a bunch of wankers rolling up to Glasto. I can't wait.

Poppy jumps out to give me a kiss. She looks fantastic as ever, in her Ibiza denim hot pants, cowboy boots, sage green long-line vest and the trilby she had on the other night. If anything, she seems even more hyper than I am, chattering away at such speed I can barely follow what she's on about.

'If you can shut up for one moment, I have something for you,' I say, proffering the card. Pops looks at it properly and a big smile crosses her lovely face.

'Oh Belles, you are so talented. I wish I could draw like that. Look, darling, at what Bella's made for me.' She shows it to Damian.

'Bloody brilliant. You've captured my missus perfectly, gorgeous little jet-setter that she is.' He gives the card a kiss and props it up on the dashboard.

'Thanks guys!' I bask cheerfully in their praise.

Poppy opens the boot and there is just enough room for my rucksack and tent.

''Fraid you'll have to put Mark's stuff on the back seat,' she says. 'Never mind – you can put it between you like a wall to stop his groping hands.'

'I really don't think Mark's going to be interested in groping me,' I say, still mindful of what I just read in *Stadium* and thinking, irritatingly, of the Brazilian twins and the young intern with the pierced nipple.

Damian laughs, the sun bouncing off yet another pair of designer shades. 'You're female, aren't you?'

I get into the back of the car via Poppy's passenger seat. We get going and within minutes I am rummaging for something to tie my hair back with. Driving west out of London is great. People in other cars hoot and the odd pedestrian waves. My elation is building to a disquieting crescendo and we haven't even started on the intoxicants yet.

'So where are we picking Mark up from?' I shout over the wind and music.

'Richmond,' shouts back Poppy.

'How very respectable,' I laugh.

'I know – seems unlikely, doesn't it?'

'By the way, Bella, big respect for what you said to Alison the other night,' shouts Damian. 'The look on her face when you chucked your drink at her! She started ranting about getting you to pay for dry cleaning after you'd left.'

'Oh, she wants more than that. She wouldn't contact me directly, of course. She told Andy to tell Max that her shirt was ruined and she wants me to replace it. It was Jil Sander apparently. Fuck knows how I'm going to afford that.'

'They've got identical shirts in Primark for a fiver,' says Poppy. 'And you can cut the label out of my old Jil Sander coat if you want. Bet she won't notice. Insensitive bitch.'

We all crack up at this. God, life is good.

'So what's this shoot Ben's on tomorrow?' I ask, unable to resist the temptation of talking about him.

'Abercrombie and Fitch,' says Damian. 'He said the last one was great – the director got them all stoned, then just filmed all these pretty young things laughing unselfconsciously together. Money for old rope if you ask me.'

'Yeah, like *you* work your fingers to the bone. Comparable to mining is the life of a *Stadium* columnist,' says Poppy, as I try to banish from my mind the image of Ben getting stoned with a load of nineteen-year-old natural beauties. I really wish I hadn't picked up that bloody magazine.

After a while we turn into a tree-lined street of semi-detached Edwardian houses with perfectly kept front lawns behind box hedges. It's the sort of street where dads wash their cars on a Saturday morning.

'This can't be where Mark lives,' I say in bemusement. 'It's so . . . so . . . suburban.'

'Oh he's all talk and no trousers, our Marky,' says Poppy. 'Underneath all the bullshit, he's as conventional as they come.'

Mr Conventional swaggers out of No. 42. Bare-chested, he is wearing very tight, very faded jeans, a leather thong around his neck, Aviator shades and a cowboy hat.

'He sooo waxes his chest,' says Poppy under her breath.

'Auditioning for the Village People, Marky?' shouts Damian.

Mark grins. 'You're just jealous I can carry it off,' he shouts back, and makes his way over to the car, pausing to say hello to a couple of little girls on tricycles.

He chucks his huge rucksack into the back seat as effortlessly as if it were made of foam, then saunters back inside and returns with a crate of Stella, which he throws in on top of the rucksack. Winking at me, he mouths, 'Hello gorgeous.' I smile. For all his manifold faults, there is something about Mark you can't help liking.

We resume our journey and soon excitement is mounting again.

'Beers, anyone?' says Mark.

'Better not mate,' says Damian. 'But the rest of you go ahead.'

'Poor love,' says Poppy, leaning over and helping herself. 'I'll drive on the way back.'

'Yeah, when a drink'll be the last thing you want,' laughs Mark.

'Dammit, you've rumbled my cunning plan.'

I open my can of Stella and pour the golden liquid down my throat. 'Mmmm, nice and cold.'

'Straight out of the fridge,' says Mark. 'They won't stay cold for long in this weather though, so we'd better drink 'em quickly.'

'Ooh twist my arm, why don't you?' laughs Poppy. 'Tell you what, why don't we have a sing-song?'

As we can't agree what to sing, she plugs her iPod into the Merc's speakers and soon we are bellowing out everything from Bowie to Amy Winehouse to Stevie Wonder to Blur to – erm – The Carpenters.

'Poppy?' Asks Damian. 'What the fuck . . .?'

'Ooops sorry, my guilty pleasure. Shall I skip it?'

'No no, I love it,' says Mark. 'Karen Carpenter – what a voice, man.' And he starts singing along in a surprisingly tuneful tenor to the cheese fest that is 'Close to You.'

When it gets to the chorus, we all join in. I tilt my head back and look up at the unblemished sky, happiness washing over me like a great big Cornish wave. Ben, Ben, Ben, I think. How am I going to get through the anticipation of the next twenty-four hours? The only answer, as it always is at Glastonbury, has to be to get wasted. I finish my beer in a huge gulp and ask Mark for another.

'Oooh look, I've spotted the first fellow Glasto car,' says Poppy, pointing at a battered old Mini whose back window is almost completely obscured by piled-up rucksacks. We overtake and wave. The driver, a forty-something woman in plaits and tie-dye, grins and waves back.

'I'm feeling it already,' says Poppy, in pseudo mystical tones. 'Are we all feeling the luuurve, man?'

'Fucking hippy,' says Mark, but he's smiling. Because, joking aside, she's right. There is something about Glastonbury when the sun shines that really does make you full of love and slushiness towards all mankind. When it rains, it's simply a case of survival.

As we progress, the ratio of festival-goers to normal law-abiding citizens gets bigger and bigger. Finally we get to the Tesco megastore, that indicator that we're on the final strait.

'So who needs what?' asks Damian.

'Another crate of Stella,' says Mark, as we seem to have pretty much demolished the last one in the three hours it's taken to get here.

'Bin bags and loo roll,' I say, stupidly pleased with myself to have remembered.

'We could do with some boxes of wine for the tent,' says Poppy. 'And I could do with a pee after all that beer.'

'I'll stay here and man the fort then, shall I?' says Damian, picking up a copy of the *Daily Star* from the car floor.

'You do that, my darling,' says Poppy, uncharacteristically not commenting on his choice of reading material. She's up to something. She leans over and kisses him. 'Thanks so much for driving so well.'

We go into the supermarket, still playing 'spot the fellow festival freak', which is getting too easy to be much fun by now. We stand at the checkout till, me with my loo paper, bin bags and a couple of litres of Diet Coke to mix with my vodka, and Poppy with a 3-litre box each of red and white wine and a long stack of plastic cups. She leans up and whispers, 'Come to the loo with me. The time is ripe for a mind-sharpening snifter.'

I grin. 'OK. What about the boys though?'

'Damian won't risk it until he's finished driving, bless him, so it's probably kinder not to tell him. Mark can fend for himself.'

'Okey-dokey.' It crosses my mind that it would probably be kinder still to wait until we're all in a position to partake, but such noble thoughts soon pass as my weak flesh follows my oldest friend to the salubrious environs of the Tesco megastore public toilets.

A middle-aged lady in a floral frock, with the kind of perm that you only ever see outside London, is washing her hands. She smiles at us in the mirror.

'You'll be going to the festival. Lovely day for it.'

'Thanks,' I smile, while Poppy, ever more voluble than me, even before the coke, launches into, 'Yup, we've come down from London, and we're so excited, we can't wait to get there. Especially after last year, which was such a disappointment with all the rain and mud . . .' Yadda yadda yadda . . .

'Well, word has it that this sunshine is going to stick,' says the friendly woman. 'So you make sure you enjoy yourselves. There – you've got a local's blessing. It's a good omen in these here parts, you know.'

She's laughing at us now, with our presumed city prejudices. Or sending herself up. Either way, it's a nice introduction, and once she's left the loo I say to Poppy, 'What a lovely woman. I almost feel guilty now for sullying her local supermarket with our dodgy wares.' Poppy raises her eyebrows at me.

'Almost, but not quite,' I say and, giggling, we pile into one of the cubicles before anyone else can come in.

Walking back outside, the sun seems hotter and brighter

than ever, glinting in sharp angles off the parked cars. The haze from the tarmac underfoot is practically shimmering, as it does in movies about the Wild West.

'There they are,' says Poppy, pointing at the Merc, and she skips towards it, dangling a wine box from each hand, the plastic cups clenched between her teeth.

'There you are, my little chickadee,' says Damian, lowering his shades and looking at her over the top of them. 'Feeling a little livelier, are we?'

Poppy laughs. 'Oh darling, you know me so well. Couldn't resist, I'm afraid. You don't mind, do you?'

He kisses her nose. 'I just want you to be happy, my love.' Awww, I think, wishing this moment was happening between me and Ben.

'Though I'll be bloody glad to get there now. Let's hope the final traffic isn't too crazy.'

We climb back into the car, crack open some more beers and set off once again on our way. It's very hot indeed now, and I hold my Stella against my burning forehead, glad of the wind in my hair. I am experiencing life in glorious surround-sound technicolour. The fields we pass are absurdly bucolic; The Clash shouting from the speakers relentlessly, incongruously rock 'n' roll. I cannot stop smiling.

Mark looks over at me and laughs.

'What's so funny?'

'You,' he says simply. 'With your big eyes and messy hair and little freckles on your nose. You look about twelve.'

I grin at him some more, not feeling like such an old hag after all. I then remember I'm wearing shades – so how can he see my big eyes? – and nearly say something, but think better of it. *Don't wreck the moment, Bella.*

Eventually we reach the car park. We disembark and begin the long trek o'er field and o'er dale to the camping ground. All around us people are smiling – despite at least an hour's tough exercise, and possibly disastrous frisking, before anyone can get anywhere to relax properly. A lot of the men are, like Mark, bare-chested, which improves my mood still further. In case the weather breaks, we head for our usual place, at the top of a hill, to the right of the main Pyramid Stage.

We are all huffing and puffing when we reach our chosen field, even Mark. Even though he's ridiculously fit, he has inexplicably opted to bring a rucksack so heavy I can't even lift it off the ground. For a minute I suspect it's simply for showing-off purposes, then reflect that surely even he couldn't be that dumb.

'It's a good job we got here today,' says Poppy, looking around. She's right. The field is extremely overcrowded already, but we find a space just big enough for our three tents.

'What are we going to do about Ben's tent?' I ask.

'Can't be helped at the moment,' says Damian. 'He'll have to share with Mark. Or you of course, Bella,' he adds slyly. I look up at him and he's laughing. How much does he know, I wonder?

We pitch our tents and I lay out my sleeping bag and pillow inside. I like the ritual of making it a little haven before we start, knowing what a hellhole it'll be before long. After last year's tent was so revoltingly flooded, I abandoned it. This year, Max has let me have the one we used to use as teenagers, as he's hiring a yurt, the ponce. The tent bears some embarrassing graffiti that we clearly found hilarious at the time, but is in pretty good nick other than that, considering it's nearly twenty years old. One of Dad's expensive guilt-gifts, I seem to recall.

After another swift line, Poppy and I get started on the vodka. It's nearly five o'clock now but as it's almost mid-summer's day it'll be light for a good few hours. We gaze down over the surreal Camelot-like scene below us, stretching out further than the eye can see, more like a little town than a temporary festival structure. Almost everything has been put up now, ready for the first acts to start in the morning. The Pyramid Stage looms, white and angular, down to our right, with the Big Top-like swirly red and blue stripes of the dance tents beyond it. Directly in front of us are more fields of tents, sloping down to the main eating, drinking and shopping fields. The shopping always surprises me. I mean, who actually goes to a festival to purchase wind chimes and dream catchers? Beyond them a distinct, snaking lane demarks the Green Fields, with their multicultural veggie offerings, runes, healing stones and the like.

It's all too exciting. I'm desperate to go and mingle, and I let the others know by waving my arms about foolishly and tripping over one of Mark's guy ropes.

'Careful, lovely,' says Poppy.

'I think she needs another sobering line,' says Mark, as he bashes his tent peg back in with something very heavy from his rucksack.

'Oh go on then,' I say. 'But let's go soon. I can't wait to get down there and start exploring.'

'Four fucking aces,' says Mark, shaking his head. 'You are one lucky bitch.'

'My cards may have been good, but my bluffing skills are beyond compare,' I boast, ludicrously pleased with myself after my poker win. We emerge from the casino tent we found an hour earlier in one of the festival's many peripheral fields. Its other attractions include an old-fashioned carousel, a ghost train, coconut shies and fire-eaters.

We plundered the complimentary dressing-up box before

our game of poker and Poppy is wearing a top hat and pink tutu, Damian an antelope's head and Mark a Red Indian headdress. I'm sporting a contraption that combines a big nose with Groucho Marx specs and moustache. If Ben were here I'd have been more conscious of trying to look pretty, but now I don't really give a fuck. We are seriously wasted.

'Where's my mummy?' screams a little voice, and we all try to refocus. A small boy, only about four or five years old, is wandering around, lost, crying and helpless. He has long, curly hair and looks absolutely terrified. I bend down to take his hand and he backs off, sobbing even more.

'Take the Groucho face off, Belles,' says Poppy, as Damian removes his antelope head. God, I'm a stupid cow. I whip the contraption off my face and sit down on the grass, so I'm eye level with the poor little bugger.

'What's your name?' I ask.

'Kestrel.'

'And where are your mummy and daddy?'

His sobbing abates a bit, now he can see my normal face, and he wipes his nose with the back of his hand.

'I haven't got a daddy. I don't know where Mummy is.' He looks around defencelessly again. Everywhere we look are crowds of people, off their stupid fucking faces, none of them taking any notice of the forlorn child in their midst. Poppy starts calling out, 'Hello! Has anyone lost a little boy?' into the mob, to no avail.

'I want my mummy.' Kestrel starts crying again and Mark scoops him up into his big, strong arms.

'Don't you worry, mate, we'll look after you. Your mummy's probably just gone to the toilet or something. She'll be back in a minute.' He whispers at Poppy and Damian over Kestrel's head, 'Go to the information tent and see if anyone's reported a missing boy. We'll stay here with

90

him in case his mum comes back.' Poppy and Damian race off in what I hope is the direction of the information tent.

I try desperately to think of something that might make little Kestrel feel better. Looking around, I spot the rock-'n'-roll diner, which, as its name might suggest, serves burgers and milkshakes to a soundtrack of Fifties rock 'n' roll.

'How'd you like a chocolate milkshake, while we wait for your mummy to get back?' I say, and Kestrel looks ever so slightly more cheerful.

'I like chocolate milkshakes.'

'Well, that's great then, isn't it?' Mark nods at me, giving upraised eyebrows of approval. 'We'll all have a nice chocolate milkshake, while we wait for your mummy.'

Kestrel looks suspicious. 'Mummy says I shouldn't go with strange people.'

'Mummy's completely right about that,' I say, ruffling his hair. 'But we're not going anywhere, we're staying here. I'll just pop in there and get us all a milkshake.'

When I emerge from the diner with three chocolate milkshakes, Mark is still carrying Kestrel, making him giggle as he points out all the silly-looking people jiving to 'Chantilly Lace'.

I sing the few words that I remember at Kestrel, putting my hair into a ponytail with my hands and then letting it hang down. He stares at me for a second, then buries his face in Mark's shoulder again. Fuck, I'll have to do better than this. I stroke his curly hair, trying to focus my addled brain on making him feel less scared. I must say that Mark seems to be doing a far better job than I am. He'll make a great dad one day, I surprise myself by thinking.

'Don't worry, darling, Mummy will be back soon,' I say hopefully.

'Tell you what, mate, you're quite a big boy and I've had quite a long day,' says Mark, winking at me. 'How about we all sit down on the grass to drink our milkshakes?'

Kestrel nods and we sit down cross-legged in a circle.

'Why do you have that on your head?' he asks Mark, pointing at his headdress.

'Because I'm a Red Indian, and this is my woman, the lovely Moon Rising,' says Mark, putting his arm around my shoulder. I smile, feeling as though I've wandered into the pages of a Hunter S. Thompson book.

'Mummy says we have to say Native American,' says Kestrel seriously.

'Oh of course, sorry,' I say. 'Do you want to play cowboys and Native Americans?'

He giggles and puts his right hand into a gun position.

'Bang bang, you're dead, you Native American punk and your Moon Rising ho!'

I fall back on the grass as if I've been shot and Mark puts his arm out to grab Kestrel, who has started to run around us, air-shooting.

'I'm Kestrel the Kid, catch me if you can!'

'I've gotcha, Kestrel the Kid.'

Kestrel wriggles in his grasp but Mark holds on to him tightly. 'Stop it, mate. What if you get lost again, and then your mummy comes back? That would be a shame, wouldn't it?'

'S'pose so.' He sits down sulkily, then starts sobbing his little heart out again.

After what seems like forever, my phone rings.

'Belles, we've found his mum,' says Poppy. 'She was at the information tent, asking them to put out a tannoy message. She was absolutely hysterical but she's calmed down a bit now. We're on our way back.'

'Oh, thank God for that. We've found your mummy,' I say to Kestrel, who smiles broadly.

Now he's feeling safe again, he becomes quite chatty, telling us how Mummy let him stay up past his bedtime as a special treat as she wanted to see the rest of the festival and none of her friends wanted to stay back at the tent to look after him. Mark is getting more and more stony faced as this story unfolds, and by the time Kestrel's mother turns up he can hardly bring himself to look at her. Probably a couple of years older than me, with plaited strawberry-blonde hair, flared jeans and a slight air of otherworldliness about her, she swoops on Kestrel with tears running down her face.

'Oh Kes, darling, my baby. Are you all right?' she cries. 'Thank you so much for looking after him,' she says to me and Mark, her eyes shining. I can't help but notice how enormous her pupils are.

'That's OK, we're just glad you've found each other again,' I say. 'We've had quite an adventure, haven't we, Kes?'

'The nice lady and man gave me a yummy chocolate milkshake and we played cowboys and Native Americans,' he solemnly informs his mother. He really is a dear little boy.

'That was very kind of them. Thank you so much,' she says to me again, rummaging in her jeans pocket for some cash. 'How much do I owe you?'

'Oh nothing, just happy to have helped,' I say, embarrassed that Mark is still maintaining his stony silence. When he breaks it, it hardly helps.

'Well, now you've deigned to come back, I'm ready for a drink. Let's hit the bar, guys. Goodbye, little man. I think he needs his bed now,' he adds pointedly to Kes's mother, who looks utterly distraught. We all shake Kes's hand goodbye and, as we walk away, I turn once to give him a wave. As soon as we're out of earshot, Mark explodes.

'How fucking irresponsible can people be? That stupid cow was totally off her tits. Did you see her eyes?'

'She was also worried sick,' I say. 'And who are we to cast the first stone?'

'We don't have kids, and she bloody well should have been worried sick. Dragging the poor little sod out in the middle of the night because none of her mates wanted to babysit. She should be fucking arrested. Festivals are no places for kids.' Mark is absolutely fuming. I've never seen him so angry. In fact, I don't think I've ever seen him angry about anything before. I do agree with him about festivals being no places for kids, but it seems a bit rich to be proselytizing about substance abuse on the first night of what is promising to be a very lost weekend for us. Besides, I felt genuinely sorry for Kestrel's mother. Her obvious terror and subsequent remorse must have been pretty tough to bear.

I open my mouth to respond and Poppy nudges me.

'Yeah Mark, you're right,' she says. 'Bloody irresponsible behaviour. Now can we please find a bar before I die of thirst? I am absolutely *gagging* for a drink.'

Chapter 7

I'm dreaming that I'm being slowly roasted in a giant wood-fired oven, like an oversized version of the one in the Ibiza villa. Skinny Alison is taunting me with the fact that I don't have a proper job, while all my friends laugh and chuck more logs on the fire. Somewhere in my peripheral vision, my father and Ben are having a three-some with Kimberly who is cackling maniacally and saying, 'Don't you just love a good roasting, Bella?'

I wake up with a jolt, pouring with sweat in the intoler-able sauna-like conditions of my tent. I grab the Evian bottle nearest me and take a huge swig, only to gag and spit it out all over my sleeping bag. Vodka. Why oh why didn't I label the bottles?

I find the real Evian bottle and pour it down my throat. God it's good. I turn my rucksack inside out looking for my olive green string bikini, then lie down on my back to get into it. Crawling out onto the grass, pulling my sleeping bag behind me, I see I'm not the only one to have had this idea.

All around people are lying outside their tents, not quite ready to get up but unable to bear another second inside their synthetic hovels-from-home. The fresh air is gorgeous. The sun's not really that hot yet, though it looks as though it's going to be another scorcher. I lie down on my front and go straight back to sleep.

When I wake up again, several hours must have passed. People are sitting up and talking now, making breakfast on portable stoves or heading towards the loos for the morning freshen-up. I crawl back inside my tent for my ancient khaki combat-style mini and white vest top, grab my toothbrush and toothpaste and head up the hill towards the facilities. I am in remarkably high spirits considering, and realize I must still be pretty wired, which is all to the good as I don't want to waste any time on hangovers here. If I can stave them off till I get back, so much the better. Though it will be a humdinger of a comedown.

The less said about the loos the better. I try to hold my breath for the duration, then queue up for the taps outside to clean my teeth. Back at the tent, I clean off yesterday's make-up with wipes and brush my hair, trying to get some of the grease out with dry shampoo. My armpits are given a good going-over with more wipes. A squirt of deodorant and my toilette is complete. I am just getting out my make-up bag when Poppy emerges from the neighbouring tent, looking staggeringly fresh faced.

She is wearing a red and white striped towelling playsuit – a strapless, hot-pant jumpsuit with a slight blouson effect at the waist. The very short shorts show off her slender brown legs and her hair hangs just above her shoulders in silky blonde plaits. On anybody else this would look ridiculous, hideous or both, but Poppy manages to look incredibly cute, like a Swedish Seventies porn star, pre-shagging.

'Morning gorgeous. How're you feeling?'

'A bit shaky, but nothing a couple of drinks won't sort out. How 'bout you?'

'Fine,' she grins. 'Long may it last.'

I take a mirror out of my make-up bag and start doing my face.

'We should probably have some breakfast, or we'll be feeling like shit later,' says Poppy, producing some apples, wholemeal rolls and a wedge of cheddar from inside her tent. Damian often has to remind Poppy to eat breakfast – forcing bowls of muesli and homemade smoothies on her as she races out to meetings – but it's somehow typical that she should remember now, for the purely practical purpose of fuelling our debauchery.

We finish our breakfast, perusing the programme of events and deciding who wants to see what when. It transpires that none of us is really bothered until 4 p.m., when Poppy wants to hit the dance tent, Damian wants to check out some up-and-coming indie band he's thinking of putting in the mag, Mark is keen to watch the Mongolian deep-throat singers and I'm just happy to see where the mood takes me.

Which means we have three hours to kill.

'In that case, it must be time for some mushroom tea,' says Poppy.

'Fuck yeah,' says Mark. 'Do the honours, babe.'

So Poppy sets up a portable stove in the clearing between our three tents and puts a pot of water on to boil.

'How wholesomely Girl Guide,' I say.

'Always be prepared,' she agrees gravely, tipping the contents of a brown paper bag into the pot.

Down the hill, we can hear excitement growing as the first band of the day prepares to play on the Pyramid Stage. Music has been blaring from the main speakers all morning in a comforting, yes I am at Glastonbury kind of way, but this is the real deal. A kerr-rash of drums, a huge roar from the crowd, and they're off.

We grin at one another.

'Vodka anyone, while we wait for our tea?' I slosh the contents of my Evian bottle into a plastic cup and top it up with Diet Coke.

It's a unanimous yes, so I pass the first cup to Poppy, then pour three more, balancing them precariously on the sloping grass.

'Morning,' says our neighbour, sticking his head out of the tent. 'Beautiful day.' He has sandy hair and a Scouse accent and we met him when we got back last night. I cannot for the life of me remember his name.

'Apparently it's going to stay like this,' I say, thinking of the woman at the Tesco megastore. 'Would you like some vodka?'

'Now you're talking.' I pour another cup. He gets out of his tent and stretches fully, which isn't very far, as he's probably around my height. He looks around short-sightedly. 'Where'd I put my glasses?'

'Are these they?' asks Poppy, holding up a horn-rimmed pair lying next to her tent.

'Too right they are. What are they doing over there? Never mind, thanks,' he says, good-naturedly. He has a lovely smile. I hand him his vodka.

'Cheers, love. Cheers all,' he says, nodding and smiling around.

'Cheers,' we chorus. 'Happy Glastonbury,' I add.

'What have you got planned today, mate?' asks Damian, who clearly can't remember our neighbour's name either.

'My mates are arriving round four. Till then, nothing much. I want to see Primal Scream tonight though.'

'Ooooh yes, me too,' I squeak as my friends laugh. It's a standing joke that after a certain level of drunkenness, Primal Scream will always get an airing at my parties. It reminds me of being a teenager, *pre-art college*, and I do like getting my rocks off after all.

'Don't get her started,' says Poppy. 'Could you pass me the cups, Belles? The tea's boiling.'

'Don't say you've got shrooms!' says the Scouser, his lovely smile lighting up his face. 'You selling?'

Mark goes into some kind of elaborate transaction with him, bartering mushrooms and a bit of K for MDMA as far as I can tell. I let my thoughts drift to Ben for a moment. I wonder what he's doing now. Then I remember he's on the Abercrombie & Fitch shoot and put an abrupt halt to that train of thought. He'll be here in a matter of hours, though, and after that, anything is possible. It's a shame I won't be looking my best by then, but that's the nature of Glastonbury, and I'm certainly not going to sit waiting soberly in my tent for him. Ben's seen me looking like shit many times before anyway, I think, remembering the Hogarthian gin hag photo. All the same, I make sure my make-up bag and hairbrush are in the mini-rucksack I'll be carrying around with me today.

'Earth to Bella!' Poppy waves at me and hands me another plastic cup. 'Careful, it's hot.'

'Thanks.' I balance it on the grass next to my vodka and drag myself back to the present. 'Can we go and see Max after this? I'm dying to see his yurt.'

'Yeah, why not?' Poppy takes a swig of her tea and grimaces. 'Yuck, that's foul.' She washes it down with some vodka and Coke.

I pick up my phone and dial Max's number. He answers on the first ring.

'Hey Belle, how's it going?'

'Oh, it's all wonderful! Last night I won at poker – I had FOUR ACES – how cool? We also reunited a lost little boy with his mother, quite the Good Samaritans.

Now we're having the first drink of the day and some mushroom tea. How 'bout you? How are the yurts?' My words are toppling over themselves, such is my excitement.

'Sounds like you're having fun,' Max laughs. 'The yurts are pretty cool actually. There are some absolute knobs in here, of course, but my yurt itself is a definite improvement on our childhood tent, I have to say.'

'Which in itself is a definite improvement on the tent I had last year,' I laugh. 'Are you going to be hanging around there long? It's just that there's nothing any of us really want to see till around four, so we thought the yurts were as good a place to start as any.'

'And I can't wait to see you either,' says Max drily. 'You flatter me, sis. Yeah, I'm having a lazy start – come on over. Should be here for at least an hour.'

'Cool – see you soon,' I say, and hang up.

Around forty-five minutes later we are ambling through the Green Fields, vaguely, we hope, in the direction of knobs in yurts. Rainbow-coloured peace flags flutter overhead, wind generators churn gently in the breeze and the tips of thousands of teepees fill the skyline.

'Aren't those yurts?' asks Mark, pointing at them.

'They're teepees, fool,' says Poppy. 'Yurts are more squat. You know – circular wooden lattice frames, covered in felt made from yaks' wool.' Mark's look of bemusement is suddenly highly amusing. The mushrooms are having the desired effect.

We amble some more, passing stalls offering all manner of mystical claptrap, from astrology to chakra diagnosis to crystal healing. A batik and 'legal highs' stall is playing 'I Am the Walrus', so we sit down on the grass next to it and sing at each other.

100

The song seems to go on for hours but nobody's complaining as the lyrics are great and it's comfortable on the grass here, the lovely sun warming us right to the depths of our souls, it seems. I am having A Moment. The music changes to 'Here Comes the Sun' and my pleasure levels shoot right off the barometer.

'Beatle heaven man,' says Dave, for that's what our Scouse neighbour is called. 'Let's hear it for the 'Pool. I love you guys.'

'We love you too, man,' I grin back at him, any semblance of urban cynicism I might once have possessed having been swept away on a rush of hippy drugs, feel-good music and sunshine. Poppy tries to look superior but fails, relaxing with us into the deeply uncool but utterly blissful moment.

A man in top hat and tails with purple hair rides past on a unicycle. He looks about nine foot tall.

I wave up at him, singing along to George Harrison.

He waves back. 'Look, no hands!' and cycles round and round in circles in front of us. Damian looks at me, laughing.

'Is this really happening?' he asks.

'Not quite sure,' I respond. 'Fun though, isn't it?'

We hang out with the beardy batik people for a while, sampling their legal highs, which are, frankly, useless, so we give them some mushrooms instead. We're enjoying a companionable joint – not saying much, just basking in the sunshine, marvelling at the brightness of the colours – when Mark says, 'Weren't we meant to be looking for a yurt?'

'Oh bugger, Max,' I say.

'He'd have called if he was moving on somewhere,' says Poppy. 'Check your phone.'

I delve into my mini-rucksack, which has its own unique

take on the infuriating handbag tardis tendency, to see a missed call and a text.

'Bet you waylaid. Gone to get fags. See you at yurts at 3. Max,' I read out.

'You don't happen to know where the yurt field is, do you?' Poppy asks Beardy No. 1 with her most winning smile. He doesn't know, but seems to have taken a shine to her, as he walks round the various neighbouring stalls asking. He returns with a map.

'Look, not far at all. Just go to the other end of this field, turn right, then a sharp left and you're there. Can't miss it,' he says, pointing it out to her.

'That's wonderful. Thank you so much.'

She jumps to her feet and the rest of us follow suit. Exchanging effusive goodbyes, we depart.

'Is it me, or is that tree changing shape?' I ask no one in particular, pointing at a stupendously lush old oak, whose trunk is gently pulsating. 'Look, its leaves are dancing!'

'Go on leaves, dance for the madwoman!' says a laughing voice in my ear.

'Max!' I turn around and give him a big hug. 'Isn't everything just amazing?'

He laughs again. 'Lovely to see you all.' He's wearing a faded yellow sleeveless T-shirt, raffia flip-flops and three-quarter-length cotton pants that he picked up in India. All standard-issue ethnic clothes are three-quarter-length on him. His golden curls stand on end around his sweet face.

'This is Dave – he's in the tent next to ours,' says Damian, as I seem to be incapable of making introductions. Or, indeed, sense.

'Nice to meet you, Dave,' smiles Max, holding out his hand. 'What do you make of this, then?' He gestures around the field. Around fifteen yurts, just as Poppy described them, squat at regular intervals throughout the field. Each has a diameter of probably twenty feet. Delicious meaty smells are coming from a barbecue at the far end of the field and some worried-looking long-haired beasts are grazing in an enclosure nearby.

'Are they yaks?' asks Poppy, laughing.

''Fraid so. Gotta be authentic,' laughs back Max. 'Anyway, come and see my yurt.'

We follow him to the middle of the field. He opens the door with a flourish and we all pile in.

'Bloody hell, Max,' I say. 'Your yurt is positively palatial.' I then start giggling and repeating 'positively palatial' to myself until Max tells me to shut up.

'Positively palatial' may be an exaggeration, but it's bloody comfortable for Glastonbury. A large futon with crisp white sheets, plumped-up pillows and a sheepskin (yak skin?) throw dominates the interior. There is coir matting underfoot and a couple of mushroom suede bean-bags slouch underneath the window in the far wall.

'Bedside tables, man. Cool,' says Damian, gesturing towards a couple of low tables made out of some expensive dark wood, supporting opaque white glass lamps that vaguely resemble Barbara Hepworth sculptures.

'I know, it's great, isn't it?' says Max. 'And the pièce de résistance . . . !' He whips back a white linen curtain that has been set up at the other end of the yurt from the futon to reveal . . . a mini Smeg fridge.

'Fuck me, they've given you a mini-bar,' says Mark. 'Cunting result.'

'Cunting? Are you sure that's a word?' Poppy gives him a look.

Max bows and opens the door. 'What can I get you all?'

'Surely cocktails would befit the glamour of our surroundings,' says Poppy. 'Do you have ice and glasses?'

'Of course.' Max opens a cupboard hewn from the same expensive dark wood as the bedside tables. 'There's some sugar in here, too.'

'And a big bunch of mint and some limes in the fridge,' says Poppy. 'Awesome – we can make mojitos. Though I'm baffled as to why anyone would think they'd fit with the yurt theme.'

'Probably some ditzy PR getting Central Asia confused with Central America,' says Damian, to all-round hilarity.

'Talking of Central America,' says Poppy. 'It would be a travesty to let these lovely smooth surfaces go to waste.'

'Here, use mine.' Dave gets a wrap out of his pocket. 'You lot have been well generous to me.'

'Very noble of you, sir,' says Damian, as Max goes to shut the yurt door.

After some rather hefty lines, Poppy and I set about making the cocktails with enormous enthusiasm.

'A tad more sophisticated than last year, wouldn't you say, Belle?' she says, chopping mint like Marco Pierre White on speed.

'Fuck yeah,' I respond inelegantly, squeezing limes as I perform a little shimmy. 'In fact, so far I'd say this is the best year ever!'

The cocktails prepared, we head out into the sunshine and sit down on the grass.

'Well, thank you, Max, for providing such a civilized interlude,' says Poppy, raising her glass. 'Cheers.'

'Yes, thanks Max, cheers,' we all chorus.

'What's the idea behind the yurts?' Dave asks Max, who starts to laugh.

'A new reality TV show where they shove a load of people with mental health problems into a great big yurt in Kazakhstan, and manipulate their neuroses for the delectation of the Great British Viewing Public.'

104

As we all crack up, Max shushes us and mouths, 'No, really.'

We lounge in the sun with our cocktails, surrounded by people who look as if they should be on the roof terrace at Shoreditch House. After a bit, Poppy checks the time on her phone and yelps.

'Cinderella time. Sorry to love you and leave you, but I really do want to see DJ Dawg who started his set at four. And I told some of my colleagues I'd see them there. It's quarter past already.'

So Poppy goes in search of the dance tents, Damian his next-big-thing indie band and Mark his Mongolian deep-throat singers. We all agree to meet at the Pyramid Stage for Primal Scream at 10.30, but to stay in mobile touch for any pre-Primal hitherto-unforeseen excitement, phone-coverage-dependent, of course.

'Great as it is amongst the yurts, Max,' I say, 'I feel the urge to get down with the people a bit more – do you know what I mean? A bit of the old group-hug mentality that you get in the fields around the main stages?'

'I certainly do. Come on, let's go. What are your plans?' he asks Dave, who is checking his phone.

'Just got a text from my mates. They're stuck in traffic and probably won't be here for at least another couple of hours. They say it's dead grim.'

'Yeah, it would be,' says Max, and I think of Ben. Bugger. 'Hang out with us some more, why don't you?' he adds, and Dave's face lights up with his lovely smile again.

It's baking hot now, as we make our way, with thousands of others, towards the main stages. All around us people are disrobing. As my initial mushroom madness has given way to light euphoria and a certain lack of inhibition, I take off my vest top (I *am* wearing a bikini underneath) and use it wipe my sweaty brow.

'That's attractive,' says Max, removing his own T-shirt to do the same. I notice Dave gawking at my brother's impressive chest, and for the first time it occurs to me that he might be gay too. Excellent, I think, matchmaking plans already formulating in my befuddled brain. I've grown rather fond of Dave in the few hours we've known him, and Max could certainly do with some success in his love life.

We stop at a beer tent for some plastic pints of Stella. The queues are so long, we get two each, even though they'll warm up in no time. After weighing up the options, we all agree we'd rather face warm beer than more time standing in line. We find a space looking down at the Pyramid Stage, far enough away from it to be able to sit down on the litter-strewn grass without being trampled. Then, suddenly and wonderfully:

'Bella? Max? Is that you?'

I look around. 'Ben! But how did you get here so quickly? What about the traffic?' I ask, all a-fluster.

'It was a stroke of luck actually,' he says, smiling that devastating smile of his. 'Susie, the director, offered me a lift in her helicopter. She's covering the festival for some US TV channel, so they had to get her here quickly. We landed at Babington House.'

'That's pretty cool,' says Max, getting up and shaking Ben's hand. 'Good to see you, mate.'

'Isn't it funny how easy it is to bump into people here, considering how huge it is?' I stammer, entirely unprepared for seeing him so soon. 'Though it wasn't that easy for Kestrel's mum to find him last night, poor woman. God, she must have been out of her mind with fear . . .' I am babbling with idiotic nerves.

'What on earth are you on about?' Ben laughs, not actually wanting a response. He is looking predictably gorgeous in slightly baggy faded jeans that hang off his narrow hips, though a battered brown leather belt stops them sliding halfway down his bum – the US jailbird look that has been taken up by teenage boys in Surrey. His almost obscenely perfect V-shaped torso is bare and brown, and last year's cowboy hat protects his beautiful face from the sun.

'Aren't you going to give me a kiss?' he continues, and I get to my feet, intending to give him a peck on the cheek, but he puts his hands round my exposed waist and pulls me closer, landing me a smacker right on my lips. My skin burns under his touch.

'You're looking great,' he says. 'Green suits you.'

Behind him, Max raises his eyebrows at me and grins.

'So how was the helicopter ride?' I ask, trying to ignore my galloping heart and racing libido. 'That's so glamorous!'

'It was fun. Fantastic views over Stonehenge and it certainly beat being stuck in traffic for hours. Had a bit of trouble fending Susie off, though.'

'I can imagine, dressed like that,' says Max wryly, apparently forgetting that he is wearing even less than Ben is. 'Would you like a beer?'

'No offence mate, but I'd rather have a cold one,' laughs Ben. 'I'll be back in a moment.' And he saunters down the hill, oblivious (or perhaps not) to female heads swivelling as he passes.

'Bloody hell. He. Is. Fit,' says Dave, confirming my earlier suspicions. He's been silent for the whole encounter.

'That's an understatement and a half,' laughs Max. 'So what's going on with you two, Bella? He was very touchy-feely.'

'He was, wasn't he? Thank God I'm not imagining it.' And I find myself telling them about the kiss the night after I left Max and the others at Osteria Basilico.

'Hmmm,' says Max thoughtfully, once I've finished.

'Well, I can see why you're tempted – hell, who wouldn't be? – but I don't want you to get hurt. Be careful, sis.' His big brown eyes are serious.

'Why would I get hurt? We've been friends for ages, and now he seems to be noticing me *as a woman* –' both Max and Dave wince at this – 'too.'

'It's just that blokes like him who could have anyone aren't the easiest people to go out with. And look at you, Belles, you're head over heels already. Anybody can see that.'

'Don't you think you're jumping the gun a bit?' I say hotly, but now both boys are shushing me, as Ben is returning with his beer. As ever it's taken him a fraction of the time of anyone else to get served.

Ben sits down between me and Max and leans back on his elbows, his long, denim-clad thigh brushing mine. I feel as if I'm in the most wonderful dream and I never want to wake up. The sunshine, the atmosphere, the music, the chemical euphoria and now *this*? Bloody hell.

'So what have I missed?' asks Ben, once we've introduced him to Dave and explained where the others are. 'Such a bore, having to do that shoot this morning.' Sometimes he talks as though he were in a Noël Coward play, a RADA affectation that I might just find a teensy bit pretentious in a lesser man, despite my continuing affection for the 1920s and 30s.

I start telling him about my poker win and little Kes, when suddenly I remember. 'Oh shit. We couldn't put your tent up. By the time we got to the field there was literally just enough room for our three tents. Sorry.'

Ben smiles and directs his startlingly blue, long-lashed gaze at me. 'Never mind, darling. I'm sure we'll make do somehow.' Am I imagining it, or is the pressure from his leg increasing? Max looks over at us sharply and changes the subject.

'Have I told you the latest about Andy and Alison's wedding?'

'God, what a bitch,' says Ben. 'What does he see in her? I mean, he's a bit dull but he's not a bad bloke.'

'He's not dull,' says Max irritably. 'He's highly intelligent and extremely principled. He was great fun at Cambridge.'

'OK, sorry,' says Ben, smiling and putting his hands up in mock surrender. 'I forgot he was a good friend of yours. I've probably been listening to Damian too much.'

'Damian has a severe case of professional jealousy,' says Max. 'Anyway, apology accepted.' He smiles back. It's impossible to be cross with Ben for long. 'Back to your original question. Well, Alison is also highly intelligent and she claims to be extremely principled. Which is difficult to believe, given her chosen profession.'

'She's a lawyer,' I say to Dave, who gives a gratifying guffaw.

'She was something of a star at Cambridge,' continues Max. 'Head of the Law Society, double firsts right the way through, you name it . . . She was considered a real catch. And she didn't seem nearly so hard in those days. But yes, now I do feel sorry for Andy. Henpecked is not the word.'

'So what's going on with their wedding?' asks Ben, with his endearingly camp thirst for gossip.

'Well, so far the original florist, photographer and band have all backed out because they refuse to work with her. It's taking all of Andy's powers of negotiation to keep their chosen venue, and the vicar has taken to drink.'

'Noooo . . . !' I gasp, gleefully.

'Yes, really,' Max laughs. 'I've been to the venue three times to check things out for the catering. It's Hambledon

Hall, Bella,' he adds, naming a beautiful seventeenth-century manor house in the next village to where our mother lives in Oxfordshire.

'Oooh nice.'

'Yes, very. Anyway, every time I've been to the village pub for lunch, the vicar's been in there, knocking back the Scotch and complaining about the lawyer woman from London who's making his life a misery.'

'Wow, she sounds scary,' says Dave.

'I chucked a glass of red wine over her last time we met,' I boast, to a chorus of 'Respect!' and high-fives. Yes, this is fun.

'Oh, and you should see what she's trying to make poor Alison wear.'

'Her bridesmaid is also called Alison,' I say to Dave. 'Oooh, go on.' It's appalling really how much I enjoy a good bitch.

'For a start, it's charcoal grey. No, make that pewter. Correct me if I'm wrong, but aren't bridesmaids meant to look joyous and celebratory? Anyway, it does absolutely nothing for her complexion.'

'No, it wouldn't,' I say, remembering Alison's pink skin and mousy hair.

'Then there's the cut. It has a high neck, which makes that rather buxom bust of hers look vast and low slung.' This is one of the great things about having a gay brother. 'There are cut-away armholes, which show off the plump arms nicely, a calf-length bias-cut skirt which clings in all the wrong places, and – get this – a drawstring waist. The proverbial sack of potatoes. It's as if she's deliberately chosen all the elements that flatter her friend the least.'

'But why would she do that?' I ask.

'Why d'you think, Razor?' It's short for Razor-Sharp Mind and a hangover from our childhood. I pull a face at Max as Ben says, sagely,

110

'She's probably one of those women who'll do anything to ensure she doesn't get upstaged on her wedding day.'

Max nods. 'That's about the size of it. And poor little Alison doesn't have a hope in hell of standing up to her about it. If anybody dares to disagree with her, she starts screeching "it's my big day" like some demented banshee.'

'God, remind me never to get married,' says Ben with a shudder, reaching out and stroking the inside of my elbow. Great tingles of pleasure shoot through my whole body and I try not to gasp. Why is he doing this to me?

'Shit, I shouldn't be laughing about it,' says Max, shaking his curly head and looking guilty. I turn to stare at him again. 'I really hope it's just pre-wedding nerves, combined with the pressure of her job. If anyone deserves to be happy, Andy does. He's had a tough time of it.'

'Well, he should have had better taste than to get involved with her in the first place,' jokes Ben.

'No, I mean before. Christ! Anyway, I told you, Alison wasn't always so bad.' Max sounds unusually angry, for him. I suspect he's cross with himself for getting carried away bitching.

'Why, what happened?' I ask, intrigued now.

'In a nutshell, both his parents died in a car crash when he was seventeen. He was an only child, and very close to them – they were both teachers . . .'

'Oh God, poor Andy. How awful.' Hearing about such tragedy in our sunny festival surroundings feels horribly incongruous.

'He was forced to grow up very quickly, which is why he sometimes seems so serious,' Max goes on.

'What caused the accident?' asks Dave.

'A pissed truck driver who got less than a year in jail. Andy was so angry about it when we first met at Cambridge. It was only a year after his entire life had been wiped out.'

Max wipes his sweaty face on his rolled-up T-shirt again. 'It's one of the reasons he got into journalism – he's passionate about exposing the truth.'

'OK, sorry, you're clearly the right man for best man then,' says Ben lightly. 'And let's hope you're right about Alison's pre-wedding nerves.'

'Sorry for bringing the mood down,' says Max. 'But I love that guy and won't hear a word against him.'

We are all silent for a moment.

Trying to get back to where we were, I repeat the Glastonbury mantra, 'So, what's on the menu for the rest of the day? Does anyone want to see anything in particular over the next couple of hours or shall we just chill?'

Max, who has just picked up his programme, gives a little shriek, then laughs. 'Well, I'm sorry to revert to stereotype quite so dramatically, but I'm afraid I *must* see the Scissor Sisters. They're on the Other Stage in twenty minutes, and it'll take twenty minutes to get there. Anyone else up for it?'

'Oh my God, I'd forgotten about the Scissor Sisters,' says Dave. 'Yes, I'm definitely up for it.'

'Having just got here, I'm more inclined to chill for a bit,' says Ben, looking at me. 'In fact, I think I've got a bit of catching up to do, retoxification-wise.'

'Well, Belle's the girl to help you with that,' says Max, who seems to have relaxed his protective attitude somewhat. 'You two have fun. We'll see you later.' And he and Dave get up and walk down the hill together, chatting away companionably.

Taking a deep swig of my repulsive, hot beer, I say, 'So a bit of retox is what you need, eh? Are you stone-cold sober apart from the hot beer?' Sweet-talking charmer, that's me.

Ben laughs. 'Not exactly. We had a few beers and spliffs

on the shoot, and Susie and I had a couple of lines in the helicopter.' I briefly envisage scratching Susie's eyes out. 'But the rest of you have had a twenty-four-hour start on me.'

'In that case, you need something a bit stronger than this horrible beer, don't you? I've got some vodka in my tent . . . Actually, no! We could have mojitos in Max's yurt. I'm sure he won't mind,' I gabble, praying he won't. 'And there are some lovely flat surfaces in there too.'

'Well, that sounds like a great idea. If you're sure Max will be OK with it. Shall we chuck these?' He gestures towards the now gently festering Stellas. I nod, and he helps me to my feet as I attempt to retrieve our rubbish.

'Here, let me take those,' he says chivalrously, taking the plastic beakers out of my hands, touching my fingers as he does so. My heart starts racing again as he holds my gaze for far longer than necessary.

'Are you sure you don't want to find Damian?' I ask, worried suddenly that I'm hijacking him.

'Surer than I've ever been,' he says with a wink and, just for a minute, I relax.

There is, on my part, a slight sense of déjà vu as Ben and I mix mojitos in Max's yurt. And, again on my part, a definite sense of disappointment. After all that delicious expectation, now we are alone together, Ben hasn't touched me at all. He's been perfectly polite and properly impressed by the yurt. We've shared a couple of lines. But all that hands-on flirtiness? *Nada*. Zilch. *Rien*. I'm beginning to wonder, yet again, whether I imagined it. Were the drugs stronger than I thought, perhaps?

Still, I'm incredibly aware of his presence. And, to be honest, feeling extremely horny. That final line has left me teetering precariously close to the edge.

'Well, let's take these drinks outside.' Ben holds the door open for me. That's it then. No more ecstatic expectation. Oh well, it was fun while it lasted.

Outside, I cheer up a bit. I'm still at Glastonbury, the sun's still shining and I've still got Ben to myself. All is not lost.

'God it's hot,' I say, fanning myself with my programme.

A random stranger in Speedos, who happens to be speed-walking past, his arms doing that silly pumping movement that speed-walkers' arms do, looks over his shoulder at us and says, 'I'm heading towards the cold showers at the end of this field. Highly recommended!'

Ben and I look at each other and burst out laughing.

'Shall we?' he says.

'Oh yes, a cold shower's exactly what I need,' I say, perhaps a little too truthfully.

As it's getting to the time of day when the main acts start to come on stage, the field is relatively empty, and there's no queue for the showers.

'Last one in's a sissy,' says Ben, taking off his jeans to reveal a close-fitting pair of grey marl Dolce & Gabbana boxers. I step out of my miniskirt and we both run, giggling, into the showers.

'Fuck me, that's good,' I exclaim as the cool, clean water sploshes down over my overheated limbs, washing away the sweat and the grime. But not the lust. I open my eyes to see Ben gazing at me again. Water is dripping off his long dark lashes as, excruciatingly slowly, he moves towards me and bends his head to mine.

Kissing him is like nothing I've ever experienced before. When his hands aren't moving over my slippery body, they are holding my face, as if he never wants to let me go. The sun is still beating down on us relentlessly, the sky almost as blue as Ben's eyes. Once or twice he pulls away and gazes at me again, only to resume, seconds later, his exquisite exploration of my mouth.

Of course, he's had a lot of practice, says an unwelcome voice in my head. I shut it up and concentrate on the quite wonderful matter in hand.

'Oi you two, get a yurt, why don't you?' shouts some wag. We let go of each other reluctantly and start laughing again. Ben takes me by the hand and leads me purposefully back to Max's yurt.

'We'll drip all over it,' I say, regretting it as soon as the words are out of my mouth. Moron. Ben shakes himself like a wet dog to get most of the water off and says,

'There's bound to be a towel in there. He's got a mini-bar, after all.' He emerges seconds later with a huge bath sheet. Soft, white and fluffy, of course.

'Dry your hair with that, darling.' Darling again! I can't believe this is happening to me. Inside the yurt, he lays a fresh, dry towel on the floor and gestures for me to sit down next to him.

'I don't want you scratching yourself on this rough floor.' He traces the outline of my face with his finger.

I try to be more *compos mentis*, with little success.

'Why didn't you do this when we first got here?'

'I was afraid that if I touched you, I wouldn't be able to control myself – thank God for cold showers.' Ben laughs. 'I do have some standards. I'm not going to fuck you in your brother's yurt.'

My face drops.

'But we can do a hell of a lot of other things.'

He kisses me again and moves one hand gently down my body. Up and down, up and down my torso, firmly on my hip, my waist, my rib-cage, then feather-light on the underside of my left breast, yet never touching the rest of me, the other bits that are crying out for attention. I try to touch him back, but he pushes my hands away and says, 'Easy babe,' manoeuvring me gently towards the floor until I'm fully supine.

He strokes me all over, across all the hitherto non-erogenous zones, untying the strings on my bikini until I'm lying naked in some kind of erotic trance, every nerve ending on red alert. Just as I think I can stand it no longer, his fingers brush my left nipple and I gasp, loudly.

'Oh,' he laughs. 'Nice, is it?'

I am incapable of speech so gasp some more. He moves down and takes my swollen breast in both hands and starts sucking, then nibbling gently. I am trying to do things to him, but it's impossible. All I can do is throw my head back, pull at his gold-streaked hair and moan.

'Pleeease, Ben, pleeease.'

He pulls himself up to look me in the eye. 'Pleeeeease Ben what?' He is smiling, and teasing me in every sense of the word. His beautiful, high-cheekboned, full-lipped face, the face I have loved for so many years, is inches from mine.

'Oh please just fuck me, I can't bear this.'

'You are a very naughty girl,' Ben murmurs, gently pushing my legs apart. I'm desperate for whatever is going to happen next, not caring how wanton I look, not giving a fuck about anything else ever for the rest of my life.

'I told you, I'm not going to fuck you in your brother's yurt.' He tweaks my left nipple hard. It hurts and turns me on even more. Then he lowers his head between my legs and starts licking, sucking, stroking. Two, three fingers inside me at once.

'God, you dirty bitch, you love it, don't you?'

It sends me right over the edge and I push against him, wanting more and more, crying out so loudly as I come that Ben shoves his other hand over my mouth, roughly.

116

'Shhhh, darling. Remember we're in Max's yurt.' His voice is more gentle than his actions.

Eventually I come to my senses and gaze at him, still unable to believe what has just happened. Ben lies down next to me and kisses me again, pushing my damp hair off my face.

'Wow. I always thought you'd be sexy, but . . . Jesus, Bella . . .'

I wrap both arms and legs around him, burying my burning face in his shoulder, trying to hide my sudden shyness. We stay like that for a couple of minutes, until, still throbbing and vulnerable, I ask, 'Erm – shall we have another drink now?'

'Great idea. I'll mix the mojitos if you chop out another line.' Ben kisses me again and winks. Now he's diffused my unwelcome attack of self-consciousness, I think I might, actually, have died and gone to heaven. I lie on my back, looking up at the celestial yurt ceiling, listening to the festival sounds outside. Are we really still at Glastonbury?

Once Ben's mixed the drinks and we've snorted yet another line, we lie back down, smoke and talk about our respective childhoods.

'Damian was my saviour,' he says as he strokes my back with his lovely long fingers. 'Working-class Wales in the early Eighties wasn't a great place to grow up if people thought you were different. There was still a lot of racism around, but Damian dealt with it really well. He was academic, and laid-back – well, you know how he is – and took everything with the most extraordinary good humour. Eventually everybody loved him.'

'I can imagine that, he's such a star. But I want to hear more about you.'

'I was the runt, when it came to macho things. I was always very pretty – my mam and aunties absolutely doted on me.' He's reverted to his Welsh lilt, which makes his story all the more compelling. 'When I was a toddler, they had to keep my hair very short so people didn't think I was a girl. As you can imagine, this didn't go down too well at school. They called me and Damian the poofter and the Paki. They used to beat the shit out of us. Luckily, once I started to take an interest in drama I was big enough to fight the fuckers back,' he laughs, and my eyes fill with tears at the thought of the gorgeous little boy being beaten up by clod-hopping, non-artistic bullies.

It's no use, I have to kiss him again.

At one stage, he gets up to pour us another drink and I am admiring the perfect curve of his buttocks, when I ask, a tad pathetically, 'Why me? When you can have your pick of gorgeous women the world over?'

He laughs. 'Don't you realize how gorgeous you are, Bella?' He's back to his normal voice now.

'Erm. Nope,' I say, honestly.

'Perhaps that's what it is. All the women I meet through work are so full of themselves. Insecure, yes, and desperate to be reassured that they're gorgeous all the time, but they do know they're gorgeous, simply by virtue of what they do. Once a model agency accepts you, you're a fully validated member of the beautiful people.' It's testament to Ben's enormous charm that he manages to say this without sounding like the most egocentric prick on the planet.

'I've always liked you,' he continues. 'You're fun and funny and talented and you always light up parties with your slightly kooky take on things.' *Kooky? Just because I'm not an identikit plastic blonde?* I possibly bristle a little as he says, 'Like the dwarf pinching your dress. No one else I know has such funny stories.' I smile at him, so he goes on, 'And you're gorgeous without knowing it. I think it was when Kimberly was being such an idiot in Ibiza that

I started to realize you meant more to me than just a friend.'

He kisses both my nipples in turn, again and again. 'And you have fucking amazing tits.'

I giggle, totally overcome with happiness.

'You are insatiable, woman,' he says, a little later. 'There's plenty of time for this when we get back to London. As long as you still want to, of course.'

And I kiss him some more, as if my very life depended on it.

It's dark when we emerge from the yurt. Everyone has been texting us, trying to arrange to meet at the beer tent next to the Pyramid Stage in time for Primal Scream. We walk in, Ben's arm around my shoulders, both of us looking, presumably, pretty obviously loved-up. Or should that be sexed-up?

Poppy says, less quietly than I imagine she intended, 'Oh my God! Sorry, Belles, I'm too fucked to be subtle, but you two . . .?'

Ben smiles and squeezes me harder. 'Got it in one, Pops.'

Everyone is smiling and congratulating us.

'Man! Now we're practically brothers!' says Damian, laughing and enveloping Ben in a huge hug. He extends his left arm to include me in a group hug. 'Guys, guys, what can I say?' Squashed into his armpit, my face is fixed in a beatific smile.

'Couple of slags deserve each other,' is Mark's charmless summary of the situation. I extricate myself from the group hug, remembering his kindness to little Kes last night, and plead, 'Be happy for me, Marky?'

'Course I am, babe.' He smiles but it doesn't reach his eyes.

Dave gives me a hug and whispers, 'Fair play to you, sweetheart – he's fucking gorgeous!'

And Max gives me the biggest hug of all. 'I'm happy as long as you're happy, Belles. Just look after yourself.'

And then the unmistakeable strains of 'Rocks' start, and we all stumble out into the field to be part of the experience. The air fizzes with excitement as the band teases us with old Stones riffs before launching into it full throttle.

It's not exactly what you'd call a romantic little ditty, but for dancing around in a field with 30,000 other drug-crazed pleasure-seekers, the song is pretty unbeatable. Searchlights scan the thrashing bodies; the band is a group of stick people with overwhelming presence. There is absolutely nothing in the world to compare with live, *loud* rock 'n' roll. I dance and dance, swishing my hair around and grinning like a maniac. Poppy, eyes shining, keeps dancing up and hugging me, saying, 'Oh Belles, I'm so happy for you.' And all the time my darling, vulnerable Ben is never more than a foot away, his hand never far from my waist or shoulder.

Afterwards, we stagger up the hill to our tents, tripping over guy ropes in the dark. Outside her tent, Poppy gives me another enormous hug.

'Don't do anything I wouldn't, lovey. I think that probably gives you carte blanche.'

Laughing, totally high on everything, I hug her back.

'God I love you, Pops.'

'I love you too, Belles.' She crawls into her tent and Damian, who has been exchanging a similarly sentimental goodnight with Ben, follows suit. Ben looks at me.

'I guess I'm sleeping outside then?'

'Oh really, enough with the bloody teasing!'

'Sorry. But I would like to wait until I'm invited into your humble abode.'

'Dear sir, may I interest you in my humble abode? It's not much, but it serves me well. I think you'll find it

120

sufficient for your needs.' I ruin the effect by staggering as I try to curtsey on the sloping grass.

Ben takes my hand.

'In that case, fine lady, I would be honoured to accept. After you.' He gestures into my tent and I try not to imagine what my arse looks like as I crawl in. Ben crawls in after me. It's dark, and there is very little room for manoeuvre. There was only just enough room for me last night, with the rucksack and bottles taking up so much space.

Ben reaches over to kiss me, and I'm lost again in the magic of being with him, his lips, his skin, his hair. Our hands are all over one another as we attempt to disrobe in the awkward space, the darkness making all the sensations even stronger. After everything he did to me earlier, I am determined to give Ben some pleasure too. I push him down onto my sleeping bag and start licking the tip of his cock, gently, with little flicks to start with. When he starts to moan, I take it in my mouth and suck and suck and suck, unable to believe I have Ben Jones's cock in my mouth. I could suck it forever.

'Don't stop, please,' he breathes as I start running my fingers up and down his inner thighs, balls and perineum, up and down, his cock in my mouth all the while.

'Oh please, Bella . . .'

'Please, Bella what?' I ask, loving the power I have over him and remembering him saying the same to me earlier.

'Touché,' he laughs, breathlessly. 'Just please fuck me, you gorgeous thing.'

Even though I can't see it, I can feel that his cock, just like the rest of him, is quite staggeringly perfect. I lower myself down onto it and take a sharp intake of breath.

'Oh God, that feels so good,' says Ben, holding me firmly by the hips and thrusting up inside me. My eyes are starting to get accustomed to the darkness and I can make out that his head is thrown back in ecstasy. I lower myself up and down with deliberate slowness initially, then start upping the pace to match his, reaching down to kiss him. Then we are biting, scratching, pulling one another's hair in absolute animal abandonment, our pelvises fused together, rocking, thrusting, acting entirely independently of our minds, it seems.

Ben comes first, letting out a deep groan. Seconds later, feeling his cock still throbbing inside me, I come too.

'Happy Glastonbury,' I say, light-headed with euphoria, collapsing on the edge of my sleeping bag next to him and kissing him again.

'Happy Glastonbury, my love.' He kisses me back and tightens his arms around me.

It's not 'I love you', but it's a bloody good start.

Chapter 8

The bored-looking peroxide blonde looks me up and down with the contempt of a schoolgirl in a communal Topshop changing room. She is wearing white skinny jeans, layered long-line vests in clashing purples and oranges, and stacks of bangles the length of her emaciated arms. She must be all of nineteen and a half.

'He's in an editorial meeting. I'll see if he can break away,' she says eventually, over her shoulder, as she mooches off. Her legs are so thin there's a large gap where they should meet at the base of her arse.

I have come to the *Stadium* office in my lunch hour to return some limited-edition vinyl that Ben borrowed from Damian ages ago. They all think they're DJs, these metrosexual media men. Ben has asked me to do his dirty work as I'm still temping in Mayfair, a ten-minute walk away from the AMAP headquarters in Soho; he's shooting in South London today.

Yes, the unthinkable has happened. Ben is officially my boyfriend. The lease on his rented flat in Belsize Park was due to expire any day, so he moved in with me a couple of days after we got back from Glastonbury, still feeling rough as badgers' arses.

I can't help wondering if it's a bit *too* convenient, but hey. *Shut up Bella, it's just your God-awful hangover messing with your head.*

I perch uncomfortably on the *Stadium* sofa, the backs of my thighs sticking sweatily to the black leather.

When Ben first moved in I was ecstatic, utterly overwhelmed after years of unrequited longing. We shagged all over the place, I cooked every evening and even got up early a couple of times to make us breakfast in bed before heading out to work. But only a month on, things aren't quite so rosy, loath though I am to admit it.

The sound of hysterical laughter around the corner of the L-shaped open-plan office interrupts my self-pitying internal monologue. The editorial meeting.

'How about a feature on fuckable feminists?'

'Hahahaha! It could be called Feminists I'd Like to Fuck! FILF!'

'Can you imagine how many humourless harridans we could offend?!'

More guffaws.

'Slight problem though,' one wag pipes up. 'There aren't any!'

They can hardly contain their mirth at this.

'Actually, that's not true,' says a lilting voice I recognize as Damian's. 'Poppy and her friends refer to themselves as feminists.' Bless him.

Much ribaldry and phwoars follow, then somebody says,

'There's that one who wrote *The Beauty Myth*, Naomi something; she was pretty hot . . .'

'And Germaine Greer . . .'

'That mad old bat? Are you off your rocker?'

'Not now, you twat, back in the day. She was well fit when she did that nude cover of *Oz* . . .'

This is how Damian earns a living? Well, it certainly beats binding, and I allow myself a grudging soupçon of envy as I look around the untidy office. The walls are papered in old shots from the magazine (practically all naked or nearly naked women, with the odd 'iconic' male – George Best, Bill Clinton, David Beckham, Oliver Reed, Richard Burton; you get the picture). In one corner are a table football, pool table, various PlayStations and a glass-fronted fridge stocked with cans of Stella and Red Bull. Some obscure house thuds from somebody's iMac speakers. Think what you want of them, these boys are living the dream.

'What is it, Lara?' a voice cuts through the raucous male laughter. 'Oh OK, thanks,' and a minute or so later Damian appears from round the corner. It's the first time for ages I've seen him not wearing shades and I'd forgotten how extraordinary his eyes are – deep pools of black, slanting slightly downwards at the corners.

'Bella, great to see you!' He gives me a hug. 'Thanks for bringing these over. That lazy good-for-nothing boyfriend of yours has had them for months now and I'm on the decks at Hoxton Cunt tonight.'

I laugh. 'Hoxton Cunt?'

'Yeah. Remember that satirical magazine *Shoreditch Twat* I worked on years ago? Hoxton Cunt is a club night *en hommage*. Pretty aptly named.' And pretty knowingly self-referential, if you ask me.

Damian came to London to study English at King's in the late 90s (he and Ben are a couple of years younger than me and Poppy). There, I gather, he soon became part of a terrifyingly cool crowd, DJ-ing in various union bars and editing underground college music mags. It wasn't too difficult then, post-graduation, with his contacts, easy manner and – oh yes – good way with words to get work as an unpaid intern on *Shoreditch Twat*, an irreverent listings mag for the East London club 333. A gig as junior writer on *Stadium* soon followed and, from there, his unstoppable upward trajectory.

A vision in a long silk dressing gown prances, Noël Coward-like, around the corner. I recognize Simon Snell from his large by-line picture in the magazine. He once underwent £25,000 worth of plastic surgery and orthodontics for an article, yet still looks like a hobbit with a peculiarly fetching smile. He lives very close to Damian and Poppy. A proper Hoxton Cunt.

'Who's this lovely girl then, Damian?' He fondles a silk lapel.

'Bella, my missus's best mate. Now shacked up with my best mate, Ben.'

'Very incestuous – almost *Flowers in the Attic*,' says Simon and I laugh. 'Loving the skirt, babe. The classic knee-length pencil skirt is my favourite shape of all time.' And he saunters off, leaving me wondering how a straight man can possibly have a 'favourite skirt shape' (unless it's short and tight). Simon makes it very clear in his column that yes, he may be partial to a bit of Botox, but he is emphatically *not gay*.

'Well, I'd better go and get something to eat before I shuffle back to my hellhole,' I say to Damian. 'I'm feeling like shit, to be honest.'

'Still suffering from the weekend?'

'Yup. Aren't you?'

'I made one of my recuperative curries last night and Pops and I are right as rain today.'

Damian is a wonderful cook, having learnt all about spices at his Indian mother's apron strings. He is also a strong believer in the medicinal properties of garlic, ginger and chilli, not to mention turmeric, cumin and coriander. I'm not 100 per cent convinced that reversing the effects of one's debauchery can be that simple, but it's a yummy way to pretend.

'God, I could do with one of your fabulous curries right now,' I say with feeling.

'Oh Belles, you are feeling rough, aren't you?'

'I feel even rougher than I look, if that's possible.'

Damian laughs. 'You look fine. But the weekend was worth it, surely?'

I'm starting to wonder. Yes, it was a good weekend: drinks at Max's bar on Friday night, a picnic on Hampstead Heath on Saturday, followed by a fancy dress pirate party on a boat on the Thames. Ben and Damian looked outrageously sexy in their long boots, tight black trousers, ruffled shirts and eye patches; Poppy ditto in tricorn hat, hot pants and over-the-knee suede boots; the stuffed parrot on my shoulder kept ending up with its beak in my cleavage. As we'd been drinking all day, we needed some coke to stop us getting too pissed at the party, which then, *due to* the coke, went on all night. Some stuff about vicious circles hovers on the periphery of my addled brain.

Sunday lunch at The Cow in Notting Hill was meant to make us feel better, but in fact involved so much restorative red wine that by Monday I was completely buggered and could hardly drag myself out of bed. I still haven't recovered and am horribly aware that the older I get, the less able I am to cope with excesses that were formerly, if not exactly a breeze, at least easier to shrug off. Even my usual 'think Keef' mindset when trying to deal with hangovers doesn't seem to be working.

What's more, since Ben moved in, I haven't had time to do any exercise (horizontal variety aside), which is making me feel repulsive. Always naturally lazy, I caught the fitness bug in my mid-twenties, mainly as it means I seem to be able to eat pretty much what I want and still fit into my clothes. And it's the only guaranteed hangover cure I know. I have had my exercise phases – Pilates, yoga, weights, swimming, spinning, body sculpt, some horrible martial arts classes where I shrank from every potential blow – but now favour running and my own version of yoga in Hyde Park. I always used to feel wonderful after my yoga classes at the Life Centre in Notting Hill, but one day realized I couldn't stand my fellow immaculate and snotty patrons a moment longer. Getting out into the great outdoors not only has the inestimable advantage of being free, but is also a perfect antidote to the seedier aspects of my life. Or it was.

Ben, not having to waste eight hours a day in an office, has plenty of time to hone his body to perfection in the gym. This week's modelling project, which involves having his photo taken with members of the Royal Ballet, doesn't start till late afternoon. The dancers can't miss their morning practice sessions, which is handy for Ben as he loves his morning lie-in. Don't we all.

'S'pose so,' I say. I give Damian another hug and bugger off.

'Fuck, fuck, FUCK,' I shout as I trip over one of Ben's trainers. He has an eclectic and vast collection, which, along with his CDs, T-shirts, hair products and *vinyl*, appear to have taken over my flat. And that's before we get to the jeans. Yeah, so he needs to look good for work, but he looks gorgeous in everything, for fuck's sake – surely he doesn't need thirty pairs of almost identical denim trousers? I'm not kidding – *thirty pairs of jeans*. I have four, two of which I never wear.

If it was difficult to keep my flat tidy before, with Ben *in situ* it's impossible. Apart from his actual stuff, the evidence of two people living a relatively debauched life is everywhere. Overflowing ashtrays on every available surface, nearly empty bottles of wine, beer cans, a *lot* of dirty glasses. Clearly every time we want a drink we simply get out more clean glasses instead of (God forbid) considering washing up. Oh lovely, a used condom on the bedroom floor and an empty wrap of coke on the bedside table.

I open the windows to get rid of some of the stale smoke/sex/sweat smell and notice that several of my geraniums are dead. I take an empty wine bottle to the kitchen, fill it with water from the tap and give my poor parched babies a drink. I know how they feel, so pour myself a large glass of water too, before setting about tidying up. I really want nothing more than to collapse on the chaise longue with a trashy novel, but know I'll feel better once the purge is completed.

Resentment starts building slowly as I chuck yet another pair of grey marl D & G boxers into the laundry basket. There are boxers and dirty black socks strewn all over the flat – which I understand, to an extent. I leave clothes and knickers where I've just dropped them too. But right next to the laundry basket, when it would have been just as easy to drop them inside it? Is it some kind of Palaeolithic statement? *I am man. You are woman. You put my stinky pants in basket?*

Ben had most of yesterday and today while I was at work to tidy up. Surely it's not beyond him to make the bed or rinse a few glasses? Or at least put the used condom in the bin? The place is a fucking tip. OK, I'm not the tidiest person in the world, but if I was living in somebody else's flat, good old-fashioned shame would force me to make the effort. And while we're on the subject of Ben's uselessness, I haven't seen him offer to pay any rent yet, either. It's not as if he can't afford it. He was paid what I earn in a month for his last photoshoot, which can hardly have been gruelling.

Fucking vain tosser, hanging out with loads of other fucking vain tossers, telling one another how gorgeous they are. The one morning Ben actually had to get out of bed at the same time as I did, he spent so long in the bloody bathroom (*my* bloody bathroom) that I didn't even have time to wash my hair. My suggestion that we showered together was met with a 'Not now, babe; it's important I look my best today.'

Just as I'm working up a full head of steam, I bend down to pick up his 'Book', or modelling portfolio, which falls open at a black and white ad he did for Banana Republic. He's standing against the stern of a yacht somewhere like the Hamptons, looking up into the middle distance through his gorgeous lashes, his full, kissable lips slightly parted. His broad chest is bare, as it often is for these commercials, his shapely legs clad in a pair of baggy surf shorts. His beauty is so staggering that I sit down on the bed with a bump, just gazing at the photo for a few minutes. After a bit I kiss it, then chide myself for expecting such a god of a man to do anything as mundane as his own washing. This Adonis is my boyfriend, I remind myself, and I should count myself bloody lucky.

On an impulse I pick up my phone and type a quick text.

'Hope your day's been better than mine. Glad it's over and can't wait to see you. Love you xxx'

I press send and instantly feel the panic that I know will not be assuaged until I hear back from him. If I am not given constant reassurance that I am on Ben's mind, *my* mind runs riot with images of what (or, more importantly, *who*) he is doing without me. His job is probably the worst thing possible for an insecure drip like me. Daily I

picture him with actresses and models who are, by defin-
ition, an awful lot more gorgeous than I am. Despite what
he said at Glastonbury, I'm not convinced that my less
obvious qualities are enough to stop his attention
wandering.

And now . . . Well, the models were bad enough, but
now he's hanging out with fucking *ballerinas*. Jesus, what
have I done to deserve this? The poise, the grace, the
ability to put their legs behind their ears . . . I have a
picture in my head of a classical beauty with large,
almond-shaped eyes and hair drawn back in a tight bun
that would look hideous on anybody with less than perfect
bone structure. She hails from somewhere like Kiev and
has a dancer's lean, taut body. She is engaging Ben in a
passionate discussion (in sexy Eastern European accent,
of course) about – oh, I don't know – Chekhov, and he
is reminded that they are both, after all, classically trained
performers, with so much more in common than . . . It's
no good, I can't be left at the mercy of my own thoughts
any longer or I'll go mad.

I pick up my phone again and call Poppy. She takes some
time to answer, but finally, just as I'm about to hang up,

'Hey gorgeous, how's it going?'

'Not that well, really. I feel like shit, my flat's a dump
and I can't get the fucking ballerinas out of my head.'

Poppy laughs. 'Right, you need to tackle these things
individually. First, the flat: tidy it up. You know you'll feel
better once it's done. Second, you feeling like shit: run
yourself a lovely warm bath with plenty of smelly stuff and
pour yourself a nice big glass of wine – not big enough to
make you feel rough again tomorrow, just big enough
to take the edge off.'

'Thanks lovely, that's just what I will do. But what about
the fucking ballerinas?'

Poppy sighs. 'That one's more difficult. Listen, Belles, you're just going to have to accept that hanging out with other attractive women is part and parcel of what Ben does. Models last week, ballerinas this week; it may be Hollywood actresses next. He wants to be with you, and you're going to have to start to believe it or you'll push him away. And if it helps, picture the ballerina with her tights and leotard around her ankles, changing a tampon.'

I start to giggle. Wonderful Poppy.

'What are you up to tonight?' I ask. 'It's awfully noisy your end.'

'The Savoy Bar, darling. Très posh. We're having drinks here before heading to the ballroom for the Neptune Music Awards.'

'You and your job are so bloody glamorous. Talking of which, I saw Damian in his professional habitat today. Most illuminating.' We are both giggling about Hoxton Cunt when Poppy says, 'Oh bugger, there's my boss. Listen babe, I've really got to go, but have a nice chilled evening, yeah, and everything will seem so much better tomorrow. It is Bluesy Tuesday after all.'

'Yeah, true. Have fun tonight and don't do anything I wouldn't do!' I hang up and instantly feel depressed again, but concentrate on making the flat look pretty. He said he wouldn't be back till nine-ish, so I've got time to nip down to the fishmonger's on the corner to pick up something simple and delicious to cook for dinner, and *still* have time for my recuperative bath.

I look in the fridge for inspiration, but find little. The dregs of a bottle of Sauvignon Blanc that has been open on the floor since Sunday, a couple of cloves of garlic, around quarter of a pint of milk, some nearly rancid butter, half a packet of streaky bacon, half a lemon and a bag of baby spinach that needs to be cooked today before becoming slimy beyond redemption. And then it hits me.

I race down to Golborne Fisheries and buy a dozen scallops, which nearly wipes me out financially, but I'll be using up the contents of my fridge so it's kind of an economy really. I pop into the corner shop across the road for a loaf of wholemeal bread, two bottles of mediocre and overpriced Soave and some milk for the morning. Then, on a whim, a bunch of rather sad white roses that I'll somehow manage to perk up once I get them inside.

Feeling quite the domestic goddess, I re-enter my now pristine flat (I've hidden most of Ben's gubbins behind the bedroom door). I pour myself a very welcome glass of wine, arrange the roses in an old crystal vase I picked up in the market and plonk them on top of my chinoiserie red chest. Then I put on a load of washing and run a bath, pouring in liberal glugs of the divine-smelling Miller Harris oil Poppy gave me for Christmas. Ella Fitzgerald croons classic Cole Porter from my old CD player, which is a relief after Ben's constant thudding techno. I must be getting old, I reflect for the second time today.

The food won't take a minute: pan-fried scallops with crispy bacon on a bed of wilted garlicky spinach. Yum. And it should impress Ben, who has distinctly expensive tastes for a boy from the valleys. I check my phone for the twentieth time since I sent the last message. Nope, still no response. Oh well, he's probably on his way home, I tell myself, trying to quash my rising panic. I take a huge swig of wine, pick up my trashy novel and make my way to the bathroom.

By 9.30 I've drunk most of the first bottle of wine, rearranged the cushions on the chaise longue four times, read three chapters of my book, wilted the spinach with some chopped garlic and fried the bacon till crisp. Bugger this, I'm going to give him a ring.

'Oh, hi sweetheart, I was just going to call you.' There are female voices and laughter in the background.

'Where are you?' I ask, trying to keep my tone light.

'In the pub. The photographer suggested it would be better for tomorrow's shoot if we all got to know each other a bit better, so we're out for a couple of drinks.'

'What shall I do about your supper?' *Don't sound like a nagging wife, you silly cow.*

'Oh, you didn't say you were cooking! I'm sorry, darling, you must be starving. Oh just a sec – yeah, mine's a pint of Stella, babe.' He addresses me again. 'Sorry Belles, I'll call you back in five.'

I stare at my phone, the evil instrument of doom, for a few seconds. I very much doubt that he'll call me back 'in five'. Bloody wanky expression. Five what? Years? After ten minutes of silence, I call back and he's switched his phone off. Consumed with a terrifying jealous rage, I type out a furious text, which includes the phrases 'half-witted fucking dancers', 'lazy, useless cunt', 'spineless moral fucking vacuum' and, worst of all, 'how do you think this makes ME feel?'. Then I come to my senses and hit delete.

There's no point in cooking his scallops now. They should be eaten immediately and at £1.50 apiece I'm not going to risk ruining them. So I heat some butter with the remains of the bacon fat and chuck in six of the plump little bivalves for me, which I admit is a tad greedy, but I reckon I could do with a bit of spoiling right now. I turn them over just as they're starting to caramelize, then plonk a pile of spinach in the middle of a plate, with a few rashers of golden bacon and a lemon quarter stacked to one side. The scallops cooked to juicy perfection, I arrange them around the greenly seeping spinach, and pour the last of the Soave into my glass.

I go out onto the balcony with my drink and plate.

As I start to eat my little bit of home-cooked luxury, I think about a pregnant homeless woman I gave some money to yesterday, and feel slightly ashamed of my earlier internal tantrum about Ben. I need to get a grip, some perspective. I'm a fucking lucky bugger, sitting here on my balcony on such a balmy night with my scallops, and if my gorgeous boyfriend – *boyfriend!* – has to do some networking with ballet dancers then so be it. It's not the end of the world.

Then I picture the dancers again and start to cry.

Chapter 9

I wake up feeling wonderfully refreshed. Glancing at my clock radio I see it's only 7.15 – still quarter of an hour until my alarm goes off, which is almost unprecedented. Ben is cuddling me from behind, which makes me very happy indeed, until I recall the events of last night. I've been out for the count since my head hit the pillow, so I've no idea what time he came in. He kisses my shoulder in his sleep and I squirm with pleasure, before steeling myself and gently extricating myself from his grasp. Nope, I'm getting up and getting on with my day. Things to do, people to see. I try not to feel too depressed that these things involve nothing more exciting than more presentations and binding, then remember that we're meeting Max later, which perks me up a bit. I look for something in my wardrobe suitable for both a Mayfair hedge fund company and a Hoxton lounge bar. Difficult, nay fucking impossible, so I settle on my trusty pale pink shift dress, with a ditsy printed floral ra-ra skirt and plain white vest in my handbag for later.

I look around my lovely tidy flat with satisfaction. Morning sun is streaming through the muslin curtains in the sitting room; it's going to be another beautiful day. Emboldened, I switch on the radio in the kitchen. Ben doesn't like to be woken up by the radio when he doesn't have to get out of bed for a few more hours, and he definitely doesn't approve of Radio 1 (*way* too mainstream), but bugger him. It's my flat. I make myself some tea and get ready at a leisurely pace, which is another new experience for me. I'm normally so desperate for another half-hour's kip in the mornings that I end up growling and lashing out like a grizzly bear disturbed mid-hibernation. Not to Ben of course, but inanimate objects, the imbeciles on the wireless, the sub-humans on the Tube – they are all, in the general course of things, fair game for my self-inflicted jittery wrath.

Showered, dressed and made up, I eat some toast on the balcony, then leave Ben a polite note about what to do with the scallops in the fridge should he want them for lunch (resisting the temptation to suggest he shove them up his arse if that proves too difficult). I go and gaze at him for a minute before leaving the flat. His skin is caramel smooth and brown against the white sheets, his long lashes brush his cheeks. His light brown hair, still streaked with gold from the Ibiza sun (and a little help from his hairdresser), flops against the pillow. With great difficulty I resist kissing him goodbye, then skip out of the door with a surprisingly light heart.

I sail through the day, working incredibly efficiently. I restrict my internet usage to a brief email exchange with Poppy and even manage to smile at a clearly perplexed Stella. The woman whose job I'm covering decided a few weeks ago to extend her maternity leave, so they asked me if I'd like to stay on. I really can't imagine why. Most temps would probably be an awful lot more efficient and less surly than I am, but I am good at the design stuff.

Much as I'd have loved to say no, having Ben living

with me has been a big drain on my already meagre finances, and in the current dreary climate finding temp work isn't as easy as it used to be. So I've resigned myself to the drudgery for the time being. Despite Ben's large modelling fees, there always seem to be new trainers, designer clothes and – yes – bloody *vinyl* for him to buy. The mortgage and bills just don't cross his mind, and I pathetically haven't brought them up, not wanting to sound like a bourgeois, suburban housewife. But I do resent giving up on my art, albeit temporarily. Still fired up, I resolve to have a serious talk with him tonight.

By the end of the working day, Ben has sent me eight texts, each more contrite than the last. The final one says: 'Darling, please speak to me. I am so, so sorry. I had no idea you were cooking such a feast. The scallops were delicious, btw, but not as delicious as they would have been if you'd cooked them. The flat looks wonderful. I can't wait to see you. What time are we meeting at DC? Love you xxxxxxxxxxx.'

I type back, 'I'm going straight from work, so should be there around 6.30. Turn up whenever you want. You'll probably have to bond a bit more with your dancer friends, so I'm not holding my breath.'

A minute after I've sent it, my phone starts ringing.

'Yes?'

'Oh Bella, come on.' He's laughing slightly. 'I'm sorry we didn't eat together, OK? I do have to do a certain amount of schmoozing for work, you know. This shoot should be over soon. What's that, Katarina?' He puts his hand over the mouthpiece and says something I don't get. 'Where was I? Oh yes. Tonight I'll be a good boy, I won't join the girls for drinks, won't pass Go, won't collect £200 and I'll be with you by seven. OK, sweetheart?'

'I suppose it'll have to be,' I say huffily, but unable to

sulk for much longer. He's managed to make me feel a bit silly.

'Great, great!' I can hear him smiling boyishly down the phone. 'Listen darling, I've really got to go now, but I'll see you later, yeah? Love you.' And he hangs up.

During my fairly hellish journey across and under town I have time to reflect on why I get so wound up about things that other women (well, Poppy at least) would be able to take in their stride. It doesn't take Freud to work out that my philandering father has to be at least part of it. Even though I was too young to remember my parents' break-up, Mum and her female friends were of the 'all men are cheating bastards' school of thought for much of my childhood. And as Dad had a different girlfriend, some-times two, every time Max and I went to visit him in Mallorca, I had no cause to think any differently.

I've had boyfriends before, of course, but none of them that meant as much to me as Ben, who, let's face it, is a pretty bloody brilliant catch. I lost my virginity at seventeen on a one-night stand, had several student dalliances with gits for whom cool was all and who didn't give a toss about me, and fling after unsuitable fling in my twenties. My last proper boyfriend, dull Rupert, was a banker (I know) who dumped me for not being 'corporate wife material'. He actually used those words. Since then, a lot of the men who've tried it on with me in bars and clubs have been either married or in long-term relationships, which has given me little reason to believe that my mother was wrong.

Divine Comedy, Max's bar, is, as I said, situated in Nan's old terraced house on the Hoxton/Dalston borders, with an extension built into the back garden where the outside loo used to be. Really. The rest of the street is a curious mix of old and new East End. Most of the neighbouring houses have been bought and done up by Hoxton Cunt types, thrilled to be living in the same street as the hippest bar in town. A launderette, pie-'n'-mash shop and ugly council estate at one end of the road give authenticity kudos to the glottal-stopped 'keeping it real' crowd (the council estate residents thoughtfully keep themselves to themselves). A fantastic Bangladeshi curry house at the other end offers the newer residents a reassuring whiff of ethnicity. Pops, Damian and I once went there, and even Damian admitted the curries were good. Though we reassured him after we left that they weren't nearly as yummy as his.

The bar on the ground floor is opulently done up in a manner that might be deemed English Eccentric, all swirly aubergine wallpaper, battered velvet sofas, sparkling chandeliers and giant candles in wrought-iron candlesticks. Into the mix Max has thrown disco glitter balls, Russ Meyer film posters, tiger skins and stuffed moose heads (in a nod to the current charming taxidermy craze), with dazzling results. The first floor is home to the restaurant, which, as a temple to seasonal, grow-your-own minimalism, is as different to the bar stylistically as it's possible to be.

The Members Only lounge area on the top floor, which used to be the loft, is Sixties-futuristic, with white leather bean-bags, large plastic spherical chairs in neon colours hanging from the ceiling (by means of pleasingly bounce-inducing spiral wires), deep white wall-to-wall shag-pile carpet, a vast aquarium and Perspex bar. But the real inner sanctum is the swimming pool in the basement, which Max will absolutely only open if he's in the mood, which is once every couple of months at the very most. Rumour has it that he turned Scarlett Johansson away as he didn't like her attitude.

Turned Scarlett Johansson away . . . Ludicrous that I should be related to somebody capable of that.

It's such a lovely day that someone has shoved some mismatched tables and chairs into what used to be the tiny front garden. They are all occupied by people for whom conventional is a dirty word (they all look exactly the same), so I go inside to look for my brother. It takes a few seconds for my eyes to adjust to the gloom, but then I spot him perching on the arm of a leather chesterfield, chatting animatedly to Charlie and Plump Alison, neither of whom I've seen since Ibiza. My heart sinks slightly.

'Alison, Charlie, what a nice surprise,' I slime sycophantically, kissing them both on both cheeks. 'Hey, Maxy.' I give him a big hug.

'Hey, Belles.' Max hugs me back. He stands back to look at me. 'You're looking well. Have you lost weight?'

'Don't think so, but I had an early night and just the one medicinal bottle of wine last night, which probably accounts for it,' I laugh.

'Is Ben joining us?'

'He said he'll be here by seven, but I'll believe that when I see it.'

'Ooooh. Trouble in paradise?' There's not quite as much sympathy in Max's voice as I'd have liked.

'Whatever gave you that idea? Can I get anyone a drink?'

'We've just opened this,' says Alison, pointing at the enticing bottle of Pouilly-Fumé in an ice bucket on the marble-topped table in front of them. 'Do you want to share it?'

'Thanks,' I say, as Max goes to get me a glass from behind the bar. 'I'll get the next one.' There is a pause.

'I can't believe how great this weather is,' I say, fanning myself with the cocktail menu, for want of anything better to say.

'I know, it's blissful, isn't it?' sighs Alison, who is looking quite pretty today in a floral cotton skirt and pale blue T-shirt that matches her eyes and makes her hair look more blonde than mouse. She is definitely one of those English girls who look better in England.

'We should be sitting outside,' says Max, returning with my glass.

'All the tables are taken,' I say. 'You really shouldn't have become so successful, Maxy.'

He laughs, 'Leave it to me,' then disappears through a side door. He staggers back carrying a Victorian love seat – a two-seater sofa, upholstered in bubblegum-pink crushed velvet. 'Charlie mate, give me a hand?'

Charlie bounds up like an eager dog and the two of them return with an identical love seat, only this one's upholstered in lime-green satin.

'Aren't they gorgeous?' says Max proudly. 'I picked them up in Paris and got them covered just around the corner, but I haven't worked out where to put them yet. For this evening, they can go outside.' So we heave the garish antiques out into the early evening sun.

'Sorry folks, you'll have to budge up a bit,' says Max to the clones sitting around the tables. 'Make room for my sister and my mates, please.'

There is some huffing and puffing as tables get shoved around, but it's all good-natured. This is partly why Max is such a success in the hospitality business. Now he's grown into himself, confidence-wise, he's just innately likeable, and people warm instantly to that easy-going exterior (behind which lurks the inevitable steely business brain).

We settle down in the love seats, Max and I side by side in the pink, facing Charlie and Alison in the lime green. The wine bottle sits between us on the floor in its ice bucket. We all smile at each other.

'This is brilliant,' says Charlie enthusiastically. 'Remind me next time I'm a fresher to befriend the speccy swot all the cool guys are shunning.'

'If I remember rightly, it was Andy who first took pity

142

on me,' says Max. 'One speccy swot to another. You were too busy trying to ingratiate yourself with the rowers.'

'Actually, they were trying to ingratiate themselves with me,' says Charlie. 'I was a brilliant addition to the light blues.'

'Did you actually compete in the Boat Race?' I ask.

'My finest hour.' Charlie looks wistful for a second, then laughs. 'Apart from the fact we lost that year.'

'I remember Andy was so worried about how you'd cope with defeat – he had a three-point plan about how we were going to help you deal with it.'

'God bless the bloke. We just went out and got monument-ally rat-arsed!' Charlie chuckles again.

'Poor Andy,' says Max. 'I hope he's not about to make the biggest mistake of his life.'

'That bloody woman,' says Alison, which takes me by surprise.

'I thought she was your friend?' I say, taking a large swig of wine. It is ice cold and delicious.

'*Was* being the operative word,' says Alison. 'And that was only really because she was Andy's girlfriend. She wasn't too bad before the engagement, but I wouldn't have actually *chosen* her to be my friend for all the tea in China.' The old-fashioned expression suits her, I think, registering the almost Victorian-doll-like quality of her face.

'I take it this is to do with being her bridesmaid?' I say, remembering what Max told me and Ben at Glastonbury, and feeling suddenly sad as I recall how intensely happy and excited I was then. It was only a month ago. Charlie laughs, bringing me back to the present.

'The woman's turned into a complete psycho.' He puts an arm around Alison's shoulders. 'Tell her, Ali.'

'Where do I begin?' sighs Alison, pushing a stray strand of fair hair out of her eyes. 'Oh yes,' she starts to laugh. 'When she asked me to be her bridesmaid, she made it quite clear that I was third choice, that her two *best friends*, who are very clever, glamorous, and *slim*, are living in New York and won't be able to do it.'

'Don't sound much like best friends to me, if they're not prepared to cross the Atlantic to be her bridesmaid,' I say.

'That's EXACTLY what I said,' says Charlie, slapping his robust rower's thigh.

'Yes, well, she practically told me I should be honoured to do it. Then she started bombarding me with emails and phone calls about my "duties". I didn't realize bridesmaids had duties. When I was my cousin Clare's bridesmaid when I was eight, all I had to do was turn up and look pretty.'

'That's all I had to do when I was my aunt Tabitha's bridesmaid, too. And Max was the most adorable page boy.'

'She put me in silk knickerbockers with a sailor collar,' sighs Max, to which Charlie gives a great whoop of delight.

'I bet you LOVED that, you poof!'

'Charlie, don't,' says Alison, looking agonized. Max smiles at her.

'Don't worry, Ali, he's about the only person in the world who can say that to me.'

'Apparently I have to follow her around on the Big Day,' Alison goes on. 'Touching up her make-up and carrying an "emergency kit" which includes a needle and thread, mints, shine blotting papers, nail varnish . . .' She ticks them off on her fingers. '. . . and – get this – a spare pair of knickers. In case she shits herself, perhaps?'

This is so unexpected coming from mild-mannered Alison that I burst out laughing.

'Are we really talking about the same high-flying, glass-ceiling-breaking superwoman?' I say. 'Who somehow turns into a pampered imbecile incapable of doing anything for herself just because she's getting married?'

'It has been known,' says Max drily. 'Oh by the way,

Belle, I got a postcard from Dad this morning. Did you know he's in Rio?' He reaches into his pocket and hands me the postcard, which has a stunning close-up photo of colonial roof tiles against an azure sky on the front. I turn it over.

Hey kiddo, Dad has written in his beautiful sloping handwriting. *Didn't think you'd appreciate one of the countless photos of girls in thongs! The real thing's even better though – Copacabana Beach has to be seen to be believed. Yesterday I drove into the jungle. Awesome, man. The beauty of the towering plants made me feel small and humble. The poverty of the favelas breaks your heart, but apart from that this country has everything – ocean, jungle, great food, fantastic climate, some amazing architecture, the Carnival spirit . . . and (of course) the girls!*
Love you Maxy,
Dad xx
PS Thought you might like to know there are plenty of handsome young men here too!!!

I laugh and hand the postcard back.

'I had a very similar one, though he didn't mention the girls quite so much. Mine had a beautiful painting on the front that he saw in some gallery and thought I'd appreciate.'

'Dear old Dad.' We both smile. The combination of culture, nature appreciation and unabashed lechery is just like him.

'Your dad's great,' says Charlie. 'Remember when we stayed at his place in Mallorca with Andy, Max?'

'How could I ever forget it?' They both smile.

'When was this?' asks Alison.

'Summer holidays between the first and second year at uni,' says Charlie. 'We hired motorbikes and drove all over the island. We thought we were so cool. God it felt great, the speed and the wind in your hair.' He looks dreamy for a minute, and I try to picture the three of them, so young and full of exuberance. I imagine Charlie was the looker of the group in those days. Max, certainly, was all gangly limbs and glasses; Andy, from what I recall, much the same.

'I take it this was pre-Alison?' I say.

'Yeah, they met in the second year, I think,' says Max.

'D'you remember, every night, when we got back to the Hermitage, your dad rolling the most enormous joints I've ever seen and getting us all monumentally stoned . . .'

I start laughing. 'At my twenty-first, my boyfriend at the time turned up with his two brothers. They were a bit provincial and straight-laced and said no to a spliff, so Dad got completely paranoid and chucked them out, thinking they were policemen.'

Everyone laughs at this.

'He seemed a real character in Ibiza,' says Alison, draining her glass.

'He is.' I smile and pick up the empty bottle. 'Though Ibiza was probably not his finest hour.'

Alison and Charlie laugh.

'Oh, you mean all that crap with the model?' says Max, pulling a face.

'U-huh,' I respond, thinking about Ben. 'Shall I get a refill?'

'Tell Ellie I said it's on the house,' says Max.

I am standing at the bar, waiting to be served by a girl with blue hair and a tartan eye-patch, when I feel a strong pair of hands around my waist.

'Hello gorgeous,' whispers Ben, nuzzling the back of my neck. I turn round and throw my arms around him in delight, completely forgetting I'm meant to be cross with him when he's standing there looking and smelling so warm and ridiculously edible. In a plain white T-shirt, jeans and trainers, which doubtless cost a fortune and took him an hour to choose this afternoon, he is nonetheless the epitome of nonchalant, no-effort sexiness. He is carrying a battered brown leather jacket, which it's way too hot for but which I imagine looked suitably moody and macho in the photos.

'Let me get this round,' he says as the bar girl comes over immediately. 'What are you having?'

'It's OK, it's on the house. Max said to tell you,' I add to the girl. 'Another bottle of Pouilly-Fumé, please.'

'Great,' says Ben. 'In that case I'll have a pint of Stella.' We settle back down outside.

'No worries, I'll have to go and mingle in a bit anyway,' says Max, perching on the pink loveseat's arm and making room for Ben. His legs are so long that his feet, in plaited flip-flops, sit squarely on the floor.

'Thanks, Maxy, for the on-the-house stuff,' I say. 'I'm buggered, money-wise. Thought I'd be OK till Friday, but I gave a hundred quid to a homeless woman the day before yesterday.'

'What? WHY?' All four of them speak in unison.

'Because she was pregnant, and her boyfriend had been beating her up. I just felt – you know – a bit guilty about everything. What's a hundred quid to me, really, in the grand scheme of things . . .' Max raises his eyebrows at me. 'Especially if my darling brother keeps giving me drinks on the house . . .'

'Yeah, thanks mate for that,' says Ben, giving Max his most winning smile. He turns to me and laughs.

'Oh Bella, Bella, you are so bloody naive, aren't you? Did you really believe her spiel? She must have seen you coming a mile off.'

'She was pregnant and covered in bruises. It spoke for itself.' I stick stubbornly to my guns.

'And she's just spent the hundred quid on booze and

drugs, so the baby probably won't live anyway,' says Ben. 'Jeez, Belles.'

'You weren't there. I believed her. And how much fucking money do we spend on booze and drugs, anyway?'

'We don't have to beg for them,' says Ben, looking and sounding so unutterably smug that for the first time since I've known him I want to kick him in the balls.

'I think it's really nice, what you did,' says Alison, smiling at me.

'Well, maybe it wasn't entirely altruistic. Maybe doing things like that just makes you feel better about yourself. Y'know, that we're not all such shallow fuckers after all . . .'

'I don't think you did it to make yourself feel better, Belles,' says Max. 'Remember I've known you since you were born. You did it to make *her* feel better. If you feel better as a result, then that's a bonus, but I bet the initial impulse was to help the poor cow.'

Ben starts tickling my feet.

'Well, yeah, maybe.' I am uncomfortable with so much attention on me – foot tickling aside, of course.

'So how have you been, mate?' Charlie asks Ben, deflecting the attention, thank God.

'Great, thanks. Life's good. You know I've moved in with this gorgeous Mother Teresa thing.' Ben picks up my left foot and kisses it. I hope it's not too sweaty.

'Yes,' says Charlie, raising a thick blond eyebrow suggestively. 'Nice work!'

'And work's going OK. Mainly modelling at the moment, but there are a couple of acting things in the pipeline that I'm keeping my fingers crossed for . . .'

'Oooh, how exciting,' breathes Alison. She looks as if she could eat Ben up, and I can't really blame her, I think, snuggling closer to him proprietorially, all thoughts of homeless people out of my head. Lust is a bad, *bad* thing.

'This week I've been shooting with the Royal Ballet for the *Sunday Times* Culture magazine,' says Ben. Charlie laughs.

'You get paid to hang out with ballerinas all day? You lucky sod. Beats bloody auditing!'

I don't know whether Alison or I look more put out. Then we catch one another's eye and start laughing.

'Bloody men,' she says, hitting Charlie on the arm. 'Let's leave them to it. What do *you* do all day, Bella? I don't think we ever really got a chance to talk properly in Ibiza.'

'No,' I say, guiltily remembering how Poppy and I lumped the Alisons together as a deeply uncool double act, without bothering to get to know either of them better. 'What I *do* all day and what I *am* are two entirely different things,' I start pretentiously, topping up both our glasses. 'I'm an *artist*, darling, but I'm temping at the moment. It bores me shitless, but I have to pay the bills somehow.'

'What kind of art?' asks Alison.

'It's not terribly fashionable, I'm afraid. Which is probably why I haven't sold anything for months.' I laugh, embarrassed again, as I always am when trying to justify my painting. Alison smiles encouragingly.

'I mainly work in oils – detailed studies of the natural world, but not absolutely literal. Not conceptual either, come to that.' *Oh brilliant, Bella, you're really selling yourself.* I rally. 'I like to think of it as a kind of modern impressionism.'

'You mean like . . .' Alison reels off the names of a couple of little-known Spanish artists whose work I admire hugely.

'Wow, if I could be halfway as good as either of them, I'd be laughing. You do know your stuff. How come?'

'Well, I studied Fine Art at the Courtauld—' Alison starts, but she is interrupted by Charlie, who has stopped leching over imaginary ballerinas.

'She's too modest as always. Ali's just opened her own gallery. It's really cool.'

'Really?' I'm impressed. 'Where?'

'Oh just around the corner from here, in Shoreditch,' she says airily, and I am stunned into silence and vow never again to judge people on first impressions. Mousy, Sloaney Alison owns a gallery in Shoreditch? Well, bugger me.

'What kind of things do you exhibit?' I ask.

'A range of stuff, but I'm always looking for new, contemporary talent. I'd love to see your work. Why don't you give me a ring, and we can discuss it.' She delves into her Mulberry handbag for a card.

'This is fantastic,' says Ben, giving me a little squeeze. 'I think we should celebrate this possible new direction in Bella's career. She's brilliant, Alison – you won't be disappointed. Any chance of a discount on a bottle of house champagne, Max?'

'Don't worry,' says Max, who has just come back outside. 'It's on the house. I'm thrilled – could be a great opportunity for you, Belles.'

'I'm not promising anything,' says Alison, throwing her hands up in mock horror. 'But I'm very happy to take a look.'

She smiles at me and I feel all happy and warm and excited again.

Four hours later, the sun has long since gone down and we're upstairs in the Members Only bar, pleasantly pissed. Alison and I are bouncing in a couple of the hanging chairs, talking about art, shoes, *EastEnders*, cooking, lipstick, the Middle East, corrupt politicians – your usual conversational mishmash. We're also doing a lot of bitching and giggling about Skinny Alison, delighted to have found a common enemy. Charlie and Ben are sitting on beanbags playing Risk with Mark, who turned up unannounced around 9.30, and a random German bloke they met at the bar. Max is flitting around being sociable, keeping the cogs of his lucrative machinery oiled the best way he knows.

'How are you boys doing?' asks Alison.

'I've just taken Irkutsk,' says Charlie, staring at the board, engrossed.

'Ahhhh,' says Alison soppily. 'Boys will be boys.'

'Hans here has already taken Poland and Czechoslovakia. He's threatening to establish a Fourth Reich,' says Mark obnoxiously, and I start to giggle.

'That is quite funny,' says the German. 'But my name is Jürgen.'

'I've got to go to for a piss,' says Ben, staggering to his feet. 'Sorry guys – don't stop play.' He seems, if anything, even drunker than everyone else, which does nothing to detract from his charisma. He's just like an overgrown puppy, I think lovingly, watching him lurch across the room, leather jacket draped over one shoulder. As I watch him, something drops out of the upside-down inside pocket.

'Ben, darling, you've dropped something,' I shout after him, but he doesn't hear and opens the door to the men's loo.

Giving Alison yet another 'men – bless 'em' smile and shrug, I jump to the floor and go to retrieve whatever it is that Ben has dropped. It's his phone. It suddenly bleeps to tell me he has a new picture message. Sender: Veronique.

Heart pounding, knowing I shouldn't but totally unable to stop myself, I open it.

That fucking French *salope* is lying stark-bollock-naked on an unmade bed, black hair tangled against the pillows, laughing into the camera. Her legs are akimbo, displaying a neat Brazilian and what looks like a pierced clitoris.

As far as I can tell, she's having a bloody good wank.

Chapter 10

'Darlings,' says my mother, greeting us in a strange waft that combines Joy by Patou with hints of patchouli and garlic. 'I'm *so* glad you could make it. Just leave all your stuff there, and let's have a lovely big drinkie before we even *think of* anything else.' And Poppy, Damian, Ben and I follow her out into the garden.

After I found the photo of Veronique, I'm afraid I flipped. Not wanting to make a scene in Max's bar, I abruptly said my goodbyes, then dragged my reluctant shit of a boyfriend out into the street. Once we were around the corner, I let rip. Veering wildly from sobbing to heavy sarcasm ('so I suppose you think it's *appropriate* to encourage fucking French sluts to send you pornographic pictures of themselves') to screaming insults, all my jealousy, hurt, anger and insecurity came tumbling out, expletive upon expletive. Ben finally calmed me down by showing me his Sent Messages folder, insisting that he hadn't encouraged Veronique to send him anything since getting together with me.

'You could easily have deleted everything,' I snivelled, wiping my nose on my wrist.

'What do I have to do to convince you?' He gave an exasperated sigh and handed me a hanky. 'Here, darling, wipe your nose on this.' The way he said it reminded me of our first night together in Glastonbury and brought on fresh floods of sobbing. Then he took me in his arms again. 'Shhh, shhh, baby, everything's going to be OK.'

The wrangling went on all night and for the next day too. (I called in sick to work and made an enormous fuss when he went off to his 'bloody moronic dancers' in the evening. To give him his due, he returned from work very promptly that night.) He deleted Veronique's number from his phone in front of me, and eventually, exhausted with fighting, we settled into a kind of uneasy truce.

Now it's Saturday, and the four of us have come to spend the weekend with my mother in Oxfordshire. I mooted the idea when Ben and I first got together, thinking what a lovely, relaxing, rustic time we could all have. Ha bloody ha.

The house, which was built at the end of the seventeenth century out of warm, golden Cotswold stone, used to be a working mill. It was seriously ramshackle when Dad bought it for Mum and us to live in when he moved to Mallorca in the late Seventies, but Mum has put her own inimitable stamp on it over the years. We pass through the kitchen, the walls of which still have the felt-tip pen drawings Max and I did when we were little (mine were *much* better, of course). The garden, Mum's pride and joy, is overblown with old-fashioned English blooms: hollyhocks and sweet peas, roses and peonies, poppies, primroses and foxgloves, in a disorganized riot of joyous summer colour. Bees hum in the sweet-scented honeysuckle bush that hugs the stone wall to the left of the stable door leading from the kitchen. A hammock made out of old decking material hangs from an apple tree. I did all of my A level revision in that hammock. The sloping lawn is as overgrown as ever; the stream, flanked by reeds and bulrushes, gushes as blissfully as ever down one side of it. Mum has laid the garden table with a blue and white checked cloth, on which sit a huge jug of Pimm's, several glasses, and bowls of Kettle Chips, hummus, tzatziki, pistachios and olives. The Mamas & the Papas are crooning 'Dream a Little Dream of Me' from an ancient CD player. I'm home.

Mum pours our drinks and we make ourselves comfortable around the table.

'How lovely to have you all here,' she beams, and I look at her properly for the first time today.

My mother is wearing what can only be described as a kaftan. And it's not a Melissa Odabash tastefully retro-inspired piece. Its orange and purple paisley, keyhole collar and nasty synthetic fabric mark it out very clearly as one of her original hippy numbers. She has piled her chocolate-brown hair up into a messy bun and lined her dark, expressive eyes with kohl. Her still-beautiful face is positively glowing.

'It's lovely to be here, Olivia,' says Ben charmingly. 'And may I congratulate you on your garden? It's looking quite wonderful.'

'He's right, Mum, it looks great,' I say. 'It's good to be home.'

'Thanks, darling. Now, I want to hear all about everything that's been going on in your life – apart from stepping out with this gorgeous boy, of course! Do you know, Ben, I always rather hoped you'd take an interest in my daughter. What's taken you so long?'

'Muuuum,' I groan.

'And Poppy, darling, how lovely to see you, looking smashing as ever.'

Smashing. Bless her. Actually, Poppy is looking rather

smashing, channelling Kate Moss today in her summer uniform of J Brand denim cut-offs and a customized Dior Homme waistcoat with nothing underneath. Her hair, long and loose, gleams, butter-coloured, in the sunlight.

'Thanks, Olivia. You too.' Pops kisses my mother fondly on both cheeks.

'How's Ken?'

'Getting worse, I'm afraid. He didn't recognize Damian last time we visited.' I look over at her, startled. *Shit.*

'Oh darling, I'm so sorry to hear that. He still knows who you are, though?'

Poppy nods. 'It's only a matter of time though.'

'How's Diana coping?' Mum's voice is concerned. She and Diana Wallace were thick as thieves when Pops and I were at school, though they drifted apart after we both left home.

'She pretends to be as upbeat as ever, but I know it's tearing her apart. Apart from the ongoing sadness of seeing Dad like that, the relentless monotony of looking after him really grinds you down. It's definitely time for him to go into residential care now. As long as he's living at home, Mum doesn't have a life.'

I remember Poppy saying that if it was down to her, her father would stay at home indefinitely. Things must be bad. I've been so full of my own woes recently that I haven't had much time for my oldest and dearest friend, whose problems make mine fade into insignificance. Guiltily, I remember pouring my heart out to her about Veronique's photo. Her measured reaction made my histrionics seem a little absurd.

'Oh my poor love,' she said. 'I can see it must have been awful actually seeing the skanky cow in all her glory – I bet she stinks, by the way. But Ben did say she'd been sending him photos and there's no reason to assume he was reciprocating.'

155

'Oh poor Diana,' says Mum now. 'I must give her a ring.'

'Did you go to see that care home you were talking about before?' I ask Poppy, aware that I should know the answer to that, were I any kind of friend worth my salt.

'Yup, the weekend after Glastonbury. It was actually very nice, in so far as these places can be. The people genuinely seemed to care, and there's a fountain and an aviary in the back garden, full of lovely colourful birds. It's just a case of persuading Mum now.'

'When you've lived with someone for nearly thirty-five years, it's bound to be an enormous wrench to let them go,' says Mum gently. 'Even if your father barely resembles the man he once was.'

Poppy smiles sadly at her.

'Thanks for understanding.'

'Coo-ey,' trills a voice from the kitchen.

'That'll be Jilly,' says Mum. 'She's come down from London for the weekend. Don't look like that, Bella, she's one of my best friends.'

'With friends like her . . .' I mutter under my breath.

'The door was open, so I let myself in,' the newcomer is saying, as Mum ushers her into the garden.

'Bella's come down for the weekend with some of her chums. We're going to have quite a full house.'

'How divine,' says Jilly. Then, as her gaze falls on Ben (and, to a lesser degree, Damian), 'How di-*viiiine*.'

Jilly Templeton lives in Chelsea. Five to ten years younger than my mother, she has been married three times and is permanently on the lookout for her fourth victim. Absurdly well-connected, she works in what she refers to as 'networking, darling'. Mum met her when they were both involved in that pyramid-selling craze for well-spoken women that swept SW3 and the Home Counties a few years ago. Until it ran its inevitable course, and a lot of

156

irate ladies lost rather a lot of money. Mum and Jilly, by virtue of being in it from the beginning, actually *made* rather a lot of money, and, after giving me and Max £500 each to 'spend on something totally frivolous', blew the lot on a month in the south of France. There the friendship was forged.

Jilly strides across the lawn towards us. Naturally slim and athletic, she works very hard at keeping herself trim, and likes to show off the results in tight jeans, high-heeled boots, little T-shirts and fitted leather jackets. Mutton dressed as mutton, if you will, so ubiquitous has the look become amongst women of a certain age and type. Her expensively blonde hair is short and artfully messy. A loyal disciple of Dr Sebagh, her face has seen more knives than the victim in *Murder on the Orient Express*, though she really should have laid off the collagen lip-job, I think as I look at her now. She looks as if she's been punched in the mouth.

'Hi Bella darling,' she says, kissing me on both cheeks. 'Aren't you going to introduce me to these perfectly yummy young men?'

'Hands off, Jilly, they're taken,' I say, laughing. 'This is my boyfriend Ben . . .' How proud I feel when I say these words, even if he is a no-good, lecherous tosser, just like my dad. Jilly looks at me with something akin to respect. 'And this is Damian, my friend Poppy's boyfriend. And this is Poppy,' I finish, thinking *but you don't really care about that*. 'This is Jilly, everyone.'

'Hi Jilly,' they all say as she does the rounds. Ben embarks on his second-nature routine flirting, then stops abruptly when he sees the look I give him.

'Do you want a drink?' I ask, reaching for a glass.

'No offence, darling, but I've brought my own,' says Jilly, producing half a bottle of Scotch from her handbag. 'You'd be better off drinking your own piss for all the kick you'll get from a Pimm's.'

'I'm pretty sure Mum spikes it with gin,' I start, but Jilly isn't listening.

'Can I cadge a ciggie, please? Thanks, darling girl,' as I give her a Marlboro Light. 'I'll get some from the village later.' Of course you will.

'How was your journey?' asks Poppy.

'Bloody nightmare,' drawls Jilly. 'Pigs tried to do me for speeding, but I outran them.'

'You gave the police the slip?' asks Damian, laughing. 'Excellent.'

'You don't know the half of it, young man,' says Jilly archly, winking and stroking his knee.

'Where did Mum get to?' I ask, looking around. I haven't had enough to drink to cope with Jilly without her quite yet.

'I'm here, darling,' Mum calls from the kitchen. 'Our next guest has arrived.'

'Fresh blood – I hope he's fit,' says Jilly, and we all laugh.

My mother floats across the lawn, followed by a very tall, large man. His balding head has been shaved to domed, egg-like splendour and his eyes are hidden by a pair of expensive-looking shades. A tropical print short-sleeved shirt hangs, tent-like, over his belly. His lower flanks look uncomfortably cramped, in tight white jeans and Italian loafers over which his fattish feet clearly long to spill. A flashy, diamond-encrusted Rolex completes the ensemble. He is sweating profusely.

'Everyone, this is Bernie Bradshaw,' says Mum. 'Bernie, meet my daughter Bella.'

Bernie lowers his shades to take a better look at me on introduction. His eyes are small, sparkly and very humorous. 'Lovely girl,' he rasps. 'Nearly as beautiful as your mother.' He's a dead ringer, aurally, for Frank Butcher in *EastEnders* (RIP).

Once the introductions are over, Mum says, in a ridiculously girly voice for a woman who used to tell me to despise women who act differently in front of men, 'Oh! I've forgotten to light the barbecue! I've made a few salads, but I thought the men should be in charge of the meat!'

Bernie, Ben and Damian puff out their chests in suitably hunter-gatherer fashion. Bernie looks as if he wants to drag my mum by her hair to the nearest cave and give her a good seeing-to.

'I'll do the sausages,' says Damian. 'Sausages are my speciality.'

Mum winks at me.

'The sausages are in the fridge, Damian love. There's also some lamb and a couple of poussins.' Thus the boys are dispatched to bring meat from the kitchen while Bernie sets about lighting the barbecue, down by the apple tree, out of earshot.

'Mum!' I say, excited for her. 'Who is he? How did you meet him?'

'At a dinner party a few weeks ago up at the manor. I think he's rather nice.' She's blushing. Bless.

'Bernie Bradshaw . . .' Jilly is musing. 'Where do I know that name from?'

'You haven't screwed him, have you?' asks Mum, looking anxious.

'No no, darling heart, far too fat for me. And too common. But . . . oh yes, I've just remembered – he was on the *Sunday Times* Rich List last year. Well, Liv, he may be fat and vulgar, but he is absolutely loaded. You go girl!' This last bit delivered in the manner of the feisty African American momma Jilly patently isn't.

'Shhh,' says Mum, putting her finger to her lips and

laughing. 'Please don't refer to him like that. Not all of us think only about body shape and wealth. He makes me laugh.'

'Laughing all the way to the bank,' says Jilly.

'So how did he make his money?' asks Poppy.

'Oh I don't know,' says Mum vaguely, as Jilly chimes in, 'Bit of this, bit of that. Officially import and export, but the word from people in the know . . .' She taps her nose and leaves a dramatic pause. '. . . is ARMS AND DRUGS. Or possibly professional malpractice. You know, FRAUD.' I don't imagine she intended the bathos.

'Just shut up, for once, please Jill.' Mum looks pissed off.

Blithely Jilly changes the subject. 'So how is that gorgeous boy of yours? I've always had a soft spot for Maxy. Are you sure there's no way I can convert him?'

'It's not a lifestyle choice . . .' I start defensively, then laugh. She's taking the piss, and her heart is in the right place.

'He's wonderful as ever,' says Mum. 'My boy . . .' She drifts off into an irritating trance. 'He's doing frightfully well, you know. There was an article in *Vogue* describing him as one of the young movers and shakers on the London party scene. Just like his father used to be.' Grrrrrr. It's only with reference to Max that Mum can be nice about Dad.

'Anyway, enough about my lot,' says Mum. 'What's new with you, Jill? Any men on the horizon?'

'Actually, there is one,' she says coyly. 'He can't get enough of me – keeps taking me away on terribly stylish trips. Cape Town last week, Buenos Aires next month. And he buys me the most *divine* underwear from Myla. He says I have the body of a twenty-five-year-old.'

'Maybe she wants it back,' Poppy whispers to me and I try not to giggle.

'He's married, isn't he?' says Mum. 'You've got that guilty

look about you. How many times have I told you that's a one-way ticket to Nowheresville?' Where *does* she pick these expressions up?

'Yes, but his wife is dark and I'm blonde, so I have a distinct advantage over her,' says Jilly, bloody rudely in my opinion, considering the current company. 'You and I are so lucky to be blondes, aren't we Poppy?'

Poppy just looks at her, not knowing what to say, and my mother kicks me under the table. 'Don't think luck had anything to do with it, do you?' says Bernie, who has returned from his barbecue-lighting exertions. 'Spot peroxide a mile off, I can.'

A few hours later, The Mamas & the Papas have been succeeded by Carole King, Carly Simon and Creedence Clearwater Revival, and we've all been fed like sultans. Mum's 'few salads' were couscous with pistachios, rose-water and mint, some courgettes she chargrilled yesterday with a lemon, garlic and thyme dressing, and a fabulous, smoky baba ghanoush. She shot herself in the foot, in the 'oh, I'm so unprepared' schtick by having spatchcocked the poussins and dry-marinated the lamb with garlic, chilli, cumin and coriander. She dragged me and Max round many a souk in Marrakesh when we were little. We moaned at the time but have certainly reaped the culinary benefits over the years.

'You're not just the most beautiful face I've ever seen, Princess,' says Bernie. 'But you cook like an angel too.'

'You did the meat,' says Mum, 'which was perfect.' She catches me looking at her, then says, 'Can you help me clear the table, darling?'

Inside, I start to expostulate: 'Mum! What's up? I can see he's a very nice man, but you don't have to lose your personality completely, you know. You haven't mentioned your poetry all day.'

'Truth is, I'm stuck. The only thing I can think of to rhyme with pudenda is agenda, which sounds horribly business-like. Also, the English language is in dire need of more words with which to express the ultimate delight. "Come" is pretty workaday – ghastly if you spell it "cum" – and orgasm's just too clinical.'

'Rhymes with spasm though,' I laugh. 'But come on Mummy, you're prevaricating . . .'

Mum gives me a look. 'All right Belle, I'm enjoying a man's company for the first time in God-knows-how-long, and I'm doing what they taught me at Lucie Clayton. Being an independent-minded free spirit never got me anywhere with your father, after all.'

Back outside, the mood is raucous. We finished the Pimm's hours ago and have got through several bottles of wine since then.

'I'm feeling quite pissed, Olivia,' says Damian, whose shades are looking ever so slightly wonky. 'What *did* you put in that Pimm's?'

'Oh just a bit of gin,' says Mum, wafting her hands about. Bernie looks sheepish.

'I put some in too. Sorry, Princess, I thought a posh bird like you wouldn't know how to make a proper drink.' Instead of being cross, my mum simpers. Wow.

The gin-spiked Pimm's and blazing sunshine seem to have gone to all our heads as the conversation becomes increasingly silly. Jilly has been flirting outrageously with Ben and Damian all afternoon, having received very short shrift when she tried it on with Bernie, who seems absolutely besotted with my mum. It's turning into one of those lazy, hazy, crazy days of summer that Nat King Cole sang about.

I'm feeling much happier than I have for ages. Ben has been wonderful company all day, warm and loving towards

162

me, charmingly polite to Mum, blokily pally-wally with Bernie. Even his flirting with Jilly I can live with, as it takes a brave man to snub her constant stream of innuendo. I look around contentedly. On a day like today it's heavenly here. At the top of the garden the mill stream cascades over the rocks, evening out as the lawn gets flatter into a fairly sizeable pool. On less perfect days than this, the old weeping willow provides shelter for the family of ducks that resides there. Today, it gives an intensely green shade, almost unbearably picturesque.

'The water's starting to look mightily inviting,' I announce. 'I think I fancy a swim. Anyone going to join me?'

Damian, Ben and Poppy are all up for it, so we stagger upstairs, laughing and talking nonsense, to change into our cossies.

'This really is turning into the most blissful day,' says Ben, in *Brideshead* mode, as we reach the first-floor landing. 'Your mother's a star, Bella. And her new chap is priceless!'

'I think he's great. And he seems to genuinely adore her.'

'Like I genuinely adore you,' says Ben, taking my face in his hands and kissing me. 'Am I forgiven yet?'

'Of course you are,' I smile back at him, so happy I think I might explode. 'Come on, let's get changed. The stream is beckoning loudly.'

We go into my old bedroom to find Poppy chopping out four hefty lines of coke on the kidney-shaped dressing table Dad bought for my eleventh birthday. Its pink lacy skirt has seen better days.

Jesus, Pops. Do you ever let up?

I'm about to protest – this is my *mother's house*, for crying out loud – when Ben cries exultantly,

163

'A girl after my own heart! Good thinking, Pops.' She hands him a straw and he takes a hearty sniff.

'For fuck's sake, Poppy,' says Damian, pushing his shades off his face and into his black hair. 'I thought we were having a weekend off.'

'Oh don't be such a bloody killjoy,' says Poppy. 'You're no fun any more.' She makes to cuff him on the shoulder and he grabs her little fist. She shakes him off testily, blowing on her hand as if he's hurt her. Damian stares at her.

'Don't be ridiculous. We don't have to have coke for every fucking occasion, you know. It's quite possible to enjoy ourselves without it.' He looks angry and genuinely concerned. 'Or isn't it these days?'

'Listen, *darling*,' Poppy hisses back. 'I have spent the last year watching my father lose his mind. If I want to have a bit of fun blowing my own mind, then I bloody well will. You don't mind us doing it here, do you Belles?'

It's blatant emotional blackmail, but I feel so guilty about not having been a better friend since hooking up with Ben that I shake my head.

For a moment Damian glares at her, then his sangfroid returns and he shrugs.

'All right then. Do as you please, my silly little cokehead. You can leave me out though. I'm having a good enough time as it is.'

Poppy laughs and kisses him on the shoulder she's just tried to punch.

'All the more for us then! Belles?'

'Not for me thanks.' It really does seem seedy when I look at it all chopped out on my old pink-skirted dressing table.

Poppy and Ben hoover up the last two lines, then she and Damian go next door into Max's old bedroom to get changed. I hope that's the end of the bickering.

I devour Ben with my eyes as he changes out of his jeans and into his trunks. I cannot imagine ever taking his beauty for granted. I put my arms around his lovely warm brown body from behind. Moving them further down, I feel his cock stiffen.

'Bella,' he groans, turning round. He pushes me onto the floor and shoves a cursory couple of fingers inside me. Finding me wet already, he mutters, 'God, you're sexy. You always want it, don't you?'

Only with you, I think (not entirely accurately), but then all thoughts are gone as he thrusts into me. I can feel his cock getting even bigger and harder as he goes deeper and deeper. I start bucking against him, wrapping my legs around him, helpless against the sheer force and momentum of the sensations gathering into an explosive knot inside me. Within less than a minute we have both come. My mother's right. There should be a better word to 'express the ultimate delight'.

We collapse in a pile of sweaty limbs, laughing into each other's eyes.

'Come on, we'd better get out there,' says Ben, kissing me for the first time since I instigated the quickie. It's a while since he paid me the kind of mesmerizing sexual attention he did that first time in Glastonbury, but I try not to dwell on it. I pull my bikini on and, hand-in-hand, we make our way to the garden.

'Wham bam thank you ma'am!' shouts Jilly coarsely from the table. She is staggeringly drunk now.

'I was just showing Ben some of my old drawings,' I say primly.

'Showing him your etchings?' sniggers Poppy, who seems to have recovered her good humour. 'Come on Belles, you can do better than that!'

Everyone laughs at this, me and Ben included.

'Right,' says Poppy. 'Last one in's a sissy!' And she runs down the lawn as fast as her dainty little feet will carry her, performing a perfect swallow dive into the mill pool. She's been here enough times to know exactly where it's deep enough for diving. Ben takes a run and dive-bombs her. She squeals dramatically. Damian and I follow, leaping into the pool with abandon. The water is cool and delicious against my skin. My friends' faces are green in the shade of the old willow as we muck about, splashing each other and generally not acting much like grown-ups.

Then, 'OK chaps, here I come,' barks Jilly, and before we know it, she has flung off her clothes with a whoop of glee and is running, totally starkers, down the lawn towards us. Her body is very impressive for her age (actually for any age), though as she gets closer you can see the telltale scars on the underside of her tits. Splash!

'Just another quiet day in the countryside,' says an amused voice.

'Maxy darling!' cries Mum. 'We weren't expecting you . . .'

'So I see,' he laughs, taking in the scene. 'But I was helping Andy and Alison out with wedding planning – you know they're getting married at Hambledon Hall, Mum? So we thought we'd pop over and say hello.'

From the pond, I see Andy and Skinny Alison walking just behind Max. The three of them look very tall from this angle. The sun is illuminating Max's curls, so he looks even more be-haloed than ever. My sainted brother. Even from here I can sense Alison's disapproval. Fuck, I still haven't replaced her shirt. Still, I can't imagine she's losing any sleep over it. Today she's exuding scowling Parisian chic in stone-coloured Capri pants and a Breton-inspired T-shirt in muted shades of khaki, grey and lavender. She likes her horizontal stripes, does Skinny. A lavender scarf knotted at her thin neck adds a jauntiness entirely at odds with the rest of her miserable demeanour.

'Andy, Alison, how lovely to see you,' says Mum, flustered now. 'This is Bernie Bradshaw, everyone. Bernie, this is my son, Max . . .' Her voice is proud. '. . . and Andy and Alison, friends of his from Cambridge.' She likes to get the Cambridge reference in wherever possible. 'They're getting married in a few months' time, which must be awfully exciting for you.' She beams at Alison.

'Not really,' says Alison. 'At the moment it's just exhausting. There's *so* much to do.'

'But fun things, surely?' persists Mum, who evidently hasn't seen Alison in wedding mode up till now.

'Not when you're dealing with halfwits,' says Alison sharply. 'Especially when you also have to deal with drunken imbeciles ruining your work clothes. Is it all right if I get myself a glass of water? I'm parched.'

'There's a jug of cold in the fridge,' says Mum. 'Then do join us for a nice glass of wine.'

'Thank you.' Alison is so lacking in warmth compared to the well-lubricated over-familiarity of the rest of us that Mum sits down, looking hurt.

As Alison makes her way to the kitchen, Max and Andy walk down to the pond.

'Maxy!' shouts Jilly, rising from the waves like Venus to give him an eyeful of her impressive chest.

'Hi Jilly,' he smiles, looking determinedly over her shoulder. Andy, beside him, doesn't know where to look, so I wave at him.

'Hi Andy,' I say, wading over to give him an affectionate if soggy greeting. I haven't forgotten how kind he was to me that night in Ibiza with Mark, the Brazilian twins and the dwarf. 'Maxy, second time in a week! You could have told me.'

167

'I didn't know myself until today,' says Max. 'Alison needed an – erm – *emergency* meeting with the musical director . . .' He tails off delicately and Andy shakes his head.

'I'm sorry, mate, I really don't know why it was necessary for you to be there today.'

'I'm your best man, aren't I? Anyway, it's such a lovely day it was nice to get out of London. And just think, I'd have missed all this fun if I'd stayed behind.' He gestures at us all and says solemnly, 'My sister and her mates at play are a joy to behold, don't you think?'

Andy looks at me and smiles. 'Yes they are. In fact it looks so inviting in there I might have to join them. Al,' he shouts up the lawn. 'Do you fancy a swim?'

'No thanks. I don't imagine it's very hygienic.'

'There's nothing unhygienic about my stream,' huffs my mother. 'The mill keeps the water moving all the time so it doesn't have a chance to get stagnant.'

'Well, I think I'll pass, all the same,' says Alison. 'And I'd rather you didn't risk it either, Andy.'

'I'm hot and bothered after yet another day of wild-goose chases,' he snaps. 'And I'm going to cool off.' And without further ado, he takes off his jeans and T-shirt and wades into the water in his navy blue boxers. Automatically, I check out his physique. Not bad at all. 'Bugger, my glasses,' he says, wading back and putting them on the grass verge. He ducks under the water for a minute, then emerges, gasping with pleasure. 'God, that's good!'

Ben and Poppy, who have been involved in a game of frenetic splashing, greet him enthusiastically, Damian less so.

'Well, I think I've done my cooling off,' drawls Jilly. 'And I'm gasping for a ciggie. See you back at the table, darlings.' And she rises again from the waves, this time giving us an eyeful of her pertish buttocks, and strides languidly, brazenly, back to dry off in the sun.

Ben swims up behind me and grabs me round the waist, kissing the back of my neck. I think I might pass out from pleasure. Mother Duck swims right past us, followed by five little ducklings, which are beyond the fluffy yellow stage but pretty damn sweet nonetheless.

'Oh my God, how adorable,' I whisper. The scene is so idyllic that we all just watch them in silence for a minute or two, then burst into spontaneous applause and laughter.

'Jesus, anyone would think we were American,' says Poppy. 'Well, for me that moment cannot be bettered, so I'm buggering back to the feast.'

As usual, Poppy has put into words what everybody else was thinking.

By the time it's dark it's also starting to get chilly. I have glamorously put one of Max's old fleeces on over my bikini but still I give a little involuntary shiver.

'Darling, you're freezing,' says Mum. 'Why don't we all go inside? I've got some lovely cheeses if anyone's still hungry.'

'Now you're talking,' grins Bernie, patting his paunch. 'Hostess with the Mostest, that's what you are, Princess.'

We troop into the sitting room, which Mum has done up like – you guessed it – a Moroccan souk. Ethnic throws and cushions in myriad shades of orange, red and pink cover up the old holey sofas and armchairs, kilims warm up the flagstoned floor and flea-market lanterns and candles give off a flattering soft light.

'Oooh, I'd forgotten about your piano,' Poppy says to Mum, who is lighting a joss stick. 'Can I have a go, please?' Poppy got up to Grade 8 at school and still plays beautifully. Well, she would, wouldn't she?

'Of course darling,' says Mum. 'Be my guest.'

'Actually, I play the piano too,' says Andy mildly. 'Perhaps I could have a go once you've finished, Poppy?'

He and Alison surprised us this afternoon by being a lot more fun than usual, after a couple of drinks had loosened Alison up. Bernie has been bringing her out of her uptight shell, asking her about boring legal stuff, and she's blossomed under the attention, waxing lyrical about the complexities of various landmark cases, all of which went right over my head.

'Very bright young lady, that,' I overheard Bernie saying to Mum, who looked as if she was still smarting from Alison's earlier *froideur*. Then her good hostess gene kicked in and she rallied.

'There's plenty of room here if you two want to stay the night, Alison. It's a long drive back and you've both been drinking.'

'Thank you very much,' said Andy. 'I was thinking we'd have to find a B and B.' I remembered what Max told me about his parents' death. Of course, there's no way he'd drink and drive.

'Oh no, what a ridiculous waste of boodle,' said Mum. 'You two can have the spare room and Jilly will be fine on the sofa. No Jilly, I've set up a camp bed for Max. Behave.'

Now we settle down comfortably as Poppy embarks on the first of several of Chopin's études. She follows these with some spirited Scott Joplin ragtime, to which Mum, Jilly and I perform an impromptu Charleston. Ben, who has been riffling through the sheet music on top of the upright rosewood piano, suddenly exclaims, 'The Noël Coward songbook! Can we? I played Elyot in *Private Lives* at RADA.'

'Talking of Noël Coward,' I say to Damian, who is watching Poppy proudly, 'what the fuck—'

'—does Simon Snell think he's up to with the silk robe?' Damian finishes my sentence, laughing. 'Your guess is as good as mine, babe.'

Then Ben embarks on 'A Room with a View', and we all watch, entranced. He is absolutely brilliant, capturing perfectly the clipped, patrician tones of the maestro himself. He runs through 'I'll See You Again', 'Mad Dogs and Englishmen' and 'Poor Little Rich Girl', before declaring himself, still in character, 'utterly pooped'.

'Why don't you take over, Andy?' says Poppy. 'I'm sure I've delighted you all enough.'

So Andy starts to play. Searing, jazzed-up rock 'n' roll and boogie-woogie fill the air as his fingers race across the keyboard. With Poppy it's always about the performance – she was laughing and joking with us, hamming it up as she trotted out our old favourites. Andy, by contrast, seems completely lost in the music.

'Blimey, you're a talented bunch,' says Bernie. 'I can't listen to this without dancing. May I have the pleasure, Princess?' And he and Mum take to the floor in a remarkably proficient jive. Soon we have all joined in, even Alison, wearing that unnatural grimace that passes for a smile, but that's probably only as Ben has asked her to dance – Jilly has annoyingly claimed me as her partner. Just as Andy has come to a break, and the rest of us are out of breath and laughing, an unmistakeable sound jars through the air. It's Ben's ringtone.

'I'll take this outside,' he says, as icy fear grips my heart. In the last few days I have come to view Ben's phone with the utmost apprehension. The next few minutes are hell as I imagine all kinds of conversations with all kinds of people, all of them female. I light a fag, trying to appear nonchalant.

Ben races back in and swings me up in the air, twirling

me round and round. 'I've done it, my darling, I've done it! I've got the part! I've beaten five thousand actors to the lead in *People Like Us*, Channel 4's most eagerly anticipated sitcom since *This Life*. Fame and fortune, here I come!' As he punches the air, and everybody crowds around, congratulating him, I am ashamed of my reaction. I should be ecstatic he's got his big break, I know I should. But I can't help feeling very, very scared of what the future may now hold.

Chapter 11

Over the next few weeks, my fears seem largely unfounded. Ben's due to start filming soon, so he spends most of the day holed up in my flat, learning his lines, ready for me to test him in the evening when I get in from work. The rest of his time is spent working out at the Third Space gym in Soho. It seems rather a lot of his body will be on show in *People Like Us*, and I try not to dwell on the sex scenes he'll doubtless have to shoot. The weather continues to be glorious – it's the best summer we've had for years – so we hang out on my balcony, ordering in sushi, as we don't want to be cooped up in the kitchen, which gets unbearably hot. Sometimes I meet him in Hyde Park or Primrose Hill, with a picnic he's chosen from a local deli. Sometimes friends join us; sometimes it's just the two of us, going over his lines and snogging. There's a lot of snogging. It's a blissful, relaxed time, and I'm starting to feel like part of a real couple. Perhaps, just perhaps, I think with cautious optimism, we can make it work after all.

I'm still temping, but can just about tolerate it in the knowledge that I'll be able to stop just as soon as Ben starts being paid for the sitcom. He's promised me that. Plump

Alison's card burns a hole in my handbag. I still haven't got around to showing her my work. All my spare time is taken up with Ben, but as soon as I can stop the bloody desktop publishing, I'll call her, I assure myself.

The only real fly in the ointment is Poppy, who is being elusive in the extreme. Horribly aware that I've been neglecting her of late, I'm constantly suggesting meeting up, but there always seems to be some glamorous work do for her to attend. To be fair, she's also travelling a lot with the new job and spending most weekends with her parents, trying to take some of the pressure off her mother. When I think of summers past, of the picnics and barbecues and beer gardens, the endless laughs and drinks we've shared, I feel terribly sad. We used to meet every Wednesday without fail, rain or shine, and generally most weekends and probably another week-night too. Obviously I understand the time she has to spend with her parents, and have offered to accompany her on her trips home, but she always says no, she has Damian for that. She is hugely protective over Ken and, I think, wants me to remember him as he used to be.

On the odd night we do meet, she seems completely wired, and I'm convinced it's coke keeping her going from showbiz party to glamorous job to sick father and back again. One evening Ben and I decide to head east and see Max and the crowd at Divine Comedy. The *Stadium* boys are there – Damian, Mark and Simon Snell, who only wears his silk dressing gown in the office, I have subsequently learned. Today he appears to be channelling a South Kensington-dwelling French child, immaculate in navy blue Bermuda shorts and a Lacoste navy and white gingham shirt. The effect is ever so slightly disturbing on a fully grown man.

'Hello boys, what a nice surprise,' I say, perching on one

of the Victorian love seats. 'Poppy's not with you, is she, Damian?'

'I was going to ask you the same thing,' says Damian morosely. 'Hardly ever see my missus any more.'

'Probably shagging someone at work,' says Mark in his usual sensitive manner. Damian rounds on him.

'Don't you *dare* fucking say that, you prick.' Then he laughs slightly self-consciously and adjusts his shades, embarrassed at losing his cool. 'Nah, she's just doing really well with her job, which is great. Who says we have to be joined at the hip anyway?'

'How's her dad?' I ask.

'Worse than ever. He went AWOL the other night. Somehow managed to get out of the house and was found wandering round the village in his pyjamas. He has no concept of day and night any more, just looks at you blankly if you point out that it's dark outside. Diana was out of her mind with worry.'

'Oh Jesus, I can imagine. Poor Pops.'

'Yeah, it's hitting her hard.'

'I wish there was something I could do to help.'

'There's nothing anyone can do. That's the tragedy of it.'

Damian sounds weary and for the first time I realize the strain he must be under too.

We hang out in the sunshine, chatting. I'll give them one thing, these *Stadium* boys, they can be bloody good company. And, much though I'm missing Poppy, it is nice to be the only girl for once.

'Those pictures of Heidi Klum made me feel sick,' says Mark, of the supermodel who posed for the magazine shortly after giving birth. 'She looked like a middle-aged, suburban housewife trying to act sexy.'

'That's a bit harsh,' laughs Simon. 'The woman had just had a baby', just as I am marvelling at the absurdly high expectations of female beauty that working in such an environment bestows.

At that moment there is a commotion as a large crowd of fashion freaks and transvestites makes its way through the garden to the front door.

'Poppy,' I cry, spotting her at their centre. She is looking seriously sexy (if a little OTT) in a black peaked leather cap, Agent Provocateur black corset, skintight American Apparel PVC leggings, fingerless lace gloves and five-inch platform ankle boots by Christian Louboutin. She looks over at me for a moment before recognition crosses her face.

'Belles!' she cries, tottering over in her boots and flinging her arms around me.

'It's great to see you,' I say. 'It's been *ages*. In fact, I think the last time was when we all went to Mum's for the weekend.'

'Yeah, I know.' She doesn't quite meet my eye. 'There's been so much on with work. Tonight we're promoting a new series on Fashion TV. Damian,' she says, suddenly noticing him, startled. 'You didn't tell me you were coming here tonight.'

'You were still asleep when I left for work this morning. And knowing how we like to keep each other updated with romantic little texts all day, I didn't think I needed to.' Uh-oh.

'Hi Pops. Loving the get-up,' says Ben.

'Pure trash, isn't it?' she grins, suddenly sounding more like her old self. 'Hi Mark, hi Simon. Listen guys, I've really got to go and schmooze, but I'll give you a ring, Belles, and we'll make a proper date, yeah?' She gives me a brief hug and kisses Damian. 'Bye babes, see you at home later.'

And she buggers off back to her fashion freaks and transvestites.

* * *

176

A few weeks later, I am at a loose end. It's Saturday and Ben has flown to New York to be interviewed by *Vanity Fair* for a piece on new Brit talent. His profile really has shot up since he landed the part in *People Like Us*. I was meant to be spending the weekend at Mum's but Bernie has swept her off on a surprise romantic getaway. Damian's gone on a stag weekend to some Eastern European city where the girls are impossibly beautiful and the beers are impossibly cheap. Poppy, as a result, has taken herself off to Babington House for a weekend of 'pampering and general detox. Christ do I need it,' she told me on the phone a few days ago. In the old days she'd have asked me to join her, I think sadly.

Fumbling in my bag for my cigarettes, I come across Plump Alison's business card. Clutching at straws – it's Saturday, she's probably got plans, but you never know – I dial the number on the card.

'Hello?'

'Alison, hi. It's Bella, uh, from Ibiza, you know? Remember we met at Divine Comedy a month or so ago?'

'Bella, how are you?' Her voice is warm and friendly.

'I'm fine thanks, never been better in fact. Um, are you still interested in seeing my paintings?' I ask directly, hating having to sell myself but not knowing how to beat about the bush.

'Yes, of course. When were you thinking?'

'Um . . . today? Look, I'm sorry, I know it's short notice and you're probably really busy, it's a stupid idea . . .' I tail off.

'No, no, I'd love to see you. Why don't you bring your portfolio to the gallery and then we can go and get some lunch?'

'That sounds great. What time?'

'Around two? The address is on the card, but I can give you directions if you like.'

'No that's OK, I'll find it in the A–Z,' I say. 'Really looking forward to it.' And I am.

I took the Hammersmith & City line from Ladbroke Grove to Aldgate East, so am wandering down Brick Lane. I always get lost around here, and find myself meandering through eighteenth-century Huguenot weavers' terraces, their perfect proportions such an incongruous juxtaposition to the hideousness of Commercial Road, with its traffic and trade clothes shops that call themselves 'fashion'. There's a great buzz to the area, with its eclectic boutiques, cool bars and curry smells – as well as Spitalfields, of course. But a lot of it's just ugly. Maybe I'm not cool enough to get it.

I walk for bloody ages, convinced I'm lost, around streets that have lovely names but horrid buildings – lots and lots of soulless concrete monstrosities, as far as I can see. Just call me Prince Charles. I am walking along Fashion Street when I ask an evident local (she is wearing neon green leggings and leopardskin) where Alison's gallery is. I show her the card.

'Just round the corner, babe.'

I find myself in yet another back street, with big nineteenth-century industrial buildings, old factories and the like that have been revamped. An awful lot easier on the eye than the last, modern lot. The biggest is very impressive. It's Alison's gallery.

I go in. Whitewashed (of course), its front windows span two floors, making it feel beautifully spacious. The top storey is suspended from steel girders, so both floors benefit from the wonderful light streaming through the skylight that is positioned directly over the spiral staircase that connects them. Alison is finishing some business with a Chinese man in bondage trousers and Jackie O shades, so I take a look around.

Somebody has had the inspired idea of making huge simulacra of the characters from *The Magic Roundabout* entirely out of dyed cotton wool, which I suppose is quite fun, though I'm not convinced my life is enriched by knowledge of their existence. Several pinball machines, depicting scenes of graphic sexual violence via Manga cartoons, are clearly making a very serious point indeed. There are some asymmetrical sculptures well within the grasp of anyone who's done A level Art. But they've sold for around sixty grand, as far as I can make out by the red stickers. So far, so predictably preposterous.

I turn around and see a wall covered with some of the most brilliant abstract paintings I've seen for a long time. As I get closer, I recognize the name of a notoriously obnoxious, but incredibly successful New Yorker.

'Bella, how lovely to see you,' says Alison, kissing me on both cheeks. She looks cool and unruffled in rolled-up jeans, sequined flip-flops and a flattering wrapover tunic top, geometrically patterned in shades of blue. 'What can I get you? Tea? Coffee? Or there's a rather nice bottle of Sancerre in the fridge, if you prefer . . .'

'What are you going to have?' I ask, not wanting to look like a lush in front of her, until I realize that after Ibiza she's unlikely to be under any illusions.

'Well, I've had quite a successful morning, so I think I deserve a glass of wine. Let's live dangerously!'

'Good idea,' I smile.

We settle down onto a white suede cuboid sofa that must have cost a fortune. I am starting to feel extremely embarrassed at my presumption in coming here. Out of my depth doesn't come close.

'So . . .?' she asks, smiling at me. 'Aren't you going to show me your portfolio?'

'Actually,' I cringe, 'I really don't think I want to show you after all. I mean, look at this place! Sorry, it was ridiculous of me to think that you'd be interested.'

'Well, we won't know until I've had a look, will we?' she says reasonably. Then, as I hold on to the book stubbornly, she laughs. 'I'm not going to bite. It's me, Fat Alison from Ibiza.' She takes advantage of my shocked horror to grab my book. 'You should see your face,' she laughs. 'You were calling Alison Price Skinny Alison the other night, so it stands to reason I must be Fat Alison.'

'Oh God,' I groan. 'I am such a git.' Should I tell her she's Plump, not Fat, or will that just dig me deeper into the hole?

'Of course you're not fat,' I say desperately. 'But you must admit she IS very skinny, and it was just a way of differentiating you: Skinny Alison and – er – Alison.'

'Whatever,' she says, and I wish the ground could swallow me up. 'Let's have a look at these paintings.'

I sit squirming on the soft suede as she goes through my book painfully slowly. *Just say something, for fuck's sake.* Eventually she looks up and smiles at me.

'I like it,' she says, and it's all I can do not to throw myself at her jewelled feet and shower them with kisses. 'OK, some of it's a bit raw, but there's definite talent there, and it's great to see such joyous use of colour. I love these ones – different interpretations of the same view, throughout the year.' She's talking about the view from my balcony. I laugh slightly wildly, unable to believe what I'm hearing.

'Really?' I say. 'Really, really, really?'

'Really, really, really!' she laughs back. 'And I think if you worked on them, *and* painted a few more, there might even be scope for an exhibition here. In fact they'd look rather good over there, don't you think?' She points to the first wall you see as you enter the gallery, which is the one exhibiting the famous, obnoxious New Yorker's work.

I take a huge gulp of my wine, my face breaking out in the most enormous grin. 'In that case, lunch is on me.'

The late afternoon sun beats hot on my shoulders as I amble slowly in the direction of Hoxton. I am so excited about the possibility of something actually happening with my art that I can't really take it in properly. This, this *thing*, this dream I've had ever since I was a little girl, but which has never really happened, suddenly looks within my grasp. I've tried calling Ben, Poppy, my mother, my father and Max, and none of them are answering their bloody phones. Typical.

Lunch was great, if expensive. Perhaps it was foolhardy of me to offer to pay, but soon I'll be earning proper money, if the prices in Alison's gallery are anything to go by. Alison is a member of Shoreditch House, so we sat on the roof terrace by the pool, eating pizzas from the wood-fired oven (which didn't break the bank) and drinking Chablis (which did, but I could hardly order the cheapest plonk on the menu, as I normally would).

Alison is worlds away from the drip I took her for in Ibiza; she, in turn, admitted to having been a bit scared of me and Pops, which made me feel horrible. I mean, I'm glad to have finally been accepted as part of the cool gang, but scaring people was never part of the plan. I remember the bitchy girls at school and all my terrifying peers at Goldsmiths and cannot really believe that this is how I might be perceived these days, like one of the people I used to detest. Maybe I've gone a bit too far in the trying-to-be-trendy game. I still feel just as insecure inside.

Now I have decided to go to Poppy's flat to pick up the canvases and paints I left there just before we went to Glastonbury. I still have her spare key, even though I haven't once taken advantage of her offer to use the spare room as a studio. *Great way to repay a friend's kindness, Bella.* But I needn't worry about that any more, I think, cheering up instantly. Alison likes the view from my window!

Life really is looking up, I think, as I turn the corner into Hoxton Square, my mind reeling with images of me and Ben, the glamorous artist with her devastatingly handsome actor boyfriend. Oh, I can't *wait* to tell him! I've missed him more than I thought possible in the last twenty-four hours. Still, it'll be worth it for the look on his face as I tell him my news. I give a little skip.

Hoxton Square is a riot of multicoloured skinny jeans, cruelly exposing flat arses and skinny legs (the boys), and a variety of root-vegetable-shaped legs, from carrots to parsnips to one unfortunate turnip (the girls). There is little extraneous fat on either gender of course (turnip notwithstanding), but even so: of all the ubiquitous trends over the last ten years or so, the skinny jean has to be the least flattering. I stroll across the grass, happily taking in the large groups playing Frisbee and football, swigging from bottles of Magners and cans of Stella, probably bought from one of the many shops around the periphery of the square announcing CHEAP BOOZE in enormous letters.

I love the ability of Londoners to turn any sunny day into an excuse for a proper piss-up. It's been a boozy old summer so far. As I emerge from the grassy interior, I see a just-married couple outside the Church of St Monica, on the corner of the square. The bride is radiant in a net-petticoated scarlet Fifties prom dress, with an emerald green veiled pillbox hat and matching emerald platforms. Her make-up is proper Fifties starlet, all porcelain complexion and matte red lipstick. The groom sports an emerald green teddy boy suit and the guests applaud lustily as he takes his new wife in a classic Hollywood clinch. How Hoxton, yet how sweet, I think soppily.

I let myself into Poppy and Damian's flat and look around with amusement. From the exposed pipes and brickwork interior walls to the lack of extraneous decoration and colour, it couldn't be more of a contrast to mine. It's a great place for a party though, I think, remembering Poppy's thirtieth birthday, which went on for three days. Most of the flat is open plan, with the main bedroom housed in a state-of-the-art glass igloo-type thing in the corner of the living space. The spare bedroom is the exception. I make my way down the corridor towards it. A sudden sound stops me in my tracks. Is there someone in the flat?

Don't be silly, Bella, everyone's away. It's probably just the traffic outside.

So I open the spare-room door, and the sight that confronts me will stay with me for the rest of my life. With her back to me, Poppy is straddling Ben, her perfect, slender torso moving backwards and forwards on top of him, her streaky blonde hair swishing against her lovely brown back. Ben, his eyes shut in ecstasy, is groaning and thrusting as he holds her firmly by the hips. They are both so beautiful and so clearly into each other that they resemble a Danish erotic art-house movie. Or something like that. My canvases, mocking me, are stacked up neatly in one corner with my easel and paints.

I must have made some kind of noise, as Ben suddenly opens his eyes.

'Shit!'

Poppy turns to look at me over her shoulder and a look of utmost horror crosses her flushed face.

'Bella!'

I am frozen to the spot for what seems like minutes, drinking in the scene with masochistic attention to detail, before turning on my heel and running as fast as I possibly can down the corridor and out of the flat. I can hear Poppy running after me, but even she can't follow me outside with no clothes on.

Once I am outside, the tears start streaming down my face and I am gulping, coughing, sobbing so hard I can hardly breathe. The pain, betrayal and humiliation are so great I have absolutely no idea what to do. I let out an awful scream, much to the amusement of some cunting twenty-somethings (thanks for the adjective, Mark) sitting outside Zigfrid, then continue to run, head down, blindly, through the square, not caring who I bump into or send flying; in fact, wanting to cause as much fucking damage as I possibly can. Then . . .

'Whoa whoa, stop that, babe, stop it.' A pair of well-manicured, freckly hands has grabbed me by the shoulders. Their owner lifts my chin up to face him. I don't know which of us is more surprised.

'Bella,' says Simon Snell, taking in my tear-stained face and lunatic lack of control. 'What on earth has happened to you?'

I start sobbing even more heavily at this, and he leads me back to Zigfrid, where he orders two triple brandies. 'Just fuck off,' he says menacingly to the cunting twenty-somethings who laughed at me. They oblige.

Somehow I manage to tell him what has just happened.

'Jesus,' he says, giving me a huge hug and stroking my hair, which starts me off again. 'Sssh, sssh . . . Here, do you smoke?' He gets out a silver cigarette case and lights me a Gauloise. Through my tears I register that he is dressed to the nines in a beautifully cut cream linen suit, navy V-necked T-shirt and Panama hat with a navy and white striped band around it. He is carrying a silver-topped cane.

'You look smart,' I quiver. 'Am I keeping you from some big do?'

'Not at all. Just popped out to get a paper. *Some of us,*' he sniffs, looking round the square at the be-jeaned masses, 'like to uphold certain sartorial standards.' I don't reply, lost in my own misery once more, so Simon continues,

'I must say I'm surprised at Poppy. Ben's too good-looking to trust further than you can throw him, but I did think better of Damian's bird.'

'Christ!' I look up in horror. 'Damian!'

'Yes. Christ, Damian, indeed. But for the moment let's worry about you. Do you want me to take you home? I'll stay with you if you want.'

Simon turns out to be an absolute star. He pays the bill, hails a cab, stops at one of the CHEAP BOOZE places for a bottle of brandy, and takes me home. Once I'm inside, the sight of Ben's stuff sets me off sobbing again.

'I'll deal with all of this, little shit,' says Simon. 'Do you have any bin bags?' I nod numbly in the direction of the kitchen. He returns with the black roll of plastic and starts, 'Oxfam, Oxfam, Oxfam – actually this is rather nice, can I have it?' This raises a watery laugh, so: 'Oxfam, me, Oxfam, me, Oxfam, me, me, me, me, me . . .'

We settle into the brandy and Simon asks if I want him to call anyone. 'No, I feel too stupid,' I sniffle pathetically. 'But I'll probably want my mum tomorrow.'

He stays with me until we have finished the brandy and he has systematically divided all of Ben's stuff into bags for Oxfam or himself.

'Damian,' I slur.

'I'll let Damian know,' says Simon grimly, 'though I can't

say I'm looking forward to it. You get some rest. Take these, sweetie.' He hands me a couple of pills.

'What are they?' I look at them suspiciously. They look just like Es and it hardly seems the time or the place.

'Valium. I always have a couple on me in case I need to fly somewhere urgently.' Blimey. Jet set or what? 'It's the only way I can get to sleep on a plane – I really need to be horizontal.' Or maybe not so jet set.

Simon goes into my bedroom and comes back with an old pink T-shirt with a picture of a kitten on it. Oh dear.

'High sartorial standards, that's what I've got,' I manage to smile up at him. He laughs, pats me on the head and goes into the kitchen while I fumble to pull the twee garment over my head. It takes several minutes.

'Done?'

I nod and Simon leads me to my bedroom. He tucks me up like a child and I am asleep within minutes.

Chapter 12

It's Monday and I am crying over Ben's portfolio, the one thing that Simon missed, as it was under the bed. What did I do wrong? I ask myself pathetically, gazing at his beautiful face, before asking myself *what the fuck did I miss?* I go over and over the lovely times, picking the proverbial scab. Getting together at Glastonbury – that's probably the most painful. But then there are more recent things, the little things, domestic details, the way he'd kiss my shoulder just before nodding off, that wonderful closeness I thought we shared when I went over his lines with him. Was the whole thing one great big fucking lie?

Then I go over and over the lovely times with Poppy, which are far, far more, as we've known one another for more than twenty years. I gaze at Ben's face in his book, then tear out the pages with another howl of grief. I have always scoffed at idiotic men in boys' films throwing things at walls, but now I'm just as bad as them, chucking crockery about, left, right and centre.

How long has it been going on? How much have they been laughing at me? I recall all the times I've confided in Poppy with my insecurities about Ben and feel so sick I wish

I could vomit, but sadly I'm cursed with the constitution of an ox. She told me I was stupid to be jealous of him. But it never occurred to me to be jealous of *her* with him.

Why would I have? She was my best friend, the person I trusted implicitly – so all of those 'silly insecurities' as she put it, are magnified somehow into something so horrible I cannot imagine I'll ever trust anybody again. I take little comfort in the fact that I was right all along about the lying scumbag. I think about her squealing when Ben dive-bombed her at my mother's house. *My mother's house.* Was he groping her under the water then? After we'd just shagged? Maybe they've been laughing at me since Glastonbury. Maybe it's been going on since Ibiza, even before Ben and I became an item . . . Maybe . . . Fuck, is it too early for a drink?

I scour the flat and eventually come across an old encrusted bottle of ouzo that I brought back from a Greek island-hopping holiday with Poppy about eight years ago. That'll do. 'Cheers, old buddy.' I toast her with heavy irony. My own thoughts are too grim to suffer alone so I switch on the telly.

'It's all about natural beauty,' says some cunt who is trying to pretend that the redhead on the box isn't wearing any make-up. Yeah right, her eyelashes would be white were she truly *au naturelle*. Some people are better looking than others and that's that. Then I remember that Poppy is naturally far more beautiful than I am and start sobbing again. How could I ever have been arrogant enough to think that someone as gorgeous as Ben could be satisfied with me? Of course Poppy is far more in his league.

I take a huge swig of ouzo and take a look in the mirror. I look gratifyingly hideous: greasy-haired, blotchy and red-eyed. I start to make gurning faces at myself, just to prove that I am the ugliest person in the world. I take all my clothes off and slouch, sticking my belly out and making my entire body look grim beyond belief. It gives me weird satisfaction. Yes, I am ugly, ugly, UGLY . . . I sit down on the floor and get stuck into the bottle.

There is someone at the door. Poppy has been calling my mobile so I've switched it off. Ben, the cunt, hasn't even bothered. I've told the hedge fund people they can shove their job where the sun don't shine. No bridges burned there then.

'FUCK OFF,' I shout down the speakerphone.

'Bella, let me in,' says Damian, sounding more Welsh than I've ever known him sound. 'I've brought your art stuff for you.' I quickly put on a horrible old greying towelling dressing gown and let him in.

If anything, Damian looks even worse than I do. His brown skin has taken on an ashy pallor that has turned it almost green, and his deep, mournful eyes are red and swollen. It speaks volumes that, today of all days, he hasn't bothered with his habitual shades. He is staggering under the weight of my canvases, paints and easel.

'Let me take those,' I say, trying to relieve him of his burden. Everything crashes on the floor and we both start laughing uproariously. As we stoop, simultaneously, to pick it all up, we both start crying.

'Oh Christ, Damian, I'm so sorry . . . You've been with Poppy for years.'

'Yeah, and she's been your friend for your whole life, just about. As . . . HE has mine . . .'

'D'you want some ouzo?' I brandish the crusty bottle.

'I've brought some Scotch with me.' Damian holds up an Oddbins carrier bag. 'Don't mind, do you?'

'Fuck no, bring it on,' I screech wildly, picking up some of my art stuff and dropping it again.

'Shall I get some glasses?' he asks, as I stumble about, too pissed already for two in the afternoon.

He pours us each a huge whisky and we sit down cross-legged on the floor, among the mess of my art stuff and broken crockery debris. Bright shafts of sunlight illuminate the sorry scene. I feel like a right old wino drinking whisky in my repulsive old dressing gown, but perversely it feels right, somehow, to wallow in the squalor.

'So do you know how long it's been going on?' I ask, dreading the answer.

'No fucking idea. Simon met me at the airport and gave me the news. Great timing with the stag-do comedown, but it was good of him. It would have been worse to hear it from anybody else.'

'So what did you do?' A tiny part of me is hoping he's killed them both and chopped them into pieces.

'I wanted to punch the fucker's lights out, but he'd disappeared like the cowardly little shit he is. Pops was waiting for me at home. She just looked up at me with those big green eyes and said sorry, but I couldn't bear to look at her, so I packed a bag and went to stay with Simon.'

'What are you going to do about the flat?' I light a fag from the butt of the one I've just finished.

'She can pay the fucking rent on her own. I never want to set foot in it again. Knowing Ben, he'll probably move in with her. It didn't take him long with you, did it?' Seeing my eyes fill with tears again, he adds, 'Oh sorry Belles, I'm not thinking straight.'

After a bit, I say,

'Believe it or not, I thought he was sweet and vulnerable . . .'

Damian laughs bitterly, showing gleaming white teeth and pink gums, the only bits of him that currently look remotely healthy.

'He didn't give you that shit about the poof and the Paki, did he?' he asks, downing his drink in one and pouring another. 'For fuck's sake, the cunt could have spared you that. He decided years ago that it would help him pull susceptible women. For the record, we both had very nice, middle-class childhoods with many privileges. And no bullying whatsoever.'

'Did Poppy know?' I ask, sadly. Damian thinks for a while.

'Yeah, I told her. We used to laugh about it. Oh, fuck, Bella, what am I going to do without her?' He starts crying again, great, heaving sobs convulsing his entire body. 'I'll never again meet someone as beautiful, intelligent, fun-loving . . .'

'. . . treacherous, poisonous, backstabbing,' I finish for him, and we both laugh madly.

'I remember when we first met, I thought I'd never seen anything quite so beautiful in my entire life,' says Damian, looking away from me, out of the window.

'That was on Koh Phangan, wasn't it?' I say, remembering all too well, but realizing Damian just needs to talk for a bit. It'll be my turn soon enough.

'Yeah, full-moon party.' Damian lights a fag and takes a deep drag. 'The sun was just starting to rise, and there she was, dancing in the sea in a tiny crochet bikini, looking like some sort of golden hippy sea goddess with her hair all wavy round her shoulders.' I wish he'd stop going on about how fucking gorgeous she is but I bite my tongue. It must be worse for him, after all.

'We'd all been up all night and most people on that beach were pretty wrecked, but Pops was entirely lucid. Smart and funny, full of quick comebacks and double entendres. I wanted to fuck her right there, on the beach.'

'You did, several hours later, didn't you?' I interrupt, hardly able to bear much more of this Poppy eulogy.

'Couldn't believe it when she came back to my hut with me.' Damian goes all misty-eyed again, then angrily bangs his fist against the wooden floorboard.

'Sorry Bella.' He slumps forwards with his face in his hands as I recall Poppy telling me all about her holiday. She'd had a gap between finishing one job and starting the next (though the next was all lined up, of course), so decided to take herself off for a month, travelling around South East Asia on her own, as she thought she hadn't explored it thoroughly enough on her world trip. The Thai island of Koh Phangan was only one of the many stops on her itinerary, and, from what I remember, Damian was only one of several notches on her bedpost that month, though she recalled him fondly enough to me when she got back. It was only once they'd been seeing each other properly in London for a couple of months that she started to get serious about him. I decide not to share this information.

To my relief, Damian gets angry again. He gets up and starts pacing around the room. 'I should have known something was up. She's been a fucking bitch ever since she got that fucking job. And I've been giving up all my bloody weekends to hold her hand and comfort her when we go to see her father.'

I look up in surprise. It's most unlike Damian to utter such an ignoble sentiment. He sees my look and gives a snort of laughter.

'Of course I didn't really resent that. It's been horrible seeing the old lad deteriorate. But it would have been nice to have had a little loyalty in return, don't you think?'

I nod and he looks even angrier.

'If she wanted to fuck my best mate, couldn't the slag have had the decency to dump me first? How long have they been shafting us, Bella, *HOW LONG?*'

We sit there going over and over it all afternoon, finishing the whisky, moving back to the ouzo, smoking so much that Damian has to go downstairs twice for more supplies. We veer jaggedly from pain to anger to booze-enabled black humour, back and forth, over and over. And it really helps. I know that I'm only delaying the evil moment, but for now Damian and I are on another planet, anaesthetizing ourselves with hard liquor, each the only one that knows what the other is going through. Soon it's dark.

'Thanks for this afternoon, Belles, it's really helped,' says Damian.

He leans over to hug me and before I know what's happening we are kissing passionately, devouring one other with a hunger bordering on the insane, tongues that have spoken to one other for years as friends now exploring one another's mouths with mounting excitement. Damian fumbles at the belt of my horrible old dressing gown and I help him, laughing shakily as our fingers fail to obey our brains. I grab the bottom of his T-shirt and drag it over his head, marvelling at his smooth brown chest. He is much slighter than Ben, but by God is he male and fit and gorgeous. Damian pushes my dressing gown off my shoulders and we resume kissing, torso to torso, hands running up and down each other's arms, shoulders and backs, stroking faces, necks, hair.

I don't know how long the kiss lasts, but by some kind of mutual understanding, whatever it was that overcame us slowly starts to ebb away. When we pull back to look at one other, tears are pouring down my face.

'Don't cry, sweetheart.' Damian kisses them away. 'I think it's probably best if we stop now, don't you?'

I nod and lay my head against his chest. His heart is thumping as loudly as mine. He gently puts his arms around me and we lie like that amongst the broken crockery and art stuff and ashtrays, until we've both fallen into a deep, troubled sleep.

When I wake up it's still dark and Damian is nowhere to be seen. My head is throbbing, my mouth tastes vile and my shoulder is hurting from sleeping in a funny position. I sit up gingerly.

'Water?' asks Damian, emerging from the kitchen with a pint glass. He's put his black Stussy T-shirt back on and I wrap my dressing gown more tightly around me.

'Thanks.' I take the water from him and down it in one. I can hardly look at him. He lights a cigarette and goes and stares out of the window, over the treetops of West London.

Fuck, I think miserably. I've now blown it with one of the few good friends I have left.

'Bella,' he says awkwardly, turning round to face me. 'I don't think anybody but us need know what happened earlier. Do you?'

'Oh no, I quite agree, I . . . Actually Damian, what the fuck *did* happen earlier? I mean, I do remember, I wasn't *that* pissed, but . . .'

'We both just needed a bit of comfort, that's all.' Smiling, he comes and sits down next to me on the floor. He puts an arm around my shoulders, and kisses the tip of my nose.

'You know I love you as a friend.'

'Thanks.' I smile up at him, relieved. 'You too.'

'Well . . . what are friends for? Thanks Belles, for helping me get through one of the worst days of my life.'

'Well, I think we're pretty square on that front,' I laugh. 'Thank you too. Listen, it's far too late for you to go back to Si's now. Do you want to stay for the rest of the night? It's far more comfortable in my bed than on the floor. But no funny business, OK?'

'No funny business,' Damian agrees, as we make our way to my bedroom.

Things get a lot worse before they get better. Once the hangover kicks in and reality bites, I realize I have never been so unhappy in my life. I mope around my flat for days on end, not answering the phone, getting stupidly cross at the rubbish on daytime TV (especially the ads that imply you need to start wearing incontinence pads in your thirties), counting the minutes to 6 p.m. when I can open some wine as, even though my life is, effectively, over, I don't want to end up in The Priory. I cannot be arsed to shower or wash my hair, though I do clean my teeth as it just tastes too horrible not to. I cannot imagine being arsed really to ever do anything again.

I also spend a hell of a lot of time crying. I've always been a bit of a soppy fool, weeping at weddings, old movies and the like, but now absolutely anything can set me off. Happy things, sad things, indifferent things. Old episodes of *Friends* that I've seen a thousand times before, news stories about cruelty to children, radio adverts with particularly moving jingles – all are given equal precedence in my unstoppable weep-athon.

Poppy has been calling incessantly, which is one of the reasons I've turned my phone off. She's also emailed several times, but all the fucking bitch can say is 'Sorry'. No explanation, nothing to make me feel better, nothing to answer the thousands of questions rattling round my brain. She can fuck off and die for all I care.

One day, I am lying on the chaise longue, morosely watching Jeremy Kyle and wondering if I should appear on it, when the doorbell rings. I try to ignore it, but my uninvited guest is tiresomely persistent. Eventually I get up off my bum and answer the bell.

'Open up darling, I know you're in there,' barks an unmistakeable voice. It's Jilly Templeton. For fuck's sake, this is the last thing I need. Reluctantly I buzz her in.

'Hi Jill, what brings you here?' I ask charmlessly.

'Your mother called me from Paris. She's worried about you, and quite right too.' Jilly gives me a hug and recoils in disgust. 'Ugh, you stink. Really, Bella, you needn't let your standards slip quite so drastically. As far as I'm aware, nobody's died. Or have they? It certainly smells as if something has,' she adds, unnecessarily in my view. She's looking disgustingly fit and fresh in straight-legged white jeans, strappy wedges and a little turquoise vest top with contrasting lime green lace trim. She's deeply tanned, presumably from her illicit trip to Buenos Aires.

I shake my head, feeling mutinous.

'Then it's time to snap out of it. Yes, your Ben was a gorgeous hunk of manhood, but frankly they're all shits, and as for that little madam . . . Really darling, you're better off without them.'

At this I start crying and, briskness evaporating, Jilly hugs me again, trying to hold her breath to avoid smelling me. 'There there poppet, I've been there, it's horrible, I know it is, but you've got to get on with your life. And you can start by getting into the shower.'

Her bullying has the desired effect. Getting the grime out of my hair and stale sweat off my body is blissful. As I shower, I suddenly think of the pregnant, battered homeless woman I gave the money to and feel slightly ashamed of my pathetic levels of self-pity.

When I emerge, Jilly has cleared away all the mugs, glasses, dirty plates and ashtrays that have been littering my sitting room.

'Right, I've made some inroads, but it's a beautiful day out there and you and I are going for a walk,' she says. 'Put some make-up on, there's a good girl, I don't want to be seen with you looking quite such a fright.'

We walk down Portobello Road and she's right, it does make me feel marginally better. I'd forgotten about the real world, the market traders and the tourists and the well-heeled locals with shades on their heads. In the last week or so I've only ventured as far as the shop on my corner for trashy magazines, Diet Coke, wine, fags and the most basic of foodstuffs (I have developed a taste for Heinz tinned ravioli with grated cheddar on top). As we approach the Electric Brasserie, Jilly looks at her watch.

'G and T time, I think,' she says, and we nab one of the outside tables. It's surprisingly pleasant sitting out here in the sun, people-watching.

'I'm going to tell you a little story,' says Jilly. 'I've never told you about Mr Templeton, have I?'

'Nope. He was the last one, wasn't he?'

'No, he was number two. The last one was Mr Al-Saud, whose name I decided against keeping for obvious reasons. Ghastly,' she shudders. 'But loaded. Anyway, Mr Templeton and I lived the life of old Riley at Cap d'Antibes. We had the cars, the yacht, the villa. I assumed it was all coming out of his pocket, but it was all on the never-never. He was a bloody swindler, after me for *my money*, can you believe?' she asks, looking so affronted it's hard not to laugh. The waiter brings our G and Ts and we each take a sip.

'That's better,' says Jilly. 'Anyway, one evening I was dressing for dinner – Mr Templeton was away *on business*, or so he would have me think, when I heard a sound coming from the ground floor. I went down to investigate, and there were all these men in balaclavas pointing guns at me. Of course I told them they could have whatever they wanted, but they tied me up and pistol-whipped me. When I woke up they had gone, but I was bleeding from my head. All I could see was red mist,' she adds dramatically.

'My God, how horrible,' I say, thinking *why are you telling me this now?*

'Yes, v horrible.' She leans in closer over the table, drawing me in. 'But the punch line is that Mr Templeton had set it all up. They should have killed me. Life insurance.' She taps the side of her nose and I look at her, aghast. 'It was meant to look like an armed robbery gone wrong, but when I spoke French to them they panicked that they might be killing one of their own – the Frogs don't care so much about Johnny Foreigner. So you see, darling, you don't have the monopoly on betrayal.'

'No, I suppose not. Your story does put things into perspective a bit. Bloody hell Jilly, how . . .?'

'Good, good,' she says briskly, taking my hand and turning the focus back to me. She's awfully good at this. An unlikely counsellor, but an effective one. 'So how are you going to get on with your life? Don't you have a job you should be going to?'

'I don't think I'll ever be working through that agency again,' I sigh, remembering how I'd told them exactly what I thought of their poxy jobs. 'I've almost run out of money, so I guess I'll have to start looking for another temp agency.' My heart falls into my shoes at the thought. 'What I'd really love to do is start painting again though.' And to my surprise, I would. I am actually capable of feeling enthusiastic about something. Result! So I tell her about Alison and her offer.

'Well, that's just wonderful, darling! What a fantastic opportunity! You mustn't let a little thing like money stop you. That brother of yours has pots of it, hasn't he? I'm sure he'll tide you over, and you can pay him back when you're successful. As they say, "success is the best revenge of all"!'

And suddenly the future doesn't look quite so bleak.

Chapter 13

'Loving the new bag, babes. Balenciaga?' one edgy fashion chick asks another.

'Yeah,' affirms the second. 'Investment shopping, you know? In these post-credit-crunch times, it's all about buying *quality* items that *last*. It's really lame how many people waste their money on useless tat that's going to fall apart, like, yesterday. On a buy-per-wear basis, this bag is the economical option.' She strokes it smugly.

The bag in question cost upward of £1,000. I know, because Poppy was lusting after it. Right about the same time she was lusting after my boyfriend, now I come to think of it. Bitch, bitch, BITCH. I clench my fists under my desk. And next season the bag will not be nearly as covetable, so the fashion chick is talking shite in terms of its longevity. In fact, anybody who uses the word 'economical' in the same sentence as 'Balenciaga handbag', unless prefixed by 'not at all', is clearly brain-dead.

'And people should stop and think about the damage they're doing to the planet, and like, the kids in the sweatshops in – um – Sri Lanka or Africa or somewhere, before they buy *cheap stuff* from places like *Primark*,' spits the second fashion chick in disgust.

I try to slip my battered old Gap denim holdall under my desk unnoticed and hope my little green tea dress doesn't scream Primark too loudly. Simon Snell has been kind enough to commission me to do some illustrations for *Stadium*, and I've come into the office to complete them. The only spare desk was in the corner where the fashion chicks (or 'fashion department') sit. They have roundly ignored me since I've been here. The only other women in the office are the editorial assistant (read: editor's dogs-body) and the fortnightly rotating work experience girls who man the reception, open the post, and write the odd caption for the odd article. Occasionally there are excep-tions, though, as Simon told me last week.

'We've been after a female sex columnist for ages,' he said, laughing behind the vintage monocle that was that day's fashion affectation. 'So sometimes when we have a female intern who can actually write – which isn't very often – we ask them to do a couple of sample columns. You know, opinions on things like porn and threesomes, interspersed with graphic first-person recollections. We do encourage them to be as explicit and left-field as possible, as there's nothing worse than *obvious* observations about sex. We've got quite a collection – they're a great laugh when the lads come round for a smoke. We could probably publish a book of them one day.'

'So you mean, you never intend to give any of them the job in the first place?' I asked, horrified. Since my world was turned upside down, I've been thinking of Simon and Damian as the good guys. I don't want my neatly simplistic, black and white outlook to be rocked like this.

'Course not,' he said, laughing at my naivety. 'We'll only go for a known writer. But the girls don't know that, and it gives them a huge confidence boost to think that they've been considered for a column at such an early stage in their journalistic career. And *we* get to read about their sordid exploits. So everyone's a winner,' he concluded, winking and depressing the hell out of me.

Three weeks have passed since Jilly bullied me out of my torpor, and I've thrown myself into my art. Max has very kindly lent me a couple of grand, which should cover my bills and mortgage and tide me over until the exhibition, which is due to take place in a month or so. If it's a complete failure, I'll have to think seriously about what to do with the rest of my life, but for the moment even admitting the possibility of failure isn't an option. Over and over, I paint the view from my balcony, capturing it at different times of day and night, trying to look at it through different eyes for each of the new pieces. It's great to be painting properly again, and I have vowed never to return to desktop publishing, even if the exhibition flops.

I have also started running again, and getting out amongst the trees and geese and swans and squirrels and occasional horses that populate Hyde Park is remarkably therapeutic, though I could do without the happy couples canoodling on the grass or sharing boats and ice creams on the Serpentine. The humiliating, brutal truth of what has happened will not leave me for a long time. But for the time being much of my pain and self-pity has turned to anger, which is a lot more bearable.

It irks me that I'm missing Poppy far more than I'm missing Ben. She, of course, was always the first person I'd turn to when Man Trouble reared its ugly head. I don't appreciate the irony, and have turned to my other female friends for lengthy, wine-fuelled bitching sessions about my former best mate. Most of them are happy to oblige, having been jealous of Poppy for years for her looks and apparently effortless success. They're also delighted to offer their opinions about Ben. Well, let's face it, most of them must have thought at some stage, 'How on earth did she manage to hook *him*?'

As I've ignored all of her calls and emails, Poppy tried sending me several Facebook messages but as all she could come up with was her broken record of 'sorry', I've defriended her. I really don't want my nose rubbed in whatever's going on in her social life anyway. According to Damian, all their mutual friends have shunned her, which gives me a glimmer of *Schadenfreude*, but she's always got her adoring fashion freaks, transvestites and workmates. And of course Ben.

I haven't spoken to Ben since D-Day, but he had the nerve to send me an email saying he was sorry I had to find out like that, but it was probably for the best, and when would be a good time for him to pick up his stuff from my flat. Telling him I'd given all his precious designer clobber to Oxfam put a smile on my face for the first time that day.

The fashion chicks are now discussing what they've eaten today. 'I had an egg white omelette sprinkled with flaxseed for breakfast,' says one. Oooh decadent. 'And a shot of wheatgrass juice – it's great for your colon, you know.'

'Oh great, great – protein-tastic. Yeah,' says the other one sagely. 'I had porridge with soya milk and dried apricots. I'm lactose intolerant, you know.'

'Yeah babes, I can tell by the bloating. You should be careful of those dried apricots – they're packed with sugar. My body finds it really hard to digest fruit.' She rubs her concave belly with satisfaction. 'My metabolism can get really sluggish if I'm not careful.' I smirk to myself as I bend over my drawings, loving the pseudo-scientific codswallop.

'I'm having a superfood antioxidant salad with quinoa

and goji berries for lunch,' says the other one. 'I'm wheat intolerant and quinoa's such a great energy-giving grain.'

'And I'm idiot-intolerant,' whispers a voice in my ear. I look up to see Simon, resplendent in his mauve silk robe, smiling his beautiful, cosmetically enhanced smile at me. 'Life's way too short for quinoa to be a dietary staple,' he says out loud. Both girls laugh sycophantically. Simon has considerable influence at *Stadium*.

He checks out my drawings, which are for a piece called *Beware: 10 things that can drag you down on your way to the top*. The illustrations are fairly stylized, depicting the imaginary *Stadium* reader – urban, expensively moisturized and successful, yet rugged, manly and possessed of an excellent trainer collection – climbing a mountain. Beautiful, scantily clad girls, evil, backstabbing colleagues, pints of beer, football pitches and lines of coke all conspire to bring him back down. I'm rather pleased with them and wonder why I haven't considered making money out of my illustrations before.

'These are great, Bella,' says Simon enthusiastically. The fashion chicks look at me with dislike. 'I'll leave you to it. You don't fancy coming to Hoxton Cunt tonight, do you? Damian and I are on the decks. It would do you good to get out.'

'Thanks,' I say, not wanting to be an object of pity, and not really ready to see Damian yet either. I was hugely relieved to be told he wasn't going to be in the office today. 'But I'm going round to dinner at Max's. I think he's cooking for a few of us.'

'Great.' Simon pats me on the shoulder. 'Have a good one.'

I finish my drawings and go over to give them to Mark, who, as Art Director, will decide which ones will go in the mag. I haven't seen him since The Day of Doom and now he looks at me awkwardly, clearly embarrassed by the situation.

'You all right?' he mumbles, shuffling his feet.

'Sure!' I grin brightly. And then, I can't help it, my eyes fill with tears. Christ, what a prick I am, crying in the *Stadium* office.

'Oh babe,' he says with concern, holding out his huge arms. 'Hug?' And I melt into his strong frame, not sobbing, but unable to stop the flow of tears for a minute or so. I can feel the fashion chicks' sneers burning a hole in my back.

'If I ever see that prick again I swear I'll deck him,' says Mark. 'Damian has gone to pieces over what he's done.'

'Thanks,' I sniffle. 'And while you're at it, could you cut Poppy's tits off please?'

'Done,' grins Mark, high-fiving me.

'Right, I'd better get going. Let me know which pic you're going to use, yeah?' And I make my way out of the office into the steaming hurly and burly of Soho in late August.

I always start to feel sad around this time of year that summer is nearly over, just as I am always happy and excited in May and June that endless long sunny days seem to stretch out ahead enticingly. Of course in recent years this hasn't been the case at all, with miserable rain, floods and even hail in July and August, followed by unfeasibly hot Septembers and Octobers. This year has been a wonderful exception, though it would have been nice to enjoy the latter part under different bloody circumstances. The papers and radio have reacted with predictable hysteria to the lovely weather by printing and broadcasting government warnings about how much water we should drink and SPF we should slap on. The best bit of advice I've read yet is 'stay in the shade if you get too hot'. No shit Sherlock. How do they think people manage in Greece? Or Dubai?

It's only 4 p.m. and I'm not due at Max's flat till 6.30. We're starting early to give us a good hour or two of sunshine on his roof terrace. It would be silly to go home now and come all the way back out again, so I start to walk east towards Lincoln's Inn Fields, where I can sit on the grass and chill out for an hour or so. I can then get the Central Line from Holborn all the way to Liverpool Street and walk the rest the other end.

I go into a newsagent's for an ice cream and something to read while I while away the time under the trees. As I walk over to the freezer, the front page of the *Evening Standard* catches my eye. More specifically, a small column to the side of the day's main headline, with the caption *TV heart-throb spotted with mystery blonde. See Page 3.* Underneath it is a photo of Ben and Poppy leaving some club, looking absurdly glamorous. Masochistically I open the paper.

Gorgeous Ben Jones, star of the much-hyped forthcoming sitcom People Like Us, *was spotted last night leaving Bungalow 8 with a stunning mystery blonde . . .* I shut the paper, then go and have a look at the newsstand. Oh, for fuck's sake, they're also on the cover pages of *The Sun*, the *Mirror*, the *Mail* and the *Express* (right next to an 'Exclusive', revealing 'new facts' about aliens killing Princess Diana). Don't any of them have any real news to report?

I buy the bloody lot, my desire for an ice cream melting as quickly as it would have done in this heat, then make a dash for it towards Kingsway, cursing the relentless stream of traffic that makes it impossible to cross the horrible, fume-filled road. I briefly consider throwing myself in front of it, but it's more of a self-pitying, knee-jerk, *that'll show 'em* reaction, than a real desire to do myself in. Finally I reach Lincoln's Inn Fields, where I collapse on the yellowing grass and allow myself to peruse the papers properly.

First, the *Standard*. I pore over the photo obsessively, trying to analyse every bit of body language, and not coming to terribly satisfactory conclusions. Ben has his arm proprietorially around Poppy's slim shoulders and she is laughing up into his face. They look fucking gorgeous together. Poppy is wearing an almost obscenely short black sequined shift, with bare brown legs and gladiator heels, her long shiny hair loose around her lovely face. Ben is in black tie, though he's discarded the tie itself and undone the top couple of buttons of his shirt. Or maybe Poppy undid them for him? *Oh do stop it.*

Gorgeous Ben Jones, star of the much-hyped forthcoming sitcom People Like Us, *was spotted last night leaving Bungalow 8 with a stunning mystery blonde* . . . begins the blurb. *They had been attending the Viper TV Awards where, according to insiders,* People Like Us *is likely to scoop several awards next year. The handsome actor seemed besotted with his beautiful companion, and who can blame him? But who is she? Actress, dancer or model would be our guess. Just look at those legs!*

Fucking morons, Poppy's way too short to be a model, I think, shutting the paper crossly. Taking a deep breath, I open *The Sun*. This time the photo has been taken from a different angle, as the paparazzo was clearly aiming for a knicker shot, but they still look pretty bloody amazing together.

Phwoooar! TV Hunk Beds Blonde Babe! is the headline. *Man of the Moment Ben Jones was seen taking an unknown blonde STUNNA back to his hotel last night* . . . Hotel? Have they got their facts right? *Sorry girls, it looks like Brawny Ben is going to have his hands full with this little sex-bomb. Fellas, wouldn't you like a piece of that? If you know the identity of the mystery babe, call* The Sun *on* ***** *for a £100 reward.*

What? Oh come on, I know August is traditionally a slow news month, but this is ridiculous. I flick through the rest of the papers, which report the story in more or less the same way, though the *Daily Mail* somehow manages to link it to an opinion piece that blames 'career women' and 'binge-drinking ladettes' for the decline of Western Civilization, followed by an article advocating facelifts for all women over forty.

I sit there on the grass for a bit, with the papers spread out in front of me, unable to know what to do or think. Then suddenly, out of nowhere, I start to laugh. I laugh and laugh and laugh until the tears run down my cheeks. I am spluttering, slapping my thigh, holding my sides, not giving a fuck about the odd looks I'm attracting. Eventually I pull myself together and throw the papers away.

I climb the ladder up to Max's roof terrace still giggling to myself.

'Hi Belles,' he greets me, handing me something large and cold. 'Margarita?' Barefoot in a loose white linen smock and matching three-quarter-length sailor pants, he looks a bit like the Angel Gabriel welcoming me to heaven. Alison and Charlie are standing nearby, looking quietly concerned.

'Hi guys,' I say cheerfully. 'Have you seen the papers? Hilarious, isn't it?' And I start laughing again. Charlie and Alison exchange looks as Max takes me to one side.

'Listen sis, are you OK? I thought you'd be devastated at seeing Ben and Poppy in the Press, and this manic laughter is a bit – well – weird.'

'Don't worry, I haven't completely lost it.' I kiss him on the cheek. 'No, I've done enough weeping and wailing, and you must admit that in a way seeing them in the papers like this *is* very funny. Let's not forget that in tabloid world, what goes up must come down. Tall Poppy syndrome!' I cackle again, delighted with my play on words.

'Oh I see.' Max looks relieved. 'Well, as long as you're OK with it . . .'

'I am.'

'In that case, let's get this party started!'

'Hello you two, lovely to see you.' I turn to Alison and Charlie and kiss them both on both cheeks.

Sitting on Max's roof terrace in the sun, we could almost be in Ibiza, were it not for the somewhat grittier views over East London. The whole space is whitewashed, with brightly coloured rugs, cushions, beanbags, hammocks and lanterns in abundance. The scent of rosemary and lavender from a couple of dense bushes in terracotta tubs, and some mellow beats winging their way up through the skylight from the living room contribute to the Balearic atmosphere. It's all very much a legacy of our peripatetic upbringing, a scene you can see played out by the children of quasi-hippies the world over.

'This is great,' I say to Max, throwing my head back and arms out to embrace the sunshine. 'Who else is coming?'

'I am,' says a strangely familiar voice. I turn to see Dave from Glastonbury surfacing from the skylight, somehow managing to make a Liverpool football shirt look stylish. I know one shouldn't generalize, but there is something about being gay . . .

'Dave!' I cry. 'How lovely to see you. But I had no idea you and Max had stayed in touch . . .'

'We've been out a few times.' Dave looks hurt. 'Maybe he wanted to keep me under wraps . . .'

'Don't be silly, honey,' says Max, walking over to give him a drink and a kiss. 'If that were the case, I wouldn't have asked you tonight, would I? I just like to keep my private life private, that's all.'

'Unlike some people we know,' I say, waving a copy of *The Sun* around. 'Well, you are a dark horse, Maxy. Any more rabbits up your sleeve?'

'No, the only other guest tonight is Andy. Alison's working on *another* big case, so it'll just be him.'

'Oh that's great news. It'll be good to see him without that witch trying to ruin everybody's fun.'

'Bella.' Max gives me a look. 'She's not that bad.' Then he laughs. 'But I was relieved when Andy said she couldn't make it. Another drink?' He takes my glass for a top-up.

'So how have you been?' I ask Dave. 'How long are you in London for?'

'I live here. Made the break for the Big Smoke when I came down here for uni, years ago. And yes, I know I haven't lost the accent.'

'You sound just like John Lennon,' says Charlie, in a slightly cringeworthy 'I don't meet many people from Ooop North' manner.

'Life is what happens to you when you're busy making other plans,' says Dave, doing the peace and love gesture and sounding *exactly* like John Lennon. 'Man.' We all laugh and he turns to me.

'Max has told me all about what happened with your mate and that gorgeous Ben.' With a deep pang I recall that he was there when Ben and I got together at Glastonbury. 'What a bitch, man. You don't do that to your mates.'

'They're both total cunts—'

Max interrupts me. 'Bella, as your big brother I feel I should point out that your language has degenerated appallingly since you got dumped . . .'

'OK, OK, wankers then.' I wave him off impatiently and turn back to Dave. 'Ben was Damian's best mate for years too.'

'You all right?' He gives me a sympathetic look.

'Not really, but life must go on.' I light a fag, turning away from him so he doesn't see the tears that have sprung back into my eyes. People being sympathetic are the worst thing of all. 'Let's talk about something else.'

'Let's talk about your art,' says Alison, smiling at me from under a big floppy straw hat. I imagine it's more to shield her fair skin from the sun than a fashion statement, but it looks pretty nonetheless. 'How's it coming along? I hope you're keeping up the pace. Bella's having an exhibition at my gallery,' she tells Dave, who smiles his lovely smile. 'Cool.'

'As it happens, I've taken some photos to show you.' I balance my fag on one of the turquoise ceramic bowls that Max has put out as ashtrays and delve into my Gap holdall for my phone. I scroll down to the Images folder and pass it to her. 'I know the quality of the photos isn't the best, but you get the gist.' The photos show the last two paintings, one of which I've finished since last seeing Alison, and one of which I've started. They depict the view at dawn and at dusk, and are surprisingly different from one another, in terms of what's going on as well as the more obvious variations in light.

'The dusk one's still a work in progress, of course,' I say, worried as she hasn't passed comment yet.

'Looks like it's coming along a treat.' Alison hands the phone back to me. 'And I love the way you've finished dawn with those clean lemony strokes. Very evocative.'

'Thanks!' I smile, thrilled because I was particularly pleased with the lemony strokes myself.

'Let's have a look,' says Max, handing over my drink in exchange for the phone. Which is doing the rounds, with everybody oohing and aahing, when Andy arrives.

'Hello everyone,' he smiles, poking his head out of the skylight. He is wearing an olive green T-shirt that hugs his broad shoulders and skims his flat stomach, his long legs clad in their habitual faded Levis. The green is good with his dark colouring, I catch myself thinking, remembering his nice torso in Mum's mill pool. I pull myself up short.

Don't be ridiculous, Bella, you haven't even recovered from the Ben debacle and you're eyeing up other men already? You are over men; you'll never trust another of the fuckers in your life. Especially one that's about to get married, you moron.

'Mate, how are you?' asks Charlie, shaking one hand and putting the other arm around Andy's shoulders in a brief man hug.

'Bloody knackered,' says Andy. 'I've spent the last few weeks researching a feature on Albanian sex-traffickers and now my main interviewee – a girl who escaped from one of the brothels – has changed her mind about being interviewed as the poor little thing is so terrified of her pimps. And of course every other minute is devoted to planning the Wedding of the Century. So tonight is a very welcome night off.'

'You sound like you need this,' says Max, handing him a margarita. 'Sit down and relax, mate.'

'Thanks. That's just what I intend to do.' Andy sits down next to me.

'Hi Bella, lovely to see you,' he smiles. 'How's it going?'

'I'm fine thanks,' I smile back, the idea of girls being trafficked for sex making my own problems seem a tad trivial all of a sudden. 'Tell me more about the piece you're writing – it sounds horrible.'

'It is horrible.' Andy looks down at his drink. 'Adila was fourteen when her cousin Vasil offered her a job working at a hotel in London. Of course she thought it was a great opportunity, better life, blah blah. She was intending to send money back to her parents and younger brother. When they got to Berlin, Vasil raped her for the first time. She was a virgin, she says.'

'Jesus,' I say unintelligently.

'By the time she arrived in London, all six of the main gang members had broken her in several times. They beat her too, of course, to break her spirit – like that was really necessary,' he adds with a brittle laugh.

I don't know what to say.

'She's now sixteen and guesses that over the last two years she's seen on average ten punters a day, which by my reckoning is around seven thousand in total. Her body is covered in bruises, scratches, cigarette burns.' He lights a cigarette and looks at me. 'When she looks you in the eye, it's impossible to hold her gaze for more than a second. It makes me ashamed to be male.'

'But these guys are monsters, not normal men.'

'One of the punters helped her, so it must have been fairly obvious that she wasn't what you might call a willing participant,' he says, and it clicks. I feel sick to the stomach.

'So six thousand nine hundred and ninety-nine-odd other punters either got off on the fact they were fucking her against her will, or didn't care, as long as they were getting their end away?' He nods grimly and I pull a face. There are no words.

'She's staying at a women's refuge but is terrified that her family back home is at risk if she agrees to be interviewed. The awful thing is, she's probably right, and I really don't see how I can try and persuade her otherwise.'

'Couldn't you interview her anonymously?'

'I could, but I've now decided to hand over everything I've discovered to the police and hope that they get the sick bastards. If we published anything now it could put the case in jeopardy.' He takes a swig of his drink. 'So that's weeks of hard work down the drain.'

'It's not down the drain at all!' I say hotly. 'It's absolutely brilliant! If they manage to catch the fuckers because of your research, think of all the other girls who might be saved.'

'That would be fantastic, if extremely unlikely. And I'm afraid it doesn't wash with Alison. The piece would have paid bloody well and getting married is an expensive business.' He takes off his glasses and rubs the bridge of his nose. He does look tired. I reflect that, for a human rights lawyer, Alison seems to have pretty skewed moral priorities. 'My editor's not best pleased with me either,' he says with a rueful smile.

'Well, I think you've done the right thing. Cheers.'

'Cheers.' We clink glasses.

'So how's the wedding planning going?' I ask, bringing the conversation back down to my superficial level.

'We're getting there. I can't believe it's only a month away. Poor Al is quite stressed about things but I'm sure it's going to be great.' He smiles determinedly and I want to give him a hug.

'I'm sure it'll be wonderful. Hambledon Hall is gorgeous. And you've got the honeymoon to look forward to, too. Where are you going?'

'Eco-trekking in Indonesia,' he says, his eyes shining with real enthusiasm. 'It looks amazing. We'll be staying in a hotel on the edge of a lake, which was built to blend in with the rocks around it, so it's now part of the landscape, with monkeys perching on the balconies and bats swooping down the corridors at night.'

'Wow, sounds incredible,' I say, wondering if the swooping bats aren't a step to oneness with nature too far.

'Oh, and the bit I'm most looking forward to is that one of the infinity pools is at treetop height, so you're swimming at eye level with tropical birds!' His deep voice sounds almost boyish with excitement.

'Oh, I'd love that.' This time I mean it.

We hang out on the roof terrace for another hour or so, and for the first time since The Day of Doom I really enjoy myself, even managing to forget about Ben and Poppy for a full five minutes at a time. Max and his mates are gentle, intelligent company, and Alison is well on her way to becoming my New Best Friend.

'Well, I think we can safely say we've milked the last drop of sunshine from today,' says Max. It's practically dark now. 'Shall we adjourn for some food?'

Andy's phone rings.

'Hi darling,' he says. 'How's it going? Oh I see . . . you poor thing. Yes, I understand that must be very annoying . . . What's that? No, I'm still at Max's – we're just about to eat. Who . . .? Well, Charlie and Alison, and Dave, who you don't know, and Bella. Yes, darling, I'm sure I told you. Calm down, sweetheart . . .' He raises his eyebrows at us apologetically. 'Yes . . . yes . . . oh come on Al, that's not fair. Yes darling . . . Surely that can wait till the morning? No, no, no, of course not, sweetheart. Calm down. Yes, I'll pick them up. Don't worry, you just concentrate on your work. OK, bye then. See you later.' And he hangs up.

Turning to us all, he says, 'I'm sorry, guys, I'm going to have to go. I've got to pick the Order of Service up from the printers, which shut at nine. Listen, I'm not stupid, I know what you all must think of Alison's recent behaviour, but you know she's not like that really.'

'It's none of our business, mate,' says Charlie.

'But I want to tell you,' says Andy earnestly, and I think what a nice man he is. 'Al's been under loads of stress recently with work. She's working on a really upsetting case about child abuse and she's been under huge pressure since her promotion last year. On top of all that, she is putting *herself* under huge pressure for the wedding to be absolutely perfect – I'd just as happily get married on a

214

beach, to be honest, but Al is a real perfectionist. Her parents are being a nightmare too.'

'God, I remember them,' says Charlie. 'Religious nutters, aren't they?'

'Well, very strict old-school Christian. The fact that we've been living in sin for the past thirteen years hasn't exactly gone down well. Now I'm finally making an honest woman of Al, they very much want it to be their show, even though we're paying for the whole bloody thing ourselves. They have an opinion on everything from our choice of hymns to how much wine we serve at the reception – they think more than one glass per head is the work of the devil.' We all laugh at this.

'Anyway, I'm sure that once the pressure of the wedding is over, we can relax into being happily married. Alison's a very good person, you know. She tries very hard to make the world a better place.'

Could have fooled me, I'm thinking, when we are interrupted again, this time by Max's phone.

'God, we're never going to eat at this rate,' laughs Max, before answering it. 'Hello? Dad? How are you? . . . WHAT?' His tone is shocked and I experience a sharp stab of fear.

'What is it?' I mouth at him, but he waves me away. 'Bella's here with me. Yes, of course, we'll come over right away. What's the address? Oh OK. Yes I know it. Don't worry Dad, keep calm, I'm sure we can sort this mess out. We'll be with you as soon as we can.' He hangs up and I cry in panic, 'What is it? Is he OK? What's happened?'

Max takes a deep breath. 'Dad's in police custody. He's been accused of rape, but he swears he didn't do it.'

'What? By whom?' I ask, my mind racing.

'Dad says you know her. Her name is Kimberly.'

Chapter 14

Charlie is the first to speak.

'But didn't they leave Ibiza together? Surely she wouldn't have gone with him if he'd raped her? And why leave it till now to report it?'

'*Her?*' says Max, the penny dropping. 'The model who was going out with Ben, then was all over Dad once she realized who he was?'

'That's the one,' I say, as Charlie, Alison and Andy nod. 'God, the lying bitch! How fucking *dare* she?'

'Well, that's just ridiculous,' says Max simultaneously. 'Didn't sound like rape to me . . .'

'Of course it wasn't rape,' I say. 'She really was all over him. God, it was repulsive.' And I tell them about witnessing Kim's heavy come-on from the kitchen garden.

'However provocative somebody's behaviour, no should still mean no,' says Andy, and I round on him.

'Of course it should, you pompous idiot. But do you really think she would have dumped Ben for my dad like that if she wasn't going to shag him? It just doesn't make sense . . .'

'Well, we need to get over to the police station now,' says Max. 'He's being held at West End Central.'

'Do you want a lift?' asks Andy, who moved on to lime and soda after the first two margaritas.

'Thanks mate, much appreciated,' says Max. 'Looks like the party's over, folks.' We bid a subdued farewell to Charlie, Alison and Dave, who head to the minicab place on the corner to share a cab back to North London.

Inside Andy's comfortable dark green Renault, I tap him on the shoulder and say sheepishly, 'Sorry I called you a pompous idiot.'

He turns his head briefly to smile at me.

'It's OK. It must have been an awful shock for you both. It's probably best not to speculate on what might or might not have happened until you hear what your father's got to say, don't you think?'

He thinks Dad's guilty, I think miserably. But what do I think? Of course I don't think my father's a rapist. He's a kind, gentle man. He's my *dad*, for Christ's sake! But he *has* always had an eye for the ladies. Which doesn't make him a rapist. And I saw them together; I heard what she said to him. But what if she was playing some prick-teasing game for reasons best known to herself? Though what would she have to gain by doing that, especially as it meant losing Ben? Or are boyfriends as gorgeous as Ben two-a-penny when you look like Kim? Jesus Christ, I don't know what to think.

'Looks like I picked the wrong month to give up glue-sniffing,' I say in a desperate attempt at gallows humour.

Andy drives well, steadily but as fast as he can within the speed limit, neatly avoiding the traffic hotspots of the West End. At last we reach Savile Row and all three of us walk into the police station.

'We're here to see Justin Brown,' says Max to the hatchet-faced WPC behind the desk.

'Well, you can't,' she says sourly. 'Visiting hours are between three and five p.m.'

'What are you talking about?' I ask frantically. 'Surely he's only being held overnight? You can't just lock people up with no evidence!'

'Please, we're his children,' adds Max. If he was hoping this would soften her up, he was very much mistaken.

'Do you know what your father is accused of doing?'

'Yes, but—'

'I said, do you know what he is accused of doing? It's a very serious crime and he can be held for up to three days without charge.'

'Please, just let us see him,' I beg, tears threatening to spill. It's like banging my head against a brick wall. The policewoman walks away from the desk, leaving us standing there like idiots.

'I don't often do this,' says Andy quietly, 'but I do believe in innocent until proven guilty. Excuse me!' he shouts after the policewoman. 'Press.' He holds up his Press pass. 'I'm writing an article on how the elderly are increasingly marginalized in this country. A story about a pensioner being locked up for three days without evidence might just illustrate my point nicely.' I look at him in awe, though I don't think Dad would be too happy about the pensioner bit. Whatever, it works.

The WPC looks at him with acute dislike. 'You've got five minutes,' she says to Max. 'Sarge! Take them to Cell Fourteen. No more than five minutes, you understand?'

'I'll wait here, shall I?' asks Andy.

'No mate, you go home, you've done more than enough,' says Max, as I remember:

'Oh God, what about the stuff you had to get from the printers?'

'That can wait,' says Andy firmly. 'Listen, you'll need to get home once you're done here, right? I'm here, and I've got a car. I'm very happy to wait another five minutes.'

We thank him again and follow the sergeant towards the cells, behind a shackled drunk shouting incomprehensible abuse. The sergeant opens the heavy metal door and lets us in, then shuts it behind him with a large clank.

'Can't you leave us alone with him?' I ask, distraught at the sight of my father.

'Sorry love, we're doing you a favour letting you see him as it is. Don't mind me,' he says kindly, turning his back to us.

Dad is sitting hunched on a bare bench, wringing his hands, his eyes bloodshot and saggy. I realize with a jolt that I've never seen my father cry before. His long grey hair is straggly around his shoulders, his skin almost yellow in the harsh light of the cell. The vertical lines on his strong, hawk-like face seem deeper than ever, pulling the corners of his eyes and mouth down. He looks very old and very tired. I remember how he used to look – my big, handsome Daddy – and my heart breaks a tiny bit more.

'Kiddos,' he says, getting up and opening his arms to us. We both walk into them, all three of us crying now. Standing here like this reminds me of how Dad used to play with us in the sea, picking one of us up in each strong arm and hurling us, giggling and screaming, through the air back into the water. He had a very specific, comforting smell. The smell of wet Dad.

'I didn't do it, I didn't,' he is saying. 'I didn't rape her.'

'Shhh Dad, it's OK, we know you didn't,' I say. 'Why don't you tell us what happened?' We sit down either side of him on the bench.

'It started the night we went to Manumission, Bella. When we got back to the villa, we made beautiful, passionate love under the stars.' Oh yuck. 'But I didn't rape her, she was enjoying it just as much as I was. She *was*, kiddos, I promise.' Oh Daddy, she saw you coming, you poor old love.

'Once it got light, we thought that under the circumstances – you know, the business with that pretty boy Ben –' Max gives me a sympathetic glance – 'it would be better to go home to Mallorca. Well, you know that anyway. She spent a few days with me, I told her I'd try and get her the cover of Italian *Vogue*, and we parted on good terms, I thought. We're both adults, we knew where we stood.' He looks at me and Max in turn. 'But I *never* forced her to do anything she didn't want to do.' Thank God, I believe him. But will everybody else? *There's no smoke without fire . . .*

'But it's my word against hers. Who's going to believe me? Look at me and look at her,' says Dad pathetically, and I feel horribly sorry for him. This is a man who used to have girls at his feet all the time, and not just because of what he could do for them. 'I know I'm not the handsome bloke I used to be. But if hot chicks like Kim want to throw themselves at me because they think I can help them get on in the biz, who am I to say no?'

And all of a sudden not quite so sorry for him. Unbidden, an image of Poppy's father pops into my head, shuffling his tragic way to total loss of faculties through absolutely no fault of his own. The contrast in their respective situations makes Dad's mess look more than a little seedy, despite his innocence.

'When is she saying the rape took place?' I ask, forcing myself back into loyal daughter mode. 'The fact that she spent so much time with you surely makes it look unlikely . . .'

'In Mallorca,' says Dad. 'The date they've got is her last night in Mallorca. I don't get it, she was just as willing then as she was the rest of the time.'

'Why would she make it up?' asks Max. 'I don't understand. Did you get her the cover of Italian *Vogue*?'

Dad shakes his head. 'I tried my best, but they weren't

interested. Told me they thought I'd lost my touch. Used to introduce them to classier birds than that.' At this I bite my lip to stop giggling, despite myself. I am feeling deeply peculiar.

'What are you doing in London, anyway?' I ask, trying to quell the incipient hysteria.

'Photo shoot for *Esquire*. I flew in this morning, did the shoot, went back to my room at the Lanesborough and was just thinking of ordering room service when the coppers came knocking at my door . . .'

'Time's up!' says the sergeant. Max and I hug Dad goodbye.

'Don't worry, Dad, we'll get you out of here,' says Max.

'Of course we will,' I agree, trying to smile.

'Thanks kiddos,' says Dad, also trying to smile. 'I feel better already, seeing you guys . . .'

Once the heavy door has clanked shut again, I burst into fresh floods of tears. What a fucking hideous day.

Andy gets up as we walk into the police waiting room. 'How is he?'

'As well as can be expected,' says Max. 'We'll tell you everything in the car.'

'Where do you want to go?' asks Andy.

'Back to Bella's is probably closer from here,' says Max. 'Is it OK if I sleep on your floor, sis?'

'Course it is.' We all get back into Andy's car.

During the journey west, we give him the full story.

'Mate.' Max suddenly turns in the front seat and lays his hand on Andy's arm. 'Say you'll help us. You're brilliant at digging up dirt on people. It's what you do for a living.'

'I don't think I could in this case,' says Andy slowly. 'It would be all about discrediting the alleged victim, which usually involves bringing up her sexual history. Which is, as we all know, wrong.'

'Oh for Christ's sake, can't you forget your fucking principles

221

for one minute?' shouts Max, unusually passionately for him. 'This is our *innocent father* we are talking about!'

We are all silent for a few more minutes. Andy turns into Portobello Road and asks for directions, which I give, mulishly. We arrive outside my front door and are about to get out of the car, when Andy says,

'Listen, I'm really sorry to have to ask – I know he's your father, but I've got to be objective when looking at the facts . . .'

'Why?' I ask, chin jutting.

'In case I want to help you.' He smiles and my heart leaps. 'I promise I won't ask again.'

'What?' Max and I say in unison.

'Are you one hundred per cent certain he is innocent?'

'YES!' we both shout.

'In that case,' he says, 'why would Kimberly make something like that up? It's not as if she was some wet-behind-the-ears virgin who suddenly regretted her actions . . .'

'Revenge!' A metaphorical light bulb goes on over my head. 'It's revenge pure and simple, I'm sure of it. Because Dad didn't get her the cover of Italian *Vogue*!'

'Surely that's a bit over the top?' says Max cautiously, though I can tell he's dying for it to be true.

'I reckon she's capable of it,' I say eagerly. 'I wouldn't put it past her to be spiteful and vindictive if she didn't get her own way. You met her, Andy, you must agree!'

'She wasn't the nicest person in the world,' he muses. 'But trumped-up rape charges? Oh, I don't know.' He sighs and runs a hand through his dark hair, making it go all spiky. 'I'll sleep on it. You two get a good night's sleep too, OK? Give me a ring in the morning, Max, and let me know how it's all going.'

'Thank you so much for everything tonight,' I say, kissing him through the open window. 'You've been so kind. I hope you don't get into too much trouble over picking up the printing.'

'Don't worry about that, Al will understand,' he says, smiling bravely. And with a final wave, he is gone.

'That, I very much doubt,' says Max.

'My beautiful babies,' says my mother theatrically, enveloping me and Max in a cloud of Joy and incense. 'What a pretty pickle this is and no mistake.' She's in shock, I tell myself, that's why she's spouting rubbish. A *pretty pickle*?

It is lunchtime, and we have convened in The Cow for a crisis meeting. Max called Mum first thing this morning and she and Bernie dropped everything to drive up to London. Mum is wearing flared jeans, a floaty purple tunic top and long ropes of jet and amber beads, her longish dark hair in the half-up/half-down, shaggy fringe style she's been sporting, on and off, since I was born. She looks very pretty and rather cool, in a knit-your-own-lentils kind of way.

'Can I get you a drink, Mum?' asks Max.

'A glass of white wine would be lovely. Thanks darling.'

'So let's get this straight,' rasps Bernie. 'This young lady – who don't sound much like a lady to me – was there with another geezer. She then started courting your dad, and now she says he raped her? Thanks son, I'll have a Scotch and water, no ice.'

'That's about the size of it,' I say.

'And you say your old man definitely wouldn't do it?' He takes off his wraparound shades and looks at me intently through his beady little eyes. In his lurid tropical print short-sleeved shirt, he'd fit right in on the terrace of an ex-pats' bar on the Costa del Crime.

'Bernie, Justin wouldn't dream of it,' says Mum, taking him by the hand. 'He may be a dirty old man – Christ knows, if anyone knows, I do, I was married to him long enough – but a rapist? No. Never.'

'If you say so, Princess.'

'You should see him, Mum, he looks awful,' I say, tears welling again. For fuck's sake, I thought I'd cried enough in the last few weeks to last me a lifetime.

'Poor geezer must be shit scared,' says Bernie. 'Rapists don't have a good time of it in the clink.'

'Oh my God, I hadn't even thought of that,' I say. 'Poor Dad.' I have a horrible sudden image in my head of burly, tattooed thugs queuing up to bugger my dear, arty father. No. It cannot happen.

'So. We've got to get this – what's her name, Kimberly? – to withdraw her statement,' says Bernie. 'Do you want me to get the boys to put the frighteners on her?' Thank God Andy isn't here yet with his tiresome principles.

'Thanks, Bernie, but I don't think that would be the right way of going about it,' says Max, returning with the drinks. 'Can you imagine if it got out? The Press would have a field day.'

Jesus. The Press. That's something else I hadn't thought about, even after Andy's inspired intervention in the nick last night. Dad has a high enough profile and the story enough unsavoury loucheness for it to be headline news. The tabloids would probably illustrate it with Kim's *Playboy* centrefold, juxtaposed with a picture of Dad looking particularly old and seedy. And photos of all the models he has shagged over the years, of course.

'We must do everything we possibly can to keep this out of the papers,' cries Mum, identical thoughts clearly passing through her mind.

'In that case, keep your voice down,' says Max quietly.

'Walls have ears,' mutters Bernie.

'In this place, that's probably truer than you realize,' says

Max, and I look around. This lunchtime, there are only a few other patrons. The Westbourne across the road is doing a roaring trade thanks to its beer garden; The Cow, with its cosy interior, all dark wood and vintage posters, tends to get more crowded in winter. However, any one of the few customers in here could easily be journalists, judging by their shared air of studied dishevelment. And the fact that they're drinking at lunchtime.

Andy walks into the bar, looking neither studiedly dishevelled nor much, come to that, like a lunchtime drinker. So much for my sweeping generalization.

'Hello, Olivia, sorry to have to see you again under such distressing circumstances.' He bends down to kiss Mum on the cheek.

'Hello, Andy darling. Thank you so much for agreeing to help us.'

'Well,' says Andy, looking Mum straight in the eye. 'I've said I'll see if I can find out anything about Kim's background that might indicate a predisposition for dishonesty. Anything that might support the idea that she is liable to make things up; that she's spiteful, vindictive.' Is he quoting me directly? 'What I won't be doing is digging up dirt on her sex life.'

'Why's that, son?' asks Bernie.

'Because I genuinely don't think it's relevant. The idea that promiscuity somehow makes somebody a more "deserving" victim, that she might have been "asking for it", is a dangerous one. Nobody asks to be raped. What is important is who's telling the truth.'

'Thank you *so, so much*,' I say warmly, reassured by both his presence and his moral integrity. There seems to have been rather too much filth in my life of late. 'I know how busy you are, what with the wedding and everything.'

'Max has been a great friend to me over the years.' He

looks over at my brother. 'If I can help, within the parameters I've described, I will.'

'Thanks mate,' says Max, coming over all emotional. He had a dreadful night's sleep, even though I made the floor as comfortable as I could with cushions and blankets, and looks really washed out. He gets up and gives Andy a man hug and I can see he's blinking back the tears.

'What's the next step?' I ask. 'Will Dad get bail until the court case comes up?'

'I've called David Simpson,' says Mum, referring to the lawyer who managed to make my parents' divorce as cheap and hassle-free as possible. 'He says it'll probably be decided this afternoon, but Dad needs to be prepared to face a hefty sum – *if* he actually gets it.'

'Don't worry, Princess. I'll stump up and he can pay me back,' says Bernie, and she gives him a big kiss.

We stay in the pub until 2.30, when Andy has to go back to work, and Bernie drives Mum, Max and me to the police station in time for visiting hours.

'Darling, how are you apart from all this ghastliness?' Mum asks as we sit in the back of the car together. 'I saw Poppy and that bastard in the paper yesterday. I do hope you're getting over it.'

I shrug, trying to hold back the tears again, as we should be focusing on Dad right now.

'I hope you don't mind, darling –' Mum looks dreadfully worried and I'm suddenly scared at what she might say – 'but I've been back in touch with Diana.'

I laugh with relief. 'Course I don't mind, Mum. My situation with Poppy has nothing to do with your friendship with Diana.'

Mum beams. 'I knew you'd see it like that. Well, I'm not excusing her behaviour, and Diana is utterly mortified, of course, but I really don't think Poppy's in her right mind at the moment. Ken's situation has been really difficult for her, you know.'

'Yes, of course I know, and I hope you're not bloody well excusing it,' I say hotly, as the pain, betrayal and humiliation I felt when I saw Ben and Poppy fucking flood through my body all over again.

'No, darling, I'm not.' Mum takes my hand. 'But for what it's worth, I don't think Poppy's very proud of herself. Apparently she keeps telling Diana how sorry she is that she hurt you, how much she misses you.'

'Yeah right,' I snort. Mum gives me a look and continues.

'She refuses to talk about Ben, and he never accompanies her down for the weekend, unlike dear Damian.'

'That figures,' I say, thinking of Ben's complete self-centredness. Visiting an elderly man who's losing his mind is unlikely to be top of his list of fun/cool/self-promoting things to do at the weekend. Just for a moment I feel a glimmer of sympathy towards Poppy.

No, she made her bed and now she can bloody well lie in it.

'You know, at the moment, I couldn't care less about either of them,' I add, almost honestly. 'I just want to see Daddy acquitted. Let them get on with their sordid tabloid lives.' I had a couple of pints with my lunch and am feeling expansive.

'That's the spirit, darling. And we *will* make everything OK. I have great faith in Andy, don't you? I've always thought he was such a lovely boy . . .'

'Yes,' I smile. 'I do.'

Ten minutes later, we get out of Bernie's pale blue Roller.

'I'll come back in an hour, all right, Princess? Things to do, people to see. And your old man don't need me hanging round.'

As we walk down the grimy corridors of the police station, which are starting to become more familiar than

I'd like, Mum says, all of a panic, 'Do I look OK? I haven't seen Justin for years . . .'

'Mum, you look gorgeous,' says Max. 'And don't be silly. You're not exactly meeting him for a date.'

If anything, Dad looks even worse than he did yesterday, which is understandable, given the lack of grooming facilities in the clink. Mum takes one look and starts to weep, gently.

'You silly old sausage. How did you get yourself into such a pretty pickle?' This time the expression seems apt.

'Thanks for coming, Liv,' says Dad softly, as she goes over to give him a hug. 'You're looking great, old girl.'

Max and I decide to leave them to it for a bit.

Chapter 15

'I think that's sixty-two points to me,' says Charlie, who has just put a Q on a royal blue triple letter score, next to an I to its right and another one below it. Bugger. Should have seen that coming. There aren't many letters left, and neither the Q nor the Z has been played till now.

'What kind of word is that? Qi?' Alison pronounces it like the French interrogative pronoun.

'I'm afraid he's right,' I say. 'It's pronounced chee and it is valid. It's to do with chakras and stuff.' Eloquent and knowledgeable as ever.

'I want to look it up.' Alison stumbles to her feet (we're sitting on the floor) in search of a dictionary.

Charlie and Alison's ground-floor flat in Highgate is just what you'd imagine from such a nice, well-read, well-fed couple. Plumped-up sofas from Heal's, books, CDs and DVDs, neatly contained in their respective shelves, standard-issue middle-class polished wooden floorboards. It's Sunday, and with, I suspect, some prompting from Max, who was worried about me worrying about Dad, they have kindly invited me over for an afternoon of late lunch and board games. Alison's rare roast beef, crisp-edged potatoes and airy Yorkshires were fabulous, if not exactly summery.

After the recent events of my somewhat sordid existence, it's lovely to be welcomed to warmly reassuring normality. Looking at them, so comfortable and happy, I feel a brief envious pang, then remind myself I'm lucky to be here, under their hospitable wing. I take another swig of my red wine.

'OK, you're right.' Alison admits defeat. 'But I still think foreign words have no place in the English dictionary.'

'Come on babe, we all know the best thing about English is that it's constantly evolving. That's why it's the most expressive language in the world,' says Charlie. 'And why we're better than the fucking Frogs with their Académie française and innate xenophobia.'

Alison laughs. 'You do realize what you've just said, you Alf Garnett you? Innate xenophobia indeed. Physician, heal thyself.'

I laugh and Charlie turns to me.

'Good to see you looking a bit happier, Belles.' It's nice he's using the affectionate version of my name. 'The last few weeks must have been bloody grim for you.'

'Bloody grim is about right, but I'm OK at this precise moment, thanks to you two. You're absolute stars.'

'Apart from this cheat with his made-up dirty foreign words,' says Alison, kissing Charlie. I look at them, trying to enjoy their happiness vicariously. Alison is wearing boyfriend jeans, which don't really flatter her, and a pale pink, low-cut top, which does. Her rosy cheeks (which are getting rosier by the glass), round face and blondish hair put me in mind of a seventeenth-century serving wench.

'You look just like a shaggable seventeenth-century wench,' I say, too much booze having already loosened my lips.

'I've always wanted to look exotic and slim, like Lucy Liu or – what's that Bollywood one called? Freida Pinto?'

'Phwoaaargh yes, she's gorgeous,' says Charlie, chuckling. God, men can be insensitive bastards. I say to Alison innocently,

'He's got a point. Those dark, slender, high-cheekboned *men* can be nice too – like Jude Law? Or Johnny Depp?'

'Oh yeah, God, Johnny Depp.' A lusty smile creeps over Alison's face. 'He's one of my all-time fantasies . . .'

Charlie looks surprised and offended, while I shout, delighted,

'You mean you *wank* over him?'

At this moment I hear somebody shutting the front door quietly; Alison said she was leaving it on the latch as Andy and Alison might pop by. A few seconds later, Andy's head pops round the corner. Oh great.

'Sounds like you guys are having a good night.' His dark eyes look amused behind their specs.

I stand up to greet him and knock my red wine onto the floor with a stray foot. 'Oh bugger, sorry, sorry Alison.' I bend down idiotically. What am I intending to do? Slurp it out of the grooves in the floorboards with my tongue?

Alison laughs, 'Hey no worries, this is the best thing about not having a carpet,' and goes to get a cloth.

Andy crouches behind me and looks at my Scrabble letters, which are a measly TNREARI. No big hitters at all. Quietly he rearranges them into TERRAIN, then gives me a little nudge to show me what he's done.

Yay. That extra fifty for making all seven into a word might just give me the edge on Charlie. I scan the board for somewhere to place the word and spot an S, with a double word score too. I grin up at Andy, wanting to kiss him. Strangely, it looks as if he might want to kiss me too.

'Well, it's my turn now,' I say, dragging my gaze away. Luckily Alison and Charlie are too engrossed in their own letters to notice. I plonk down TERRAIN and nudge Andy back.

'That is *so* not fair,' says Charlie, like a stocky Valley Girl who specializes in bought ledgers, pushing his thick blond hair away from his forehead. 'Bella wouldn't have had any idea what to do with those letters . . .'

'Oy mate, calling me thick?' Bloody cheek, I'd have got there eventually.

The doorbell rings. Andy must have left it off the latch.

'That'll be Al,' he says, jumping up and adjusting his glasses. 'We're off to The Wolseley tonight, which should cheer her up. She's been working all day.' He goes to let her in.

Alison walks in looking stunning (as long as you don't look at her face, which is trying to smile) in rolled-up safari shorts and a white silk vest that would look gross on anybody with an ounce of flesh on them. And who was capable of sweating.

'Hi Ali,' she says, walking over and giving Alison a kiss. 'You look pretty.'

'Thanks Al,' says Alison, trying to mask her surprise. 'You look great.'

'I'm so tired you wouldn't believe it. Hi Charlie.'

'Hi Al.' Charlie gets to his feet and gives her a dutiful peck.

'Bella.' She looks over at me. 'Thanks for the shirt.' Feeling guilty about not replacing the Jil Sander number after Andy had been so kind about Dad, I maxed my dodgy Egg card on a new one and gave it to Max, who had it delivered to her office by one of his eager Dalston minions. 'Better late than never, eh?'

'Yeah, well, I'm sorry for being so stupid . . . I s'pose you don't need me to tell you I was pissed?'

'No, that was quite clear. But I may have been a bit out of order too,' she concedes, accepting a glass of merlot from Charlie. 'God, what a day.' And she sits elegantly on one of the plump sofas, pale slim legs displayed to good effect against the navy blue twill.

'Why? What's happened?' I am so glad to be forgiven that I'll accept any scraps. I may sometimes (in my cups) be a bit of a loose cannon, but generally I can't bear to think of people not liking me.

'Apart from the child torture case I'm working on, you mean?' She smiles briefly and I can see the strain on her face. 'Oh I'm sorry, but one just gets so caught up in the hideous details of these things that one forgets other people only read the bits they can actually publish in the papers.' Jesus. Puts me in my place.

'Shall we talk about the wedding instead?' says Ali. 'I had a look at the flower girls' trial bouquets today and they are totally adorable.'

'Thanks Alison, but you know what? For once I'd just like to forget about the wedding.' Andy's head jerks up in surprise and the rest of us follow suit. 'On top of everything else, I've had my bloody mother on all day, and she goes on and on and ON . . .' She bashes her forehead against her palm in time to her words. Good God, she's human after all.

Andy laughs, putting an arm around her shoulder. 'My future mother-in-law is a bit of a control freak.'

'You know what they say,' says Charlie, laughing drunkenly and slapping his thigh. 'Look to the mother-in-law to see what you'll be lumbered with in years to come!'

It's too close to the bone and we sit in uncomfortable silence for a moment or two, Groove Armada reminding us to think of sand dunes and salty air rather too loudly.

'Can you talk about the case?' I ask Alison, changing the subject.

'Shouldn't really, except to say that some people shouldn't be allowed to procreate.' She looks sad again and I almost see what Andy sees in her. Without the frown or Gordon Brown fake smile her features fall naturally into a droopily pre-Raphaelite version of beauty.

'So, Bella.' She turns to me again, and I am terrified, as if I'm about to be summoned to the headmistress's office. 'I heard about your dad. I'm sorry. Andy and I both agree that even though your father – may I say it? – has *issues*, that silly little whore was absolutely out for everything she could get.'

'My father doesn't have issues!' I am immediately in defensive mode. There is silence apart from Groove Ar-fucking-mada, who are now singing about 'shaking that ass'. 'Well, OK, maybe. But he's not a rapist. Thanks for the vote of confidence anyway.'

'Bella,' says Skinny, looking me straight in the eye. Am I about to get detention? 'I know we haven't always seen eye to eye, but I appreciate what you must be going through. Occasionally the legal system really sucks. Your father being named, whether he's guilty or not, while Kimberly keeps her anonymity, for starters.'

'Yeah, I know. I really don't see how that's fair.'

'And if your father had raped a thousand times before – hypothetically, of course – they couldn't bring that up in court . . .' She's on a roll now, her voice rising. 'And in this case I'm working on, even though the stepfather of the child that's just been tortured to death actually raped a baby girl less than a year ago, I'm not allowed to bring THAT up in court either.' She puts her head in her hands again and I notice, shallowly, how silky and shiny her black hair looks. Andy strokes it.

'Darling, we do know that everybody is entitled to legal defence, however horrific their crime. It's one of the first things you learn at law school. It's part of our constitution.'

'Shut up, Andy, you're sounding like a Yank,' says Charlie. I'm glad he said it.

'But how can you do it?' I ask, for it is something that has bothered me for years. How can the cream of the country's intelligentsia actually get people off heinous crimes, knowing they're guilty, and live with themselves?

'You know what?' Alison looks up. 'I honestly don't know any more. It's all about gamesmanship and beating your fellow lawyers, which I'm very good at.' She laughs, slightly bitterly. 'But it's not about justice, which is what I signed up for.'

Nobody knows what to say to this, so Charlie changes the subject clumsily, asking Andy to go next door with him to look at something manly and utterly incomprehensible on his computer.

Ali gets up to go to the loo. I top my glass up from the bottle of merlot on the table and offer some to Alison. She puts her hand over her glass and shakes her head.

'Don't you think you've had enough?' Her eyes are glittering with malice, just as they did that time at Osteria Basilico.

'I'm not sure it's any of your business.' I am so surprised I don't know what else to say.

'And don't you think you've outstayed your welcome? Charlie and Alison only invited you to lunch, and it's nearly eight o'clock now. I know they both have to get up early tomorrow.'

'What, you mean with their *proper* jobs?' I say, utterly unprepared for such a volte-face.

'Oh come on, I've apologized for that. I just think it can't be nice to be a millstone round people's necks, constantly dependent on their kindness and goodwill. I mean, just look at you. You drink far too much, you look an absolute mess, your so-called *career* –' she does the inverted commas fingers sign, smiling evilly – 'is only just starting to go somewhere because Ali feels sorry for you. Quite frankly, I'm surprised Ben stuck around for as long as he did.'

Jesus. Just as I start to think she's not all bad, she comes out with *this*? She must have just been trying to fool the others into thinking she's human. Well, I won't be making the same mistake twice. Traumatic job or no traumatic job, she's a fucking bitch and I hate her.

She's right about me looking a mess though. I'm in flip-flops, holey old Levis with fraying hems as they're too long if I don't wear heels, and a faded T-shirt that used to be a vibrant shade of green. My clothes are hanging off me (the only good thing to come out of my recent traumas), my hair is tied up in a messy ponytail and my fringe is so long that I can hardly see out. I try to curl my feet up under my legs as I notice how badly chipped the ancient red polish on my grotesquely long toenails is.

I am trying to work out how to respond to the wounding personal attack when Ali comes back into the room, followed by the boys. She offers more drinks all around, but Andy shakes his head.

'Thanks, but we'd better get going. The table's booked for eight thirty.'

They drain their glasses and walk out, Alison back in gracious and charming mode, her small bottom and long legs looking far too attractive for my liking in the khaki shorts.

'Bugger me,' says Charlie. 'She's almost the Alison she used to be at Cambridge.'

'Slim and dark,' says Ali wistfully.

'BUT NOT EXOTIC!' I shout, also wistfully – if it's possible to shout wistfully. Pride prevents me from repeating what the bitch has just said to me as I secretly suspect she's right on every count. 'God, what a horrid job. I'm so glad I just paint pretty pictures for a living. It will be a living, won't it?' I ask Ali, touching wooden floorboards.

'There are no guarantees, but I reckon so.' She smiles. 'Shall we finish this silly game then?'

Mindful of what Alison has just said, I tell them I should be going, but they insist I stay to finish the game, at least.

I lower the tone and cheer myself up by putting down an F next to RIG and happily plonking ROT underneath, giggling to myself.

Charlie wins with ZEN, then asks, 'How about a game of Trivial Pursuit?'

'You and your bloody oriental mysticism. Zen indeed,' says Ali. 'I'm a bit tired, but you're welcome to stay if you want, Belles.'

I'd love to stay for Trivial Pursuit (which I know I'd win, trivia being my specialist subject, after all) and more booze, but, hating the idea of being a millstone, I feign tiredness too. Charlie, by dint of twisting my arm, persuades me to stay for one more drink, but soon it's time to say goodbye.

'Thanks so much for a lovely day – it's the best I've had for months. And that food was exceptional, Ali. Byeeee and thanks again!'

The minicab driver puts Magic FM on the radio at my request and we sing along to things as random as Carole King's 'You've Got a Friend', Jet's 'Are You Gonna Be My Girl', the Kinks' 'Waterloo Sunset' and, best of all, Dolly Parton's '9 to 5' – to which our mutual screeching is as heartfelt as it is unharmonious.

When we get to Portobello I notice a couple of photos of children in school uniform on the dashboard.

'Gorgeous kids! What are their names?' I ask effusively.

'Harrison and Rhianna. They're my angels.'

I so don't want tonight to end; I so don't want to be reminded that everybody except me has someone to love. And as I walk up the rickety staircase to my empty flat, I don't think I have ever felt so alone in my entire life.

Chapter 16

The next few days are a blur of lawyers and police, and countless crisis meetings with my nearest and dearest. Dad has been given bail, on the condition that he doesn't leave the country, so Mum is putting him up until the trial; the date has been set a month from now. We all agree that the most important thing is to try and keep the story out of the Press for as long as we can. Once the case comes to court, it will be nigh on impossible, which doesn't bode well. As Dad says, 'Even if I am acquitted, I'll be ruined. Shit sticks, and I'll always be known as the photographer who was tried for rape. *No smoke without fire . . .*' That bloody expression again. It appears that Bernie has friends in high places who so far have stopped any police leaks, for which we're hugely grateful.

Dad has only told a handful of friends whom he thought he could trust, but two of them, on the instigation of their wives, have actually stopped speaking to him. If this is the reaction, even pre-trial, I can't bear to imagine the global vitriol that will be poured on him once the papers get hold of the story. There are bound to be judgemental editorials, commenting with pious disapproval on every aspect of Dad's life. Old girlfriends (of whom there are literally hundreds) will no doubt come out of the woodwork. So much of his career is based on image that not only will the lucrative commissions stop, but a shadow will be cast over his entire lifetime's body of work. I can imagine people looking at all the photos he's taken of nude models over the years and speculating over which ones he might 'also have raped'.

And this is the good version, the 'Not Guilty' version. If he's found guilty . . . Well, let's just say I can't get Bernie's comment about rapists 'not having a good time of it inside' out of my head. I honestly cannot imagine my father surviving it. He is such a free spirit, such a traveller, such a lover of nature and beauty. Being banged up for years for something he didn't do will absolutely destroy him. And that's before you start thinking about the prison buggery potential.

So Andy is trying to find out if there's anything about Kim that might preclude the case coming to trial at all. It transpires that she claims not to have shagged Dad *at all* until the final night in Mallorca, when she says he forced her. She only went with him to Mallorca, she says, for professional reasons. Which is of course true. According to Dad, he did take some photos of her in his studio there, so this might hold water. On the other hand, we all know that she's a lying cow, and I, for one, am willing to stand up in court and testify to what I heard from the kitchen garden.

It's a horrifically tense time, clearly, but it has at least taken my mind off Ben and Poppy. Now the pain and madness have worn off I probably miss being part of our cool little gang more than anything. Poppy, Damian, Ben and occasionally Mark were the hub of my social life for

239

much longer than my ill-fated romance (if it can be called that). And after spending my formative years in what might kindly be termed a social wilderness, I loved the feeling of being in with the in-crowd.

So I fill the void with painting, determined to give the exhibition my best shot.

One balmy evening I am standing on my balcony, glass of white wine in one hand, paintbrush in the other, when my phone rings.

'Hey Maxy.'

'Belles, listen.' His voice is excited. 'Are you free tomorrow afternoon?'

'Erm, yes. Why? What's going on?'

'I've been doing a bit of detective work of my own and I've found something out about Kimberly!'

'Bloody hell, what is it? Tell me, quick!'

'I think she's part of some weird cult.' *What?* 'They've got some sort of ritual sacrifice going on tomorrow afternoon in a wood near the South Downs. We've *got* to go and see what dirt we can get on her.'

I laugh. 'Maxy. Don't you think that's clutching at straws?'

Max laughs too. 'Well, don't you see we've got to at least go and see what they're up to? We might find out *something* about the bitch.'

He goes on to tell me he overheard Kim's name being mentioned in Divine Comedy, in connection to whatever this ritual sacrifice thing is. The whole thing sounds extremely far-fetched, but I can absolutely see where my brother is coming from. We're both dying to do something to help, and anything is better than the constant impotent waiting.

'Apparently the ceremony starts at three, so I'll pick you

up at twelve thirty. That should give us plenty of time to get there. Oh and sis . . .'

'Yeeesss . . .'

'Wear something that will blend in with the woodland surroundings.' His tone is hushed.

'You mean camouflage?' I laugh. 'I'll see what I can do.'

The next day I am looking in the mirror, wondering whether I should paint camouflage stripes on my face with some greasepaint I bought for a fancy dress party a couple of years ago. I am wearing the khaki combat-style mini that I wore at Glastonbury, a camouflage-print vest top and an olive green baseball cap. My hair is in plaits, my feet in old grey Converse and an oversized pair of shades covers half my face. I think my urban warrior look is rather cool, and decide the greasepaint might ruin it.

I am doing martial arts stalking-type movements in the mirror when the doorbell rings.

'I'll be right down!' I shout.

Outside, I am in for a surprise. Instead of Max in his flash new Lotus, Andy is sitting there, in the driver's seat of his old green Renault. He takes one look at me and bursts out laughing. I am so glad I didn't bother with the greasepaint.

'Glad you find it amusing,' I say, holding my head up high and going to kiss him through the window. 'So what's up? Where's Max?'

'He called me an hour ago in a total panic. Geronimo has gone nuts with a knife, and Max has to stay behind and pick up the pieces.' Seeing my look of horror, Andy laughs again. 'Not literally. But he has to calm him and the rest of the staff down, which he says could take several hours and all of his powers of negotiation.' Geronimo is Max's very temperamental chef. I shudder.

'Poor Max, but surely he didn't need you to come and tell me that in person? Why didn't he just give me a ring?'

'Because he knows you can't drive, and he is desperate for this – er – mission to go ahead. So today, Bella Brown, I am your chauffeur and fellow sleuth. Lewis to your Morse, Cagney to your Lacey.' He's laughing again. I've never seen him so jolly. 'Jump in, then! We don't want to miss the bit where they sacrifice a virgin pygmy goat.' Ah, I get it. He's laughing *at us*.

'You must think we're awfully silly,' I say, looking at him out of the corner of my eye as we head down towards the river. 'I'm really sorry that Max lumbered you with this. It's probably a complete dead-end. Don't you have to be at work?'

'I'm allowed out and about – part and parcel of the job. If I'd had a deadline, you wouldn't have seen me for dust.'

'Well, thank you very much anyway. And you never know, we might find out *something* . . .'

'Indeed.' But he can't stop a smirk creeping up one side of his mouth.

We drive in silence for a bit, as the inner-city landscape becomes progressively suburban. It's slightly cooler today, with a lovely fresh breeze coming through the open windows and a few wispy clouds floating across the corn-flower sky. Andy puts on a CD and the opening guitar strains of Rodrigo's *Concierto de Aranjuez* fill the car.

'Oh my God, I love this,' I say. 'My dad used to play it all the time when we were kids in Mallorca. It takes me right back to the smell of lavender and rosemary and thyme. They grew wild across the mountains.' Andy looks surprised.

'How funny,' he says. 'My parents used to play it all the time too. But the smells it conjures up for me aren't nearly so exotic – freshly mown grass, Camel Lights and shepherd's pie, I'd say.' He laughs.

'Do you want to talk about them?' I ask, quickly doing the sums. If he was seventeen when they died, he's lived for as long now without them as he did with them.

'You know, then?' He briefly takes his eyes from the road to look at me. 'You know what, I'm thirty-four now. It's seventeen years since they died. I've lived as long without them as I did with them.' *What?* 'That's a really weird thing to come to terms with.'

'What were they like?' I ask.

'What's anyone like? They were my parents. I loved them. Sorry, that's not a very satisfactory answer, is it?' He smiles briefly. 'Well, Mum was a music teacher; Dad was a history teacher. They were both very keen on education. They seemed to have fun a lot too, though. *We* had a lot of fun, the three of us. I think they really loved each other. You take all that stuff for granted, when it's all you've ever known, but knowing what I know now of the world, I think my parents probably had an exceptional relationship.' A lump comes into my throat.

'What a horrible waste,' I say quietly.

'Yes.'

We drive on in silence for a few minutes, then Andy says,

'When it happened it felt like my world had come to an end. But now I am just grateful that for seventeen years I was so happy. I'm grateful every day that they gave me that. Which isn't to say that I don't still miss them, of course.' He stares steadily at the road.

'No, of course not.' The lump is getting bigger and I can sense that his is too. We are both silent again.

His hands on the steering wheel look male and capable. I look around the car. Neither horribly neat nor as messy as mine would doubtless be if I could a) drive and b) afford a car, it has a comfortable, lived-in feel about it. The back seat is strewn with newspapers – *The Times*, *Telegraph*, *Guardian*, *FT*, *New York Times* and *International Herald Tribune*. Some crosswords look as if they're completed, which impresses me. The open glove compartment is stuffed with maps, pens and unopened letters – bills by the look of them. A well-thumbed Penguin paperback of Evelyn Waugh's *Scoop* lies at my feet. I pick it up.

'I must re-read this,' I say. 'One of the funniest books ever.'

'Absolutely,' he says. 'And a must-read for all journalists. Borrow it if you want, I've just finished it.'

'Thanks,' I say, surprised. 'I'm pretty sure my copy is at Mum's.' I put it in my handbag.

Eventually, after some piss-poor map reading on my part, we reach the turn-off for the wood.

'Look, this is where it says we need to get out,' I say, pointing at the big red cross on the map Max gave to Andy.

'So it is. Well, Bella, time to put your best foot forward, old girl.'

'Good luck,' I say in my best Agatha Christie heroine voice, leaning over to shake his hand.

We sneak through the wood as quietly as we can, every twig breaking sounding like gunshot. I am such a private investigator. When Poppy and I were thirteen, a careers counsellor came to our school and, immersed at the time in Agatha and Dorothy L. Sayers, we both told her we wanted to be private detectives; we were given pretty short shrift. As the memories hit me, I find myself hoping that Pops is coping OK with her father's decline without Damian's support. I swiftly put the thought out of my head.

Soon, sounds come floating through the air, faintly at first, then gradually louder and louder. Pan pipes, a fiddle, drums, chanting . . . oooh, how exciting. I grin at Andy, and he grins back, also caught up in the excitement, by the look on his face, as he treads carefully through the undergrowth.

He stops abruptly, with his finger to his lips. Gesturing to me to hide behind the trees, he points into a large clearing.

A motley crew of face-painted tree-people and creatures that probably think they are druids or shamans are sitting cross-legged in a circle. I spot Kimberly among them, her red ringlets loose around her face, eyes closed, face lifted up to the sky. I'd forgotten how young she is – twenty-five at the very most. And how exquisitely pretty. God, I hate the self-centred moron. How dare she sit here, serenely sucking up whatever mindless bollocks this is, while my father is enduring a living hell?

Andy nudges me, whispering, 'I think we've gate-crashed a wedding.'

Oh for fuck's sake, Max.

The bride and groom are kneeling at the centre of the human circle, palm-to-palm, smiling beatifically, eyes half shut. The groom is wearing a kilt and a grubby brown shirt; the bride, faintly Grecian robes the colour of snot, with a headdress that looks like something a Red Indian squaw might sport. Statues of Ganesh, pagan effigies, Egyptian cats and Buddhas form an inner circle between the happy couple and the ersatz congregation.

A man in purple robes with a blond goatee and sideburns is saying,

'You, gentle people, were all asked to bring a stone with you, a special stone, for this very special day. The day that our good fellow planet-dwellers, Jed and Bethany, become one, with each other, and with the earth.' The crowd hollers and cheers. 'I would now like to ask you, one by one, what your stone means to you.'

A chap with a greasy grey ponytail stands up and says, 'So this pebble, this little anti-capitalist pebble – or should I say, *little Rock of Ages that says FUCK YOU, TORIES . . .*' There are appreciative sniggers all round at the profundity. He puts up a grubby hand so he can continue. 'Symbolizes to me – and I think I can speak for all of us . . .' He smiles around smugly. 'Unity, harmony, peace – and above all, anarchy! Oh pebble of the people, I kiss you.'

Andy nudges me again and I bite my lip, trying to keep a straight face as the crowd erupts into cheers. Next up is an earnest-looking woman sporting frizzy, centre-parted hair, calf-length tie-dye and friendship bracelets. I imagine her shagging opportunities are few and far between.

'I didn't so much find this stone as . . .' There is a pregnant pause. Andy whispers in my ear, 'Please God, don't let her say "It found me".'

'. . . As . . . It. Found. Me.'

It's the knowing smiles and sincere nods from the other guests that finally do it for us. Heaving and spluttering, we run out of the forest, trying to contain our giggles until we reach a place of safety.

'Oh God, oh God, oh God,' I say, clutching my tummy as we reach the car. 'I can't believe Max sent us all this way for that!'

'Perhaps we should go back into the fray,' says Andy gravely. 'I'd like to see what Kimberly has to say about her stone. You never know, it could be a clue . . . Or at least give us a link to the Universe.'

'Stop it, stop it,' I plead, weak with laughter now.

'We might be missing the live sacrifice AS WE SPEAK . . .'

'STOP IT!' I turn away from him as the very sight of

him is cracking me up now and I can't breathe I'm laughing so much. Once I've regained my breath, I say,

'Good job I wore my camouflage gear, though. And if I'd done my face painting I might even have been able to infiltrate the enemy . . .'

'You weren't going to paint your face?' It's Andy's turn to laugh his bollocks off.

'Oh yes. Stripes. Only stopped myself at the last minute.'

'Well, what are we going to do now?' says Andy once he's stopped laughing. 'It seems silly to have come all this way for nothing – though I have to admit that ceremony alone was worth the drive. It's very pretty round here. Do you want to try and find a pub with a beer garden?'

'That's a brilliant idea, if you're sure you've got the time . . .'

'Thanks to that brother of yours, this afternoon's already a write-off work-wise. Let's make the most of it.' He smiles and we get back in the car. Ensconced, I call Max.

'Well? What've you got?'

'Maxy, for a very clever man you can be very stupid sometimes!' I can hardly get the words out I'm laughing so much again. 'Talk to Andy, he'll tell you.' Andy gestures to me that he can't take both hands off the wheel, so I put the phone on monitor, and soon the three of us are laughing fit to explode.

'OK, sorry,' says Max. 'I suppose she can't be done for stupidity. But it was worth a try, surely?'

Andy smiles at me and says, 'Yes, Max, it was certainly worth a try. And we now think that the excruciatingly long journey is worth a drink. A pint with your lovely sister is just what I could do with.'

Did he just say lovely?

Outside The Old Swan Tavern, I gulp my large Magners as Andy sips his pint of Pride.

'Sorry again for such a waste of your afternoon,' I say.

'You can hardly call it a waste,' he says, gesturing around at the pretty beer garden, all wooden tables and colourful hanging baskets. England is in full bloom. 'Actually, I haven't laughed so much for ages.'

Suddenly self-conscious, I remove my shades and base-ball cap, glad again that I don't have to wipe greasepaint off my face.

'Should I take these ridiculous mutton as lamb things out too?' I tug at my plaits.

'No, keep them in. You look cute.'

'Thanks.' Something is going on inside me every time he looks at me like that. I have to kill it.

'So how's it going with the wedding? It's less than a month now, isn't it?'

'Thanks for asking. Everything's going really well now. Al has stopped being so weird . . .' I try to look as if I don't know what he's on about and he laughs.

'You're so transparent. Al has been horrible, especially in front of my friends, ever since we got engaged, and it's been a real struggle. Mainly defending her to my friends, actually, as we hardly ever see one another alone with so much work on both our plates, but over the last couple of weeks she's really lightened up. It's such a relief.'

'Do you think it's to do with that awful case she's working on?' No point in telling him what the bitch said to me at Charlie and Ali's.

'Probably. And also the pressure from her horrible, reli-gious nutter parents. Christ, why should hers be alive and mine be dead?' He laughs slightly shamefacedly. 'Not an honourable sentiment, I know.'

'But entirely understandable. There's no rhyme nor

reason.' I wish I could say something more profound. 'I'm so sorry, Andy. The idea of my parents dying is just too horrific to contemplate, and I've no idea how I'll cope when the time comes. You're awfully brave.'

'What a man's gotta do, a man's gotta do.' He puts on a John Wayne voice and I laugh.

'Seriously though, it was years ago. I've had plenty of time to get used to it,' he says, taking a sip of his Pride and noticing my Magners is nearly empty. 'D'you want another one?'

'Oh yes please.' Despite the grim topic of conversation, I am enjoying talking to him enormously. Surely one more drink won't hurt?

He comes back with my bottle and its ice-filled glass and all I can think, as I look at him with the sun behind him, is how tall he is, how incredibly nice he is, how shaggable he is . . .

For Christ's sake, you absolute bloody fool. He is getting MARRIED next month.

'You look ever so handsome.' Oh Christ, I didn't just say that, did I?

He does, though. Some people look bloody awful in bright sunshine. With his high cheekbones, strong jaw and just a hint of black stubble on his clear male skin, Andy looks fantastic, even though the sun glinting off his specs means I can't see his dark eyes properly.

'And you look ever so pretty . . .' He stops himself. 'Let's not get carried away,' he laughs and starts again.

'Bella . . .' Someone is shaking my shoulder, disturbing me from a wonderful dream, during which Andy was kissing every inch of my body, while telling me how much he loved me.

'Huh?' I say drowsily and unattractively.

'You're home,' says Andy, smiling at me. I'm still in the passenger seat of his car. Must have been out for the count since we left the pub.

'Oh fuck, I wasn't snoring, was I?' Such an elegant way with words.

'Like a trooper.' Great.

'Well, thanks so much for everything today, and sorry for passing out. It has to be too much sun – two bottles of Magners wouldn't get a gnat pissed, after all!'

Andy laughs as I get out of the door. 'It was quite sweet actually. You were snoring in time to Rodrigo.' And he buggers off into the warm summer evening.

Chapter 17

It's the night of the *Stadium* summer party and I'm twitchy with excitement. It's been bloody ages since I had a proper night out, and Simon issued me with an invite a couple of days ago. Somebody probably dropped out at the last moment.

'Well, you're a contributor now,' he said, generously referring to my measly set of illustrations. The party is being held in conjunction with Agent Provocateur to coincide with the magazine's porn supplement, and will feature Dita Von Teese and various other sex workers – sorry, 'burlesque dancers' – taking their clothes off on stage. Appropriately, the venue is the Windmill Club in Soho.

The night should be a hoot. The *Stadium* boys do know how to party, and it's bound to be a glam do, with minor celebs and narcotics a-plenty. For the first time since the Ben debacle I am making a real effort with my appearance. Fuck it, I deserve a bit of fun.

'Because I'm worth it,' I mouth at myself in the mirror, striking a pose. I have blown my *Stadium* fee on a new dress from Preen (size 10 – yay!). My dress makes me drool. In the palest of shell-pink silk crêpe, it is strapless and body skimming with a subtle bubble hemline where the skirt finishes at mid-thigh. The effect is simultaneously elegant and sexy, showing off my nice brown legs and shoulders, which are satisfyingly slim after the requisite post-trauma weight loss, and all my recent running. Classy, not tarty, I think, taking an enormous swig of wine, hiking up the hem and applying yet more eyeliner.

I try not to think about Dad. Since the ridiculous excursion in the woods, Andy, Max and I seem to have drawn a blank on Kimbo muck-raking. Dad could easily still be acquitted, I've been telling myself. The jury has to believe he's guilty beyond reasonable doubt, and surely my testimony will be enough to cast some doubt in their minds. *But not in the minds of the Great British Public*, says a niggling voice in my head. *No smoke without fire . . .*

I honestly think that if we don't stop the case coming to court my father's life will be irreparably damaged, even if he's found not guilty. I can imagine him becoming a virtual recluse in his hermitage in Mallorca, hating the idea of the constant whispering and speculation, his irrepressible *joie de vivre* gone forever. There is a permanent tight knot of worry in my heart at the prospect.

I turn my attention back to my appearance. I haven't bothered to get my hair cut for months, and it currently reaches halfway down my back. On a bad day this can make me look like a witch, but tonight I have blown it dry straight and trimmed my fringe, mussing it with my fingers to sex it up a bit. I've piled on the smoky eye make-up and added some pink blusher to what women's magazines insist on referring to as the apples of my cheeks for that essential just-been-fucked look.

I'm meeting Max and Andy for a drink in Soho before hitting the party and don't need to leave for another quarter of an hour or so. I pour myself another drink, light a fag and go out onto the balcony with the *Evening Standard*. It's another balmy evening and the air throbs with excitement. All around preparations are being made for the Notting Hill Carnival, which is this coming weekend. My neighbours seem to be having a loudest music competition – reggae on one side, samba on the other. The faint strains of jungle can be heard from way down the road. You keep reading in the papers that the (white) locals hate Carnival, but I love the whole colourful, musical, messy, crowded, noisy, dirty, joyous, celebratory Caribbean shebang.

Opening the paper, I am confronted by yet another photo of Poppy and Ben. Yes, in the last couple of weeks, my two former favourite people have become permanent fixtures in the tabloids, though the last few pictures haven't exactly done either of them any favours. In this photo, they are falling out of another club, Poppy looking even more dishevelled (OK, off her head) than she did in yesterday's *Metro*. I peer at the photo with satisfaction. Yes, she really does look awful. Nothing could make that pretty little face look ugly, or that neat little body look fat, but her eyes are wide and mad, her eyeliner somewhere around her chin, hair all over the place, skirt tucked into her knickers. Ben looks as if he's having trouble holding her up. Excellent. Even better, she's flipping a V at the cameras. Oh goody, the tabs won't like that. Tall Poppy syndrome time.

Will P***ed Poppy Pack a Punch? says the headline. The blurb continues, *Ben 'opening of an envelope' Jones and his tired and emotional partner Poppy Wallace were pictured leaving The Ivy last night looking somewhat worse for wear. A word of advice, Poppy love. If you don't like being photographed, there are plenty of other places to dine in the capital. And just what ARE you famous for, anyway?*

Poppy's father was always so proud that she'd used her brains to get on in life, rather than her looks. I suppose it's a tiny silver lining on an enormous black cloud that he's been spared her transformation from high-flying TV producer to C-list tabloid fodder. No, fuck it, it's not a silver lining at all. What in God's name am I thinking? Far better he was still able to read – he'd probably just laugh it off as the idiocy of the Press. Just for a moment a wave of sympathy for Pops washes over me, but then I force the image of her straddling Ben back into my mind and the familiar bile rises in my gorge.

I harden my heart, shut the paper and go inside to finish getting ready. I clip on some dangly silver and diamanté vintage earrings, then sit down to strap on a pair of vertiginous silver strappy platforms that add at least five inches to my legs. I stand up again to look in the mirror, wobbling slightly. A vision stares back at me, dark-eyed and slim and exotic in her fabulous dress. Yes, I am gorgeous. Eat your heart out, Poppy Wino Wallace.

As I wobble down Ladbroke Grove in search of a taxi, cars hoot, men on the street do double takes and one even wolf whistles. It's all I can do not to punch the air. Such is my momentary joy of being ME ME ME that I don't notice the blessed orange light of a black cab until it speeds right past me. I hail it frantically and it screeches to a halt.

'Where to, love?'

'Old Compton Street, please.'

'You're looking lovely tonight,' the cab driver says after a while. 'Going anywhere nice?'

'Thanks,' I grin. 'It's a party given by the men's magazine, *Stadium*. Do you know it?'

'Is that the one with the naked birds on the cover?' asks the cabbie. Hardly narrows it down, but I let it pass. 'Never look at it myself. You a model then?' Yay!

'No, I'm an illustrator,' I say, feeling a huge surge of pride as I say the words. Yes, I may look like a model (if you don't know what models really look like) but I'm actually going to the party as I am a bona fide contributor to the magazine. By the time we reach Soho I am thoroughly pleased with myself.

The traffic is terrible, so I get out of the cab at the beginning of Old Compton Street to let the cabbie carry on up Wardour Street rather than get caught up in the heinous one-way system.

'Thanks beautiful,' the driver says as I tip him. 'There are going to be some very happy blokes at your party tonight.'

I make my way down Old Compton Street, past the sex shops, gay bars and tourist dives. Past Patisserie Valerie, Bar Italia, The Admiral Duncan – the old institutions that make Soho what it is. Rickshaw drivers weave in and out of the traffic, dealers deal, tourists gawp, the pink pound flexes its not inconsiderable muscle. I feel fantastic as I sashay down the road in the warm night air, my hair swishing against my bare back and shoulders. Max and Andy, sitting outside Café Boheme, do a comedy joint double take as I approach.

'Gotta hand it to you, sis, you do scrub up well,' says Max, laughing slightly.

'He's right.' Andy gets up to kiss me on both cheeks. 'You look really lovely.'

'An improvement on my urban warrior get-up?'

'Well, that had its charms too, but – yes, I'd say an improvement. What would you like to drink?'

'A glass of white wine would be great, thanks.' Andy hails a passing waiter.

I sit down and bend over to loosen the straps on my shoes. They're hurting already but I'll just have to hope that tonight's booze and the drugs I imagine I'll be offered have a numbing effect before too long.

'So how've you been since our woodland sleuthing adventure? You must be totally immersed in all things wedding by this stage.' I look at Andy and smile. He doesn't seem to realize how gorgeous he looks.

'Funnily enough, the pressure's eased off a bit now. Al was so determined to get everything right in the first few months that almost all the donkey work has been done. We're just sort of cruising along happily to the Big Day, which is far more like it.'

'Glad to hear it mate,' says Max, patting Andy's forearm, as I remember how worried he was about him at Glastonbury, bless his soppy heart.

'More than I can say for work, though – mine *and* Al's. She's worked late every night this week. The honeymoon cannot come soon enough.'

'Oh yes, Indonesia. Swimming with the birds in the treetops.' Max looks at me as if I've completely lost the plot. 'Sounds so blissful. Wish I was coming with you!'

'I'm sure Alison would be thrilled,' says Max, as I realize how inappropriate the comment was. Andy is looking at me with an unreadable expression on his face. I change the subject.

'I don't suppose you've had time to dig any more dirt on the bimbo yet?'

'Nothing that would stand up in court, I'm afraid, though she is not what you'd call popular on the modelling circuit. One thing I have learnt is that Bernie's influence must be colossal. My editor is aware of the story but he'd no more dare run it than . . . well actually I can hardly think of anything else he wouldn't dare run.'

'Blimey,' I say, laughing. 'Does anybody know what Bernie actually does? He is soooo dodgy.'

'Beats me,' shrugs Max, also laughing. 'But I reckon it's a good job we're his friends. Wouldn't want to get on the wrong side of him.'

'God no! I hope Mum knows what she's doing,' I say, worried for her suddenly.

'Bella, your mother has him wrapped around her little finger,' says Andy. 'He's totally devoted to her.'

'Well . . . long may it last.'

'Long may it last,' concurs Max. He raises his glass. 'To Bernie's dodgy contacts!'

'To Bernie's dodgy contacts!' we chorus and, as I catch Andy's eye, something in his gaze makes my heart start thump-thump-thumping.

Bella Bella Bella, he's getting married.

However many times I tell myself, it doesn't seem to sink in. It's just the excitement of the evening and my gratitude for his helping Dad. Impulsively I lean over and grab his hand.

'Thank you so much for everything,' I gabble for the hundredth time. Oh God, it's happening again. Thump thump thump. Those dark eyes staring deep into my heart. I could stare back forever.

'I think you've made your point, sis,' says Max.

I leave shortly after, pleading lateness but actually because the whole Andy thing has been disquieting in the extreme. The last thing I need in my life right now is to fall for a man who's about to marry another woman. Also, I'm starting to feel quite pissed and could do with a sobering line. Mark's bound to have some coke on him.

I saunter past a huge group of blokes wearing antlers. Unimaginative stag do paraphernalia, but there you go. They are all at least eight or nine years younger than me, and they all start chanting:

'LEGS!'

'TITS!'

'LEGS!'

Silly little buggers can't make their minds up.

'Can I marry you?' asks one of the boys, who is all of

twenty-one, by the looks of him, and I laugh, blowing them all kisses.

Fuck it, whatever I may feel for Andy is tenuous and idiotic. He is getting married and that's that. Boys much, much younger than me fancy me, and I am going to have the time of my life tonight.

Inside the Windmill Club it's dark and noisy and opulent and fabulous. The burlesque theme is carried right through from the heavy velvet curtains either side of the stage to the corseted bar staff to the stocking-ed and suspender-ed cigarette girls in their red lipstick and little pink uniforms. Even the pale pink and black cocktail menus are written in the distinctive Agent Provocateur font. I scan the gloom for a familiar face, spotting an MTV presenter and a rock star's currently-more-famous-than-her-legendary-guitar-playing-Dad's daughter as I do so.

'Bella!' I turn around to see Mark beaming at me, his arms outstretched. As I launch myself into them, he whispers in my ear, 'Christ you look fuckable tonight.' He looks pretty AOK himself, if decidedly butch-camp in tight white jeans that show off his apparently vast packet – unless he's got socks down there – and a gold-embroidered pink Indian waistcoat with nothing underneath. His biceps ripple enticingly.

'Oh go on, you big charmer.' I put my hand on one of them (bicep, not bollock or sock) and whisper into his ear, 'You don't have any coke on you do you?'

'Big charmer yourself,' he grins, punching me playfully on the shoulder and nearly felling me to the ground. 'Here you go.' He reaches into his pocket for a wrap. I thank him and make my way towards the loo. Then,

'Bella!' This time it's Damian, whom I haven't seen since the night we kissed. All of a sudden I come over all shy, but he gives me a warm hug.

'Wow, look at you,' he says eventually, holding me at arm's length. 'Being single suits you.'

'Thanks. You don't look too bad yourself.' Damian is looking very handsome in a sharply cut dark grey suit with an open-necked lilac shirt that sets off his dark skin. I don't recall ever seeing him look so smart.

'Well, I thought I'd make the effort as technically I'm on the pull now for the rest of my life,' he says, and I realize how unhappy he still is. I give him another hug.

'Been following the tabloids?' I ask. He nods.

'Me too. Today's *Standard* was brilliant, I thought.'

'I'm worried about her, Belles,' he says sadly. 'I can't help it; I know she treated us both like shit but watching her destroy herself in public is heartbreaking. And I just know that *Ben* –' he spits the word out – 'isn't helping her to look after her dad.'

'Hardly famed for his sensitive, caring side, is he?' I assent. 'I know, that's been on my mind a bit too, I have to admit. But, as far as the papers go – come on Damian, you're a hack, you know how it works. It's just an unfortunate consequence of fame by association. If any of the paps got hold of any of us after any of our big nights we'd probably look just as bad.'

'I hope you're right.'

'I am right,' I say, full of the confidence of the half-pissed and soon-to-be-coked-up. 'And talking of destroying ourselves, I must just nip to the loo.' I tap my nose and he laughs.

'I'm heading to the bar. Shall I see you there?'

'Try keeping me away,' I say, and carry on walking. I am just about to enter the Ladies, when,

'Bella!' It's Simon, exiting the velvet-curtained Gents, sniffing loudly. 'My God, you look fab-u-lous. Give us a twirl, darling.' It really is hard sometimes to remember Simon's straight, especially as he now seems to be channelling Sebastian Flyte, in black tie, with a Twenties white silk scarf draped just so. Tonight he and Mark have crossed the metrosexual 'just gay enough' line with their fashion choices. 'To die for. Really.'

'Thanks,' I say, so buoyed up with praise now that I'll no doubt be rendered quite insufferable in – oh, five minutes' time, max. 'Fantastic party!' I gesture around at the glittering crowd, dressed to impress and mainlining cocktails. Some early Sixties lounge music – Henry Mancini or Burt Bacharach – enhances the louche glamour of the surroundings.

'It's going well so far,' says Simon. 'Listen darling, I am *gagging* for a drink. Shall I see you at the bar? What can I get you?'

'Oh pick me a fabulous cocktail. Something that matches my frock.'

'Your wish is my command.' He performs a deep sweeping bow and disappears into the crowd.

Inside the cubicle, I sit on the loo and open Mark's wrap. Bloody hell, there's loads in here. I pinch a bit between my forefinger and thumb and am about to take a sniff when voices outside the cubicle stop me in my tracks. I'll wait until they've gone. It's unlikely anybody will object to my behaviour in such an establishment, but better safe than sorry.

'Did you see that photo of Ben Jones and Poppy Wallace in the paper today?' says one of the voices.

'Yeah. God, the slag's a mess,' says the other. 'I used to work with her and she really thought she was it.' She laughs nastily. 'Nice to see pride coming before a fall. Jules says she's yesterday's woman.'

'I heard she's on smack,' says the other, and my heart plummets. 'Also, between you and me, Ben's not that keen any more. My mate Sophie was at Punk the other night and she said he was chasing anything in a skirt.'

'Serves the stuck-up bitch right. I wouldn't mind a

look-in with him. He is GORGEOUS. Did you know . . .'
Their voices fade away as they leave the loo.

Ha! So Ben's reverting to type, eh? Let's see how you like it when the tables are turned, Poppy. But I can't help feeling worried. Smack? Surely not. She would never be so stupid. Then I remember what she said at my mum's house about her father losing his mind, so she should be allowed to blow hers too. I think again. Oh fucking hell.

I sit there for a minute or two, trying to calm myself down, before picking up the wrap again and taking three hearty sniffs. Maybe I should get in touch, see if she's OK.

Stop being such a soft-hearted mug. She stole your boyfriend. Fuck her, and go out and enjoy yourself.

I flush the loo for appearance's sake, leave the cubicle and check my reflection in the mirror, still feeling uneasy. I'm ashamed to say that my reflection cheers me up. I still look bloody fantastic. In fact, probably even more fantastic than I did before, apart from a telltale couple of white crumbs around my right nostril. I brush them away, ready to face my public again.

'Bella!' shouts Simon as I approach the bar. 'I have found the perfect match.' I look at the drink in his hand and smile. The colour of the cocktail is the exact pale pink of my dress.

'You're brilliant.' I take it from him. 'What is it?'

'Lychee martini, darling. Absolutely delicious and full of vitamin C. Quite cancels out the alcohol content.'

'I do hope not,' I smile, taking a sip of the delicately sweet concoction. 'Divine.' A voice comes over the tannoy.

'Ladies and gentlemen, your attention please. The cabaret is about to commence.' A hush falls over the room as a transvestite who looks like Mae West bumps and grinds his/her way to centre stage. This must be the compère. She introduces the first act with a mixture of camp innuendo and coarse bawdiness, then wiggles off the stage to drunken whoops and applause.

A pretty, pale-skinned girl with a dark Louise Brooks bob dances on, apparently naked underneath around fifty blown-up pink balloons which are somehow attached to her person. She is chased around the stage by a dastardly mustachioed Edwardian villain brandishing a giant needle. Every time he bursts one of her balloons (and somehow dispenses with the flapping bit of rubber), she strikes a pose, wide-eyed with her hand to her open mouth. It's all rather innocent and charming, harking back to a bygone age of suggestion, compared to – say – the simulated sex shows at Manumission. Eventually she is down to five balloons. The Edwardian villain bursts first one, then the second covering her boobs, to reveal a pair of black nipple tassels, which she twirls in expert circles for a minute or two, leaving all the men around me transfixed.

'Great party trick – you should learn how to do that,' Mark whispers to me. I am about to respond, when someone behind me bitches,

'God I'd kill myself if I was that fat.' I turn to see the *Stadium* fashion chicks leaning against the bar, sneering with all the venom only the professionally malnourished and terminally stupid can muster against another member of their sex. For the record, the girl on stage is probably a size 10, with a tiny waist and B/C-cup boobs at the most.

'I know – her cellulite is wobbling all over the place,' says the other one. 'Gross.'

Balloon Girl finishes her act by bursting both balloons covering her buttocks herself, then shaking her head sadly at the audience and wagging her finger as they sit in antici-pation of her final bits being revealed. With another shake of the head, she turns round and wiggles her bare bottom at them, before skipping off stage, to good-natured boos and more applause.

The cabaret does get raunchier after this (the South-East Asian girl performing with a live snake is particularly graphic), but it all has an air of performance rather than just cheap lapdancing-type thrills. Or maybe it's the coke.

I am certainly not thinking of Poppy, either of our fathers' respective plights or even my earlier reaction to Andy as I dance with Mark some time later, getting down and dirty to some late Seventies funk. I have kicked off my painful shoes and my bare feet are filthy as we writhe around the grimy dance floor.

'Come on boys,' I cry, pulling Damian and Simon up to dance too, totally off my stupid face now. They kindly oblige and I am in my element, centre of attention as I prance around with 'my *Stadium* boys' as I have come to think of them tonight.

After a bit Mark and I decide to go outside for a fag.

'Brilliant, brilliant party,' I shout over the music as we stagger up the club's dingy back staircase. 'You're all so clever. I love you all, I really do. Everything's just brilliant! Isn't it all brilliant, Marky?'

'Yes, yes, it's brilliant,' he laughs, throwing back his shaved head and giving me an eyeful of his powerful throat.

'You're brilliant!' I cry. 'You know, everyone thinks you're so stupid, but they're wrong. You're brilliant! Absolutely brilliant.'

'Thanks babe, that means a lot to me,' says Mark sentimentally. And without further ado he pushes me back against the wall and shoves his tongue down my throat. It feels amazing. His tongue is as huge and muscly as the rest of him. I respond, forcing my tongue back into his mouth so I can kiss his lips too.

He holds both my wrists up against the wall with one incredibly strong arm, so I am trapped. With the other, he pushes my dress up and starts kneading his palm against the front of my new lace knickers. The friction of the lace combined with the force of his enormous hand makes me moan into his mouth.

Mark leans back, still holding me against the wall by my wrists, and looks mockingly into my eyes.

'Fuck me, you're a sexy little thing, aren't you?'

'Don't stop,' I say.

'Would you like it if I did this?' He puts one finger just inside my knickers, not inside me, but touching the very edge.

'U-huh.'

'How would you like this, then?' He puts a large finger right inside me and I look him in the eye.

'I'd like it a lot.'

'And how would you feel if I started doing this?' He starts rubbing my clitoris with his thumb, two huge fingers now going deeper still inside me. He still has my arms pinned above my head with one hand.

'Oh Jesus, Mark, I . . .'

He lowers his head and starts kissing me again. I feel vulnerable, unable to move as he's so strong and has me pinned to the wall. His huge tongue is in my mouth, his huge fingers in my cunt, his huge thumb against my clit. Plundering never felt so good.

Suddenly, somebody says, 'Oy you two, enough of that.' Mark lets go of my arms and withdraws his other hand. A security guard is standing on the stair below us.

'Looks like you're having fun, but it's more than my job's worth to let you carry on here,' he says, looking overexcited himself. I wonder how long he's been watching us. 'If I catch you again, you're out of here.' He walks back down the stairs, probably off for a wank.

'Phew, perhaps we'd better go outside and cool off, have a fag.' I adjust my wet knickers and lean up to kiss Mark's stubbly cheek. 'But I definitely don't want tonight to finish here. You and I have unfinished business.'

'You're on babe,' he says, giving me a slap on the arse, and we make our way outside, where we immediately start snogging again. He is so huge, so strong, so virile and male that all I care about are his muscly arms around me, his stubbly jaw scratching mine, his hard-on pushing through the stiff material of his white jeans.

There have been many times tonight when I've heard my name spoken aloud, none of them less welcome than it is now.

'Bella? Is that you?'

I disentangle myself from Mark. No, no, no it can't be. Oh God in fucking heaven. Max and Andy are standing in the street a couple of feet away from me, Max regarding me with amusement, Andy with what looks like acute distaste.

'Wh . . . what are you doing here?' I ask, aware of what a slut I must look – presumably pretty bedraggled by now, with dirty bare feet and hair all tangled around my face. Max laughs.

'The back streets of Soho aren't your private playground, you know, much as you clearly think they are.' Ouch. 'We're on our way home from dinner. What happened to your shoes?'

'They were hurting, so I took them off.' I face him defiantly. I can't look at Andy. 'Is that a crime?'

'Of course not, Belles, don't be silly. Just try not to step on any broken glass. Enjoy the rest of your party!' And they walk off into the distance. Andy hasn't spoken a single word the entire encounter. Fuck fuck fuck fuck fuck. Cunting fuck.

Chapter 18

It's 4 p.m. and I am lying on my sitting-room floor, head resting on my zebra print beanbag. I got out of bed an hour ago, unable to bear the company of my clamouring thoughts in the fetid darkness of my shuttered bedroom. I tried to make myself comfortable on the chaise longue, but to no avail. I wish I could just leave this body behind, and inhabit a new, fresh, *unsoiled* one. I'm trying to read the Penguin paperback of *Scoop* that Andy lent me, but my eyes keep closing and I can't concentrate on the words.

My feet are ingrained with black – my cursory shower didn't come close to getting the muck off – and cut to shreds. They really, seriously hurt. I am also covered in bruises, especially halfway down the front of my thighs, which suggests I did a lot of walking into tables last night. I don't remember falling over, but an unsightly graze on my left knee indicates otherwise. My lovely pink dress lies on the floor just beyond the front door, where I must have left it as soon as I stumbled in. It is soiled and battered, probably beyond redemption. Just like its owner.

Worse by far than my physical symptoms are the emotional ones. Seeing Andy was the equivalent of having a bucket of cold water chucked over me as far as Mark went, and I left the party soon after. Alone. What a fucking slapper, I think, despising myself on every level. *'Unfinished business?' Aaaargh!*

And as for Andy . . . In all honesty, I can hardly bear to think about Andy. It's clear to me now that my feelings for him overstep any normal barriers of friendship, and while I know it's pointless as he's about to get married, I still don't want him to think I'm a despicable slag.

Painfully, I compare the look he gave me outside Café Boheme to the utter distaste on his face as he witnessed the unedifying spectacle of me and Mark bringing the spirit of an 18–30 holiday in Faliraki to the streets of Soho. All that was missing was the vomit. And the eighteen- to thirty-year-olds, come to that.

Why why WHY did they have to walk past just then? Oh but *why why WHY did you have to behave like that?* an unwelcome voice keeps prodding.

To stop the irksome voice, my mind wanders back to earlier in the evening and I recall, with intense shame, dragging Damian and Simon onto the dance floor as I pranced barefoot, singing in all probability, feeling like queen bee, convinced I was one hot chick. At one stage – oh Christ, stop the memories – I even stuck my tongue out at the fashion chicks, implying that the *Stadium* boys were now my territory, thank you very much. Did I actually do the wanker gesture with my right hand at them too? No, I conclude, even I wouldn't do that. It's just my mind playing cruel tricks on me to punish me for having too much fun.

I hope this isn't going to affect Andy helping with Dad's case, I think guiltily, the hangover and comedown now making my behaviour the cause of everything bad in the world. No, why should it? He's a principled man, on the side

267

of justice, helping because he's Max's dear friend. It has nothing, NOTHING, to do with you, Bella Not The Centre Of The Universe. I should call Dad, find out how he's coping, but at the moment I really cannot face talking to anyone.

Out of habit I start to think about Ben and Poppy shagging, my daily self-torture, and to my surprise it doesn't hurt at all. In fact, I just feel sad for Pops, having to deal with her father's dementia with no support whatsoever from the handsome, self-absorbed bastard I used to think I was in love with.

A silly old quote comes into my mind: *the best way to get over one man is to get under another.* Sadly it seems I've got over one man by falling in love with one I'll never get under. *Falling in love with?*

I almost laugh thinking about the differences between vain, selfish, weak, manipulative Ben and kind, intelligent, straight-laced, morally upright Andy. Even Ben's looks, which used to so enthral me, are verging on the effeminate compared to Andy's. It's like comparing Brad Pitt to Gregory Peck in *To Kill a Mockingbird*.

'Here Comes the Sun' starts playing tinnily from somewhere. My ringtone. Where the fuck did I leave my phone? I didn't take it with me last night. I gingerly get to my feet, wincing as my knee touches the bare floorboards, and look around. My head is swimming now I'm no longer horizontal. My phone sounds as if it's in the kitchen and I remember having a conversation with Alison about the exhibition in there yesterday afternoon. Yesterday afternoon, when I was clean, unsoiled, looking forward to an evening I then went on to ruin . . . *SHUT UP!*

I'm moving so slowly that my phone reaches the end of its ring span and stops, then immediately starts ringing again.

'All right, all right, keep your hair on,' I mutter, walking more quickly towards the kitchen now. As I pick it up and look at the display I draw a sharp breath. I deleted Poppy's number soon after catching her in bed with Ben, but would recognize it anywhere. All of a sudden I think of what I overheard in the loo last night, and press the green button with a feeling of foreboding.

'Poppy?'

'Bella?' Her voice sounds quavery, indistinct, blurry. 'Is that you? Oh Belles, I'm so sorry, so so sorry, sorry, sorry . . .'

'Yes, so you should be, but why are you calling me now?' She's not on smack, is she? *Is she?*

'Sorry Belles, sorry . . . Ben . . .' It sounds as if she's crying now. 'Ben, Ben, Ben, CUNT. Sorry, Bella, sorry.' Then she starts giggling.

'Poppy, what the fuck are you on?' I ask, properly worried now. Poppy never loses control.

'Pills . . . had some pills . . . ran out of coke so took pills . . . and vodka.'

'No smack?'

'Smack? You say smack? Nooooooo. We don't do smack, Belles, do we? Why d'ya think that?' She giggles in a deeply disconcerting manner. 'No smack but sorry sorry sorry sorry sorry sorry.'

'For Christ's sake, you silly bitch, are you OK? Where are you? I'm coming to get you . . .'

'Home . . .'

'You're at home? In Hoxton?'

'Yes yes, Hoxton, home, sorry, Bella.'

I try to keep her talking, putting my phone on loud-speaker as I throw some clothes on and run downstairs to hail a cab, but she goes silent on me just as I'm getting into the taxi.

'Poppy!' I shout down the phone. 'Speak to me, you stupid tart. POPPY!'

But nothing. Panicking, I call again, but it just rings and rings and rings. Jesus Christ, what the fuck do I do now? Should I call an ambulance? It's just about possible it's nothing major. And it could get her into an awful lot of trouble. But what if she dies? The very thought is enough to make me dial 999 with no more buggering about. I tell the ambulance people what has happened and give them her address. They assure me they'll send someone straight over and I lie down in the cab, very slightly comforted by the thought.

I am pouring with toxic sweat after the uncalled-for exertions and for once in my life wish this bloody summer was over; it's gone on quite long enough. Soothing rain might take me back to September schoolbooks and child-hood sobriety.

There is no sign of an ambulance as I get out of the cab in Hoxton Square. Scared at what I'll find, I make my way up to Poppy's flat, letting myself in with the set of keys that caused all the trouble in the first place. It's very odd being here again, the surroundings so familiar, yet connected with so much recent pain. I race up the stairs as fast as my legs will carry me, not allowing myself time to wallow.

I brace myself and open the door.

She is lying on her open-plan bare floorboards, much as I was earlier, only she is face-down, her usually lovely hair spread out in greasy clumps around her head. I gently lift it up to look at her face. She seems to be breathing, but is certainly not conscious. She is extremely pale and her lips are an unsettling purple, approaching blue, with a dribble of white spume at one corner.

'Poppy sweetheart, wake up.' I'm crying now, shaking her. 'Please wake up.'

She is wearing an old grey marl T-shirt, which has ridden up over her bare bottom. In a kind of trance, I pull it down and look for something to cover her up further. *She needs dignity.* The nearest thing to hand is a blue and white checked tea towel on the kitchen worktop; it will have to do. Propped up next to it is the card I made to thank her for her offer of the spare room as a studio. I open it and look at the words inside.

Thanks, dear friend xxx

The tears that started a minute ago are now pouring down my face and galvanize me into action.

I put the tea towel over her bottom but, small though her bum is, it doesn't really help, so I take off my T-shirt and wrap it around her lower quarters. I sit there in my bra on the floor, stroking her hair, saying, 'Just stay alive Pops, please. It'll be OK, everything's going to be OK.' My tears are soaking her hair and, madly, I turn her around and try to give her the kiss of life.

It always works in films, but I never paid any attention to first aid things at school and I'm bloody useless. After several failed attempts I give up and put her head on my lap, worried that I might do more harm than good if I continue. I carry on stroking her hair and trying to say positive things.

'Remember lovey, what your dad used to say, that brilliant quote from Dryden? "Happy the man, and happy he alone, He who can call today his own; He who, secure within, can say, Tomorrow do thy worst, for I have lived today . . ." Well, I don't think that your dad would think that what you've done today is living, really, would he? He would want you to go on doing the living today that he can't do any more, so tomorrow and tomorrow and tomorrow can do their worst . . .' My voice breaks. 'Go on Pops, live. For your dad's sake . . . And your mum's . . .

And mine.' She doesn't respond and I let myself sob quietly, still stroking her hair. 'Tomorrow do thy worst, Pops, for you have lived today,' I manage through my tears.

I can hear an ambulance siren approach, and look around, trying to assess the damage. An empty bottle of vodka has been knocked over on the floor, alongside a plastic prescription pill bottle, spewing its small white contents in several directions. I reach over to pick it up, trying not to disturb Poppy's head on my lap, and look at the label. Temazepam. The inevitable couple of empty coke (or smack?) wraps are splayed either side of where her head's just been. I pick one up and, steeling myself, run my finger inside. The crumbs do have the disgusting, bitter taste of coke, but then I don't know what smack tastes like.

Something else catches my eye. A transparent plastic bag, only around five centimetres square, of the type that dealers use, containing three tablets that look like Es.

'Jesus Christ, Poppy, how many have you taken?' I say aloud, holding her pale hand tightly in one of mine and continuing to stroke her hair with the other.

The ambulance men burst through the door and I hold up the bag, gabbling, 'It looks like she's taken cocaine, Temazepam, Ecstasy and vodka. Maybe heroin, but probably not. Can you pump her stomach or something? She is going to be all right, isn't she? Please say she's going to be all right . . .'

One of the ambulance men comes over and takes the two pill packets from me.

'And you are, madam?'

'I'm her friend Bella. She phoned me and I called nine-nine-nine. I've got a spare key. Is she going to be OK?'

'Try not to worry,' he says, not answering me directly. 'We'll do everything we can for her. You did the right thing calling us.'

I watch numbly as they pick Poppy up off my lap, strap her to a stretcher and carry her out of the door. My T-shirt falls away from her nether regions. So much for dignity. I try to reclaim mine by retrieving the crumpled garment from the floor and putting it back on.

'Can I come with you?'

'No, sorry love, but make your way to St Barts and go to A & E. They'll point you in the right direction. Try not to worry,' he says for the third time, his words having quite the opposite of their intended effect.

My journey to St Barts seems to take forever, even though it's no distance at all as the crow flies, and all I can think is *live, Poppy, please live. Please God, make her be all right.* I really couldn't care less about Ben any more. Fuck this mad summer. Fuck it.

I think of the day we got our A level results, which meant Pops had got into Oxford; going out and celebrating in the village, then coming up to London for a very naughty weekend of booze and snogging desperately uncool boys, giggling over everything the way only teenage girls can. ('Mine's worse than yours'; 'No, mine's really, *really* gross!' We were late developers, remember.) I think of her skipping through the car park en route to Glastonbury, a wine box in each hand, plastic cups clenched between her teeth. I think of her holding my hand at my nan's funeral, squeezing so hard it hurt but made me feel better. I think right back to our first day at school together, Poppy with her slightly too-big uniform, pristine white socks, angelic face, tufty bunches and wicked sense of humour. I think of endless days of laughter and fun and kindness and friendship and wish more than I've ever wished anything that neither of us had ever set eyes on Ben bloody Jones. *Live, Poppy, live.*

I suddenly remember that Mum is back in contact with

Diana, Poppy's mother. Shit, she needs to be told. I dial Mum's number.

'Darling, I was just thinking about you,' she says in her dear, familiar voice. 'I must have evoked you.'

Five hours later, Mum, Diana, Damian and I are sitting in the A & E waiting room, on our seventeenth cup of horrible NHS coffee. I have never seen anybody look as distraught as Diana does now. If I could wipe that look out of my memory bank forever, I would.

'I thought life had struck me a pretty unkind blow, when I found out about Ken's illness,' she said earlier, in her lovely measured Radio 4 tones. 'But nothing – *nothing* – prepares you for the idea that your child might die before you.'

She broke down then, crying out, 'Not Poppy, please God, not Poppy. Please don't let my beautiful baby die . . .'

Mum took her off for some strong coffee, brandy out of a cow-hide hip flask and some soothing words as only my mother knows how. When they returned, Diana was dry-eyed, beyond tears, an automaton. She's remained like that since, but the pain and fear etched on her face are almost unbearable to behold.

The doctors pumped Poppy's stomach but the coke, booze and pills had already done their worst (there wasn't any smack, which is one blessing, I suppose). She hasn't regained consciousness yet, and if she doesn't wake up soon, there's a possibility of permanent brain damage. And of course, she might not wake up at all. The words *lethal cocktail of drugs* keep swishing round my mind.

Damian starts pacing the hospital corridors, out of his mind with fear. He called Ben to establish just what had happened and Ben eventually admitted that he'd left Poppy for one of the actresses on *People Like Us*. I wouldn't like to be in his shoes when Damian gets hold of him.

A doctor in a long white coat, stethoscope hanging around his neck, walks towards us down the corridor. I experience a moment of pure dread.

'Mrs Wallace?'

Diana starts running towards him like a madwoman.

'Tell me my baby's OK, please, please, tell me she's OK.'

The doctor smiles.

'She's just regained consciousness, and she's asking for you.'

'Does she seem . . . OK?' None of us has been able to bring ourselves to speak the words *brain damage* out loud.

'Well, the tests are still inconclusive, but judging from her vocabulary, I'd say she's on the mend already,' says the doctor, with a twinkle in his eye.

'Oh thank God, oh thank God, oh thank you thank you thank you God. Oh Jesus. Oh thank Christ.'

Diana, a lifelong atheist, falls to her knees and finally lets herself go, sobbing her poor old heart out in the middle of the cold, sterile hospital corridor.

Mum, Damian and I look at each other and smile, tears streaming down all our faces.

The tubes coming out of her nose and arms are unreal. I feel as if I'm in an episode of *Casualty*. But the words coming out of her mouth are pure Poppy.

'Christ I'm a contemptible cunt.'

'Shhh, sweetheart, just rest.' I stroke her hair.

'But I AM.' She tries to prop herself up on her elbows, then sinks back onto the narrow bed, defeated.

'Unforgivable . . . boyfriend-stealing bitch . . . primadonna near-death experience,' she wheezes hoarsely. 'As if poor Mum doesn't have enough on her plate as it is. Sorry Belles . . . I really wasn't trying to kill myself. More drugs just seemed like a good idea at the time. Until I started to feel really weird, and not good weird.' She coughs like someone dying of tuberculosis in a nineteenth-century novel.

'Did you really love him that much?' I ask, remembering how much I thought I did.

'No, I realized ages ago what a complete knobber he is.' She's struggling to get the words out.

'Complete knobber just about sums him up.'

She tries to grin the old Poppy grin, then stops, looking serious.

'After he went, I just sat there thinking about what I'd done, to you AND Damian, my two favourite people. For fuck's sake, Bella, remember "frolics and friendship forever"?'

I laugh tearfully, remembering our teenage chant all too well.

'Frolics and friendship forever. Yup. But don't worry now, lovely. You're OK and that's the main thing. Fucking men. Didn't we always say we'd never let the X-chromosomally challenged get between us?'

Poppy laughs, holding her stomach.

'Ow-y-ow-y-ow that hurts.'

'If it's any consolation, I feel like shit too. Hangover from hell. Can I get in with you? – it looks awfully comfy in there.'

Poppy laughs again, weakly pushing back the sheet.

'Just kidding, you silly arse.' I lean over and kiss her pale forehead. She seems to perk up slightly and says,

'Talking of the X-chromosomally challenged, have you seen anything of Damian recently? I hope he's all right . . .'

I decide not to share the memory of snogging him among the debris on my sitting-room floor.

'. . . I can't imagine he will ever forgive me, but please do tell him I'm sorry.'

276

'Actually you can tell him yourself – he's here.'

Her pale face lights up. 'Really?'

'Really,' I smile. 'He still loves you, even though you're a contemptible cunt. Shall I go and get him?' She nods, hope flickering in her eyes, and I make my way back out into the corridor.

Mum is chatting to one of the nurses. I imagine Diana's outside, having a fag. She's always been a guilty smoker – I remember her hiding her cigarettes from herself when Poppy and I were kids, then clambering on kitchen stools, trying to remember where she'd put them. She spent an hour with Poppy earlier, holding her hand as she drifted in and out of consciousness, but once Pops was fully awake she insisted on seeing me. And even lying in a hospital bed with tubes coming out of her nose, Poppy's will is a force to be reckoned with.

'Darling, how is she?'

'She's OK. Very very sorry for everything she's done but still showing some of the old fighting spirit. She wants to see Damian. Is he in the loo?'

Mum looks anxious. 'Darling, he's gone.'

'Gone? Where?'

'Once he found out she was going to be OK, he went. He looked really angry, actually. He was calling her an attention-seeking little bitch.' She delivers the last bit sotto voce.

'Oh fuck.' This scenario hadn't even crossed my mind. 'What am I going to tell her?'

'Just say he had to go. She doesn't need to know the truth quite yet.'

'OK. Thanks Mum. For everything.' I kiss her.

Poppy's face falls as I re-enter the room alone, though she tries to hide it.

'Damian had to go. Deadline,' I lie brightly.

'Bollocks. He can't bring himself to see me, now he knows I'm all right, can he? It's OK, Belles, I lived with him for five years, I know how the stubborn bugger's mind works.'

'I'm sure he'll come round in the end . . .'

'I wouldn't blame him if he never wanted to see me again. He gave up every bloody weekend to come and see Dad with me. *Every bloody weekend.* Ben wouldn't come with me once. And this is how I repay him. And you . . . My best friend ever . . . What kind of bitch am I . . .?' She is struggling to speak again, weak, white and poorly on her horribly remedial-looking bed.

'You need some rest, young lady,' says the nurse who's just walked into the room, approaching said bed with a cup of tea. She plumps up her pillows and smiles at her. 'You've given everyone a nasty shock.'

'I'll come and see you again tomorrow.' I kiss her bloodless cheek. 'Night night.'

'You don't have to, you know, but I'd love it if you did,' she replies, kissing me back.

'Oh I'll be back all right. I want some answers, and you've got some serious explaining to do. Young lady.'

'All I want to know is why. And how long it had been going on before I caught you.'

'That day you caught us was the first time, I promise.' Poppy looks a lot more like her old self today. There's some colour in her cheeks and they've taken the tubes out of her nose, thank God, though she's still on a drip. 'And maybe, if you hadn't caught us, it might have been the last time.'

'Really?' I ask, sceptically.

'Actually no, it probably wouldn't have been the last time, but it *was* the first. You've got to believe me, Belles.'

'So how did you set it up? Ben was meant to be in New

York. YOU were meant to be at Babington House, for fuck's sake!' I almost shout, angry again now that she's OK and the extent of their betrayal is coming back to me.

'Ben called me the Wednesday before. He said he thought things were moving too fast between you two and he needed someone to talk to about it . . .'

'WHAT? The little shit. HE asked to move in with ME. He kept telling me how much he loved me. I wasted hours helping him learn his boring fucking lines. He's a useless ham anyway; he's only got one cunting facial expression for grief . . .'

Poppy furrows her brow in an exact impersonation of Ben's grief face. It's funny, but I'm too furious to laugh.

'He . . . he . . . he . . .' I am lost for words, remembering with renewed rage all the faithless turd's empty promises. I may not be sad any more, but that doesn't stop me being livid at his duplicity.

'He said he'd spun you some line about going to the Big Apple for the weekend, he knew Damian was going away for Adam's stag do, so was it OK if he crashed in Hoxton with me on Saturday night.'

'And you said yes? You fucking bitch! You must have known what he was after.' Poppy can't look at me. Eventually she says, in a very small voice,

'I knew what he was after. He'd been flirting with me for ages, whenever you were out of the room, and I'd been getting off on it. As I said, I'm a contemptible cunt.'

She sees the look on my face and adds, 'Though I did try to stop seeing you both for a bit. I reckoned it would be better to put some distance between us all.' She takes a deep breath, which clearly hurts. 'I was bored. I've been with Damian for five years.'

I raise my eyebrows at her and she punches herself in the arm.

'Still thinking in the present tense, silly cow. I *was* with Damian for five years, my career *was* going brilliantly and, once I started the new job, I was doing a LOT of coke. Probably getting on for a couple of grams a day.'

'For fuck's sake, Poppy, you're a TV producer, not a bloody rock star.'

'I know, I know, Pete Doherty eat your heart out,' she says, coughing like Mimi in *La Bohème*. 'And, much as I don't want to blame the drugs for my own absence of moral fibre, you kind of stop having normal feelings if you never give yourself a chance to sober up.' I wonder how she's going to feel when they take her off the morphine drip.

'So why Ben? I know he's got a body to die for, and it must have been flattering him flirting with you, but . . .' I trail off miserably. 'I thought you and I meant more than that to each other.'

'That's the worst thing for me to come to terms with.' She stares out of the window. 'I think it was *because* he was with you. I've always been the successful one – straight As, Oxford, effortless achievements, gorgeous blokes, the full fucking Monty. I was really happy for you at first, when you and Ben got together at Glastonbury. But then . . . I don't know, he suddenly looked on the verge of A-list stardom, and I was intensely, *insanely* jealous.'

I am suddenly angrier than I've ever been in my life.

'You disgusting, conceited, mean-spirited little bitch,' I say slowly. 'Do you have any idea what it's been like, playing second fucking fiddle to you ever since we were ten? Do you think I actually enjoyed celebrating all your successes when I was only successful at art? And not even that after I left college? Do you really think I never fantasized about any of *your* gorgeous blokes? Do you think that in a million years I would ever have tried it on with any of them?'

Poppy shakes her head miserably. Something occurs to me. 'Actually, now I come to think of it, that wanker you were shagging at Oxford, Luke something or other, tried it on with me one of those nights I came to stay at Christ Church with you. He said you were too skinny for him and he needed a real woman, ha ha. What a bastard, eh? I told him to fuck off, because that's what friends do. THAT'S WHAT FRIENDS DO, POPPY.' I am now looming over the bed, shouting into her face.

A middle-aged nurse bursts through the door.

'What on earth do you think you're doing? Get out of here, at once.' She grabs my arm and tries to pull me away, but Poppy stops her, saying,

'No, it's all right, Jean. Please let her stay. I've had this coming a long time.'

'Nobody has any right to shout at you in your condition.'

'Bella has every right to shout at me whenever she wants.'

'I'll stop shouting,' I say to the nurse, as I haven't finished what I have to say yet and I'm buggered if Poppy's getting off that lightly.

'Just leave us alone for five more minutes, please?' Poppy says to the nurse. She nods, grudgingly, and walks out, shooting me another dirty look.

'Getting together with Ben was the best thing that had ever happened to me,' I start, and Poppy gives a little snort.

'Oh just shut the fuck up for once, you arrogant bitch. Yes, I do realize *now* that it wasn't the best thing ever, but at the time, my greatest fantasy had come true. Can you imagine, for once in your self-centred life, what it's like *not* to be you, *not* always to get the gorgeous man of your dreams? Can you imagine how it felt for me to walk in

281

on the man of my dreams with my best mate? Two people I loved and who I thought loved me?'

'Oh Belles, I'm so sorry . . .' Poppy is gazing up at me, tears running down her pale cheeks.

'And can you imagine how it was made even worse by the fact that he was shagging the person I'd always played second fucking fiddle to? Like of course I was never in his league in the first place? That I cried and cried myself to sleep for weeks on end because of you? Did THAT ever occur to you, when you were coked out of your tiny mind, bored with Damian and jealous of me? *Jealous* of me . . .' I shake my head at such a preposterous notion. 'If only you knew how many years I've battled with myself not to be jealous of you.' I'm crying too now, almost out of steam.

'Belles, stop it, please,' Poppy begs me. 'There was another reason, but I didn't want to say before.'

I snort. 'This had better be good.'

'That weekend before, when Damian and I went to see Dad, he didn't recognize me. Not for the whole weekend. He had absolutely no idea who I was . . .'

'Oh . . .'

'I went on a massive bender. Not the most grown-up way of dealing with it, I know, but there you go. Fuck knows how I managed to wing it at work. That Wednesday that Ben called, I was completely off my tits. I'd said no to meeting up in private so many times before, Belles, you've got to believe me. He caught me at a very, very weak moment. I guess I just thought – fuck it, he's gorgeous, it's about time I had some fun. No one need ever know. You and Damian were both meant to be away. It was never my intention to hurt either of you, I promise.'

'Oh for Christ's sake . . . why didn't you say so before?' I recall the endless phone calls and emails and Facebook messages, when all she could say was sorry.

'I didn't want to use Dad's illness as an excuse for my shoddy behaviour.'

'Which is exactly what you're doing now,' I point out. 'But I'm really sorry about your dad.'

'Don't be nice to me, Belles. I think I preferred it when you were shouting at me.' She tries to get out of bed to approach me but is hindered by the drip.

Poppy gazes at me some more, so many tears now falling that the front of her hospital gown is soaked.

'Stop crying and get back into bed. I'll probably get blamed for you catching pneumonia.'

I go and stare out of the window, trying to decide what to do next. The revelation about her father not recognizing her doesn't excuse what she did, but it does make it a hell of a lot more understandable. And I do have a grudging respect for her not using it as an excuse until now.

'If it helps, I've been bloody miserable pretty much ever since it happened – not that I'm asking for sympathy. None of my friends would speak to me, except for the druggy workmates – you know, Caz and Lucas, all that gang. I've been missing you and Damian more than I thought possible. And living with Ben was pretty fucking hellish in the end. His ego is even bigger than mine, if such a thing is possible . . .'

'So . . . not all glamorous A-list stuff? I kept seeing you in the papers.'

'Sorry about that too. But you can't help the bloody paparazzi taking photos. I did hope you'd get a bit of *Schadenfreude* at the pics of me looking like shit . . .'

I try not to smile at this.

'Oh yes, plenty.'

'I tried to call and explain, Belles, I *did*.'

'Let's change the subject. I don't think I can take much more in today.'

'Delighted to.' Poppy smiles nervously, wiping her sodden face on the arm without a drip in it. 'OK. Erm . . . what's been happening in your life since I've been so inconveniently out of the loop? Any gossip?'

I laugh slightly bitterly. 'Where do I begin?'

And over the next hour I fill her in on the last few months' events. The only thing I leave out is my growing obsession with Andy. I'm not ready to trust her with that quite yet, if ever. It's great talking to her about everything else, though. She is thrilled about my painting and horrified about Dad's arrest but determined 'we won't let the lanky bitch get away with it'.

When I tell her about the *Stadium* party and Mark she makes me feel better, just like she always used to.

'I still don't understand why you didn't shag him. But don't you dare call yourself a despicable slag. Where have your old feminist principles gone? You wouldn't use those words about anyone else, so don't use them about yourself.'

'You keep calling yourself a contemptible cunt.'

'That's a statement of fact. All you did was have a bit of slap and tickle with a fellow unattached grown-up. Nothing wrong with that at all.' She doesn't know about Damian and Andy of course, but again she makes me feel better.

'So how did Damian seem?' she asks, oh so casually. 'Was he with anyone?'

'Anyone female, you mean? No. It'll be a long time before he's interested in anything like that again. You broke his heart.'

Chapter 19

'I am not going to see her and that is final,' shouts Damian, banging his fist on the beer-sticky table. We're in the Coach & Horses in Soho, just around the corner from the *Stadium* office. A couple of old soaks turn to stare at him. He's wearing blackout shades again, so I can't see the expression in his eyes. 'I don't know how you can forgive her, Bella, after what she did to us both. You're too bloody soft, that's your problem.' The Welsh lilt is back with a vengeance.

'You were there like a shot when you thought she might die. Anyway, I haven't forgiven her, but she's my oldest friend and I missed her. What's the point in holding on to grudges? Her dad didn't recognize her, Damian, you of all people should understand how hard that must have hit her.'

'I know exactly how hard it hit her. I was there when it happened, as I was always there for her. And how did she repay me? By going on a fucking bender and shagging my best mate.'

I realize I'd better change tack.

'As far as I'm concerned, she's sorry, she nearly died, and I really don't give a fuck about Ben any more.' Damian looks murderous at the mention of his nemesis. I add hastily, 'Go on, Damian, would you just consider giving her another chance? I know she regrets it from the bottom of her heart. You two were such a perfect couple.'

'You're wasting your time so we might as well change the subject.' He takes a large swig of his pint and starts laughing. 'I have to say you're not the fashion department's favourite person at the moment.' He starts to chair-dance, sticking out his tongue and making the universal wanking gesture. The old soaks gawp a bit more as I bury my face in my hands.

'Oh fuckety fuck, I was hoping that bit was a dream.'

'Don't worry, everyone else thinks it was great. Simon and Mark adore you.'

I am walking towards the number 23 bus stop, trying to decide what to cook for dinner, when my phone rings.

'Maxy? How are you? What's up?'

'It's Andy!' Max is so excited he can barely get the words out. 'He's found something out about Kimberly, something that he says is relevant to the case!'

'Oh my God!' I stop dead in the street.

'Stupid bitch,' says the man behind me, narrowly avoiding walking into me.

'So what is it? What has he found out? It has nothing to do with cults, has it?'

Max laughs. 'He told me to tell you that it has nothing to do with cults. He wants to meet us this evening to show us the evidence. Say you're free, sis.'

'Are you insane? Of course I'm free. And even if I wasn't, I'd cancel dinner with Barack Obama to see what he's got on Kim.' I'd cancel dinner with Barack Obama just to see Andy again full stop but I don't tell Max this.

'Divine Comedy at seven thirty?'

'Can't he make it any earlier? I'll be there.'

* * *

Max and Andy are sitting at a large wooden table made out of an ancient carved Indian door. I try to be cool, sauntering over and not noticing an empty pint glass that someone's left on the floor. I trip over it and nearly go flying but Andy leaps to his feet and catches me in time.

'Wow,' says Max quietly.

Andy's arms around me are too close for comfort, so I say, with not a jot of coolness,

'OK, as I've ruined my entrance and cannot wait a minute longer, pleeeeease, Andy, tell us what you've got?'

'Are you sure? You don't want a drink first?' Andy looks at me quizzically.

'You know what, for probably the first time since I was about fifteen, I don't want a drink first.'

He laughs and takes some papers out of his slightly battered dark brown leather laptop carrier.

'In that case, sit down.'

I do as he says. I will always do as he says.

'I thought it was better to print it, as seeing things on paper always makes it more real than on a screen, don't you think?' He smiles.

'Andy, I can see you're enjoying your moment of glory, but please just get on with it,' says Max.

'OK, OK,' says Andy. 'Sorry. The thing is, we have special search engines at work that search all global news, and the archives go way back. That's one of the ways we hacks are able to dig up dirt. Things like Google don't come close.' He smiles at Max, who has been Googling Kimberly for weeks.

'So all you had to do was type in the bitch's name, and it came up?' I say, thinking ungratefully, if it's that bloody simple, why didn't he come up with it earlier?

'It wasn't quite as easy as that. You'll see why in a minute.' As he riffles through the papers to make sure they're in the right order, I steal a glance at him. He looks wonderful: tall, broad-shouldered and dependable, his intelligent dark eyes gleaming with excitement behind their geeky specs.

He hands me and Max two sheets of A4 each. We start to read. It's an article from the *Perth Gazette*, dated five years ago, about a girl working in a hardware store who accused her middle-aged boss of raping her.

Hilda Lehman, 20, broke down under cross-questioning and admitted she'd fabricated the entire story. Sykes, 56, had refused to promote Lehman to store manager after intercourse had taken place . . .

'OK, it's a similar story, but it's a different person,' I say, disappointed. 'Surely that won't make any difference to Dad being found guilty or not? It's hardly a landmark victory.'

'Look at the photo,' says Max, his smile lighting up his dear face. 'Turn the page, you idiot!'

I turn the page over and from the second a skinny, freckly girl with goofy teeth and – yes! – a ginger Afro stares back at me. She's had some work done since then (very expensive dentistry for starters) but it's Kimbo all right.

'She must have changed her name,' I say, quick on the uptake as ever.

'Models do it all the time,' says Max.

'Especially if they're called Hilda!' splutters Andy, and we all crack up, laughing till we're fit to burst, hugging and high-fiving each other. Max punches the air, whooping, his golden curls flying all over the place.

'But what about the legalities?' I come down to earth with a whacking thump. 'I bet there's some stupid law where you're not allowed to bring things like this up in court. Alison was telling us about how crap the law can be the other night, Andy . . .'

'Ah yes. That is a problem. But don't you see? Now we all know, beyond reasonable doubt, that your father is innocent.'

'I knew anyway,' Max and I say in unison. Andy smiles at us.

'So did I. But as far as I'm concerned, this proves it. Even with my tiresome bloody principles, I can see that it's a coincidence too far.' Max and I look at one another guiltily, trying to remember who coined the phrase.

'But what are we going to do about it?' I ask. 'If they can't bring it up in court, how can it help?'

Andy takes off his glasses and rubs the bridge of his nose with his forefinger and thumb. 'I'm not entirely sure. We probably need to talk to your dad's lawyer. Let me sleep on it, and I'll try to figure something out.'

The next morning, I'm looking at Facebook on my elderly Mac. Yup, found the bitch. There she is, amongst Ben's friends. Kimberly Bliss. What kind of wanky, made-up name is that? I scroll through her profile: 1,798 photos of herself. Yeah, it figures.

I've decided to take matters into my own hands as I think Kimbo needs a little push, and I just know that Andy won't countenance such a thing. He'll probably start talking about witness intimidation or something. I am hoping to find out where I may be able to confront her. Luckily for me she is one of those self-centred twats who assumes that everybody is going to be fascinated by the minutiae of her daily activity.

Yesterday, for example, she wrote, *Got up had a bath with Chanel stuff they always give me for free sooo nice to pamper myself for once I work so hard. Walked down the street and three men in a car wolf wistled!!! Day got even better when man from Pretty Polly said my leg's are the best hes seen for a long time. Ha ha long time. Like my leg's are long!!!!*

As I look at today's offering I realize the illiterate freak of nature is making it very easy for me.

Gr8 day so far 100 red rose's from secret admirer dellivere'd to my door!!!! Dont understand why I have so many secret admirer's???! Seeing agent @ Modz1 @ 3pm to pick up check then more pampering at Harvey Nix god I need it I work so hard!!! Meditation later its very important to look after you're brain :-)

Bingo. I know where Models 1 is, as it's Ben's agency too. In fact, I think that's where they met.

When I get out of the Tubc, Covent Garden station is packed with your usual annoying tourists who keep getting in the way. I try to remind myself that they're on holiday so they should be allowed to meander, but still find myself tutting, then saying very loudly to a group of French school kids who are clogging up the exit to the lift, 'That's not the best place to stand.' I'll be quite horrible when I'm an old lady.

It's very odd outside Models 1, as if one is in a parallel universe of beauty, where every single girl going in and out of the door is nearly a foot taller than the girls on the street. Some of them are quite exquisite, of course, but a lot of them just look weird, as though they belong to some kind of alien race. It's all bones, height and other things that look good in photos.

Even the weird-looking ones make me feel old, fat and ugly though. I snap myself out of it. This isn't about me, it's about Dad. I hadn't realized that I had a recording device on my phone, but having discovered it last night, I've switched it on and am standing in wait. Poppy would be proud of me, I think, as I recall our teenage private detective aspirations.

On the dot of three, I see her approaching the agency, talking into her iPhone.

'Well yeah, of course I've always been lucky with my legs! Oh babe, you're toooo kind. Yeah, I know I'm genetically blessed. But I do try and give things back too? I'm going to a charity thing tonight for L'Oréal?' She looks puzzled. 'What do you mean, what charity? I thought L'Oréal was the charity? Something to do with testing cosmetics on animals?'

I walk up to her, my trusty recording device peeking out of the front pocket of my denim jacket, and she looks even more puzzled for a few seconds. Then recognition dawns.

'You!' she shouts. 'Get away from me; I haven't got time for this. Don't you know who I am?!' A crowd is starting to gather.

'Isn't that Kimberly Bliss?' says one starstruck schoolboy.

'Oh, I think you might have some time for me once you've heard what I have to say. And I certainly know who you are, Ms Lehman. Or should I call you Hilda?'

Kimberly's mouth falls open, making her look even stupider.

'I don't know what you're talking about.'

'Oh I think you do, *Hilda*.'

'What's going on? Why's that weird woman calling her Hilda?' asks the starstruck schoolboy.

Kimbo drags me into a side street and says, 'What do you want, Becca?'

'My name's Bella. And I want to know why you're so determined to ruin my father's life.'

A really nasty, hard look crosses her pretty little face.

'Stupid old git should have stuck to his side of the bargain. Does he really think I enjoyed sleeping with him? He's disgusting. Old, and flabby, and grey. I'm so sick of these lechy old blokes, they make my skin crawl.' She gives an exaggerated shudder and I want to kill her. 'I really needed that Italian *Vogue* cover too.'

I look at her with absolute distaste.

'You really are vile. Has it ever occurred to you that one day you will be old, and flabby, and grey, too?' Kimberly looks terribly put out, as if she thinks she has the elixir of eternal youth or something. 'Dad would never have gone for you if you hadn't given him so much encouragement. I saw you in the herb garden in Ibiza. I also know about what you did back in Perth in the hardware store, *Hilda*, so you might as well tell me. You thought you'd teach him a lesson, right, just as you thought you'd teach your store manager a lesson?' Take the bait, bitch, take the bait.

'Yeah, I did. I thought I'd teach them both a lesson.' A self-satisfied smile crosses her conceited, dim-witted face. 'I don't screw fucking granddads unless there's something in it for me.' Bullseye. Straight from the horse's mouth.

'You fucking moronic cow,' I say slowly. 'How many models do you think my father has met over the years? Really? How many? What do you think makes you so bloody special? He's always said he hates ginger minges anyway.' It's not true, but I want to protect Dad. 'He actually tried to get you the cover of Italian *Vogue*, but they told him they were used to classier birds than you. I *think* I know where they're coming from . . .'

'You fucking bitch!' Kimbo tries to grab my hair but I skip lightly out of her way.

'Nope. I think you'll find that you're the fucking bitch.'

'I'll get my lawyer on you for harassment.'

'Oh I don't think you will.' I take my trusty recording device out of my jacket pocket and start playing her own voice back to her. I will always treasure the look on her stupid, smug little face.

'I think it's about time you withdrew your ludicrous allegations. Don't you?'

'Belles,' says Max as I answer my phone. 'You'll never guess what's happened!'

Try me, I think.

'Kimbo's withdrawn all her allegations against Dad! It's bloody amazing!'

'Ah – well. I think I might have had something to do with that.'

'What are you on about, sis?'

So I tell him.

'Not just a pretty face then,' he says eventually, laughing. 'Bloody hell, that's brilliant. I wish I'd been there.'

'You can listen to the recording. And if you want a real laugh, go and check out her Facebook page. But not a word to Dad, please. Promise?'

'Of course I promise. I can't believe she's so stupid she actually admitted it!'

'I know. Like candy from a baby. She's so used to mass adulation that she probably considers herself untouchable, stupid bitch. I hardly even needed my knowledge of her past.'

'Just brilliant,' says Max again. 'Ooh, before I forget, Dad wants to take us and Andy out to lunch at the Pont de la Tour tomorrow to celebrate. Suit you?'

Suits me down to the ground.

Our table's starched linen, gleaming glassware and shining silver has long since given way to creased napkins, crumbs and a cheery throng of bottles, despite the best attentions of the excellent waiting staff. As it's another perfect day, we're lunching on the terrace, with its spectacular views of Tower Bridge. The restaurant is packed, mainly with tourists taking advantage of the weak pound, though I spot several clearly illicit canoodling couples and several bailed-out-by-the-taxpayer bankers on expenses. Bastards.

'That was delicious,' says my mother, patting her mouth with her napkin. 'Thank you, Justin.'

'Yes, thanks Dad,' I say. 'Mine was really yummy.' My sea bass was heavenly, but it's the company that's made lunch today, as, giddy with relief, Mum, Dad, Bernie, Max, Andy and I have laughed and bantered our way through three courses and six bottles. I can't remember the last time I shared a meal with my parents and Max, and it's lovely how well we all still get on. Great that Bernie fits in so well. Lovelier still that . . . *Don't even think it.*

'I still find it incredible that any sister could do that. *Twice.*' Mum, who flirted with bra burning in the Seventies (a mistake with her large bust), drains her glass. 'Apart from anything else, it totally undermines the plight of genuine victims.'

'Quite,' says Andy, pouring himself another glass of Shiraz. I am reminded of his horrible story about the Albanian girl and feel slightly sick.

'Tell me again what David Simpson said?' Max asks Dad, who is wearing Bono shades, a billowing peasant smock, tight black jeans and cowboy boots.

'*Hilda*'s just dropped the charges altogether.' Dad chortles, highly amused by this detail. It seems unkind to remind him that he was once called Bert. 'What a stroke of luck. Even though you found out about her past, Andy – and I can't thank you enough, son, David said we couldn't have brought that up in court anyway.'

'Yes, a real stroke of luck,' says Bernie, looking at the three of us beadily.

'She's getting off bloody lightly, considering she could have ruined your life,' I say, swiftly changing the subject.

'You know what, angel face? I don't want the chick locked up. I just want to put the whole mess behind me. I would like to know why she did it, though.' Dad's eyes are sad, the vertical lines on his face deeper than ever.

'Come on, Dad, we've been through this. She's clearly a total basket case.'

'Yeah kiddo, you're probably right. Anyone for coffees? Brandies?'

Brandy in the middle of a weekday is a little decadent, even by my family's standards, but fuck it, we're celebrating. Six espressos, three Armagnacs, a Cointreau, a Grand Marnier and a Calvados are duly ordered. The Americans at the next table look suitably horrified. Yup, we're the 'alcoholic Brits' you've heard so much about.

'How's preparation for your exhibition coming along, darling?' asks Mum. 'It's next Saturday, isn't it? *So* exciting.'

'Yes, really exciting, but bloody terrifying too. I've just about finished all the work, but Alison is determined to make the party a great big poncy art world launch. The art world scares me shitless.' I remember being at Goldsmiths, ploughing on with my painting, while all the people around me were marinating sheep's hearts in absinthe and sneering at my 'chocolate box conformity'. There was nothing remotely chocolate boxy about my work, as far as I was concerned, but the words still stung.

'Don't be silly, sis,' says Max. 'At least you can actually paint. Which is more than you can say for half the bunch of blaggers currently out there. It's going to be great. Tell you what, if you sell more than twenty per cent on the opening night, I'll open the pool at DC for an after-party.'

'Oh wow! OK, it's a deal.' I lean across the table to shake on it, catching Andy's eye in the process. All these meaningful looks are having a disturbing effect on my equilibrium. Disturbing yet addictive.

'You're all coming to the opening night, aren't you?' I ask around the table.

'Wouldn't miss it for the world, love,' says Bernie. 'Haven't you got a clever daughter, Princess?' He lands Mum a big smacker on her cheek.

'Both my babies are brilliant,' she beams. I try not to look at Max.

'Alison's assistant, Jessie, who is very Shoreditch, has

come up with some hilarious ideas for the party, which have absolutely nothing to do with my paintings,' I say. 'Dwarfs with platters heaped with talcum powder on their heads, for instance.'

'What on earth for?' asks Mum, furrowing her brow. Dad laughs and pats her on the head, patronizingly.

'It's the old story about Freddie Mercury's legendary party where dwarfs had platters of coke strapped to their heads, surely?' says Andy. 'I always thought that was apocryphal.'

'No, that's true, all right,' says Dad, who's been dying to put his oar in. 'I was there.' Suddenly the vertical lines on his face are verging on horizontal. 'If I remember correctly I took Marie Helvin. Now *she* was one saucy bit of crumpet.' I wince. Will he never learn?

'Never!' says Bernie. 'I was security that night. Those were the days.' He slaps Dad on the back, laughing hoarsely. 'What a night, me old china. Remember the hookers? Most beautiful girls I've ever seen, present company excepted, of course Princess, and they turned out to be geezer girls . . .'

As we listen in amused disbelief to their scandalous reminiscences, Max and I both look at Andy, shrugging and raising our eyebrows, as if to say: 'Shucks, parents. What can you do, huh?'

'Anyway, it's a dreadful idea for your opening night,' says Max. 'Can you imagine your guests' disappointment once they discovered it was talcum powder? You'd have a riot on your hands.'

'I know. Jessie also suggested Balkan violinists on roller skates, which would have been fun too, but . . .'

We finish our coffees and brandies and walk down to Butler's Wharf. Bernie's part-time chauffeur/hired thug is taking the oldies back to the country, which is just as well as none of them is in a fit state to drive. Dad hugs me, Max and Andy in turn.

'If you ever need anything, son – anything . . .' he is slurring sentimentally into Andy's shoulder.

'Thanks sir, I'll bear it in mind,' says Andy, giving him a brief hug back and shaking his hand. God, what must he make of us all?

Eventually we wave them off and start making our way back towards Southwark.

'Oooh, now we're here, I'd love to pick up some *jamón ibérico* from Borough Market,' I say, aglow with afternoon sunshine and Cointreau. 'Do you know it, Andy? It's the best ham in the whole world.'

'It is mouthwatering,' agrees Max. 'And I wish I could come with you. But I'm afraid I've a very dull meeting with my accountant, in . . .' He looks at his watch. '. . . Shit, less than half an hour. I've really got to run. Great lunch. Thanks again, Andy. See you at Belle's exhibition? Byeeee!' And long legs flying, golden curls bouncing, he runs off towards London Bridge station.

'Well, I'm heading to Waterloo, and Borough Market is almost en route, so I don't see how I could possibly not stop for *the best ham in the whole world*,' says Andy, making fun of me.

'You're not in a hurry to get back to work then?' Please say you're not.

'It's four o'clock, Bella. I took the precaution of taking the afternoon off. I didn't think your father would let me get away with a sandwich and a can of Coke.'

It's much cooler in the shade of the market. Blinking in the comparative darkness, we are faced with stall upon stall of artisan breads, robust charcuterie, rainbow-hued fruit and veg; cheeses that are pungent, mild, crumbly, creamy, snowy white to tangerine and every shade of yellow in between; wobbly custard tarts, delicate millefeuilles, stodgy stollen, cutesy cupcakes; aromatic hog roasts, curries, tagines, goulashes, cassoulets, stir-fries, paellas.

The paellas signify our arrival at the Spanish stall, Brindisa, purveyor of most excellent ham.

'It's sooo good, honestly,' I tell Andy. 'It's made from black-hoofed pigs fed on acorns and it's just completely delicious.' He laughs at my eagerness, but I'm trying to deflect attention from the fact that it seems such a couply thing to do, checking out the goodies at Borough Market. The woman in charge of the stall cuts off a couple of slices for us to try. The sweet, salty, unctuous meat melts onto my tongue.

'You know what?' says Andy, looking into my eyes. 'I think that really is the best ham in the *whole wide world*!'

I laugh back at him, taking care not to touch him, my heart going so fast I'm surprised it hasn't burst right out of my chest by now.

We amble along the South Bank in the heat, picking from the packet of ham, even though we've just eaten; it really is too good to resist. Just like Andy, I think, glancing up at him.

'Your parents are great,' he says, helping himself to another oily slice.

'I'm glad you think so. They can be a bit of a pain at times, but I love them to bits really.'

'Yes, it's obvious. That bond between you all is a lovely thing to see.' I can hardly bear to think of his loneliness, as an only child, after both his parents died so suddenly.

Leafy plane trees line the path. Across the water sits St Paul's: grandly, classically, unfeasibly beautiful. I can still never get over the fact that people managed to build domes like that in those days. In the distance we can just make out the Houses of Parliament and Big Ben, glinting in the sinking sun. I love the view from this side of the river. The Thames rolls by. An enormous variety of boats, from ferries to pleasure cruisers to permanently moored pubs to police craft to kayaks to dinghies, crowds the glittering taupe water. A lone, flower-painted barge that has clearly drifted from one of the canals looks as if it is in trouble the other side of the river, which might explain the police boat.

As I point it out to Andy, one of the thousands of tourists cluttering up my wonderful city jostles me. I stumble right into Andy's chest. He puts his arms out to steady me and before I know what's happening, he is kissing me. I want it to go on forever.

'Christ.' He pulls away, still looking me in the eyes, then drags me away from the crowds, into one of the little winding side streets round the back of the Globe. He takes off his glasses, which have steamed up (I didn't realize that really happened), and wipes them on his T-shirt. Then he replaces them, catches sight of a bench, and drags me after him to sit down. I'm finding all this masterful dragging really quite exciting. Once we're both seated, he turns to look at me again. He is holding both my hands.

'Bella, I shouldn't have done that. I've wanted to for weeks now, I've got some kind of crazy – I don't know – *crush* on you . . .'

'Oh, it's not a crush, I feel the same, I—' Andy cuts me off.

'But it's got to stop. You must realize that? This can't go any further. Whatever this madness is that's taken hold of us is not real and *it's got to stop*!' He's shouting now. I nod numbly.

'I'm getting married to Alison in three weeks' time. We've been together *thirteen years*, Bella. I couldn't do anything to hurt her, really I couldn't. She's set her heart on this wedding and it would kill her if I pulled out now.'

Pulled out? Andy visibly shakes himself.

'But of course I wouldn't pull out anyway. Al and I have been through a lot together; we see eye to eye, we're two of a kind.' *Oh no you're not.* 'You and I must forget that this has ever happened. Please, Bella? I'm sorry I kissed you, it was very, very wrong of me.' He looks almost as distraught as I feel.

And all of a sudden that image of Poppy looking over her bare shoulder at me as she fucks my boyfriend forces its way into my mind. What the fuck do I think I'm doing? I, just as much as anyone, know the hell of being cheated on, and I was only with Ben for a couple of months, for Christ's sake. What kind of evil bitch am I, intruding on a thirteen-year relationship? A thirteen-year, *about-to-be-married* relationship?

I realize he is still clasping my hands and gently extricate myself.

'You're right.' I force myself to smile. 'What on earth were we thinking? I blame the brandies! And the sunshine! And bloody Dad for making me so grateful to you!' I'm trying not to cry now. 'We'll forget this ever happened, and I promise you my lips are sealed. If you don't want to come to my exhibition, I understand, so . . .' I falter, then pull myself together brightly. '. . . So I guess I'll see you at the wedding. Best of luck, Andy.' I consider kissing him on the cheek but think better of it.

It's only once I get home that the tears come properly.

Chapter 20

It's the night of my launch party and the weather has finally broken. After such a long, hot summer, the torrential rain has been welcomed by practically everyone in the desiccated land. Everyone except me. I gaze out at the sheets of water splashing down onto the slate grey streets with such vehemence they splash straight back up again.

'Nobody's going to come, are they? This sodding weather's going to keep them all away.'

'Don't worry, Bella. *Everyone*'s coming,' says Ali, pouring me a glass of champagne. 'I've hyped it up to be *the* party of the summer. No self-respecting hell-raiser is going to be put off by a little bit of rain.'

'Little bit?' I laugh, gesturing out of the floor-to-ceiling windows, through which the storm looks admittedly impressive.

'OK, perhaps more than a little bit. But honestly, try not to worry. It's going to be great. The last half-hour before-hand is always the worst.'

Ali's wearing a navy blue and white spotted Diane Von Furstenberg wrap dress that makes her look about a stone slimmer. She went to the hairdresser this morning and her hair falls in silky blonde waves to her shoulders. She looks lovely, and I think I might love her. But I am terrified.

To calm my nerves, I pace through to the gallery's back office and check my appearance for the twenty-fifth time in twenty-five minutes. In deference to the weather, I'm wearing black skinny jeans (yes, I know) and a vintage oversized Clash T-shirt which I've slashed at the neck so it falls off one shoulder. A wide patent leather belt the exact shade of Chanel Rouge Noir nips the T-shirt in at the waist and I'm teetering, as ever, on platform strappy sandals. Apart from the shoes, it's a pretty radical departure from my usual carefree summer style, but tonight I need a coat of armour against the jeers of the art world's coolmeisters.

Perhaps I'm also in a kind of mourning. Oh, that's probably too fanciful, but toughening up my image has been a conscious way of distancing myself from Andy, should he turn up. *Look, I'm Bella the edgy Shoreditch artist. What would I need with a conventional nine-to-fiver like you? OK, so investigative journalism isn't exactly nine-to-five, but . . . SHUT UP!* The only way I've been able to deal with my sadness over Andy is to block it out completely, compartmentalizing like men do. I did enough wallowing over Ben to realize that it doesn't help in the slightest, and were I to dwell on it, this pain would be far greater than anything the spineless lothario could cause. So consciously, deliberately, I put Andy out of my head (again), and turn my thoughts to my big night.

Ali has been working round the clock to promote the exhibition and I've watched in awe as she's set the cogs of the publicity wheel in motion. Journalists, art critics, rock stars, food critics, models, theatre critics, billionaire entrepreneurs, film critics, nightclub impresarios, a ghastly Geldof or two – she knows them all and nobody has been exempt from her relentless storm of upbeat endorsement. Who'd have thought mousy little Alison would have a contacts book to rival Jade Jagger's? (Oh yes, she's been invited too.)

The caterers Jessie hired wanted a themed opening, 'conceptually Palestine meets Judy Garland meets Jack the Ripper Whitechapel, with the emphasis on Gaza', but Ali vetoed it. Instead, and sadly *sans* dwarfs with coke on their heads, we've gone for England, forever England, which reflects my work to an extent and means we can have yummy miniature Yorkshire puddings topped with slivers of rare roast beef, fish and chips in little newspaper cones, tiny spoonfuls of chicken tikka masala et al. We were told by the caterers that this was 'very ten years ago', but as Ali said, with the speed with which out-of-date becomes retro fashionable, we're way ahead of the game. The waitresses are wearing Vivienne Westwood-influenced tweed bustiers with mini Union Jack bustles and a Thirties-styled band in evening dress has just started tuning up. They'll be playing things like 'A Nightingale Sang in Berkeley Square'.

I walk back out into the main space of the gallery. Its vast geometric whiteness makes a striking contrast to the tempestuous scene outside. And my splashily colourful oils create another cheery dimension of contrast. Ali, true to her word, has grouped the views from my balcony on the wall previously occupied by the famous New Yoiker, the one directly to your right as you enter the gallery. There are fifteen of them, each strikingly different to the last, from the warm purples and lilacs of late summer dusk to the bright lemons and limes of a spring dawn, via a clearly autumnal piece vibrant with vermillion and terracotta. If you look closely, it's the differences in detail – the flower seller packing up for the day, the blokes fighting outside the pub, the pregnant woman buying the *Big Issue* – that are more interesting than the seasonal variety, decorative as this makes the overall rainbow effect. Well, I hope so anyway.

Ali has deemed almost as many other works from my portfolio worthy of exhibition too: a portrait of my mother in her garden that I painted a couple of years ago; a detailed close-up of an Arum lily, dot-dot-dotted with pollen; some Japanese-inspired line drawings of Routemaster buses and London cabs that I was terribly pleased with at the time. It's overwhelming, really, being surrounded by my work. *I did all this! I haven't just been wasting my life ricocheting from pub to party to beach and back again! I am an artist!*

I turn to Ali with a huge grin on my face.

'Thank you.'

'So, Ms Brown, or may I call you Bella?' starts the food critic from the *Evening Standard*. 'How can you explain a mere art exhibition becoming the Most Talked About Party of the Season? There are more luminaries here than there were at the Serpentine summer party.'

'I don't know . . . I – well, I can't really.' I start laughing. 'And can you explain why I'm being interviewed by a food critic?'

'Our gossip columnist is having an affair and is *in flagrante* as we speak,' the food critic confides. He is plump and smiley and reminds me a bit of Ronnie Corbett. 'Shit, that was stupid of me. Please don't let on.'

'Mum's the word. So – what do you make of it?' I gesture round at the gallery, which has filled up with people in the last hour to the extent that Ali is now operating a one-in-one-out policy at the door. Every other face is recognizable from *Hello!* magazine.

'Honestly? Half these people would turn up to the opening of an envelope, but I like your paintings very much. They're easy on the eye and interesting. A bit like you, in fact.'

'Thanks,' I beam, loving the little fellow.

'Bella! That bloody woman wouldn't let us in until two others had gone and she *knows* I'm your best friend.' Poppy races through the crowds towards me, arms outstretched for a hug, and I hide a smile. Ali doesn't have much time for Poppy after her recent behaviour, while Poppy's pretty little nose has been put well out of joint by my having another best friend. I let her hug me. She looks adorable in an Inspector Clouseau rain hat and stone-coloured mini trench coat with bare brown legs and black patent ballet pumps.

'How are you?' I ask. 'Are you allowed to have a drink?' She's been in a hideously expensive drying-out place for the last couple of weeks, with no contact with the outside world.

'Does the Pope shit in the woods?' She grins and grabs a Black Velvet off a passing waitress. The food critic looks at me enquiringly. 'Sorry,' I tell him. 'But this is personal. Help yourself to everything you want and be nice about me please?'

'Rarely did one suggestion so perfectly follow the last.' He bows and heads off in search of more booze.

'Hello, Bella darling,' says Diana, who has followed Poppy through the crowds at a statelier pace. She looks very chic in a knee-length pale grey silk shift, pearls at her throat, her ash-blonde hair in an elegant chignon.

'Oh Diana, thank you so much for coming. I had no idea. Are you sure it's OK to leave Ken for the night?'

Diana smiles sadly.

'I'm afraid the time had come to listen to my daughter. I'm not the right person to look after him any more, and our home isn't properly equipped. He seems quite content in the home we've found him though, which is close enough for me to spend several hours a day with him. He doesn't even ask when he's coming home, which is what I was dreading. He seems to think that the home *is* home.'

'Oh Diana, that's a huge thing for you to have done, but I'm glad to hear Ken's happy where he is. I hope it's not too hideous a wrench for you.'

'Well, the house does seem vast and empty without him, so I'm selling up. I have to anyway, to pay the care fees, which are astronomical. But there's a little cottage around the corner I've got my eye on.' Diana smiles bravely and I give her a hug.

'Mum's been brilliant,' says Pops. 'You know it's the right thing to do, don't you Mum?'

'Yes darling, I do.' Diana smiles at her daughter and I thank God that Poppy is alive. How the poor woman would have coped with both tragedies is unthinkable.

Somebody throws a bear-like arm around me from behind, nearly knocking all the breath from my lungs. It can only be one person.

'Mark! Great to see you.' As I turn around I notice he is hand-in-hand with an incredibly pretty girl.

'This is Sammi-Jo.' He sounds almost bashful. Sammi-Jo holds out a tiny little hand. Her nails are very long and sugar pink.

'Hi. This is brilliant. You must be so excited,' she says in a husky voice, and I warm to her instantly. She is about the same size as Poppy, except for a vast pair of knockers, braless and barely contained in a cropped white vest top. Flagrantly disobeying the 'legs or tits' rule, her prettily shaped lower quarters are clad in tiny black hot pants, over-the-knee schoolgirl socks and stripper shoes. The expanse of young flesh on display (thighs, midriff, cleavage, arms) looks as if it's been dipped in caramel.

'Sorry about the get-up,' she says. 'But we've come

straight from a shoot. You did say it would be all right, Mark?' They are still holding hands.

'You look gorgeous,' I say. Her face is young and sweet, with huge brown eyes and full lips under the heavy make-up. Her waist-length straightened hair is dyed dark red.

'So you've been shooting for *Stadium*?' asks Poppy.

'Yeah, bit of a step up from *Nuts*. *Nuts* pays better, of course, but they keep trying to put me in a mortar board, which frankly looks a bit stupid when you've got your tits out.'

'Sammi-Jo is studying philosophy at London Uni,' says Mark proudly.

'Cool.' Poppy looks at her with new respect. 'Shall we all bugger off for a bit? Maybe get some canapés? I think Bella might have to mingle some more. Belles?'

'Thanks.' I'm dying to talk to all of them more, but she's right. I really need to focus on the punters.

'Great,' says Sammi-Jo. 'If I don't have something to eat soon I'll start biting my acrylic nails again. This is the third lot I've got through this month and my agent is starting to get *really* pissed off with me.' Mark laughs and kisses her full on the lips. Undeterred, she continues. 'They're tough buggers to bite through and I'll probably wreck my teeth too if I go on at this rate . . .' They wander off in the direction of the bar.

'Bella, I want to introduce you to Philip Henderson,' says Ali, gesturing to the very distinguished-looking gentleman at her side. Tall and slim, sporting well-cut grey hair and an equally well-cut grey suit, Philip Henderson, who's probably around fifty, exudes expensive charm. You can just tell that his shoes are hand-made.

'Delighted,' he says. 'And may I congratulate you on a first-class body of work?'

'Thanks.' I'm not sure what else to say; I can hardly start

307

asking him to put his money where his mouth is. As it happens I don't have to, as Ali butts in, 'Philip is interested in buying your line drawings of the buses and taxis.' A sale? Yippee! I try to stay cool but am probably betrayed by the huge grin on my face.

'They're quite beautiful,' says Philip. 'And very clever to use the Japanese medium to depict something so quintessentially London.'

'Well, that's what I thought at the time, but then I started wondering if it's not a bit . . .' Ali silences me with a look. Christ I'm stupid. 'That's the general idea,' she says firmly, as I wonder, insanely, if I could write a Cockney haiku to go with them.

'So which ones do you want?' I ask.

'All of them.' He produces a Coutts chequebook and says, 'I think I'd better snap them up before anybody else does. I'm assuming a cheque's OK?'

Ali is rushing around with red stickers, giving me a discreet thumbs-up, when I spot Andy and Alison through the crowds. Alison is looking sickeningly elegant in a short and sleeveless teal silk shirt dress cinched at the waist with a tan leather belt, which makes the most of her slim figure and shows off her thoroughbred legs. Flat tan sandals and an oversized man's watch add a touch of nonchalant chic to the ensemble, and make me feel like a scruffy schoolgirl in my Shoreditch artist fancy dress.

'Alison!' shouts Philip, spotting her and surprising me. 'What are you doing here?'

'Oh, my bridesmaid owns the gallery,' she says, proffering her cheek for a kiss. Bitch. 'And Bella's our best man's sister.' Yup, *my* exhibition is all about *your* wedding.

'Hello Andy,' Philip nods at him. Andy nods back, and seeing my look of confusion says, 'Philip is a senior partner at Alison's firm. Hi Bella.'

'Oh right. Hi Andy.'

God it's horrible, standing here giving each other such curt greetings, when all I want is to hurl myself into his arms. The feelings haven't gone away one bit.

'And I've just bought these sensational drawings,' says Philip, indicating them. 'Aren't they beautiful?'

This is just too excruciating.

'How's the wedding planning coming along, Alison?' I ask, as if I don't dream every night about fucking her fiancé. She puts a skinny arm around Andy's waist and smirks.

'Oh, it's going to be quite wonderful. We had a few hitches to begin with but now everything's going like clockwork, isn't it darling?' She kisses his cheek and I want to kill her. 'They might even want to do a spread on it in *Harpers*.'

To his credit, Andy also looks as if he wants to die.

'Well, that's great. I'm really looking forward to the big day,' I say, wondering if my nose has grown a foot. 'But do you mind if Philip and I just complete this deal?'

Very coolly done. Pat on the back for me.

Flushed with the success of my first sale, I put Andy and Alison firmly out of my mind (again) and work the room like a pro. Success breeds success, and soon the Arum lilies have been snapped up, while Bernie buys the portrait of my mother.

'Almost as beautiful as the real thing,' he says, stroking Mum's face as if he still can't quite believe his luck. It's really rather sweet, this elderly love thing. Mum is endearingly thrilled for me and my nascent achievement. Although she wouldn't let on in a million years, it's been painfully obvious to me that since adulthood Max has been the success story of the family, while I've stumbled along, having a bloody good time but not really impressing anybody in the process.

The importance of this exhibition – in changing, well, my whole life really – cannot be overemphasized but as yet nobody has wanted to buy any of the views from my window. It suddenly strikes me why: when grouped together like this they are so stunning that individually they don't quite match up to the sum of their parts, and these days not many people have the cash to shell out for fifteen paintings in one go. For the first time, I start to question Ali's judgement.

I'm desperate for a pee now so head towards the loo in the private, 'Staff Only' bit of the gallery. There are two cubicles, and I selfishly go for the disabled one, as there is more space and a mirror in there. None of the staff is in a wheelchair anyway. Just as I'm pulling my excruciatingly tight jeans back up, I hear a lilting Welsh voice.

'Poppy, what the fuck do you think you're doing?'

'I'm sorry, but I had to get to talk to you in private.' Poppy sounds sincere, and a little breathless. 'This is Bella's big night, and I don't want to take any of the attention away from her.'

Awww, bless you Pops, I think.

'So you drag me into the toilet? If you're so worried about upstaging Bella, who has been such a wonderful friend to you (which is more than I can say for you), why didn't you do this another night, then? You know where Simon lives, where I live now. *We* used to live just around the corner, *together*, remember?' His voice drips sarcasm.

Actually, Damian's right. She didn't have to do this tonight, fucking little attention-seeker. Grrr.

'Oh God, Damian, if you only knew how many times I've been round to see you in Hoxton and bottled it at the last minute . . .'

Bottled it? Damian seems to share my scepticism as he says,

'Come off it, you've never bottled anything in your life.'

'I've never hated myself in my life before now,' she says simply. 'There was no reason to bottle anything. But every time I got to Si's place, everything I'd planned to say to you sounded so empty and hollow in my head. I've been such a bitch, and hurt my two favourite people so badly . . .'

'Bella seems to be forgiving you.' Damian's voice is softening slightly.

'Bella's a saint.'

Yay. I'm starting to enjoy this, utterly transfixed, even though I know I shouldn't be eavesdropping. But I can hardly walk out and reveal myself now.

'Yeah she is,' says Damian. 'So what do you want?' His voice is harsh again.

'I just want to tell you how sorry I am, and I wondered . . .' Her voice breaks. 'No, I'm being stupid. I'm a contempt-ible cunt . . .'

Get some new vocab, Poppy.

'You wondered what?'

'I wondered if there was any way you might consider us trying to make a go of it again?'

Damian laughs bitterly. 'I don't think you quite under-stand what you put me through. What was it about Ben? Was he a better fuck than me? I know he's got a bigger cock than me, I remember from the showers at school.'

'Oh babe, no no no, none of that,' she says, her voice breaking again. 'Nobody's ever been better than you.'

Carly Simon singing 'Nobody Does It Better' comes into my head and I bite my lip to stop myself giggling. Or worse, singing it out loud. That would surprise them both.

'SO WHY THE FUCK DID YOU LEAVE ME FOR HIM?'

311

'Well, our hands were kind of forced. I don't know what would have happened if Bella hadn't walked in on us . . .' she starts. 'Don't look at me like that. I was off my fucking tits, Damian, out of my mind with grief. With Alzheimer's the grief starts a long time before the person you love actually dies, *you know that*. But you and I were together for five years – FIVE YEARS, my love. Once I was living with Ben I realized what a horrific mistake I'd made. He's such a selfish, arrogant fucker. He never came with me to see Dad, and you were always so supportive, you couldn't have been kinder. Ben couldn't even be arsed to shag me, once I was just another conquest.'

I suspect that this will sway Damian, as his hurt male pride was the only thing really getting in the way of any reconciliation. Sure enough, he says softly,

'But how can I ever trust you again?'

'Because I would never do anything to risk losing you again. You're the only man I've ever loved.' Damian is silent, and Poppy adds, 'I could ask you to marry me.'

What? OK Poppy, now you are stealing my fucking thunder.

'And I could say no . . . Jesus, Pops, what are you doing?' Damian starts laughing, and then says, 'I did think that looked like a flasher's mac.'

She's clearly got nothing on underneath. Now they stop talking and there are muffled giggles, moans and sounds of snogging. The door of the other cubicle slams shut and I wait until the coast is definitely clear before emerging stealthily from mine.

As theirs isn't a disabled loo, there is a gap between the bottom of the door and the floor, and I can see Poppy's raincoat lying by their feet next to the loo as I try to ignore their sex noises.

All of a sudden I am tempted to put my hand under and pinch the raincoat, just as the dwarf in Ibiza did with my dress. I'm slightly ashamed to admit that the only thing stopping me is the fact that, if I did, Poppy coming out into the gallery naked would *definitely* steal my thunder.

Good God. Randy and the dwarf in Ibiza. Is it really still the same summer? So much has happened since then, it seems several lifetimes ago. I tiptoe towards the mirror and shake my head upside down to muss my hair up, looking myself in the eye as I come up again. Now is not the time for reflection, Belles. It's your big night. I am actually extremely pleased about Poppy and Damian but now I need to go back and face my public.

Back in the gallery, I make my way towards Mum and Bernie. Somebody is making an entrance. The excited hubbub of chatter is hushed and people are turning to stare in the direction of a statuesque blonde.

'Blimey, that's Natalia Evanovitch,' says Bernie. He whispers in my ear, 'I knew her when she was a very expensive hooker, but don't tell your mother that.' He must be pissed out of his mind to offer such juicy info.

Natalia Evanovitch is certainly striking. Her white-blonde hair is pulled back into the kind of high ponytail that only those with impeccable Slavic bone structure can carry off. The very bone structure I envisaged Ben's ballerinas having. You could slice cheese on those cheekbones. Her slanty grey eyes survey the room coolly. She snaps her fingers and one of her minions appears at her side with a glass of champagne.

Part of the reason we are all gawping is that much of the Ukrainian goddess's six foot plus is swathed in a halterneck Pucci catsuit in eye-searing swirls of pink, purple and orange. She turns around to reveal a swooping low back with just a hint of buttock cleavage. She is dripping in what I assume are diamonds.

'So what does she do now?' I whisper back to Bernie.

'She invested her hooking money in property overseas and is now worth billions. Good on the girl, I say. She always did have plenty of spirit.' I rather wish he'd kept this to himself.

'Fere is artiste? I font to see artiste,' Natalia demands imperiously. I hurry over, aware of two hundred pairs of eyes watching.

'Hello, I'm Bella. Is everything OK?'

'OK? It is MAGNIFICENT! Dat fall! Dat fall dere . . .' She is pointing at the wall with the views from my balcony. 'Colors. I font!' I look at her catsuit again and twig. Clever Alison.

Once we're nearer the wall, she says quietly, in a slightly Americanized accent, 'Sorry for the dramatics. I find they help keep the reputation mystique. And I DO lof the paintings. All of them. Color is my thing, you see.' Clever, clever Alison.

'Well, thank you.' Again I don't know what else to say. 'Ummm . . . we could probably give you a discount if you want all of them . . .'

'Do not be ridiculous. I haf money and I font to pay. Never undersell yourself. I learnt that from ferry young age.'

'OK,' I grin. 'You mean you . . . really . . . want to buy all the paintings on this wall?' It hadn't occurred to me that anyone would buy the whole bloody lot, so I quickly do the sums. Put it this way, I won't be going back to desktop publishing any time soon. Looks as if Alison was right, too, about pricing high.

'That's fot I mean, girl. I haf recently acquired small villa in Ibiza. I can see them there . . .' She waves her hands in the air. 'In my rainbow chill-out room.' It sounds pretty ghastly actually, but what do I know? I'm only the artist.

314

Alison appears at my elbow, all smiles, proffering her hand.

'Hi Natalia. I'm Alison, I own the gallery. I was on the phone to your people earlier in the week . . .'

'Ah Alison!' Natalia swoops on her like a long-lost friend, air-kissing manically to keep the patent lip gloss intact. 'Congratulations! You haf made big sale!'

Alison raises her eyebrows at me over Natalia's shoulder. *She wants all of them*, I mouth back. A huge smile crosses Alison's sweet round face. She composes herself and says to Natalia,

'Well, that's fantastic news. Of course, we'll have to keep them up for the duration of the exhibition – it wouldn't be much of an exhibition without them, after all . . .' Only the increasing pinkness in her cheeks betrays her excitement.

'Off course!' Natalia waves her hand in the air dismissively. 'And then maybe I commission more! I like idea off own personal artiste, like European Royal Court . . .' Seeing the shock on my and Alison's faces she lets out peals of throaty laughter. 'Or maybe I joke!'

'Ahhh ha ha ha ha ha! Well, I think we can complete this transaction in the back office, don't you? Why don't you take Natalia through, Bella, and I'll get a bottle of champagne?'

I am about to do as I'm told, when Natalia lets out a low whistle and breathes, 'Who is that beeeoootiful man?' I follow her gaze and cannot believe my eyes. It's Ben, looking quite the dandy artist in a purple velvet suit and floral shirt. The sheer, unbridled nerve of the man. What's more, he appears to be chatting up Sammi-Jo, who for some reason Mark has left on her own for a minute. Ooooh, I'm looking forward to this.

It all happens in slow motion. Mark gives a great roar

as he lumbers across the crowded gallery, clenching his fist, and drawing back his arm to— Too late. Someone has beaten him to it.

'Sorry mate,' says Damian to Mark, dusting his hands down on his trousers. 'But I think I had first dabs on the cunt. Feel free to give him a good kicking while he's down, though.' He looks down at his former best mate with absolute contempt.

'And that's better than you deserve. Go on, get up and get out. I can't imagine Bella welcomes you here.' Oh this really is too good to be true. 'And Poppy nearly *died* because of you, you snivelling little shit.' All the journos are scribbling furiously and I wonder if that wasn't a little too much information.

Ben staggers to his feet. His nose is bleeding all over his flowery shirt and he puts up his hands in surrender, like the miserable coward he is. As he backs towards the exit, the tanked-up crowd boos and jeers. One hundred and eighty.

The pool room at Divine Comedy is done up like a highly camp Roman baths, complete with fountains, statues, marble pillars. Twin mosaics of Bacchus and Priapus grin up at us from the bottom of the pool with heavy-handed symbolism. Max's 2:1 in Classics had to come in useful one day. A jungle of hothouse plants leads to the bar at the far end, which, in a contrast to the Roman theme, is what you might call Waikiki-chic, with sand underfoot, a bamboo bar, cocktails served in coconut shells and high stools upholstered in bright pink, turquoise and orange. The whole Caligula does Honolulu effect is so kitsch, with so little effort towards any semblance of good taste, that it somehow works.

The basement is packed with my friends, family and a whole raft of minor and not-so-minor celebrities. Much shrieking and splashing is coming from the pool, where, eager to show off their young bodies, a load of pissed-up rock progeny have stripped down to their underwear. The Health & Safety implications must be horrendous, which is probably why Max only opens his magnificent folly when it suits him.

The noisiest group is sharing a Jacuzzi in the far corner. My father, Jilly Templeton, Poppy, Damian and Natalia seem to be getting on like dachas on fire. I make my way over.

'Congratulations, darling!' shouts Jilly, raising her lurid green cocktail to me. It looks as if they're all starkers underneath the water. 'Didn't I tell you to get off your arse and stop moping? You should listen to your aunt Jill more often.'

'Hasn't my girl done well?' says my father. 'I couldn't be a prouder old dad.' I crouch down and kiss the top of his grey head. I'm still feeling awfully protective over him after Kimberly's horrible words.

'Well, that's all thanks to Natalia.' I raise my glass to her.

'Nonsense! That is all thanks to you and your colors.' She raises her glass back at me, smiling her feline smile.

'Anyway the highlight of the night was when Damian punched Ben. In fact, it might have been the highlight of my life.'

I sit down on the edge of the Jacuzzi and dangle my feet in beside Poppy.

'And a little bird told me you and Damian have got some big news,' I say teasingly.

'Wha . . .? But how . . .? I wasn't going to tell you until after your exhibition . . . You don't mind, do you, Belles?' Poppy's pretty brow is knotted with anxiety.

'Actually, I think it's fab news. Congratulations, both of you.'

317

'Well, it makes perfect sense,' says Damian, who is wearing Poppy's Inspector Clouseau rain hat and has one arm around her shoulders. 'If she doesn't mend her wicked ways I'll be entitled to half her earnings.'

Poppy sticks her tongue out at him. 'Poo to you.'

'What are you, eight?'

'I've learnt my lesson. There's only one man for me.' She gives him a big soppy kiss.

'I'd better go and mingle a bit more,' I say with a touch of regret. 'Congrats again.'

En route to the bar, I pass Sammi-Jo on a lounger, wringing her hair out. As she wasn't wearing any underwear, she leapt into the pool in her shorts and crop top, which is now completely transparent. Mascara is running down her face.

'I must look a right state,' she laughs up at me.

'Alice Cooper springs to mind.' I sit down next to her. 'But I happen to know that Max caters for such eventualities.' I reach into the drawer of the marble-topped table next to the lounger and produce a pack of eye-make-up-remover wipes. It's this kind of attention to detail that has made my brother so successful.

'That's just so cool. Thanks,' she says in her husky voice. 'You must be so pleased with how everything went tonight.' There's something appealingly open and positive about Mark's new squeeze and I feel a sudden surge of affection for them both.

'That's putting it mildly.' We both look over at the pool, where Mark is showing off, flexing his muscles as he prepares to dive in.

'Isn't he gorgeous?' sighs Sammi-Jo. 'I just thought phwoargh as soon as I saw him.'

'I'm pretty sure the feeling was mutual,' I laugh. Without the make-up, she is even prettier, and very young looking apart from the bust. Mark must be unable to believe his luck, dirty bugger.

'Well, Sammi-Jo—'

'Oh Sam, please. My agent insisted on Sammi-Jo – I was christened Samantha Josephine – but all my mates call me Sam.'

'I prefer Sam too.' I smile at her. 'I'm going to the bar for a top-up. Do you want to come with me or are you happy here on your own?'

'I could sit here and watch Mark for days, but thanks for asking me. You're nice.'

'Bella! Congratulations darling, it's gone like a dream!'

Simon, resplendent in trunks that look as if they date from 1950s Hollywood – high waisted and belted, in a lurid green and yellow check – is standing at the bar with his arms outstretched in greeting.

'Thanks darling,' I say, trying not to laugh. 'I'm assuming the shorts are vintage?'

'Of course,' he says. I'm not particularly bothered by the unsavoury implications. 'I was considering giving a striped Twenties all-in-one a go, but I feared folk might not get it. People can be *so* unadventurous when it comes to fashion.' He sniffs and I laugh.

'Anyway sweetheart, I have a proposition for you,' he says. 'Can I get you a drink first?'

'Yes please. I'll have another one of whatever these are,' I say to Ellie with the eye-patch.

Simon hands over some cash and we sit down on a couple of orange upholstered bar stools.

'So what's this proposition?' I ask, intrigued now.

'Weeelll,' Simon drawls, drawing it out. 'Seeing as you're now an acclaimed artiste . . .'

'Oh come on, hardly,' I say, embarrassed.

'Take it from me, darling, I know how these things work,'

says Simon. 'You'll get rave reviews and soon you'll be a household name among the chattering classes.'

'Really?' I ask, excited but scared. 'I'm not sure I could handle that . . .'

'Don't be wet, sweetheart,' Simon drawls. He's right.

'OK, I won't,' I laugh. 'So what's your proposition?'

'How would you like to earn some regular dosh as *Stadium*'s in-house illustrator? It would probably only be about a day's work a week, or a week a month at the most, as we mainly use *very high-end* photos, of course . . .' I nod, thinking about the endless glossy nudes created by people like my father and Mark. '. . . so you'd still have plenty of time for your painting.'

I am silent, trying to take it all in. Simon clearly takes my silence as a bargaining tool and says,

'Now you're a household name, of course, we'll be able to pay you a far higher rate than we did before. And you can work from home, so you won't have to run the gamut of the fashion department.'

I start to smile, thinking how easily things fall into your lap once you've had a bit of success. I enjoyed doing the illustrations before and decide to put him out of his misery.

'Thanks Si, I'd love to.'

An hour or so later, Max and Dave are propping up the bar. They are holding hands and looking very happy. Alison and Charlie are sitting next to them, laughing and joking about something. They all seem quite pissed and very jolly indeed.

'Here she comes! The art world's Next Big Thing!' cries Max as I approach. They give me a little round of applause and I feel all warm and pleased with myself, and, frankly, invincible.

'I couldn't have done any of it without Ali,' I say, raising my glass and smiling at her. She smiles back, eyes glittering, cheeks more flushed than ever.

'Hear hear!' hollers Charlie. He gives her a big squeeze. 'Well done old thing.'

She kisses him and says, 'Thanks, old thing yourself.'

'To Ali!'

'To Ali!' We all shout.

Alison starts a new toast, raising her glass in my direction:

'To Bella and her beautiful paintings! To Belle's colours!'

'To Belle's colours!'

'I think we can safely say we work well together,' says Ali, putting down her drink briefly to give me a hug. I hug her back. She is soft and warm and comfortable.

'To continued success!'

'Continued success!'

And the drink and mutual congratulations flow on.

Chapter 21

I'm lying in the hammock in the shade of the old apple tree at the bottom of Mum's garden. The rain lasted for three days, cleansing and moisturizing the land, and now the countryside sparkles with freshness in the soft September sun. I'm very comfortable in my old summer pyjama shorts and vest, sipping a long glass of Mum's delicious homemade lemonade infused with mint. She normally pours in a slosh of vodka, but I don't want to drink booze right now.

Andy's copy of *Scoop* lies open on the grass. Tomorrow he and Alison are getting married, and I just can't concentrate. I'm forcing myself to go to the wedding, though couldn't muster my usual enthusiasm when it came to choosing an outfit. What's the bloody point? I'm hardly likely to meet the man of my dreams when he's the one up the aisle, and nobody could possibly compare.

Getting some kind of closure, I reckon, is vital. Once I've seen him pledge to love and cherish her, till death them do part, I'll be able to get on with my life with no more pathetic hankerings. I'm going straight from the wedding to Stansted Airport, where I've a seat booked on the clubbers' EasyJet to Ibiza, which lands at midnight.

There I'll be joining Poppy, Damian, my father and Jilly, all of whom Natalia invited to her 'small villa' for a couple of weeks to coincide with the closing parties.

'You should see the place, it's fucking wicked,' Poppy whispered over the phone to me yesterday. Our friendship is slowly getting back to how it used to be, although I'm still a little wary. 'Three pools, one with an island with a bar on it. A recording studio. Full DJ decks outside. Moroccan outdoor chill-out areas. Oh and Belles, you should *really* see the rainbow chill-out room she wants to put your paintings in! It's amazing!' I wonder if her work people know that this is how she's spending her recuperative sabbatical. Damian has vowed to keep her off the hard stuff, but we shall see.

I pick up the book and lie back in the hammock.

In many ways I couldn't be happier. Just as Simon predicted, my exhibition received rave reviews, as a result of which I've picked up several fairly lucrative commissions. My fee for a few drawings a month for *Stadium*, which take about three hours, is more than an entire month's ghastly desktop publishing. And thanks to Natalia, for the first time in my life I have earned myself some proper capital, which is an amazing feeling.

Unless I'm really crap with my money (which isn't inconceivable), I'll never have to set foot in an office again, which in itself should be enough to make me sing from the rooftops. Mum is very happy with Bernie, Dad seems pretty happy with Jilly, but more importantly, is not in prison; Poppy is alive. And watching Ben's humiliation was without doubt one of the best moments of my life. Yet . . .

Yesterday, masochistically, I called Ali, knowing she was already up at Hambledon Hall, helping with the wedding preparations.

'So how's it all going?' I asked.

'Surprisingly smoothly.' She laughed her easy laugh. 'Al's even lightened up about my dress and has let me have it altered so I don't look quite such a sack of shite.'

'That's great news,' I forced myself to sound as if I was smiling. 'So you won't still be skulking at the back of all the photos?'

'Wouldn't go that far,' Ali laughed back. 'Anyway, nobody will notice anyone else in the photos. Al's dress is totally stunning. She's going to look amazing.'

'What's it like?' I asked.

Just stop doing this to yourself, you'll find out soon enough anyway.

'Bias-cut, slim-fitting, floor-length ivory satin.' Every word was another knife wound to my heart. 'It's totally simple, practically backless with tiny straps made of seed pearls. Of course I'd look gross in something like that, but on Al it's fabulous. She's also got a full-length vintage veil, embroidered with the same seed pearls . . .' I'd heard enough.

Now I close *Scoop* and get out of the hammock. Trying to read is pointless. I wander down to the stream and sit with my feet dangling in the water, just staring out at the view, thinking about Andy. I think of his kindness and decency and his bravery in the face of his parents' death. I remember our sleuthing adventure in the woods, the helpless giggles and our pints in the pretty pub. I remember the way he looked at me when he said my plaits looked cute. I remember the way he looked at me outside Café Boheme. I remember our joy as he showed me and Max what he'd discovered about Kimbo. I remember him kissing me on the South Bank and my gaze mists over.

A shadow falls over me. God knows how long I've been sitting here.

'Hi Mum.'

'Erm, it's not Mum.' Just his deep, hesitant voice is enough to make my heart leap. I look up. Andy is standing above me, tall and serious in his specs and faded jeans and navy T-shirt, looking – well, just like him. Which is perfect.

'Is everything all right?' I try to keep my voice neutral.

'Well, yes and no. In a way everything's wrong, but it could all be right, if only—'

'If only what? You're talking in riddles.' I get up and face him. On closer inspection, he is flushed and slightly breathless.

'How do you feel about me, Bella? Please tell me the truth.'

Oh no, you can't ask me that, not today of all days.

'Why?' I look him steadily in the eye.

'Because the wedding's off. I'm not going to marry Alison.'

A great big light switches itself on in my heart and I stare at him some more, my smile spreading across my whole face and body.

'But w-what? Why?'

Andy puts up a hand and says impatiently, 'The whats and whys can wait. You still haven't answered my question.'

Right, this is it. This is my chance to do the right thing, not to fuck it up for once in my idiotic life. *Be brave, Bella, and tell him.* I hesitate.

'Would it help if I told you how I feel about you?' He's smiling at me now, his eyes like molten dark chocolate. I nod.

'It was at your exhibition that I realized it wasn't just a crush I had on you.' I look up at him, my heart starting to race. This cannot be happening. Despite my bare feet, I stumble a bit on the grass. Andy automatically puts out an arm to steady me.

325

'You're constantly putting yourself down, but you're not such a bad little thing, you know.' He laughs. 'Actually, I doubt there's a real bad bone in your body.'

I gaze up at him, wondering if he's got the right person.

'When I saw how well it was going for you, all I wanted to do was hold you and kiss you and tell you how brilliant and beautiful you are, how much I love you . . .'

I laugh, very shakily, 'Did you just say the L word?'

'Did I? Surely not. Well, I can't remember saying it, so I'd better say it again. I love you, Bella. Oh God, that was so easy. I LOVE YOU, BELLA!' Now he is shouting up into the apple tree, skipping around the garden. 'I LOVE YOU!' For the first time since I've known him, his seriousness has completely disappeared.

'In that case, don't you think you'd better kiss me?' I probably should have waited for him to do it off his own bat, but I've waited long enough.

'Oh I'm so sorry, I'm doing this all the wrong way round. I don't do this very often you know . . .'

We both laugh, then stop as he fixes me with that dark intense stare and takes my face in his hands. Mmmm.

After a bit, he pulls away.

'Don't stop, please.' My hands are still clasping the back of his neck. 'Come back here.'

He comes back for a few more heavenly seconds, then pulls away again.

'You still haven't answered my question.'

Through a smile that thinks it will go on forever, I say,

'I think that should be pretty obvious. And you're meant to be the clever one. Fool!'

He raises his eyebrows. 'The romance.'

'I love everything about you, from the bottom of my heart, and I think I always will.'

'That's better.' And he starts to kiss me again.

We are both sitting, hand-in-hand, with our feet dangling in the stream. Andy has rolled up the legs of his jeans, exposing a fine if hairy pair of ankles.

'So what are you going to tell Alison?' I ask. 'Isn't she going to be furious?' He'd risk that? For *me*?

Andy looks uncomfortable.

'You know I said we'd leave the whats and whys till later? Well, I suppose now is as good a time as any.' He takes a deep breath. 'Alison has been sleeping with Philip Henderson. You know, the . . .'

It takes a few seconds to register.

'The distinguished gent who bought my pictures? Yes, of course I know. But Andy, I don't understand . . . W-when did you find out?' I'm starting to feel very small and stupid. Has he just come to me as second choice because he discovered his fiancée was cheating on him?

'I found out a few hours ago. I needed to email cab numbers to some of the guests, and was looking them up on Al's laptop. While I was there an instant message flashed up, from Philip.'

'Bloody hell!' Despite myself, I get a weird thrill at the intrigue. There's more than one bad bone in my body. But my heart is sinking. I should have known it was too good to be true.

'What did it say?'

'I'll spare you the gory details, but suffice to say, it made reference to Al gritting her teeth and bearing it on the wedding night, which didn't exactly do wonders for the old ego.'

He laughs and I don't join in. I get up and start to walk away from him.

'Bella? What's the matter? I don't understand!'

He runs after me and forces me to turn round and look at him. Tears are streaming down my face.

'So you've only decided you're not going through with the wedding because you've found out Alison has been unfaithful, and your male ego can't take it? Nothing at all to do with me. How do you think that makes *my female* ego feel?' My voice is choked. 'I'll just go and see if Bella will have me instead, faithful little lapdog, waiting on the sidelines . . .' I am gulping, waving my arms around, pushing him away.

'It's not like that at all!' he shouts angrily. 'Bloody hell, why do women always have to overcomplicate things?' He pushes his hand through his dark hair, in the gesture I've come to know and love, making it go all spiky.

He takes me by the shoulders and shakes them slightly.

'You must understand that I couldn't just jilt Alison at the altar, thinking she'd done nothing wrong? After thirteen years? Because of some feelings I thought I had for you? What kind of a man could do that? What kind of man would that make *me*? Would *you* want to be with a man who was capable of that?'

I look at him, slowly starting to understand. No, of course I couldn't be with a man who was capable of that. And there's a certain noble honour about him marrying the wrong woman, out of duty, but always hankering after me, I think, cheering up again. Andy takes my hand.

'Don't you think we should just be really happy that we've been given this chance, that I was lucky enough to find out in time?'

Once he has finished kissing me again, I ask,

'So how did Alison react?'

Andy laughs. 'She made it an awful lot easier for me, actually. First of all she was horrified at being caught out, and pretended to be sorry. Then when she realized that wasn't working, she started begging me to still go through with the wedding, just to save face. She seemed to care about the wedding an awful lot more than the rest of our lives together. She promised we could have an open marriage. She even promised a divorce, after a respectable time . . .'

'What did she consider a respectable time?' I ask, kissing him again. He kisses me back.

'Six months. As I say, it made it a whole lot easier.'

'Bloody hell. And all of that . . . That big wedding . . . All those guests . . .' I gesture vaguely in the direction of Hambledon Hall. 'Who's going to deal with the fallout?'

'Al can do it,' says Andy harshly. 'I went through hell, thinking I couldn't have you, and all along she was building up to our wedding by fucking around on me.'

I think for a second. 'Shit, Andy, that must be a hell of a lot of money down the drain . . .?'

'Yes.' Andy looks bleak for a minute. Then he laughs, 'But worth every penny to be here with you now.' And he kisses me again.

Andy drives me back to London, back to my flat. We listen to *Concierto de Aranjuez*, chatting all the while. I've never known anybody I can talk to so easily without the prop of a glass and a fag in my hand. Everything he says is well thought out, intelligent and sincere. And the way he looks at me with his intense dark gaze simply melts me. It's different to the Ben lust, or the Mark lust, or even that one time of Damian lust. He just looks at me as if I am his every dream come true.

When we get to Portobello Road, I am suddenly overcome with an attack of nerves, and start babbling.

'Well, we're nearly home. Thanks for the lift. What do you have lined up for the rest of the day?'

Andy pulls into a side road and stops the car. He turns to stare at me. 'Please don't play with me, Bella. I've wanted you from the first moment I set eyes on you, nearly fifteen years ago when you came up to Cambridge to see Max. I felt like such a dirty old man. What kind of pervert did I think I was? Fixated on my mate's little sister, who was doing her A levels. In fact, you were the reason I hooked up with Alison – I was desperate to get the gorgeous, big-eyed seventeen-year-old out of my head.'

Bloody hell. No wonder Alison's always hated me so much, I think. Women tend to pick up on these things.

'Not really that perverted,' I say out loud, utterly overwhelmed by the revelation. 'You were – *are* – only two years older than me.'

'I felt a hundred years older.' I think about his horrible grief and squeeze his hand.

'But why didn't you tell me before?'

'When do you think it might have been appropriate?'

'I suppose now's as good a time as any,' I laugh shakily. 'I'm sorry it's taken me so much longer to realize, but please, please, come home with me now. I've never wanted anything more in my life.'

'Oh Bella.' He leans across to kiss me again, then stops himself. 'No. Not in the car.' He drives on until we're right outside my flat, then parks, gets out and comes round to my side of it, opening the door for me.

'Give me your keys.' I fumble in my handbag until I find them. He walks over to open my front door, then comes back, picks me up and carries me up all four flights of stairs. He must be bloody strong.

330

He carries me into my bedroom and gently puts me down on my bed. We gaze at one another.

'May I?' he says, as he makes to unzip my dress. I nod, tongue-tied. He is so gentle, treating me with the utmost tenderness. I'm so not used to this. He pulls my dress over my head and gazes at me some more.

'You're even more beautiful than I imagined.'

'You saw me in a bikini in Ibiza.' Why can't I just shut up?

'It's different,' he says simply, undoing my bra and kissing the tips of my breasts. Suddenly the gentle tenderness isn't enough. I need more, and reach up to pull his T-shirt over his head, desperate to feel his skin against mine. As his chest touches mine, Andy seems to lose control too. He starts kissing me with the utmost passion, his hands pulling at my hair as his pelvis grinds against mine. I can feel how hard he is through his jeans, and reach down to touch him.

'Oh Christ.' He moves away and looks at me. 'Oh my darling, I've waited for this moment for so many years. I wanted to take it slowly, but I'm not sure that I can.'

'It's OK,' I breathe. 'I'm as ready as you are.' I am desperate to feel him inside me and pull my knickers off as he drags his jeans down. He takes his glasses off, raises himself onto his elbows and, looking me in the eye all the while, lunges right into me.

'Oh Andy, oh my God, oh don't stop, oh oh oh . . .' I am tearing at his hair, kissing him all over his face. It's ridiculous. Within seconds we have both come. As we come to our senses, we both start laughing.

Andy kisses me on the lips and says, 'Right, now we've got that out of the way, shall we start again?'

And ever so lightly, he starts to kiss my collarbone, moving his way with deliberate slowness across my whole body, just as I dreamt about that time in his car. He certainly knows what he's doing. Serious, clever, principled Andy. Who'd have thought it? The thought of still waters running deep turns me on even more and by the time he reaches my cunt I am more than ready for him again.

'Oh please, I want to feel you inside me again.' He looks up at me and smiles.

'With pleasure.' He is hard again, and as he slides his cock into me, he takes my face in his hands, gazing at me and smiling. The sensations inside me are beyond exquisite.

'I love you, Bella Brown.'

'I love you too, Andy Marshall.'

But now the sensations are gathering momentum again and neither of us can talk as we fuck and kiss and fuck and kiss and all that matters is his cock inside me, filling me up and touching my soul until, crying out, I have the sweetest, most long-drawn-out orgasm I've ever had in my life.

Dappled sunlight filters through the shutters onto his naked body in my London bed. I savour the moment for – well, more than a moment – then, not wanting to disturb him, pad to the kitchen and put the kettle on. I'm almost hungover from euphoria as I recall the urgency, then the extraordinary sweetness of the sex. In all my years of – erm – experience, I can honestly say that nothing has ever come close. I cannot believe Philip Henderson's message to Alison about grinning and bearing it, but each to his own, I suppose. And Andy is most certainly *my own* now. If any more confirmation were needed, last night was it.

When I re-enter the bedroom with two cups of tea, he is awake and sitting up, broad-shouldered against my white lacy pillows.

'Hello beautiful.'

'Hello handsome.' If I wasn't me, I'd nauseate myself. 'Tea?'

'Let's leave it to cool down for a bit.' I raise my eyebrows. 'Oh just come here, you lovely thing.'

'Blimey, Alison and Philip Henderson,' I say, resting my head against Andy's chest. He kisses the top of it. 'Are you sure you're OK with it?'

'Apart from the old ego blow, yes.' I can hear him smiling. 'And it is a blow. Apparently it started the night your dad was arrested, when I was meant to be picking up the Order of Service from the printers. It was immediately after that I remember Al starting to lighten up.'

I giggle. 'So Mr Coutts chequebook started to make her feel like a wo-man again?'

'Shut up.' He cuffs me gently on the shoulder. 'I wouldn't be above giving him a good whack, slimy bastard.' Then he softens and puts his arms around me again. 'But that's only natural, surely? You must realize, Bella, that what I feel for you is the most important thing that's ever happened to me? Actually, I wanted to hit Mark more than I've wanted to hurt anyone in my entire life, when I saw the two of you together in Soho.'

'As soon as I saw you, I realized it wouldn't go any further than one kiss.' I kiss him to prove my point.

'Really? Mark with his muscles?'

'Yes, Mark with his muscles, who now has Sam with her tits.'

'Which are pretty nice, in a young, surgically enhanced kind of way.'

'I thought you only had eyes for me!' I'm part joking.

'Of course I have. But she *is* paid to take her clothes off in the tabloids.'

'Grrrrrrr.'

'I'm joking, silly. Come here.'

And he kisses me so thoroughly I don't care if nothing nice ever happens to me again. Presently . . .

'Aaandy?'

'Yessss?'

'Ummm . . . you know I told you I was going to go to Ibiza to get over you?'

'Yessss . . .'

'Why don't we go together? There's still time to catch my flight and there could easily be last-minute cancellations . . .'

For a second he looks taken aback, then laughs. 'OK, why not? I booked the time off work for my honeymoon, after all.' He pauses. 'But do you mind if we don't stay with your friends? I'd like to have you to myself at least some of the time. Besides, that Damian has a severe case of professional jealousy.'

Epilogue

The little stone cottage in the north of the island belongs to a mad, dreadlocked old girlfriend of Dad's, who has gone to Goa for a month. The condition of occupancy is that we look after her parrot, which, amusingly, is called Poppy. The cottage's shutters are painted cornflower blue; they match the sky and clash vividly with the bougainvillea climbing the walls. Another plant, whose name escapes us, has flowers that change from deepest purple to palest aqua, according to the time of day or night. They are now indigo, as the sun starts to set over the hills. I can just about make out the sea glittering in the distance over the fragrant expanse of pine and olive trees.

I am picking basil and rosemary from the herb garden, just outside the cottage's French windows. The haunting guitar strains of *Concierto de Aranjuez* can be heard from inside. Still in my bikini, warmth radiating from my sun-soaked body, I take a sip from my glass of rosé, whose exterior beads of moisture proclaim its delicious coolness in the still fierce early evening heat. I wave at Andy, splashing away in the palm-tree-surrounded pool that belongs to the big house. He waves back, grinning.

Today, after a pleasurely leisurely start, we took the ferry to Formentera, where we ate lobster and chips at ramshackle tables on the white sandy beach and swam for hours in the unfeasibly clear, turquoise waters. On the boat ride back, some Italians got out guitars and started playing old hippy stuff – Santana and a bit of Pink Floyd. We felt it appropriate, then, to stop for late-afternoon drinks, *jamón* and olives at Anita's Bar, the original hippy bar in San Carlos, the village just outside which we're staying.

Later we might meet the others in Ibiza Town for vodka *limóns* and the constant cosmopolitan promenade. We might join the hardcore at Space, or head to Playa s'Estanyol, a beautiful, pine-surrounded little cove where there are rumours of a beach party tonight. We might even end up back at Natalia's, as we did the other night, when she hosted the most outrageous after-party. Man, that was fun. Or we might just do nothing at all, as everything we need is right here.

Whatever we do, we'll be doing it together. And that makes me very happy indeed.

Acknowledgements

Firstly I'd like to thank my agent, Annabel Merullo, for all your help and encouragement, and being behind me, every step of the way; Juliet Mushens, for your invaluable advice on pretty much every detail of *Revelry*, and Arabella Foster, for spotting its potential in the first place.

Sarah Ritherdon, my brilliant editor – you were absolutely right about all those changes, Sarah! Also Hana Osman, for bringing everything together beautifully, and the rest of the team at HarperCollins.

My parents, Elizabeth and Christopher, for their unwavering patience, humour, support and love; my sister Caroline in Australia, for keeping me entertained and enriching my vocabulary with countless games of online Scrabble; and my lovely husband Andy, who has had to put up with night after night of me hammering away at my laptop while he makes dinner for us both and watches telly on his own.

And I would like to give a special thank you to my brother Nick, a brilliant writer himself, who persuaded me to stop wasting my time on rubbish jobs and start writing. Thanks Nick, you're a star.

Read on for an exclusive Q&A with Lucy Lord

Revelry is the first book you have had published, how did you come to write it?

I've been writing books (and not getting beyond the first few chapters) for years. With *Revelry*, suddenly the time seemed right. I had had a few summers that had been unbelievably good fun and thought that if I combined them all into one mad summer it could make a good background for a sort of light hearted romantic romp, with a flawed but (hopefully) likeable heroine. And all my friends told me I had to use the story about the dwarf!

Did you develop a particular way of writing? Describe a typical day for you whilst producing Revelry.

When I was writing *Revelry*, I was working full-time so most of it was done in the evenings. Now I am writing more or less full-time, a perfect day would be getting up between 8 and 9, going for a run and a bit of yoga in Hyde Park, having some breakfast and doing my chores. Then writing pretty much solidly between midday and 6, when it's time for *Eggheads* or *Friends*, depending on my mood (and whether I can actually quote the *Friends* episode verbatim). This doesn't always go according to plan though. I can get very carried away, writing more and more ludicrous stuff into the wee small hours, in which case I am unlikely to rise before 11, a massive editing job is in order and exercise gets pretty short shrift.

Did you always want to be an author, and if not what else did you want to be?

I have always wanted to be a writer, and have unfinished manuscripts under my bed from the age of about 11. Apart from journalism, every other job I've ever had has been a means to an end. The chapters where Bella is temping are written from the heart!

Bella's taste in men is not always perfect, and some of her dalliances were hysterical. What is the funniest dating story you have heard recently?

A friend of mine met a man at the Hampstead Heath Summer Solstice (which should have been warning enough in itself). He belonged to a men-only re-birthing group and was heavily into crystal readings. Despite all this, she went on a date with him, which was predictably tedious (although she did discover he'd studied tantric and erogenous massage). When he said goodbye to her at the tube station, instead of kissing her goodbye, he bit her neck, hard. She thought it was an odd thing to do until, sitting on the tube 5 minutes later, she started to feel incredibly turned on. Yes, he'd attacked one of her erogenous zones and here she was trying not to make it apparent to all the other passengers that she was having an orgasm on the underground. She never saw him again.

Bella has been best friends with Poppy for years. How did you meet your best friend?

Just like Bella and Poppy, I met my best friend, Emma, at school. There are a lot of similarities: we were new girls together, obsessed with the 1920s and 30s, we both wanted to be private detectives and we were inseparable until I went off to university and she became a model. The similarities end there, though – she has never seduced any of my boyfriends (in fact I can think of nothing she would like less!). She now lives in LA, and even though we hardly ever see each other, I still consider her my best friend. Corny though it may sound, my other best friend is my husband, Andy.

The trip to Glastonbury sounds incredible. Did you write about it from experience?

The last time I went to Glastonbury it rained solidly for four days and I have never been so glad to see my own bed as I was at the end of it! The Glastonbury in *Revelry* is a kind of wishful thinking and made up of bits and pieces from various wonderful (sunny) Glasto' experiences in years gone by. Sadly I have never been seduced by a drop-dead gorgeous male model at a festival.

During the summer Bella and her friends go not only to Glastonbury, but also to Ibiza. Where would your dream summer holiday take you?

Oh God, that's almost impossible to choose – there are so many amazing places I'd love to see. Obviously, I love Ibiza, and have been going for years now. Villa holidays with friends can be wonderful (or disastrous, though the less said about that the better). I love the Greek islands – anywhere with unspoilt beaches and clean, clear sea. This year, for a complete change, Andy and I will be cycling round Tuscany, tasting wine and staying at beautiful agrotourismo places – ancient farmhouses, country villas and the like. It all sounds terribly energetic, so I have insisted on one day on/one day off cycling and made sure that everywhere we stay has a pool!

Although Bella has to do a job she hates, what she really loves is painting. Are you at all interested in art?

Absolutely, and during our Tuscany trip we will of course be doing all the cultural stuff in Florence and Siena. I wouldn't say I have any discernible artistic talent, though I do get a huge thrill from finding old bits of furniture in junk shops and tarting them up. I'm currently in the process of transforming a fairly ordinary pine wardrobe into a Provençal gem, with toile de jouy panelling, new handles and distressed paintwork. I'm not quite there yet.

Revelry is the perfect beach read. What is your favourite book to read whilst you are on holiday?

I'd recommend Solzhenitsyn's *Cancer Ward* as the perfect feel-good holiday read. Seriously? Anything by Jilly Cooper – she is the queen – and I always buy a load of new paperbacks at the airport.

We hear you are writing a sequel. What can we hope to see from Bella, Poppy and their friends next?

Vanity, the sequel, starts with Poppy and Damian's boho beach wedding in Ibiza. The action then takes us to LA (where Ben is an up-and-coming film star), New York, St Tropez, London, the Hamptons and backpacker beaches in Thailand. Towards the end, Bella and Poppy find themselves on a road trip across the States in a hired Cadillac (something I've always wanted to do). You'll have to read it to find out how they get there!

An exclusive extract from
Lucy's next book

Vanity

Out January 2013

"Bollocks,' said the blushing bride, scrutinising her crotch through her wedding dress in the floor-to-ceiling mirror. 'It's too see-through in daylight, isn't it? I'm going to have to wear those bloody remedial granny pants.'

The pants in question were an exorbitantly expensive pair of sheer nude silk Myla boy shorts, hardly the passion-killing girdle the comment implied. But Poppy Wallace had set her heart on going commando on her Big Day.

'Never mind,' said her best friend Bella, topping up their glasses with Veuve Clicquot. 'Damian can rip them off with his teeth later.'

They both looked at Poppy's reflection. Transparency problem aside, she looked more beautiful than Bella had ever seen her, and that was saying something. The sheer white cotton voile dress, suspended from spaghetti straps and embroidered with daisies at the hem and strategically across what there was of her chest, skimmed her tiny body and floated to her delicate ankles. Her streaky white-gold hair flowed loose, halfway down her bare brown back, crowned with a sweet-smelling garland of white and yellow spring flowers. Her only jewellery was her vintage diamond and emerald engagement ring and an anklet fashioned out of silver daisies. She was barefoot and her lovely little face, all wide green eyes, small nose and perfect teeth, was glowing.

Bella's eyes filled with tears.

'Oh Pops, you look gorgeous. Can I hug you without ruining anything?'

'Course you can, you silly arse. Come here.' She flung her little arms around Bella. When she released her, Bella could see that her eyes were suspiciously shiny too. Poppy only cried on the rarest of occasions (unlike Bella, who found herself gently weeping like George Harrison's guitar with embarrassing frequency now she was in her thirties. Sad news stories, soppy song lyrics, old episodes of *Friends* she'd seen a million times before – it didn't take a lot these days).

'If it wasn't for you, Belles, I wouldn't be standing here today. So thanks lovely. For everything.'

They downed their champagne and Poppy added, 'Looking pretty gorgeous yourself, if I may congratulate myself on my exquisite taste. In friends *and* clothes.'

'Such a pretty dress.' Bella dabbed at her eyes with her fingers, then licked them, trying not to get any watery black residue on her cotton voile halter-neck bridesmaid's frock (she'd predictably forgotten to pack waterproof mascara). She and Poppy had spent ages choosing the exact shade of coral pink that most flattered Bella's dark hair and eyes.

'Thanks for not putting me in lilac frills.'

'It was touch and go, especially when you kept going on about having my hen do at School Disco.'

They both laughed.

'Shit, look at the time!' said Bella. It wasn't hard to miss, a fluorescent LCD display projected against one of the whitewashed walls of the ultra-glamorous, ultra-modern villa. 'Take one last look at yourself as a single woman, babe. No last minute regrets?'

Poppy shook her golden head. 'No last minute regrets.' They both looked at her reflection again, different memories racing through each of their minds. 'Let's go then. But you'd better put your knickers on first.'

Mark looked around the crowded beach and smiled broadly. What a way to get hitched, man. Playa S'Estanyol, a little sandy cove halfway up the east coast of Ibiza, was a bugger to get to, located at the bottom of a long and bumpy pine-tree-shaded track, but that hadn't fazed Mark. He'd relished bombing down in his hired jeep, sending up clouds of white dust, fucking up the tyres and making his girlfriend Sam squeal. And even his unromantic heart had thrilled at the beauty of the beach, nestled into warm yellow rocks and backed by the lush green forest. The scent of pine groves mingled with the sea air and clear tourmaline water lapped the pale shore. Further out, where the ocean changed to navy, pristine white sails breezed across the horizon.

Nudists habitually basked on the rocks and in the crystal waters at the southernmost end of the beach, but today they'd kept away out of deference to the nuptials. Spoilsports. In Mark's experience, the more a nudist wanted to flaunt their bits in your face, the older and saggier they were (Scandinavians aside), but sometimes a young chick with a hot bod slipped through the net and he wasn't above a sneaky peek. Still, it was early season, only May, and although it was a beautiful day, in the high 20s already, the sea was probably still cold enough to freeze your nuts off.

Arctic camouflage material fluttered above the stone-clad bar/restaurant area, giving a dappled shade to the tables that had been laid for the wedding feast. Sam had said it looked like crochet from a distance. Now she was ordering a drink at the bar, possibly unaware of the fact that every male eye on the beach was currently feasting on her.

That's my girl, thought Mark proudly, taking in her pretty little body in its short yellow dress, huge knockers threatening to burst through the thin floral fabric. Her long, straightened, henna-red hair was caught by the breeze as she noticed him watching her. A genuine smile lit up her sweet young face and she waved, tottering over the sand on foolish heels. Mark could have fucked her right there, in front of everybody.

'Isn't this wicked?' She breathed in her husky voice as she reached him. 'I can't wait to see Poppy's dress. And Bella's. I bet Poppy's got her something really nice to wear – they're such good mates. Not like when Karen made me wear puke green satin.' She made a face to illustrate and Mark laughed.

'You'd look gorgeous in anything, babe.'

Much as Mark couldn't believe his luck about Sam, he had long harboured threesome fantasies about Poppy and Bella: Poppy so fair, Bella so dark, both of them so fit. And he'd nearly had his wicked way with Bella a couple of times last year. But that was before she got together with Andy. And before he met Sam, of course.

Damian was doing the rounds, sweating slightly in his cream linen suit. He'd be glad when he could take the bloody jacket off. It was great seeing all their friends and family gathered on the beautiful beach, the result of months of excited planning. The planning had been amazing, without doubt the best nine months of his life. He'd nearly lost Poppy last year, in more ways than one, and the joy he'd felt when she surprised him with a proposal had been overwhelming. Relief had turned to magical excitement as they planned every last detail of what they hoped would be the best day of their lives, and he'd never felt closer to anyone. But by God was he nervous now. He was almost 100% sure he was doing the right thing.

'Not getting cold feet are you, darling?' asked Simon, his best man and fellow journalist on the men's style magazine *Stadium*. 'Here, have some of this.' He passed him his drink, an ice-cold White Russian.

'Thanks mate.' Damian took a swig. 'And no I'm not. Well – maybe a bit.' He laughed. 'But only stage fright, not the till death do us part bit, I'm absolutely convinced about that.' He looked at Simon through his wraparound rock-star shades, fully aware of what most of his friends had made of Poppy's behaviour the previous year. 'And I'm bloody hot in this suit.'

'*Il faut souffrir pour être belle.*' Simon's affected campery could be misleading sometimes. 'Anyway, you're lookin' mighty fine, dude.' And Damian was. The cream linen set off his half-Indian, half-Welsh complexion beautifully and the sharp cut emphasised his lean build. The shades, which he planned to take off during the ceremony, concealed soulful dark eyes that slanted down at the corners.

'But maybe you should have taken a leaf out of that couple's book.' Simon was now laughing in the direction of an ageing pair of ravers in matching purple sarongs. The man was bare-chested, the woman improbably pert-breasted in a gold and lilac paisley bandeau bikini top. They were boogeying barefoot in the sand to Moby, half-pissed already by the look of it.

'That's Bella's Dad and his latest,' said Damian, laughing too now and waving over at them. 'Hey Justin, hey Jilly.' They waved back, blowing kisses.

'You don't mind them not making more of an effort?' Simon was very conscious of his own and others' sartorial standards. Today he was impeccably dressed in a white open-necked shirt under a similar suit to Damian's (only in a muted café au lait shade, so as not to upstage the groom).

'Why do you think we're getting married on a beach, you twat?'

He just wished Poppy would hurry up so they could get this over with.